"Have You Ever Been Kissed?"

Jackson asked Grace.

They had climbed the stairs to the quarter gallery. The ship moved to a rocky dip, then buffeted against an oncoming wave. Grace adjusted easily to the shifting deck. Her body remembered what to do.

Jackson moved behind her, leaning close so the loose strands of her hair breezed against his face. He put his hands on the railing beside hers, so near their arms touched. He had her trapped, and from the sudden rasping of her breath, she knew it.

"Have you?"

"Jackson, what we did before—how close we came to— I swore I wouldn't allow it to happen again."

"Why?" He lowered his head, keeping his mouth close to her jaw, the curve of her neck. Close, but not touching.

He should stop before he did something he truly regretted. Yet, some part of him kept him from moving away.

"The Jackson I knew wouldn't behave so brazenly."

"This is about you never having been kissed, not my lack of manners. I don't blame you for being curious."

She tried to turn, but he grazed his lips against the length of her neck. "Jack . . ." She swallowed. "Jackson, what are you doing?"

"I'm kissing you. . . ."

Dear Romance Reader,

Last year, we launched the Ballad line with four new series, and each month we'll present both new and continuing stories set everywhere from medieval England to the American West—the kind of passionate, romantic stories you love best, written by the most gifted authors. At the back of each book, we'll tell you when you can find subsequent books in the series that have captured your heart.

This month a group of very talented authors introduces a breathtaking new series called *Hope Chest,* beginning with Pam McCutcheon's **Enchantment.** As five people unearth an abandoned hotel's century-old hope chest, each will be transported back to a bygone age—and transformed by the timeless power of true love. Kathryn Fox presents the next installment of *The Mounties.* In **The Second Vow,** a transplanted Irishman who must escort the Sioux across the U.S. border meets a woman whose loyalty to her people is as fierce as the desire that flames between them.

In the third book of the charming *Happily Ever After Co.* series, Kate Donovan offers **Meant To Be.** The spirited daughter of a successful matchmaker is determined to avoid matrimony—unless a rugged sharpshooter can persuade her that their union is no accident of fate . . . but a romance for all time. Finally, rising star Tammy Hilz concludes the passionate *Jewels of the Sea* trilogy with **Once an Angel,** as a woman sailing toward an uncertain future—and an arranged marriage—is taken captive by a man who will risk anything to save her from a life without the love only he can offer.

Kate Duffy
Editorial Director

Jewels of the Sea

ONCE AN ANGEL

Tammy Hilz

ZEBRA BOOKS
KENSINGTON PUBLISHING CORP.

http://www.zebrabooks.com

For my sister, Karen,
Because there really are angels on earth

Prologue

1774

Stone-hard pews, nearly filled to capacity, lined the majestic nave like soldiers ready for battle. Not a soul dared speak; not here. The air rumbled with a sound that was not quite a sound, like the hum of a thousand hushed voices all whispering prayers. Tall, paned windows, twenty feet above the marble floor, lined each side of the imposing room, allowing misty English light to filter in. Colorful banners hung below the windows, one to represent each family present, and the daughter they'd come to see.

Waiting in the hallway, Grace Fisk spotted her flag, a fierce lion on a field of red, his paw raised in defense, and felt her heart flip against her chest. Not her flag exactly, but one she could claim because of her sister's marriage. Gripping her hands at her waist to keep them from shaking, she took her place in line, the last of thirty-two women, all years younger than her. She tried to ignore the hurt she felt at the slight. *Being last does not mean I'm the least important.*

But, however much she wanted to ignore it, she knew an affront when faced with one—she should, she thought, straightening a perfect pleat in her soft, black wool gown, identical to the ones the other girls wore. She'd had four years experience of being spurned. She'd quickly learned that Wilmouth School for Girls wasn't for the faint of heart. It hadn't mattered that she'd surpassed the other students in their lessons, perfecting her French, excelling at writing and numbers, even though those skills hadn't been encouraged. The harder she'd tried to fit in, the more of an outcast she'd become.

Grace shut the disparaging thoughts away. Her schoolmates hadn't meant to be cruel. They simply didn't know any better. One glance at the row of women ahead of her, with their delicate hands and perfect skin, women who knew nothing of struggling to survive, and she knew her achievements weren't the reason she'd been ostracized. It was because of who she was, and *what* she was, that had kept her from ever belonging. Her blood wasn't noble, but common—worse than common—with the smell of a fisherman's daughter and the taint of a pirate.

She touched the hated *Sea Queen* dagger she secretly wore strapped to her thigh and inwardly cringed. She felt the gold-wrought hilt, the embedded thumb-size gems that shimmered like fire when held to the light. If she'd had her way the dagger would be lying at the bottom of the ocean where it belonged. She only wore it now because of Jo's infernal nagging, blast her sister. If her classmates learned of it she'd be ruined, this time forever.

Shuddering, she straightened her shoulders and forced her thoughts to brighten. Against all odds, she'd persevered—surviving poverty, near starvation, a possible hanging, years of arduous study. Finally, today was her graduation day.

She allowed a smile that felt good on her lips. The future she'd hoped for was finally within reach. After today, she would be a real lady. Not only one her sisters, Morgan and Jo, could be proud of, but a *lady* any man would covet as his wife. The rest of her dream would follow soon after: a home full of children she would love, and security—two things no one could take from her or tear apart.

"What are your plans after the reception, Grace?" Allyson Whitehall whispered. The petite young woman smoothed her hand over white-blonde hair that was arranged in perfect curls.

Smiling at the girl she'd once believed to be her friend, she said, "I'm returning to my sister's town house in London."

Sheila Foxsworth glanced over her narrow shoulder and arched a brow the color of dull wood, the same as the hair she ruthlessly braided and coiled around her head. She had sharp-boned cheeks and a full, pouty mouth that wasn't prone to smile. If not for her large, almond-shaped brown eyes she would have been plain. "I daresay you're not going to town for the season."

"Well . . ."

"Don't be silly, Sheila," Allyson interjected, stifling a giggle. "Grace is *twenty-four.*"

Sucking in a breath, Grace stiffened her back, then silently chided herself for reacting at all. *They aren't trying to be unkind. They're only stating a truth.*

The women—both eighteen and in their prime for marriage—exchanged amused glances before Allyson said, "Perhaps I'll find time to visit you, Grace. I'll be in London, as well. Not to find a husband, of course."

"I can't believe you're marrying an earl. I'm so envious," Sheila confided, her pale cheeks flushing red.

"Your day will come, and sooner than you might imagine," Allyson declared, sparing Grace a pitying glance. "Sheila, if you aren't engaged to an earl within a month, I'll set my mama to the task. Just name which aristocrat you want and she'll see you have him."

"What about you, Grace?" Sheila's brown eyes flickered like broken glass. "Do you have any prospects? Your brother-in-law is in shipping, is he not? Perhaps he knows a merchant who is looking for a wife."

A merchant, not a nobleman. Sheila was the daughter of a lowly baron, but she was still a thousand steps above Grace. She gripped her hands together until her fingers ached. Was it wrong of her to want a titled husband? One with land and an income that would secure her future, protect her from whatever crisis might surround them? *Give me the kind of home I had as a child before everything was ripped away?*

"I haven't been as lucky as Allyson," Grace conceded.

The brown-haired woman sniffed. "I won't need Allyson's mother to help me find a husband. I'll undoubtedly snatch one up long before you."

Grace said a silent prayer of thanks that Jo hadn't heard Sheila's venomous tone. If she had, the young woman would have found herself face-first on the ground with Jo's knee in her back, digging in until Sheila apologized. But Grace had never been so bold; confrontations made her stomach ache.

Smiling when she really wanted to turn away, she murmured, "I'm sure you'll find a wonderful husband."

A mischievous light glimmered in Allyson's leaf-green eyes. "What say you to a wager? Whichever one of you becomes engaged first wins."

"Wins what?" Sheila asked.

Allyson giggled, a shrill, childish sound that made Grace wince. "Her position in society, of course."

Grace wanted to tell them they were being foolish. Once society learned of the wager, the loser would be humiliated. Besides, ladies did not gamble, and certainly not on finding a husband!

"Do we have a wager?" Allyson asked.

"It's scandalous." Sheila's mouth twitched with an excited grin.

"You can't be serious." Grace tried to laugh but failed.

"Can't I?" Allyson drew her shoulders back. "To prove how serious I am, I'll have my mama host a ball to present whichever one of you becomes engaged first. And you know *everyone* attends my mama's balls."

Sheila's eyes glowed as if envisioning herself a bride-to-be, with every nobleman within a hundred miles wishing her felicitations.

The ball doesn't matter. Unless . . . unless it secures the things I want most—a home of my own, and children.

She didn't add love to her list. She'd loved a man once, for all her life it sometimes seemed, but he'd never returned her affections. And even if he had, he couldn't, or perhaps wouldn't, give her the security she needed.

But security isn't everything, a voice in the back of her mind insisted. *I want to belong.* For eight years, ever since her sister Morgan had married Daniel Tremayne, the earl of Leighton, Grace had stood on the outer rim of society, flirting along the edge, without ever being a true part.

If she could find a man she cared for, one who was respected by England's elite, then the ruling class would have to accept her. She shook her head. There were no "ifs" about finding the man of her dreams. He was out there, waiting for her. She was certain of it.

The headmistress bustled in, shushing the girls and straightening their line. It was time for the ceremony to begin.

"Allyson," Grace whispered as her classmates began

their final walk down the nave, leaving their school years behind in hopes of finding something better and new.

"Are you going to show the white feather?" the girl taunted. Sheila choked on a laugh.

"No." Grace touched the *Sea Queen* blade through her skirt. With a determination she hardly recognized, she vowed, "I'm going to win."

Chapter One

One year later

Bleached canvas sails were raised, snapping taut, running the *Maiden Fair* before the wind. The sun burned against a piercing blue sky, the color so rich and bold Grace had forgotten such brilliance existed. London was a beautiful city, but it dwelled beneath a perpetual ashen cloud—soot from too many chimneys and the incessant belching of smokestacks. But out here, riding the waves in the middle of the world, the ocean glittered like hammered gold tossed about in handful after giant handful.

It had been eight years since she'd stood on the deck of a ship, felt the rhythmic rock of wood fighting sea, heard the flap of sails, the siren cries of gulls. Smelled the salty spray that wet her tongue. She'd never thought to experience those things again; had, in fact, vowed to *never* experience them again. But here she was, on a ship by her own choosing, crossing the Atlantic and heading for her future. To the Americas, where her fiancé awaited her.

She smiled and lifted her face into the warm breeze, letting the brackish air fill her lungs. She would have laughed out loud like a carefree child had it been proper, but since it wasn't she contented herself with simply smiling and reflecting on how unpredictable life could be. Disheartening one moment, miraculous the next.

A moan of pure agony drew her attention to the woman beside her. Frowning with worry, Grace reached out, but quickly let her hand drop to her side. Once before she'd made the mistake of patting Sheila Foxsworth on the back and had received a tongue lashing for her effort. Grace considered the sick woman's ashen face. Life was not only unpredictable, it had a cruel sense of humor by confining her to Sheila's company for the five-week voyage to Boston.

"Did the dill weed tea I prepared for you not help?" Grace asked, wincing when the woman's groan turned into a sucking gasp. The ship tipped leeward, then dropped into a stomach-clenching dive. Just as quickly, the deck righted itself to meet the next wave.

Holding onto the railing with a white-knuckled grip, Sheila shuddered, then clamped a shaking hand over her mouth. Lavender would have made a better remedy for seasickness, Grace thought, troubled by the woman's continued illness, but there was none to be had on the *Maiden Fair*.

"Nothing will help except getting off this horrid ship." Sheila glared at Grace as if faulting her for her wretched condition. Ever since they'd sailed from London port three weeks past, Sheila's complexion had been as green as her temper had been black. "I feel as if my stomach has twisted around my throat."

Her mouth pinched tight, and her face became even more drawn and pasty than before. Her brown hair, always perfectly smooth and coiled in the latest fashion, now clung in sweaty strands to her jaw and neck.

Though they were far from being friends, Grace couldn't help but feel sorry for the woman. Sheila hadn't wanted to make the voyage to the Americas. But after losing their wager when Grace was the first to become engaged, Lady Foxsworth thought it a grand idea for her daughter to take a trip abroad. Grace had thought it odd that Lady Foxsworth had booked her daughter passage on the same ship that she sailed on. When she'd asked Sheila about the coincidence, she'd turned a cold shoulder and entered her cabin, slamming the door closed behind her.

"The cook might have some alfalfa," Grace said to herself, clenching her hand to keep from reaching out to the woman. She couldn't stand to see anyone in pain—even someone who didn't like her. "I could make a—"

"Don't bother. I don't trust you or your tonics. You're probably trying to poison me."

Sighing, Grace contemplated the ocean once more, though it had suddenly lost its shimmer. She didn't fault Sheila for her spiteful remark. The woman had been humiliated before all of England the night Allyson Whitehall hosted a ball announcing Grace's engagement. Allyson had spoken the truth when she'd said everyone attended her mother's assemblies. Though secretly, Grace thought Sheila was partly to blame for her disgrace. Had the woman not boasted that she would find a husband while poor, timid Grace gathered dust on the shelf, her loss might not have been so traumatic.

But Grace had not only won the wager, she'd poured salt on Sheila's wound by becoming engaged to the very man Sheila had set her sights on.

She bit down on her lip, still feeling guilty over that fact. She'd met Lord William Mason, viscount of Kensale, at a garden party Morgan and Daniel had given. He'd arrived with Sheila and her family, making it clear that he'd intended to court her. But when Daniel had introduced Grace to the viscount as his sister, the tides had turned. Within days, Lord Kensale had begun appearing at Daniel's home for dinner, and on the grounds to accompany her on her afternoon walks. She'd discouraged his attentions, but his persistence, and his assurance that he had never intended to offer for Sheila, had worn her down. But the fact was, she'd had a hard time resisting his charm.

William Mason was the epitome of nobility with his blue blood, his heritage, his tall, lithe body and patrician nose. He had deep-set, steel-blue eyes that had the power to capture and hold. His manners that were beyond impeccable. She still couldn't believe that he'd chosen her to be his wife. Her dowry of fifty thousand pounds had swayed him heavily in her favor, of course. But it was the ties to Daniel's business in trade that William valued most. Such a bond would undoubtedly help the shipbuilding enterprise he'd started in the Colonies.

The arrangement didn't bother her in the least, at least not very much; they were both bringing things of value to the marriage. She a dowry and connections; he the security and respectability she craved.

Within two months, she would become viscountess of Kensale. Just the thought of how close her dream was from being fulfilled made her smile. She didn't know William as well as she'd have liked, nor did she love him—a fact that upset both her sisters, who were madly in love with their husbands and argued she shouldn't marry for anything less. But she liked him, just as he liked her. Caring would grow after a time, and if they were lucky, love would follow.

Because of William's schedule the wedding was to take place in Medford, a town north of Boston, so all of Massachusetts's society could attend. It was almost too good to be true. Everything would be perfect. Even the name of her new home sounded like a fairy tale. White Rose. William had assured her it was as beautiful and grand as its name.

Feeling her smile fade, she drew a deep, fortifying breath. She would have felt better if her sisters had been able to make the trip with her. But Jo was expecting her first child, and her husband, Nathan, had refused to let her travel. Morgan had stayed behind to see Jo through the birthing.

The birth of a niece or nephew I might never know. She brushed the anxious thought away. She would see her family again, and when she did, she just might have her own baby to introduce.

Lifting her face into the wind and closing her eyes, Grace recalled the worry in Nathan's eyes as he held onto his wife, afraid she might fall on the slippery docks when they'd come to see Grace off. Would William be so concerned for her?

She opened her eyes and blinked against the sharp rays of sunlight. She couldn't imagine her fiancé fretting on her behalf. It took a man foolishly in love to behave so.

And she wasn't marrying for love; she refused to. At a young age she'd not only learned how dangerous life could be, she'd learned how much it hurt to love someone, desperately, with all her heart, and not have that love returned. If only Jackson—

Stiffening her spine, Grace cut off the thought, reminding herself that this was the beginning of the most wonderful time of her life; she was on the brink of having everything she wanted. She wouldn't spoil it by wishing for something that could never be.

"Admit it, Grace," Sheila demanded as she clung to the ship's rail, fighting to stay on her feet. "You're enjoying my disgrace."

"That's not true."

"You can stop your virtuous act. We're in the middle of a godforsaken ocean. It's time you showed your true colors."

"You don't feel well, Sheila. You don't know what you're saying."

"Don't I?" With a shaky laugh, she ran the back of her hand over her damp brow. "You can pretend to be one of us, but you can't disguise what you really are."

Grace shook her head, wanting to stop whatever the woman meant to say next. Though she could guess what was coming. Sheila knew about Grace's past—as did all of England.

"You're a pirate." She spat the last word like a curse. "A thief. Why you and your sisters haven't been run out of England, or beheaded, is beyond me."

"That's all in the past, Sheila. The king pardoned us," Grace said, knowing the pardon could have come from God Himself and people like Sheila still wouldn't have cared.

Nor did they care about the reasons that had driven her and her sisters to pirating in the first place. They only saw the rough, violent life she'd led, the cargo she'd stolen—from some of them personally—the laws she'd broken that were punishable by hanging. A sentence she and her sisters would have received if not for Daniel, whose love for Morgan had saved them all.

A cold tremor ran over her skin. Try as she might to ignore her fears, she could never escape her past entirely. Sheila's accusations forced her anxiety into the open, forced her to look at it and remember when all she wanted to do was forget. Morgan had always taken precautions during their time at sea, but Jo had been wild and reckless, always searching for a fight. And Jackson, he'd loved the been possessive and greedy as they'd moved over her body. She'd felt every sensation, every pearling ripple he'd caused beneath her skin, and had been certain he'd felt the same as well. She'd thought he'd wanted more than a kiss—much, much more. From her, the woman she'd become, not the little girl he once knew.

And then he'd pulled away.

She tightened her grip on her shawl. *Don't think about his kiss,* she lectured herself for the hundredth time. *And for heaven's sake, don't think about how it made you feel!* Her private reprimands had done little good over the last few days, and they did nothing to settle her unease now.

It meant nothing. He only wanted to throw me off balance, convince me to return to England.

The frightening part was that it had almost worked. For an instant, before he'd pulled away and she'd seen the self-contempt in his eyes, she'd forgotten all about William. She would have willingly followed Jackson anywhere, agreed to anything, for the rest of her life, so long as he didn't let her go.

Fool, fool, foolish girl!

Turning back toward the coast, her heart lurched against her chest in surprise. They were less than two hundred yards from shore. A row of buildings, their shapes as vague as the muted colors they were painted in, lined the coast. Some were mere lean-tos of bleached and rotting wood. Small fishing boats fought the waves as they struggled back to shore.

Her fiancé was somewhere beyond those buildings, far to the south. William wouldn't be expecting her for another week. She wondered if it would take her that long to reach him. A breath shuddered out of her lungs. It wasn't fear, she reassured herself. But the knot in her stomach and the way her skin prickled felt horribly like dread. She'd meant it when she told Jackson that she wanted to sail to lie." Angry tears shimmered in Sheila's eyes. "He should be my fiancé. *Mine!*"

"I'm sorry, Sheila."

"I don't want your pity."

"I told him the truth." Grace wished her voice were stronger, wished there were some way she could lessen the woman's anger and obvious pain. The only way to do that was to call off her engagement with William, and that she couldn't do.

"Your version of the truth, which is no truth at all."

Grace held her tongue, realizing it would do no good to repeat what she'd told William. He hadn't asked about her past, but she'd felt compelled to explain. If they were to have a happy life together, he had to know everything, beginning with the day a horrific storm nearly destroyed Dunmore, the fishing village where she'd been born. A pirate ship had washed into their cove, frightening them with its sheer size and presence. Would they be attacked and murdered? Or merely robbed of what few belongings they had left? But the vessel had been abandoned, a floating ghost ship.

Her village had been on the verge of starvation. With their crops destroyed by the king's soldiers and their fishing boats sitting at the bottom of the North Sea, the elders had decided to abandon their homes and move to London. Morgan had opposed their decision, terrified they'd all become beggars, living in the streets. But there hadn't been any other alternative.

Except for the *Sea Queen*.

Pirating had seemed an unlikely option for three young si   and a handful of aging men, but they'd set sail   ss, saving Dunmore and their homes. Their very

it had seemed like their only choice, but ered if there hadn't been another path they could have chosen, one that wouldn't have put them at such risk. Feeling Sheila's spiteful stare, she pushed the thought away. There was nothing to be done about her past now, she reaffirmed. And it didn't matter. She would be a married woman soon, and William didn't care about her time as a pirate.

"England might know about your escapades on board the Sea Queen," he'd told her before sailing to America two months ago, secure that she would soon join him. *"But no one in Boston need know."*

He wanted to forget about her past as much as she did. For that alone, she could come to love him. She would have her new beginning. Only two more weeks and she'd be reunited with her fiancé. A week following that, she would be his wife. She'd have her new life, her new husband and her own special place to belong. For the first time ever, everything would be perfect.

Sheila's sharp tongue could threaten her happiness, but fortunately Sheila wasn't staying in Medford, rather traveling further south to a town called Abington where she had relatives.

Deciding it was best to ignore her, Grace focused on the horizon. The seas were becoming restless, gathering force with the surging wind. Tilting her head back, she studied the sky. When she'd been little more than a child on board the *Sea Queen,* she'd had a way of predicting the weather, knowing if brewing clouds held a storm, or just a fistful of wind.

A band of thin, hazy white clouds had gathered off to the east, building speed beneath the dazzling blue sky. Behind them, hours away yet, thicker, peat-colored clouds billowed like soup bubbling in a cook pot.

"Shortly after nightfall," Grace mused out loud. "Or it could strike as late as midnight." She had to warn Captain Peters to batten down the ship.

"What did you say?" Sheila demanded.

Grace glanced at the woman and noted that while her mouth was still pinched tight, color had returned to her cheeks. Evidently her anger had taken her mind off her sick stomach. "You should go below and get some rest. A storm is coming."

The fire drained from Sheila's cheeks. She glared at the sky. "You're just saying that to frighten me. The day couldn't be any clearer."

Off the starboard side, Grace spotted a flash of white canvas, another ship on the same heading as the *Maiden Fair*. She watched it struggle against the building waves, its three masts full of sail, driving the vessel at a reckless pace. She'd lived through too many storms to know that this was just the beginning. The captain of the other ship needed to furl her sails, bring his ship under control or he'd never survive.

The nerves in her stomach pulled tight. *This is my last time at sea. Once I reach Boston, nothing will ever make me go near the ocean again.*

"Excuse me," Grace said absently, alternately watching the other vessel and the sky. "I need to speak with the captain."

Leaving the woman gaping after her, Grace made a list of the things that needed to be done to secure the *Maiden Fair*. A list she made out of a habit. It surprised her how readily her long-forgotten duty came back to her. Though tension coiled in the back of her neck, she was relieved that in this instance, her experience would serve her well.

She was going to reach Boston and marry William Mason, she vowed, and *nothing*, not Sheila's animosity or a temperamental storm, was going to stop her.

Chapter Two

"Grace! Wake up, for God's sake, wake up!"

The frantic voice and the jarring of her shoulder snapped Grace out of her deep, dreamless sleep. She sat upright and blinked against the flickering light. Disorientated, it took her a few seconds to remember she was on board the *Maiden Fair*.

The hull groaned around her, a loud, forbidding sound that nearly masked the roaring wind and sky-breaking thunder. Rain pelted the deck above in a battering downpour. How she'd slept through a raging gale she didn't know, and had no time to wonder. The ship keeled to the right, and would have tossed her from her bed had she not gripped the corner of her bunk. She pressed her other hand to the side of the ship, half afraid the copper rivets would tear free. The wooden strakes would splinter against the ocean's pressure, ripping a hole through the ship's belly. If she were aboard the *Sea Queen*, she wouldn't have worried about the vessel's soundness, but she had no idea if the *Maiden Fair* would withstand the strain.

"I'm dying," Sheila cried, her voice reed thin and shaking. "Please, help me."

Grace turned away from the hull, and for the first time saw Sheila sitting on the floor in a nook between the bed and the opposite wall, knees drawn up to her chest, her face waxen, her hand bone white from clenching the candle.

"What are you doing here?" Grace asked, though she knew the answer.

Trembling in her night rail, without a shawl to protect her from the biting cold, the younger woman wept, "You're a pirate. You've been through this before. Are we going to sink?"

"Of course not. It's just a storm."

"I almost wish we would. My stomach . . . How could my mother do this to me? Is there nothing you can do to help me? Please, Grace . . ."

Jumping to her feet, she took Sheila by the arms and helped her onto her bed. She took the candle from the woman's grip and blew it out. Darkness swept into the room, sealing it, intensifying the sounds of blustering wind, the raging force of the sea.

"What have you done?" Sheila gasped, panicking. "We need the light."

"Candles can cause a fire, especially during a time like this." As if to prove her point, the ship took a vicious lurch. Sheila screamed; Grace threw herself over the girl and held them both down. Once the hull leveled, she pulled the blankets up and tucked them around Sheila's body.

"There's plenty of water to be had," she said, trying to sound calm, but her hands were shaking and her skin felt tight and clammy with sweat. Memories of past storms came rushing back; whip-cracking lightning, shipmates tossed like sticks in the wind, the *Sea Queen* ravaged of sail and mast. They'd never lost a crewman, but that hadn't lessened her fear.

"Should we start a fire by accident," Grace said, ignoring the chill biting deep into her bones, "the crew is too busy to put it out."

"I hadn't thought—" She doubled over, moaning into the pillow.

Feeling Sheila's damp brow, Grace doubted the woman would retch even if she tried. She hadn't been able to eat more than a spoonful of broth at each meal since leaving London. There wasn't much she could do to ease Sheila's seasickness, but she had to try.

There wasn't any lavender to make a soothing tea, but maybe there was something else. "Wait here."

"Don't leave me," she whimpered, but Grace slipped on her robe and hurried out the door, closing it behind her.

Wind blasted though the hallway, whistling in her ears, flattening her gown to her body. Groping the walls, she dug in with her fingers, finding notches in the wood to keep her balance. She listened for shouts from above, bellowing orders for the helmsman to keep the bow into the wind, barked commands for men to work the pumps. But there was only the wind tearing through the corridor, obliterating all but its howl.

Lightning flashed, throwing grayish light through the hatchway ahead of her. Except for the shadowed doorways and cold lanterns swinging from their hooks, she was alone. There should be sailors about, she thought frantically, gripping onto a doorjamb as the ship shuddered against a wave. Everyone must be above deck, she realized, working to keep the riggings tied, fighting the wheel, saving sails if they tore loose from their yards. Still, she wished she could hear someone, see someone.

She hurried forward, the floor icy and wet beneath her bare feet. The chilled air swept beneath her gown and robe, swirling around her legs. She had to reach the galley, one level down from her cabin. She might find laudanum there, and if not that, whiskey. Considering the severity of the storm, and sensing it could last for hours yet, rendering Sheila unconscious might be the most humane thing she could do.

Reaching the ladder, she hesitated in descending and looked up through the hatchway. Stinging rain burned her skin, the cold piercing hot. It stole her breath. A gush of salty water poured through the opening, soaking her face, the bodice of her gown, both her sleeves. She gasped, shivering as the frigid wetness cut through her chest like a knife. But she held her ground and searched the deck, sighing when she spotted several crewmen gripping the capstan, though they couldn't be using the pulley to bring up cargo from below, not in this storm. So what were they doing?

They weren't wearing their baggy calico trousers and striped shirts, but dark pants, knee-high boots and long black coats. With their hair and beards plastered to their faces. she didn't recognize them, but that was to be expected.

They have things well in hand. Only slightly relieved, she turned away and hurried down the companionway. She'd ridden out countless storms before, but she swore this would be her last.

"Once my feet touch Boston soil, I'll be there to stay," she muttered to herself.

She rushed through the lower deck as fast as she could, bumping into walls as the ship thrashed and swayed. Crates had come loose from their ties, scattering across the corridor, some breaking open to spill their contents—which she tripped over, nearly skidding onto her knees.

Finally, she found the galley. Rubbing her hands over her arms to suppress the shivers, she felt her way past a basin that served as a sink. Besides that, she found the iron stove, cold now and missing the enormous pot that normally hung from a metal hook, bubbling with some creation the cook had invented.

The small, cramped room had a window the size of a cannon port, closed now, and she didn't dare open it, though some light would help speed up her search. She should have brought the candle, she thought belatedly. But no matter. If there was whiskey to be had, she'd find it.

She opened the cabinet door and gasped when the ship lurched. She expected the contents to tumble out, crash around her bare feet, but a metal bar kept everything secured on its shelf. She slid her fingers over glass jars, too short she thought for liquor. Spices perhaps, or a ration of sugar.

She searched each shelf, finding nothing, her anxiety building with each jarring pull of the ship. How much more could the *Maiden Fair* endure? The vessel had to withstand the storm, *it had to;* she hadn't braved Wilmouth, found the perfect fiancé and crossed half an ocean only to drown at sea.

Stretching to reach the top shelf, her hand closed around a tall, narrow bottle. Pulling it down, she removed the stopper, sniffed and whispered "thank you" to the heavens. Brandy, if her guess was right.

Replacing the stopper, keeping her balance with the rocking floor, she started to turn. A rough hand clamped over her mouth. Her heart lurched to her throat, shutting off her scream. She smelled sweat and dirt. He pressed harder, muffling the rush of her breath. A solid arm locked around her waist, pinning both her arms to her sides, lifting her off her feet.

Grace twisted, tried to break free, tried to scream, but her hoarse cry was buried beneath the sounds of the angry sea. She jabbed her elbow into her attacker's side. He grunted, but didn't release her. She struck out with her feet, found only air. He squeezed her ribs, cutting off her breath.

"Stop fight'n'," the smooth male voice ordered.

She wanted to smash the bottle of brandy over his head, but he had her trapped. She couldn't move. If he chose, he could easily snap her neck in two. She stilled, heard the quick rasp of his breath in her ear, felt his eyes on her, watching, inspecting.

"That's better." He eased his hand from her mouth enough for her to speak.

"Who . . . who are you?"

"Just a visitor."

A visitor? She knew the other passengers aboard the *Maiden Fair*. A minister and his wife, two businessmen, a family of five setting out to build their new home in the Colonies; none of them would do this to her. It had to be one of Captain Peters's men. Yet, she found that hard to believe. In the three weeks she'd been on board, none of the sailors had made any advances or untoward comments. Why would one dare to do so now? The answer occurred to her. With the rest of the crew fighting the ship and the storm, who would stop him from doing whatever it was he intended?

Grace shivered with equal amounts of fear and fury. For once she wished she'd taken Jo's advice, given before Grace had sailed for America. *Wear the* Sea Queen *blade at all times. You'll never know when you'll need it.*

Well she needed it now, but it was locked in her trunk, buried under a pile of silk gowns. Even if she had the blade, she wouldn't know how to use it. But she had other skills. Whether they would help her now, she had no clue.

"You've no right to manhandle me in this manner," she reprimanded in the sternest voice she could manage with her feet dangling a foot off the ground. "I demand you release me at once, or I'll report you to Captain Peters."

"Will ye now?" He chuckled, a soft mocking sound.

A chill swept over Grace. The threat should have made the man obey at once. Captain Peters kept his men in line through equal amounts of respect and fear, knowing they would be punished—undoubtedly with a cat-o'-nine-tails—if they crossed that line. If this man wasn't afraid of his captain, she had to think of another way to escape. But how? If only she could see him, read his intent in his eyes. But it was as dark as a tomb in the galley.

He took the bottle from her. She heard a faint pop, and realized he had pulled the stopper loose with his teeth. He upended the bottle, took a deep drink, then sighed.

"This is what I've been look'n' for." He laughed and turned toward the hall, carrying her with him as if she were a rag doll. "Find'n' you was a bonus."

"What do you think you're doing? Let me go!" Grace flailed her legs, reached out for the wall, the basin, the jars of sugar, anything she could use to pry herself free or use as a weapon. Her fingers closed around the doorjamb, but one forceful tug from her captor and she lost her hold, breaking her nails in the process.

Once in the narrow passageway, he started toward the ship's stern. The floor bucked beneath his feet; he crashed into the wall, losing his grip on her. The instant her feet touched ground, Grace turned to flee. He snared her arm before she took two steps, spun her around and caught her stomach with his shoulder, heaving her up like a sack of grain.

"Put me down!" She beat her fists against his back, knowing it would do no good. What did he plan to do with her? Lock her away? She prayed that were so, because the alternative turned her blood cold with fear. *I won't let him rape me. I won't!* She'd fight, scratch out his eyes. She may not be the swordsman Jo was, but she wouldn't give up and let this man molest her.

Reaching a ladder, he climbed it with ease, then continued down the corridor.

"If you put me down right now," Grace said, "I'll forget all about this."

"I intend tae put ye down, luv." His large hand tightened on her thigh, and she had to grit her teeth to keep from screaming with outrage. "When I'm ready."

He opened a door and her heart lurched against her chest. Light flooded the hallway, giving her a glimpse of the stairs. As soon as he lowered her, she would run. She wouldn't let this man abuse her; she'd fight, scream for help. Someone would hear and come to her aid.

"Look at what I found, Capt'n," her captor boasted.

Captain? Outrage burst through Grace's panic. Captain Peters would allow his man to behave like a savage, capturing her as if she were a prize? Then the reality of her situation hit her. If the captain approved of his crewman abducting a passenger, what did that mean for her?

The man bent, setting her on the floor. Grace whipped around, filling her lungs with air to demand an explanation. The words froze in her throat.

Captain Peters, wearing nothing but brown leggings, was lying on his bed, his mouth gagged with a red cloth, his hands and arms bound by a knotted rope. He shook his head at her, and tried to talk, but the rag muffled his urgent words. The ruddy skin around his left eye was swollen and turning purple with a bruise.

"Captain—my God, what—what's going on?" she stammered, starting forward to free him.

"Well I'll be damned."

A voice from her past, a voice she thought she'd never hear again had her spinning to face a wall of pitch-black windows, and a ghost from her past.

"You . . . you . . ." There didn't seem to be enough air in the room for her to draw a full breath and finish what she meant to say. Her mind tipped, or perhaps it was the ship. In any case, she felt numb from the inside out. "It can't be."

"It's good to see you too, Angel." She flinched at the endearment he used to call her when she'd been a child. The surprise in his whiskey-brown eyes quickly vanished, leaving a hardness she didn't recognize. Her gaze scanned his sun-streaked hair, wild about his shoulders, his strong and towering body. He smiled, a cocky pull of his lips, a teasing seduction that sent a warm shiver down her back. She remembered that smirk well; it belonged to the man she'd loved for nearly all her life.

But how could he be here? And why?

"Jackson Brodie," she finally managed. "It's been a long time."

But not long enough. Not nearly long enough to forget him.

A breath shuddered out of her, a tremor that held both a warning of tears and anger. Against her will, her feet moved her toward him, closing the narrow space. For five years she hadn't known where he was, had waited daily to receive word from him. And when she hadn't, she'd assumed the worst—that he'd drowned at sea. She'd struggled to put him in the past. But now she knew the truth. He was *alive*.

Her heart thudded against her chest, so hard she thought he ought to hear it, if not see the force of it beating. Stopping within a foot of him, she stared at his clean-shaven jaw, hard and tanned from the sun, his well-shaped nose, his eyes that had long ago reached inside her and stolen a part of her heart.

Then she did the one thing she swore she'd do if she ever saw him again.

She reached out and slapped him.

Chapter Three

"Bloody 'ell, Capt'n! Ye want me tae lock 'er in the 'old?"

Jackson raised his hand to stop his first mate from taking another step. Considering Macklin's scowl, he half expected the man to throw Grace over his shoulder again and cart her off. *Grace.* He still couldn't believe his eyes. What in God's name was she doing here? "There's no need, Mac. Miss Fisk is undoubtedly upset."

"Miss . . . who?" Mac's soot-black eyes widened as they slid from the damp blonde hair clinging to Grace's shoulders and back, down to her bare toes, the tips of which were just visible beneath her gown.

"Upset?" Her eyes shot blue fire, the way they always did whenever she was angry with him, which was most of the time as Jackson recalled. With his face still stinging, he wondered if she was about to slap him again.

"I was just pouring myself a drink." He picked up a tumbler and filled it with whiskey, stalling as questions spun through his mind. Of all the bloody ships she could sail on, why the devil was she one *this* one? "Would you care to join me?"

"No I don't want a drink. Your man frightened years off my life, making me think he planned to—to—" She rounded on the sailor, ready to reprimand him. Gasping, she went as stiff as a sword, her small hands clenching into fists at her sides. "Macklin Renshaw. I should have known you'd still be keeping company with a pirate. Did you not have your fill of stealing when you served with Jo?"

Grinning, Mac fingered his black goatee, trimmed to a devil's point. "What can I say? Thiev'n's in my blood. But I do apologize for rough'n' ye up. 'Ad I know who ye were . . . " He shrugged as if that explained everything.

The ship tipped violently into a rise. Everyone reached for a handhold to keep from falling. Captain Peters slammed against the wall, Mac caught the doorjamb; Jackson braced his legs and leaned into the swell. Grace missed the chair she'd lunged for and spun backward. Jackson caught her around the waist and hugged her to him until the hull leveled.

"I'd best see what's 'appen'n' above deck," Mac said, already disappearing down the hall.

Jackson hardly noticed the man's departure. Grace shivered in his arms, her slender body pressing tighter to his. Wet linen clung to her chest like a sheet of mist, shaping her full breasts, revealing shadows of darkened nipples. His hand tightened instinctively around the curve of her waist. He breathed in the warm, feminine scent of her, and felt a pull deep in his gut.

Blood thundered in his ears, rushing down to his groin where he began to harden. God, what in bloody hell was he thinking? This was Grace, his Angel, the child he'd always protected, not a woman he could lust after. Gripping her shoulders with both hands, he set her at arms length.

"What in sweet Jesus are you doing here?" he demanded, not sounding near as angry as he felt. "You're supposed to be in a blasted school for girls, learning to become a lady." *Not in the middle of a damned ocean risking your life.*

"What am *I* doing here?" Her eyes glittered with indignation. When his gaze flickered to her barely concealed breasts, she tensed and turned aside, wrapping the panels of her robe around her like a shield. "How did you get on this ship? And why have you tied up Captain Peters? Or do I need ask?"

Jackson clenched his jaw, recalling what he had found among the captain's papers before Mac had barged in with his find. "My business with the captain is none of your concern. Return to your cabin, Grace. I'll speak to you later."

Her mouth dropped open in outrage. "I haven't seen you in five years and you think you can order me about? We aren't on the *Sea Queen*, Jackson. I'm not the adoring, gullible child any longer."

He noted the high arch of her flushed cheeks, the slender length of her neck, the slope of her breasts where her robe clung in disturbing detail, outlining things he was better off not seeing. No, she wasn't a child. But she was Grace, his little Angel, and he couldn't look at her, or treat her, any differently.

"I want you to release the captain," she continued. "Immediately, or I'll do it myself."

"You aren't going near the man," he warned.

"And why not?" She'd done more than fill out with womanly curves since he'd last seen her. Her voice had lowered to a husky tone, smooth and mellow, smoky, like aged wine. The realization made his blood thrum hot through his veins. Grinding out a curse that earned him a reproachful glare, he thought it would be worth forfeiting the bounty stored in the ship's bays if he could have his young, malleable Grace back. He didn't have time to argue with the new one.

"Captain Peters is a *Tory,*" he told her, putting as much venom behind the word as he could.

"A what?"

"A Tory, Grace. A British loyalist who is aiding the king in suppressing the colonists." Jackson picked up a letter from the desk, crumbling it in his fist. It had been written with invisible stain and he would have bypassed it in his search if not for the fact that it had been in an envelope and sealed with plain wax. The paper was still damp where he'd squeezed lime juice over the body of the letter, revealing the secret message.

"Surely you've heard about the uprising in the Colonies," he added.

Captain Peters lurched against his ropes, trying to struggle upright. Twisting futilely, he mumbled something urgent and unintelligible though his gag. Grace rushed to his side.

"Leave him," Jackson barked.

She paused, but only long enough to frown at him over her shoulder. Easing the binding from around the man's mouth, she then reached for the ropes.

"Grace," Jackson growled low, drawing out her name.

This time she stopped and regarded him with a tolerant look that might have shamed a different man. "I don't care what you call the captain, he doesn't deserve to be treated this way. Just look at his face." Her brow furrowed with worry. "You hit him!"

"Get tae your cabin, Miss," Captain Peters urged. "Hurry! Arm yerself. 'E's a blackguard. Do as I say before 'e decides tae kill ye."

"Enough!" Jackson scowled at the captain, then replaced the gag around his mouth. Aye, he'd hit the man, but only to stop the captain from burying a dagger in his back. All things considered, he thought he'd been charitable. But Grace wouldn't see things his way. She only saw a man suffering, and that was something his Angel had never been able to withstand.

She gripped her hands in front of her like a proper lady, but her narrowed gaze conveyed her disapproval. "I assume you've returned to pirating."

He arched a brow in answer, though he didn't consider himself a pirate any longer, but a smuggler with a mission. Silence invaded the crowded room, relieved only by the patter of rain against the windows along the stern.

"Why do you care if he's a British loyalist?" she asked. "You're English and the Colonies are governed by England."

"Therein lies the problem," he muttered, the words thick with sarcasm. Picking up the glass he'd dropped when he'd caught her, he refilled it and downed the whiskey in one gulp, welcoming the burning fire in his throat.

"I don't understand." She tilted her head, studying him. Light from the oil lamp reflected in her eyes, making them shimmer like pale blue stones. "You've never cared about causes before. Are you saying you now care about a group of people you have no ties to, who live half a world away?"

"I've changed since we last saw each other." In ways not even he understood completely. He was driven to help the colonists win their struggle for independence. They didn't deserve to have a crazed king who passed detrimental laws on a whim. Already countless businesses had been ruined, innocent people had been sentenced to prison, needless lives had been lost. Too many lives.

Like those of my parents. But that had been during the Seven Years' War. A battle so similar to the colonists' plight, Jackson hadn't been able to ignore it.

"Yes, you have changed. The Jackson I knew wouldn't

have resorted to pummeling a helpless man.'' Though she was a full head shorter than him, she somehow managed to look down her nose, a prim, haughty pose he didn't care for at all. Undoubtedly a trait she learned while at her bloody school.

"Return to your cabin, Grace. In the morning, when the storm is over, we can talk again.'' But he hoped to be gone by then, preventing her from asking questions he couldn't answer.

"I don't know what your plans are, Jackson,'' she said, not budging one foot toward the door. "But I'm sailing to Boston and I won't have you interfering.''

"You aren't going to America,'' he said, surprising himself. Instead of transferring the *Maiden Fair's* cargo of ammunition to his ship, he'd planned to divide his crew, leaving half his men to sail the Tory ship to Newburyport. But Grace's presence changed all that.

Her eyes widened, and her cheeks fused pink with temper. "Don't you dare think to order me about, Jackson Brodie.''

"I'm sending you back to England, Angel. After I have the cargo transferred to my ship, I'll leave Macklin and enough men to sail the *Maiden Fair* back to London.''

"Who are you to decide where I'll go and where I won't?''

He slammed his empty glass on the desk. "If Morgan and Jo had known the rebellion had turned into a war, they never would have let you leave.''

As an afterthought, he demanded, "Why did you leave?''

"You're not the only one who's changed, Jackson,'' she said, her tone suddenly so cultured, the hairs at the base of his neck raised in warning.

"There's nothing for you in Boston except danger.''

"I beg to differ.'' For the first time since she'd arrived in the cabin, she smiled, a coy, victorious smile. "There is something waiting for me in Boston. Something wonderful."

"Such as?" he asked, not liking the defiant light in her eyes.

"My fiancé."

Jackson didn't move, didn't blink, yet his brown eyes sharpened, the gold specks flaring like gunpowder set to match. Blistering, fervent and deadly. The cool air circling the cabin quivered, heating against her skin. Belatedly, she wished she'd kept her mouth shut. Regardless of what was happening now, Jackson had always been her friend and protector. Spouting off that she was engaged had been a spiteful thing to do, something Sheila might have done, but not her. She blamed her lack of control on seeing him again so unexpectedly.

He stared at her, not saying a word, so still he could have been carved from stone, hammered with a chisel and mallet. When he finally spoke, his voice sounded like shards of broken flint.

"Who should I congratulate?"

"Me, of course," she said with a flippant tilt of her chin. Inwardly, she cringed. *What am I doing?* She was purposefully baiting him, testing his patience. But he was being so overbearing, she knew she had to set him straight now or he just might force her to return home.

"And the groom?" Jackson stood rooted to the floor as if immune to the pitch of the ship.

"William Mason. A viscount from England."

"So you finally have what you've always wanted." The corner of his mouth lifted with the semblance of a smile, yet his eyes seemed like those of a stranger, cold and detached.

The sound of running footsteps had her spinning toward

the door. A sailor in a large black coat, tan pants and black boots, all soaked through, barged through the threshold, though only barely. The man was as wide as the door, thick with muscle instead of fat, Grace realized.

"Macklin needs ye topside, Capt'n. Storms gett'n' worse." As if to prove his point, the ship careened to the left, sweeping papers, the decanter of liquor, a telescope and more onto the floor.

"I'll be there in a moment, Dillon." Jackson skirted the desk, not pausing as he gripped her arm, his fingers digging into her tender skin, and led her into the passageway.

"What are you doing?"

"Putting you where you belong," he growled in a voice she'd never heard before. Had five years really changed him so much? She didn't know this Jackson, or recognize the cold fire in his eyes.

"I insist you unhand me."

"Where's your cabin?" He stopped to stare down at her, waiting for her to answer. The ship rolled, making it impossible to stand still. She staggered back, butted up against the wall, but Jackson jerked her to him, so close her gown brushed the front of his clothes. She smelled clean sweat on him, whiskey, salty rain. But mostly she smelled his anger. It was hot, boiling just under the surface of his granite face, the muscles knotted in his arms.

Irritated, but refusing to show it, she pointed to her cabin. Jackson started off again, dragging her with him. Reaching the door, he threw it open.

Before he could force her inside, she warned in a voice that was both trembling and stern, "Do whatever it takes, Jackson, but don't you dare let this ship sink."

"And keep you from your fiancé? I wouldn't dream of it."

"I want your word that you won't stop me from going to the Colonies."

"It's too dangerous."

"Your word, Jackson," she stressed, gripping his arm when he started to leave. "This is my life, and I'm going to live it in Boston."

It was too dark to see his expression, but she could *feel* his scowl. "You're right, Grace. It is your life, to do with as you wish."

"I have your word then?"

"Aye." The word was so brittle, she could have reached out and snapped it in half.

Before she could say anything else, he forced her back into the black confines of her cabin. With a whoosh of air, the door banged closed, sealing her in a rolling, creaking tomb.

He wouldn't stop her from sailing to Boston, she thought, clenching her hands at her sides. He wouldn't go back on his word, not her Jackson, no matter how much he had changed. She would be Lady Kensale soon. Everything would work out just as she'd planned.

Once the storm ended, things were going to be just fine.

Chapter Four

" 'Tis bloody wicked luck.'' Macklin snatched a splintered yardarm off the deck and threw it into the air with a grunted oath.

Jackson watched the useless pole sail against the pink-tinged sky until it arched and disappeared below the railing. He vaguely heard the resulting splash as it struck the sea, now as calm as a sleeping babe after a fretful night. Though it was barely past dawn, and no one had had a moment's rest, his crew, and even a few belonging to the *Maiden,* were hauling debris that couldn't be salvaged to the sides, pitching it overboard, clearing the deck for the dangerous, backbreaking work that was to come.

From his estimation, most of the ship's sails, two of the towering masts and all but one remaining yard were damaged beyond repair. Ratlines and shrouds had vanished, the heavy ropes clipped free from the deadeyes that kept them taut. A portion of the hull near the bow had buckled. They were taking on water. The pumps were handling the seepage, but it wouldn't be long before the strakes weakened and ripped a hole larger than they could fight. If he could reach land, repairs might be possible, but they were days from any island. At most, the *Maiden Fair* had two hours before she headed for the bottom of the sea.

"Do whatever it takes, Jackson, but don't you dare let this ship sink. This is my life, and I'm going to live it in Boston."

Hearing Grace's defiant vow from the night before, he spit out a curse that had Mac raising a dark brow and pausing as he dug a sail hook from beneath a pile of severed wood.

"Put men on the capstan, Mac," Jackson ordered. "I want to be off this ship before she decides to take us with her to the ocean floor."

"Aye, Capt'n."

Turning away, Jackson headed for the stern, the highest point of the ship, to better see the destruction, though he wasn't sure why he bothered. The vessel was lost, but not the cargo, which they could unload and save if they hurried.

The tension that had him clenching his hands had little to do with the sinking ship and everything to do with the decoded letter he'd found in Captain Peters's cabin. King George was sending a fleet of ships to blockade the Americas' coast, cutting the rebels off from the rest of the world. They had to be warned. If they gathered every vessel capable of firing a cannon, they might be able to defeat the English. Adding the *Maiden Fair* to the rebels' array would have helped—

Jackson spotted his ship fast approaching from the east. He'd ordered her to move off before the storm had struck. Only half her sails were raised, but her three masts were intact, spearing into the sky like the horns of a proud beast.

He allowed a smile, the first in a lifetime it seemed. His

ship had obviously suffered some damage, but nothing too serious. He wasn't surprised. The *Sea Queen* had the luck of an infant born with a silver spoon. Or perhaps a jeweled dagger, he thought, thinking of the *Sea Queen* blade. Nothing could touch her.

Feeling a surge of pride that warmed his chest, he wondered what Grace would say when she glimpsed the vessel she'd always claimed to hate. More importantly, how would she react when she learned what he'd renamed her?

A stir at the hatchway below warned that he wouldn't have to wait long to find out. Grace eased through the portal and into the sun's soft glow. She'd braided and wrapped her white-gold hair into an elegant knot at the base of her neck, drawing attention to her slender throat and the scooped neckline of her bodice, the cut far too low for his liking, especially when every male eye paused to gawk at her. She seemed small and fragile, so much like the compassionate child he once knew. Grinding his jaw, he thought about the words he intended to have with Morgan and Jo for letting their baby sister out of their sight and without protection.

Baby sister. Remembering the annoying curves he'd held the night before, it was obvious he had to change his way of thinking. Grace was no longer a child with dirt on her face and her hair in scruffy pigtails. She'd been on the verge of blossoming into a young woman the last time he'd seen her. And blossom she had.

Jackson felt his mouth curl into a scowl. Why couldn't she have remained a little girl? Adoring? Docile? Recalling the heat of her anger when she'd first seen him, she'd not only grown up, she thought she didn't need his protection. If not for the rebellion, he'd be happy to see her. But by simply approaching the Americas' coast, they were risking a confrontation with the British.

A battle with Grace on board his ship. His nerves tightened with the possibility.

Lifting the skirt of her jade gown, revealing her ruffled shift and soft leather boots, she carefully picked her way through the rubble. Her pale brow furrowed; her full mouth compressed into a tight line of worry. She lifted her gaze, instantly finding him, as if she'd known where he'd be. He tensed, then realized he shouldn't be surprised; she'd always had the unnerving ability to sense his presence.

What did she see when she looked at him now? A pirate who destroyed and thieved? Or a man who refused to let life, *or England,* hold him down? There were accusations in her clear blue eyes, silent disapproval she didn't need to voice. She blamed him, not the storm, for the destruction of the *Maiden Fair.*

He sighed, no happier about the turn of events than she.

"What . . . what happened?" a panicked female voice called out.

A woman wearing a silver gown with a black-and-white striped Watteau overdress, emerged from below. Her brown hair, the color of old moss, was twisted around the crown of her head as tightly as her gown was buttoned at her throat. Her full, sulky mouth dropped open in outrage; her eyes bulged as she scanned the wreckage.

Seeing three men toss strips of canvas over the rails, she snapped, "You men there, what are you doing? Was that part of the sail you just threw away?"

The sailors barely spared her a glance before bending to their task again.

"We need those," she told them, her voice breaking with either panic or fury, Jackson wasn't sure which. He hoped it wasn't panic; he had no experience with hysterical women.

"Retrieve them!" she demanded, pointing to the railing. "At once!"

" 'Ere now," Macklin drawled, strolling up to the ladies, slowly inspecting the strange woman's form. "What's all the fuss about?"

When she caught Macklin eyeing her, Jackson thought it a miracle her scowl didn't burn a hole through his first mate's head. "The 'fuss' is that those men don't know what they're doing!"

"Is that so?" Folding his arms across his lean chest, the sailor braced both legs shoulder width apart. He produced a cocky, dimpled smile that he regularly used to charm his way into ladies' beds and out of brawls. "What would ye have them do?"

Tightening her spine, she said slowly and simply, "Put the sails back up on the poles where they belong."

Chuckling so hard, the morning light danced in his black eyes, Macklin said, "Now why 'adn't I thought of that?"

Jackson smiled at the absurd demand, curious as to what would happen next.

"Mac, would you please go away." Grace touched the woman's arm. "Sheila—"

The woman jerked back, leveling Grace with a furious glare. "You're responsible for this. If not for you, I wouldn't be on this horrid ship. But my mother . . ." She gripped her stomach with both hands and moaned. "It's bad enough that my sickness is coming back, but this wretched man has insulted me. These miscreants will abandon me in the middle of nowhere, I just know they will."

Losing his smile and replacing it with a scowl, Jackson stepped up to the balustrade to tower over them, and focused his glare on the woman. "Is there a problem, Grace?"

The woman whipped around, staggering slightly as her petticoats swirled around her legs. "Who are you?"

"I've just recently arrived." It amazed him that the words didn't vibrate in a growl. He'd met few women he didn't like, but hearing this one's scornful tone with Grace tempted him to toss her overboard with the rest of the debris.

"How is that possible? I've never seen you before, and we've been at sea for weeks."

"Jackson, please," Grace urged. "Sheila, if you'll let me explain—"

"Jackson? You called him by his name. Do you know this man?"

Just then the dozen crewmen working the capstan gave a cheer as the first crate of ammunition was raised from the hold below. Pushing the giant wooden spokes that were attached to a drum, much like a wagon wheel, they brought their prize into view. Another group of men, led by Dillon, whose arms were as thick as a pine tree, guided it to a clear spot on deck.

"What are they doing?" Sheila asked.

Grace squeezed her eyes shut. Jackson had a good idea as to why. She'd spent the last eight years trying to disassociate herself from pirates and thieving, and here she was, surrounded by a shipload of sea robbers stealing cargo.

"Grace," Sheila insisted in a level voice that held only a slight quiver. "If you know what is going on, I demand you tell me at once."

"They're taking the crates stored below," Grace said, fidgeting with the cream lace on her sleeves.

"Taking them where?" Lifting her hands, Sheila frowned, perplexed. Then, seeing the other vessel drawing alongside, her pale complexion faded to deadly white. Jackson had no doubt that she'd spotted the black Jolly Roger flying from the mast.

"They're pirates?" The woman hugged up against Grace, using her as a shield. "These men are pirates!"

"You've brought the *Sea Queen*," Grace whispered, her eyes wide with an emotion he couldn't read. Everything about her stilled, her face, her hands. For an instant, not even the steady breeze seemed to touch her.

"She's not the *Sea Queen* any longer," he told her, watching for her reaction. "She's the *Sea Angel*."

"Angel?" She shook her head as if unable to accept what she'd heard. "You've named her after . . ."

"After you," he said, his voice so low he wasn't sure she heard him.

She glanced at him, her eyes narrowed, almost pained, but the ship drew her gaze away as if pulling her by an invisible magnetic force.

Sheila sucked in a breath and stumbled back. "That's your pirate ship. I remember hearing about the horrible things you did on the *Sea Queen*. Stealing, murdering." She pointed at Jackson. "And you know him. You called him by his given name. Oh, dear Lord, help me. You're in league with him. You're stealing the cargo. You had this planned all along."

"No, Sheila, I—" Grace reached for the woman, but when Sheila squealed, Grace flinched and dropped her hands.

"Don't kill me. I know you don't like me, but please don't kill me."

"I wouldn't . . ." Grace's face turned ashen with disbelief. She looked to Jackson, her gaze imploring. "Do something."

"Such as?"

"Tell her you don't mean to harm her."

"You'd have me lie?"

"Jackson!" Grace said with such fury, he thought she

might choke. "Don't frighten her. She's had a difficult enough voyage as it is."

As angry as he was with the disagreeable woman, Jackson wanted to take Grace by the shoulders and shake her. She was too blasted compassionate for her own good. The few times he'd visited her in London, he'd watched people shun her, trample on her tender feelings. Because he'd known how much she'd wanted to be accepted, he'd been forced to stand by and let it happen. That was one reason he'd decided to stay away from her. His presence threatened her chance to belong.

Well, they weren't in a London drawing room at the moment, and he'd be dammed if he'd offer the shrewish woman any reassurance.

"I haven't decided what to do with her. The rest of the passengers were wise enough to remain in their cabins, keeping their tongues still and their mouths shut."

"Well, I never—" Sheila said, though with less contempt than before.

"As you can see, we're pressed for time. I must unload the *Maiden's* cargo before we sink."

"Sink?" The woman pressed her hand to her chest and staggered as if she meant to faint. Macklin gripped her arms to steady her, but Sheila made a remarkable recovery and shot him a quelling glare.

"Aye. Sinks." Jackson felt compelled to add, "And there's not enough room on my vessel for everyone."

"I can pay my way," the woman hurriedly assured him. "I have gold."

"Sheila, you don't—"

"Let her finish." Jackson crossed to the stairs and joined them on the main deck. With every step he took forward, Sheila took one in retreat. "If she has enough to tempt me, perhaps I'll take her along. If not . . ." He shrugged, giving the woman a deadly smile.

"That's enough!" Grace stood between him and the cowering woman. She tilted her head back to meet Jackson's scowl. "Since you failed to keep the *Maiden* intact, you will be taking *all* of us to the Colonies."

"And why would I do that?"

"Because you promised."

He bit back an oath. Damn his temper. He never should have promised to take her to the Americas, but now the deed was done, made worse now that the *Maiden Fair* was sinking. He had no choice but take her with him.

But just because he'd promised to take her to the Colonies didn't mean he had to leave her there. Once he delivered the ammunition and the coded message to his contact, he'd return to England, taking her with him. Which meant they would have to spend two months in each other's company. Considering the fiery temper she'd acquired since he'd last seen her, he wondered if either of them would survive.

"Now, kindly tell Sheila you were only teasing about leaving her behind, and tell her I had nothing to do with you taking the cargo."

Standing aside and folding her arms across her chest, Grace waited for him to do as she ordered. He stared down at her, saw the obstinate shimmer in her crystal-blue eyes, the unbending pout of her lush mouth. He fought the urge to smile. God, how he'd missed her. He never should have stayed away so long. But miss her or not, he wasn't about to let her issue demands. Yet he could give her part of what she asked.

To Sheila, he said, "Grace knew nothing about my . . . visit or my intentions to detain the *Maiden Fair*. And so you understand, my business here has nothing to do with pirating. This is war, and you've sailed into the middle of it. I suggest you don't forget it." Turning to leave, he paused to add over his shoulder, "If you keep your viper tongue in your head, I'll consider taking you when we sail. If not, you'll be left behind.''

"Jackson!" Grace admonished, her cheeks flushing with anger.

He walked toward the bow, allowing his grin to show, only to feel it vanish. Grace was here, with him. The reminder made every muscle tighten with apprehension. He had to convince her to return home. The British were gaining strength, seizing a wider area than merely Boston under their control. Farms and businesses, food and supplies were being seized at will. People were afraid to leave their homes, terrified they might not be there when they returned. But they were equally afraid to stay, knowing they might be shot as rebels.

And Jackson would be powerless to protect her. That duty would fall to her fiancé—the man who would give Grace everything she'd ever wanted.

"Damn it, Grace," he said softly so no one would hear the fear in his voice. "Why aren't you in London where you belong?"

"I always expect to see a 'alo over your 'ead."

Startled, Grace spun around to find Macklin leaning against the doorjamb of the captain's cabin. She hadn't heard his approach. Being back onboard the *Sea Queen* after so many years, her thoughts had become lost in the past. Smoothing her palms down her muslin skirt, she turned away, wishing she could ask him to leave; she just wanted to be alone right now.

Besides, halo, indeed!

"Why would you expect such a thing?" She fingered the blankets on the narrow bunk bed, remembering the times Morgan had let her sit there and read her books on herbal remedies. She'd imagined herself growing up to be a doctor, helping people. The Angel Doctor, they'd called her.

She shook her head, grimacing. That was so long ago, such a different person.

Macklin shrugged, hooking his thumbs into the waistband of his pants. "I suppose 'tis the way Capt'n talks about ye."

She tensed, her chest squeezing tight. "Jackson talks about me?"

"Aye, about the days you sailed together. 'Im learn'n' tae be a pirate, you follow'n' 'im around, determined tae keep 'im out of trouble. Like some sort of guardian angel."

Grace hugged her arms across her waist. The pressure in her chest didn't ease, it just turned to disappointment. *Foolish, foolish girl!* Jackson had always thought her a pest, no doubt his opinion hadn't changed.

"I did not follow him around," she said, wincing at the snappish tone of her voice. Though she *had* pursued him, shamefully, at that, in her effort to keep him safe. Hearing it from Mac made her finally realize that she'd been no better than an annoying puppy, chasing after the heels of her master. Embarrassing.

Forcing a pleasant tone, she asked, "Is there something I can do for you, Mac?"

"I've a message for ye from the Capt'n. Ye're tae 'ave 'is cabin while on board the *Sea Angel*."

"That's kind of Jackson, but you can tell him I'll use my old room."

Stroking his beard, Mac straightened to his full height. "If ye don't mind my say'n', Miss Fisk, consider'n' the black mood 'e's in, I'll 'ave your trunk brought in 'ere."

She started to argue, but Mac vacated the doorway before she could manage one word. Huffing a breath, she turned in a tight circle, feeling trapped by her frustration. The man was infuriating, overbearing. *And alive!*

For five years she hadn't known where Jackson was. He hadn't bothered to send one letter to tell her if he was safe and well. If he'd married, or had settled down. Nothing. Not one word. But now she knew. He was alive and still challenging fate, risking his life. *But then I always knew Jackson was a pirate, through and through.*

A rush of trembling emotions forced her to sink onto the thin mattress. She pressed her hands to her face as the events of the last few hours overwhelmed her. How could her life turn upside down within a blink of an eye? She stood to lose everything she'd planned for. Moving to the Colonies meant moving away from her past, escaping the rumors that had dogged her wherever she went, preventing her from being accepted.

It was bad enough that Sheila knew about her pirating days. But now the woman had met Jackson, had tangible proof of Grace's association with thieves. What hope was there that the woman would keep quiet? Grace quietly moaned, but the small sound of distress disgusted her. She might be a lady now, but she wasn't weak.

Fisting her hands in her lap, she straightened her spine, determined to look on the bright side. Nothing had really changed. She was still engaged to William, who didn't care about her past. Sheila wouldn't be able to ruin anything because she would be traveling to Abington. Once they docked in Medford, there was no reason to believe she'd ever see Sheila again.

No, nothing had changed. Her plans for her future were no different than . . . than this cabin since the last time she'd seen it. Bookshelves strung with thick cable kept books and charts in place. A single ladder-back chair sat before the heavy oak desk. She stood and ran her hand over the smooth table, scarred and faded from years of use. She found the gash where the *Sea Queen* blade had been impaled the day they'd discovered the ship. That day seemed like a lifetime ago—someone else's life, at that.

She skimmed her fingers over the groove. No, nothing had changed. She only had to look at Jackson to be assured of that.

He was still the wild, untamed man she remembered, and had foolishly loved. After all these years, he was still seeking adventure, rushing in headfirst as if relishing the chance to grab hold of danger. Gambling to see if he would beat the odds and come out the victor. Pirating had been dangerous enough, but he'd obviously moved on to higher stakes.

Why settle for pirating when you could fight a war?

Yes, he was alive, but for how long? The thought pressed the breath from her lungs, the way it always did when she thought of something horrible happening to Jackson. That's why she'd had to put him out of her mind, shut him out of her life.

She'd lost her parents and younger brother because of the Seven Years' War. She'd spent the remainder of her childhood fearing she'd lose Morgan, Jo *and* Jackson because of their thirst for adventure. It was a fear she refused to live with any longer.

She'd been right to stop pining away for him, hoping that he'd become the man she needed. He was what he was. A pirate, a man destined to test his fate. *Alone.*

Facing the bay of windows along the back wall, watching the sun beat down on the rolling sea, she reaffirmed how lucky she'd been to have found William. They made an ideal pair; he would provide her with a home, White Rose, and security. She in turn would raise their children.

The thought didn't produce the cheerful smile she needed. Instead, she felt an anxious quiver in her stomach.

"Now this is a sight I could never grow tired of."

Startled for the second time that morning, Grace somehow managed to keep from spinning around as she had with Macklin. The rich timbre of Jackson's voice wound its way inside her, making her cheeks burn, her breath turn whisper thin. Had he meant he could never tire of seeing her? She pressed her hand to her jittery stomach.

Glancing out the window, she felt her nerves harden. With bitter certainty, she knew he'd been referring to the ocean beyond, sparkling like amber set ablaze in the setting sun. The sea was a wicked, tempestuous woman—the only one Jackson would ever love. It wasn't within Grace to hate, but she wanted to hate the sea for that fact alone.

No! I have William. Jackson can have the sea for all I care! He isn't for me!

She heard the brush of his footsteps against wood, felt the air warm and tingle as he drew near. The hairs on her arms raised, danced with vibrating shivers. She rubbed the sensation away, but it persisted, spreading to her chest and up her neck. She mentally willed herself to stop reacting to his presence, but she had no control over what she felt, what he made her feel.

Stopping beside her, he sat on the windowsill and leaned against the corner, one booted foot on the seat and his elbow braced on his knee. He watched her through lowered lids as if she were a frightened mouse poised to run. "I suppose it feels strange, being back on board the *Sea Angel.*"

The *Sea Angel.* Why had he named the ship after her? For what possible reason?

"Years ago I swore I'd never sail on this ship again." She gave a mirthless laugh. "Jo warned me that I might need it someday." And the *Sea Queen* blade, as well. But Grace hadn't believed her.

"I'll keep the dagger, but I won't ever use it." Grace had grudgingly conceded five years ago.

"Don't be so sure." Her sister had smiled a secretive, mad-

dening smile. *"You're looking for something, Grace. This ship and the blade you're holding just might help you find it."*

Well, she'd finally taken her sister's advice, strapping the dagger to her thigh after her first encounter with Jackson. Though, considering she didn't know how to use it, the knife gave her little comfort. Not that she needed to use it. She already knew what she wanted and where she intended to go. Only now, it seemed fate was throwing her words back into her face, because with the sinking of the *Maiden Fair*, she had to rely on the *Sea Queen*—or *Sea Angel*, she silently amended—to take her to her new home.

"This ship is supposed to be anchored in Dunmore," she said, determined to keep an emotional distance from him. "Have you taken to stealing from me and my sisters, as well?"

"I only borrowed her for a time."

"She isn't yours to borrow. Why are you involving yourself in the rebellion, anyway? It has nothing to do with you."

He considered her for a long moment, then said, "The Seven Years' War was hard on you, was it not?"

"You know it was."

He nodded, his attention straying to the window. "It took its toll on me, as well. My father lost his life in the war. And my mother . . ."

"I know, Jackson," she whispered, startled that she could feel the grief he still carried. His mother had died less than six months after learning her husband would never return home.

"I had no one left, Grace. You had your sisters. But me . . ." He shook his head.

She remembered the fifteen-year-old boy who'd joined the *Sea Queen*. He'd been quiet with anger, the pain of losing his family vivid in his eyes. She'd been drawn to him that first day, desperate to help him. He wasn't a hurting boy any longer, she reminded herself, but a man who knew right from wrong. Somehow she had to make him see that this war wasn't his to fight.

"Because you have no family left, you've decided to take up someone else's cause?" she asked. "Risk your life for nothing?"

He angled his head, his sharp gaze piercing her. "Do you consider trying to stop the king from ruining countless lives 'nothing'? What if I could have stopped the soldiers from destroying your village? Would you have wanted me to help? Or do the safe thing and turn away?"

She opened her mouth to argue, but snapped it shut again. What could she possibly say to that?

Running a hand through his thick, sun-streaked hair, he changed the subject by asking, "Is being back on board this ship so bad?"

"Not if you keep your word." Her curt response surprised her and caused a dangerous spark to leap into his eyes. A breath hissed from between his teeth. Jackson had never, *ever*, directed his anger at her. Feeling it now, she retreated a step, stopping when her thighs bumped against the desk.

"If you're foolish enough to ignore common sense," he said, his voice grounding like coarse gravel, "I won't try to stop you."

"Not foolish. Determined."

"Call it what you will. The Colonies is no place for you."

"My place is wherever my fiancé happens to be. And at present, he's in Medford."

The muscle in his jaw pulsed, and his skin darkened beneath his tan. She'd pushed him too far, though she didn't understand how she'd done so. Perhaps he needed time to accept her engagement. He didn't know William; Jackson might be feeling protective, like the big brother she didn't want him to be.

Or perhaps it was as he'd said; he'd changed, so much so, that she didn't know him any longer.

Her gaze flickered over the stubble of his beard, specks of hard gold covering him from chin to cheek. Bruised shadows rimmed his eyes, fatigue not evident in the brace of his wide shoulders, covered by a gauzy black shirt, or the muscles that flexed and bunched along his arms where he'd rolled the sleeves back. He was like a wolf, crouched on his haunches and ready to spring. *Or a six-foot-tall overbearing ogre ready to explode.* Even the air smelled angry. Like sulfur and ash.

Well, he could be mad all he wanted, she decided, ignoring the way her stomach wound into a dozen little knots. She didn't want to fight with him. In fact, she *refused* to fight.

"Do you love him?"

The simple question, and the quiet way he asked it, took her breath away. She snatched a rolled piece of paper off the desk and twisted it in her hands.

Jackson reached out. Grace flinched, expecting him to grab her, but he pried the missive out of her grip and replaced it on the desk. "It's a rather important document you nearly strangled. Now, do you love him?"

"I'm not going to discuss William with you."

"You're ashamed of him," he scoffed.

"I am not!" she said, punctuating each word.

"Then why are you afraid to talk about him?" he asked, standing to tower over her.

"I'm not afraid of anything." She held his gaze, matching temper with temper. "Including you."

"Do you love him?"

"My feelings are none of your business."

His heated gaze nearly singed her where she stood. "Answer my question, damn it!"

"Don't curse at me, Jackson Brodie."

"Do you—"

"All right! I love him!" she shouted back, not believing the lie coming out of her mouth. Or the temper he'd invoked. But now that she'd started she couldn't stop. "I love him with all my heart. And he adores me!"

Something dark and painful passed through Jackson's eyes. She heard his knuckles pop as he clenched his hands. Then he caught her chin between his thumb and forefinger, forcing her gaze to stay locked with his. For an instant she thought he could see inside her, feel the sudden shaking his touch created. It had been so long since she'd seen him. He shouldn't make her feel anything except friendship. She didn't *want* to feel anything else. But the wild beating of her heart, the heating of her skin, the yearning for something more that opened up inside her warned her that nothing had changed. She still cared for him, too much for her own good. The realization made her want to cry.

The corner of his mouth lifted with a remorseful smile. "Can't say as I blame the man for adoring you. He'd be insane not to."

Jackson's gaze flickered to her lips. His eyes narrowed, the gold specks within flaring with a burst of fire. This new emotion wasn't anger, she realized, but something else, something she never thought she'd see in him. Grace held her breath, afraid to move, afraid to even think about where they were or what might happen next. He wanted to kiss her; she could see the need in his eyes, the uncertainty warring with a strange kind of desire.

His shoulder-length hair fell to the sides of his face, the honeyed streaks shadowing his eyes, bringing her the scents of sun and man, a musky tang she remembered so well, she often smelled it in her dreams. How many times had she seen him like this in her mind's eye? Imagining him holding her, looking at her, wanting only her?

"Stop," a practical voice urged from the back of her mind. *"He'll break your heart. William is the man you're to marry."*

She ignored the warning. Jackson wanted to kiss her, and folly or not, nothing in the world would make her stop him. If only once, she wanted to know the texture of his lips, learn the flavor of his taste. His hand slid up, rough fingers over sensitive skin, until he cupped her jaw in his callused palm. He bent closer, his warm breath brushing her lips, slipping into her mouth.

A quiver erupted in her knees, spreading a tingling numbness throughout her limbs. She thought she would either fall at his feet or float off the ground. *Kiss me, Jackson, please.* She wanted to grip his head, bring him to her, but she didn't move. *Couldn't* move.

"Jackson," she whispered.

As if her voice hadn't been an encouraging plea, but a blow to the head, his eyes widened with sudden alarm.

"Bloody hell." He straightened, putting a foot of space between them, though it could have been a mile, he withdrew so quickly and so completely. A pulse beat furiously at his temple. His eyes turned dark, shuttering out all emotion. The angles of his face hardened, becoming as unreadable as a sheet of hammered steel.

"Angel, I . . ." He stepped back, taking great pains not to touch her. Abruptly, he turned and headed for the door. "I'll leave you to get settled."

She tried to think of something to say, anything that would end the humiliation that had her shaking with cold. After a moment, she realized there wasn't any need; Jackson was gone, leaving her alone with her reproachful thoughts.

He hadn't kissed her. He hadn't *wanted* to kiss her. Wouldn't have even tried if she hadn't encouraged him. Oh, God, what had she done?

She pressed her hands to her stomach and thought she might become ill. The repercussions of what had nearly happened hit her then. She was engaged to William, her fiancé who had light blue eyes, an easy smile and perfect manners. She might not have kissed Jackson, but she'd betrayed William nonetheless.

She sank onto the window seat, horrified by her behavior.

"I don't deserve William," she whispered. He thought he was marrying a real lady, not a common girl with the morals of an alley cat.

Straightening her back, she realized seeing Jackson was just another test, not unlike those she'd taken at Wilmouth School for Girls, to prove whether or not she was ready to enter society. And this test she meant to pass. She could control her emotions where Jackson Brodie was concerned. Would, in fact, put her feelings behind her for good.

Because once again, Jackson had proven that he was not the man she needed.

Chapter Five

Her glare reached across the ship like a dagger of ice. Despite the noonday heat burning his bare chest, the sweat dripping down his face, Jackson could feel Grace's frigid blue gaze impale his back. Cold, with a keen anger meant for him alone. She stood near the wheel twenty yards away, her arms crossed, her chin tilted like a petulant child. *But a child with the body of a seductress.*

Well, her anger couldn't be helped, he thought, gripping a thick, coarse line with both hands and heaving back to raise the fore topgallant sail another foot. Two crewmen stood aside, waiting to lend a hand, but Jackson shook his head, wanting to do the backbreaking work alone. For six days, ever since he'd nearly made the worst blunder of his life, he'd been raising sails, rearranging cargo, scaling shrouds to hoist replacement ropes up the masts—all tasks normally performed by his crew—but he'd needed the distraction. Though it hadn't helped, he admitted with a scowl.

No matter how exhausted he was at the end of each day, how much his limbs shook or his hands bled from the cuts he'd sustained, he couldn't forget the moment he'd almost kissed Grace. *Kissed her!*

Or the pained look in her eyes before he'd turned and ran.

"Bloody hell!" She should have slapped him. But she hadn't. She'd leaned into him, undoubtedly too shocked to react. *But her eyes . . .* He'd seen a shimmer of uncertainty *and* expectation. Had she wanted him to kiss her? The thought had him snarling out another curse. *Don't be a fool, man.* She might have been infatuated with him when she'd been a child, but that was in the past.

He jerked the rope harder, felt the halyard catch at the top. Tying off the line, he wiped sweat from his brow and headed for the hatchway to the lower deck. The cannons needed to be cleaned and inspected. The closer they came to reaching the Americas' coast, the more likely the guns would be put to use.

At the companionway he paused—he couldn't help himself—to catch a glimpse of her. Their gazes met—clashed, more accurately. She stiffened, lowering her arms to clasp her hands behind her back. Pivoting on her heel, she turned away, her nose in the air, her shoulders straight. Every inch the lady.

Her gown, pale peach today, was cut like her others: tight-fitting sleeves, a bodice that hugged her slim waist, a gathered skirt that fell from her hips to swirl like froth around her long legs—and a neckline scooped so low as to tempt a priest.

He should forbid her to roam the decks. If she wasn't covered in freckles when they reached Medford, she'd certainly have every sailor on board in love with her by the time they docked.

"Did ye eat someth'n' bad, Capt'n?" Macklin asked, chewing around a bite of hardtack.

Jackson frowned at his first mate. "No, why do you ask?"

" 'Tis the look on ye face, as if someth'n' were pain'n' ye." He studied the hard biscuit and struggled to swallow. "I thought maybe weevils 'ad gotten into the flour again."

Jackson scowled. "Go away, Mac."

The sailor leaned against the bulkhead and sighed as if he had nothing better to do. "She's a comely lass, wouldn't ye say? Easy on the eyes."

Feeling a heat begin to burn in his gut that had nothing to do with the sun or food, he warned, "I suggest you keep your eyes focused on your work."

"Aye, but a man does get lonely for a woman's voice every now and then. Even if it might be a bit sharp-tongued."

Sharp? Jackson wouldn't know. He and Grace hadn't exchanged more than a curt "Good morning" and "Good night" in days.

"A man has to take advantage where he can. Who knows 'ow long 'twill be before I 'ave the pleasure of a beautiful woman's company."

"Stay away from her, Mac," Jackson ordered, drawing attention from the crewmen nearby. Knowing he should lower his voice, but unable to, he added, "She's too virtuous for the likes of you." *Or me.*

"Too virtuous? Ye must be josh'n' me, Capt'n. There's fire in that woman tae be sure, and she might be a lady. But virtue?" He cocked his head as if to consider the thought. "Perhaps ye're see'n' someth'n' I've missed. Could be I need tae spend more time with 'er."

Jackson grabbed the man by the shirt front and hauled him up. "Stay away from her, Macklin!"

"From who, Capt'n?" With a shrewd grin, he nodded toward the railing starboard side, where a woman was struggling to keep her parasol from flying away in the stiff breeze. "I was referr'n' tae Miss Foxsworth. She 'as spirit, that one does. If ye're of a mind tae let me go, I think the little lady might be in need of my 'elp."

Jackson released his first mate and watched in fuming silence as the sailor smoothed his shirt and headed for the English shrew.

Pausing, all traces of his smile gone, Mac said, " 'Tis as I said, Capt'n, ye never know 'ow long 'twill be before ye see such a beautiful woman again."

Damn Macklin. The man had purposefully let him think he'd been referring to Grace. And Jackson had been ready to tear Mac apart one limb at a time. He wiped his hand over his face, then snatched his shirt from atop a barrel where he'd tossed it before setting to work.

This couldn't continue, he swore to himself, clenching the shirt in his fist. He couldn't tolerate another day of her silence or his ... his ... He wasn't certain which emotion had him more on edge. Disgust that he'd almost violated the brotherly trust between himself and Grace, or anger that he couldn't rid himself of the desire to kiss her.

"Bloody hell," he growled.

He started for the stern, where Grace stood at the far rail, and pushed thoughts of his disturbing need aside. Or tried to. He couldn't forget entirely, damn his soul. The compelling temptation to touch her had been too strong to ignore. The scent of her, something soft and womanly, still filled his mind, all but wiping out the salty air, the sweaty men, the sun-baked wood.

He had to apologize. He'd been a fool not to do so six days ago. If he had, perhaps she would have forgiven him and he would have saved himself an aching back and blistered hands. They could have pretended nothing had happened and gone on as before.

He only had two days left, three at most, before they reached the Americas. She would expect him to sail to

Medford, hand her over to her fiancé, the *viscount*, a man Jackson disliked sight unseen.

I'm not leaving her behind in the midst of a war, regardless of what I promised. Which meant he had to make peace with her before he broke his word.

Climbing the stairs to the quarter gallery, he stopped well behind her. She tensed her back as if she were a rabbit sensing the presence of a wolf. Her head came up another inch. The ship took a rocky dip, then buffeted against an oncoming wave. She adjusted easily to the shifting deck. He smiled ruefully, thinking she might not have liked sailing, but her body remembered what to do.

"Grace, I think it's time we talked."

Silence.

He forced a steadying breath. "There's no reason to be stubborn."

"I hadn't realized I was being anything, Jackson," she said in a silky, cultured tone, keeping her gaze fixed on the horizon.

"Blast it, Grace, I'm trying to apologize."

"Apologize? You've ignored me for six days, Jackson, and now you want to apol—" She spun to face him, but her tirade ended as her mouth fell open. Her gaze fastened on his bare chest. As if needing help to keep herself braced upright, she gripped the railing behind her. Belatedly, he realized he still held his shirt in his hand.

She'd seen him wearing nothing more than his pants before, he thought, shifting uneasily. Countless times. *When she'd been a girl.* From the astonishment on her face she wasn't looking at him through the eyes of a child, but through those of a woman. A look similar to the one she'd worn the moment he'd almost kissed her. But he'd mistaken the meaning of that look—he was sure of it. She couldn't be infatuated with him any longer. Not after all these years.

Turning to the side, she half choked, "We may be on a ship, but there are still rules of decorum."

He jerked the shirt over his head and moved to stand behind her. The wind had pulled strands of blonde hair loose from the complicated knot at her nape. The silky threads fluttered in the wind, streaming against her neck, curling around her ears. He hadn't touched her hair since she'd worn it in braids. It looked softer now, fairer. Just like the woman she'd grown into.

"The wind's been with us. We should reach Massachusetts within two days." He didn't know why he'd brought that up. Their destination was the last thing he wanted to discuss. But he no longer knew what to say to her, or how to act. His unease was an irksome thing. She'd become a lady since he'd last seen her. If he tried ruffling her hair or tickling her until she cried mercy, she'd probably slap him.

She faced the bow and squinted her eyes to study the sky. "So soon?"

The hesitancy in her voice surprised him. "Having second thoughts about seeing your fiancé?"

Gifting him with a tolerant smirk, she said, "I just thought it would take longer, is all."

"Grace," he began, "about the other day. I feel I should explain."

She looked at him, her features smooth, carefully void of all emotion.

"I don't know what I thought I was doing."

"You almost kissed me," she said, far too boldly for his liking. But then he'd always confused her gentleness with timidity.

"But I didn't. That's the important thing."

"It would have been a mistake."

"Exactly."

"Because I'm to be married soon," she reaffirmed with a stubborn tilt of her chin.

"There's no need to remind me." Her belonging to another man was a fact he didn't think he'd ever forget—or accept.

Pursing her lips thoughtfully, she asked, "Miss Foxsworth isn't engaged. Would kissing her have been a mistake?"

"Aye, of the worst kind." Scowling, he glanced at the woman in question just as she turned a cold shoulder to Macklin. The sailor wasn't daunted, however, but stepped up to Miss Foxsworth and whispered something into her ear. To Jackson's disbelief, she faced Mac, her pouty mouth drawn in a superior line. She didn't move away, but said something in return that had Macklin laughing with delight.

"It sounds as if you oppose kissing any lady."

"I've known my share of women," he blurted, then wished he hadn't when her eyes flared with surprise. She quickly looked away, making him regret his decision to seek her out at all. "Why all these questions? Can't you just accept that I regret my behavior and let it go?"

"I'm trying to understand you, Jackson." Grace sighed, a deep, breathy sigh that lifted her chest and stretched pale rosy-peach fabric against her creamy breasts.

Jackson's mouth suddenly went dry. He forced his gaze to stay on her face. "You're trying to test my patience, is what you're doing."

As if she hadn't heard him, she asked, "Why don't you want to kiss Miss Foxsworth?"

"I find nothing about her attractive."

"And me?" she asked. "Do you find me attractive?"

He ground his teeth, fighting back the answer that pushed to the fore of his mind. *Attractive* didn't do her justice. She was beautiful, innocent and alluring, everything a man could want in a woman and more. But nothing on earth would make him say as much. "You're fair enough."

"But not fair enough to tempt you."

"Is this about me almost kissing you, or does this involve your viscount?" The image of a man, any man, touching her set something loose inside Jackson, a furious emotion that jolted him to the core. "Has your fiancé kissed you?"

She gasped. "How could you ask something so personal?"

"He hasn't, has he?" He saw his answer in her wide, nervous eyes. "Is that what this is all about? You're curious?" He took a step toward her. Grace took a hasty step in retreat. "Do you want me to show you how it's done?"

"Don't be obtuse," she insisted, drawing herself up, her blue eyes glittering like wet crystals left in the sun. Butting up against the railing, she spun around and gripped the balustrade. "The only thing I want from you is to be taken to Medford."

He moved behind her, leaning close so the loose strands of her hair breezed against his face. He put his hands on the railing beside hers, so near their arms touched. Despite the layers of clothing between them, he could feel the heat of her skin, the small shivers that raced through her body. He had her trapped, and from the sudden rasping of her breath, she knew it.

"What are you doing?" she demanded. "Everyone will see us."

"If they look, they'll only see me." She was so small, he blocked everything except the lower portion of her skirts. Bending close, feeling a wild heat erupt in his body, he whispered, "Have you ever been kissed, Grace?"

"This is inappropriate—"

"Have you?" Ignoring the warning racing through his

head, he grazed his mouth against her ear, resisting the urge to smile when she sucked in a gasp.

"Jackson, stop, please. What we did before—how close we came to—I swore I wouldn't allow it to happen again."

"Why?" He lowered his head, keeping his mouth close to her jaw, the curve of her neck. Close, but not touching. The clean, honeyed scent of her filled his lungs, made his mind spin with thoughts he had no business thinking. This was Grace he was teasing. His Angel. The one person who had worked her way into his heart after he'd shut everyone else out.

He should stop before he did something he truly regretted. Yet, however much as he tried, some baser part of him kept him from moving away.

"Why do you want me to stop?" he asked again when she didn't respond. *Because it's the sane thing to do,* his mind insisted. Yet, he felt compelled to move closer, wanting to turn the idea of kissing her into something real.

"I don't know why you're doing this. The Jackson I knew wouldn't behave so brazenly."

"I thought we were talking about you never having been kissed, not about my lack of manners."

"Jackson, please stop."

He would have pulled back if her voice hadn't dropped to a whisper, losing its force. "I don't blame you for being curious."

"I'm not."

"Are you sure?"

She tried to turn, but he grazed his lips against the length of her neck. She straightened, inadvertently pushing her back against his chest. "Jack . . ." She swallowed. "Jackson what are you doing?"

"I'm kissing you."

"That's not . . . how. I thought . . ."

He would have laughed if he'd been able. But the idea of

her never having been kissed, and some wretched viscount being the one to teach her, made him want to lock her in a cabin and sail for the Caribbean. To make matters worse, she didn't just smell like honey, she tasted like it, too. Sweet and fresh and much too pure for a bloody nobleman with soft hands.

And she's too pure for you. He ignored his inner voice and skimmed his lips up to the curve of her jaw, nipping her with his teeth just below her ear. When she tilted her head back slightly, giving him better access, he had to stifle a groan.

He shifted his arms around her and held her in an unfettered embrace. Beneath the rush of wind, he heard his men moving about behind him, humming as they saw to their chores. He even felt the eyes of the few who were watching. Since the righteous Miss Foxsworth hadn't shrieked in outrage, he assumed Macklin still had the woman well occupied, for which he was grateful.

He should stop, he thought distantly, end the spectacle and save Grace the embarrassment that was sure to follow. But stopping meant taking his arms from around her, moving far enough away so he couldn't smell her, couldn't feel the softness of her skin against his lips. Never in his life had he known a woman who felt like satin.

"Tell me what you want," he said, strangely pleased when he felt her shiver.

She angled her head to look at him, her mouth parting with an obvious retort, but she didn't utter a word. Her eyes widened, leaving them clear and so readable he could almost hear her thoughts as if she'd spoken them out loud. Yet, he found her silent message almost impossible to believe.

The infatuation she'd borne him so many years ago hadn't faded; it had turned into a woman's need. He saw the yearning in her eyes. She wanted him to kiss her, was silently begging for him to. Mistake or no, he would give her what she wanted. Taking what *he* wanted in the process. A kiss, and nothing more.

Holding her slender back flush against his chest, so her soft body fit the hard length of his, he could almost believe she'd been designed solely for him. Asinine thought. Grace wasn't for him; he belonged to the sea, she belonged to society, and nothing would change that. He cursed himself for the disastrous path he'd embarked on, but he couldn't let her go. Not until he kissed her, as thoroughly and as deeply as he could, showing her how a real kiss was meant to be.

"This is wrong, you know that don't you?" Her gaze shifted to his lips, intensifying, pulling him to her as if by an unseen force. Her hand came up, and her fingers grazed over his unshaven cheek.

"If you want me to stop, say so. Now."

"You almost kissed me once, Jackson. But you left. Why do you want to kiss me now?"

"God help me if I know." Desire roared through his limbs, burning his veins, heating a path to his core. His skin tightened. His muscles flexed, knotting with the effort to control the hunger building with frightening speed. With both of his arms around her, he held her tight as the ship rolled and swayed, the rocking turning their embrace into a sensual rhythm.

She rested her head against his shoulder, all but making herself vulnerable to his touch. Like a woman who knew what she wanted. This wasn't the cool and distant sophisticated lady he'd watched during the last few days.

Nor was she the Grace he'd known for most of his life: a child who possessed a guileless heart regardless of what trials she faced.

He didn't care who she was or what she'd become. He only knew that she'd never been kissed and he wanted to be the one to teach her. Already he could imagine the taste of her in his mouth.

"Jackson—"

"Ships ho! Capt'n! Ships ho! Leeward!"

The repeated shouts wove through the purpose burning in Jackson's mind. *A ship?* The flush on Grace's cheeks paled as she, too, registered the harried cries.

He straightened, silently cursing when she hurriedly pulled out of his arms. They both moved to the right side of the ship to scan the horizon.

Macklin came running up the steps, a telescope in hand. "Seems our wicked luck 'as decided tae stick with us."

Taking the bring-me-closer, he found the twin vessels and ground out a curse. He sensed Grace's disapproving look, but wasn't about to apologize. Not when two British warships were directly in his path, and changing course to intercept him.

"Macklin," he said, snapping the telescope closed. "Change the flags. Raise the *Maiden Fair*'s standard."

"What if that doesn't fool them?" Grace followed him to the ladder leading down to the main deck.

"It will." Landing on the lower deck, he helped her down. "For a time at least."

"Jackson Brodie, don't you dare placate me," she admonished. All signs of the woman he'd been about to kiss had vanished. Her eyes were dark, frightened, as if she'd just seen a ghost from her past. "I may not have your thirst for pirating, but even I know what will happen if we're stopped by a warship. They'll search the *Sea Angel* and find your prisoners. And you can be certain Miss Foxsworth won't hold her tongue."

"I knew I should have left her to sink with the other ship."

"Jackson!"

"What's going on?" Miss Foxsworth pointed her closed

parasol at him as if it were a sword and she were challenging him to a duel. "What is all the shouting about?"

"Take her below, Grace," Jackson ordered. "And keep her there."

Miss Foxsworth harrumphed. "I'm not going anywhere until someone answers my questions."

"Now, Grace." Turning away, Jackson lowered his voice to speak with Mac. "Have Dillon man the cannons. All of them."

"I take it we aren't goin' tae let 'em board."

"No, we aren't."

"Jackson." Grace caught his sleeve, forcing him to stop. "We're lighter. We can outrun them."

"You want me to take the coward's way out?"

She shoved him back—or tried to—then fisted her hands at her sides. The blue of her eyes blazed like cold fire. "What I want is for you to live another day!"

"I intend to. Now go below. I have to see to my ship."

As he turned to leave, she called after him, the anger in her voice cracking like a whip. "You'll never change, will you, Jackson? You're as reckless as you ever were. Determined to put yourself in danger's path, dragging all of us down with you."

"I won't let anything happen to you, Grace. You know that."

She gave a sardonic laugh. "How do you intend to keep me safe when you're planning to fire on *two* British warships?"

"He's going to do *what?*" Miss Foxsworth shrieked and spun to face the approaching vessels. "They're British? That means I'm saved. Oh, thank heaven."

They both ignored her. Grace held his gaze. "Promise me you won't attack them. Please, promise me."

He hadn't kept his word about keeping the *Maiden Fair* whole so she wouldn't sink, and he didn't intend to keep his promise about leaving Grace in Boston. The least he could do was reassure her that he intended to avoid a heated battle with a larger, stronger and better gunned enemy.

But that would be a lie, too.

He took her hands between his. "Go below, Angel. You'll be safe there."

She flinched, pulling back as if he'd slapped her. She stared at him for a moment, swaying as if she were in a daze. "Perhaps today will be the day then."

"What day is that?" he asked, knowing he shouldn't, knowing too well what the fear in her eyes meant.

"I always knew it would come. That's why I stopped loving you." In a tone void of emotion, she whispered, "Today might be the day you die."

Chapter Six

Shouts echoed through the ship's belly, a frightening mixture of fear and excitement.

Thick wooden strakes groaned a language of their own as the vessel caught the wind and raced over the shifting sea. The floor tilted to a vicious pitch beneath Grace's feet. Instinctively, she adjusted her weight and kept her vigil on the foaming wake the *Sea Angel* left behind.

She touched the paned windows lining the rear of the captain's cabin, feeling the smooth glass, cool beneath her fingers. She heard Sheila, who sat on the bunk bed, alternately bemoaning her sore stomach and making threats that Grace and her pirates would all be captured and hanged.

Grace held herself as rigid as the *Sea Queen* blade she wore secured at her thigh. If Jackson failed to defeat the approaching ships, she wondered if the British captain would try to arrest her. If Jo and Morgan were in danger of becoming prisoners, they wouldn't have stood by and let it happen. They'd have defended themselves, brandishing the dagger, loading the cannons, whatever it took to protect themselves and the ship. But fighting had never been her way.

The pounding of feet and snapped orders broke through her warring thoughts. She angled her head, listening to the distinctive, grinding roll of cannons moving over a sanded deck. The thuds that followed told her they'd been secured in their gun ports.

He's going to attack.

Cold sweat layered her skin. She had to think, do something, somehow convince Jackson to turn back before it was too late. Yet she stood frozen to the floor, numb both inside and out, certain this was another of the grisly nightmares she'd suffered since childhood. She would wake up soon, in her bed at Morgan's town house in London. Safe. She'd be safe, and so would Jackson.

Morgan had been sly when they'd pirated on the *Sea Queen,* devising ways to board merchant ships before the other crews knew what had happened. They'd never fired on another vessel; they'd never had to, though Grace had always feared it would come to that one day.

Evidently, today was that day.

"They're going to rescue me," she heard Sheila declare. "And when they do, they'll take me back to England immediately."

"I don't believe the commander of a warship will see you home," Grace stated, disturbed by the hollowness of her own voice. "Not as soon as you'd like, at any rate."

"Once he learns who I am and what your pirates have done to me, they will."

"My pirates?" Grace turned from the window. "What, exactly, have 'my pirates' done to you?"

"They kidnapped me!"

"They did no such thing." Grace frowned, suddenly

afraid Sheila would be as much a threat to them as the cannonade they would soon face.

"They sank the *Maiden Fair.*"

"The storm caused that tragedy." Not until she heard the words from her own mouth did she realize that she, too, had blamed Jackson for destroying the merchant ship. She would have to apologize to him—should they survive. "We were fortunate the *Sea Angel* came upon us when she did, or everyone on board would have perished."

"You're defending those rakes?"

"I'm speaking the truth. Regardless of what you think of Jackson and his men, they'd wouldn't cause us harm." *But that's not true! He's taking us into battle when he could run.*

The *Sea Angel* shuddered, groaning wildly as she lurched in her fight against the sea. Grace braced her hands against the windowpane to keep from falling. Sheila screamed. Clothing, books, plates and cups went flying, crashing into the opposite wall, then crumbling to the floor.

The sun blazed across the sky in a fiery orange ball as the stern whipped around. They were changing heading. Had they encountered the warships already? She had to know. Without any plan or thoughts for her own safety, Grace ran from the cabin, using the desk, the chair and doorjamb to keep upright. Sheila shouted for her to come back, but Grace hurried for the stairs.

She had to stop Jackson. She had to try. There might still be time to turn away.

She ran through the companionway and ducked through the hatch, her heart pounding against her ribs. Blinking against the sudden glare of light, she scanned the deck, now cleared of all tack and equipment and prepared for battle. Men hurried in all directions, adding to the chaotic hive of activity and the noise that seemed to roll like a wave of thunder. Sailors were hauling up buckets of water in case of fire, others were pulling lines to change the sail's angle as the helmsmen ordered. Every man was armed with pistols, odd knives and swords that glistened with dangerously sharp edges. At bow and stern, and to both sides of the quarterdeck, crewmen crowded around cannons already loaded and packed to fire. They only waited for the command from their captain.

She found Jackson standing near the wheel, his tall, muscular body braced against the temper of the ship. His attention was directed starboard, toward the oncoming vessels, she assumed, though she couldn't turn her head to see. She was caught, snared by the deadly, challenging twist of Jackson's lips that was more snarl than smile, held by the wild, almost maniacal gleam that shot hatred from his eyes.

In that instant, she realized she didn't know this Jackson, how he thought or what he wanted. Where had his loathing come from? Why had she never seen it before? When he'd sailed with Jo, he'd opposed her when she'd insisted on attacking Nathan's ship to seize his gold, wanting to use Morgan's cunning methods instead. What in heaven's name had happened to Jackson in the last five years to make him risk his life for a cause that had nothing to do with him? How could a man possibly change so much?

Or was this the man he'd always been, and she'd been too blinded by girlish love to see it?

She crossed the deck, lifting her skirts as she hopped over coiled ropes and piles of powder and shot. When Jackson saw her, his expression turned cold with fury, making her hesitate in mid stride.

He caught her by the arm and led her toward Macklin. "You've no business here, Angel. Go below. Mac, see to it."

He turned away, dismissing her "Helmsman, I want to pass within three hundred yards. Dillon! Ready the cannons."

"Aye!" came dual replies.

Grace twisted free, surprising Macklin, and spun around, backing up. To her horror, twin warships were fast approaching, their sails filling the sky, their cannons visible through their gun ports, glinting like black steel in the sun. Their bows cut through the ocean as if they meant to ram the *Sea Angel* and split her in two. "I'm not going anywhere until you turn this ship away. Attacking is insanity, Jackson, and you know it."

"You should trust me, Angel. I know what I'm doing. I want you safe below." He moved toward her, reaching out to take her arm. "Go with Mac."

"Don't come any closer, Jackson!" She held her hand out, knowing the futility of that stopping him. "I'm warning you! This ship is mine and I won't have you taking her into battle."

"Yours, is it?" Jaw clenched, he spared a glance at the fast approaching vessels. "I don't have time for this."

"We're turning away, Jackson. Give the order now, or I'll do it for you."

His brow dipped with a threatening scowl. *"I'm* the captain of this ship, and I'll give no such order."

Frantic to find a way to make him listen, she jerked up her skirt, a part of her horrified that she was exposing most of her bare leg, and pulled the *Sea Queen* blade free. "This knife says otherwise. You took my ship without my permission. I'm the rightful captain. Macklin," she called, "turn this ship about."

Jackson's scowl was already so severe, she hadn't thought it possible that the menacing lines around his mouth and eyes could become even more frightening. But they did, causing her to take a step in retreat.

"Where did you get that blade?" His voice was low, seemingly calm, but the words were a clipped demand.

"From Jo when she turned this ship over to me. She

even taught me to use it," Grace lied. "So unless you want to feel its point, I suggest you support my order and instruct the helmsman to turn sail."

For once, she wished she were more like her sisters. Her hand was shaking so badly it was a wonder she could hold onto the hilt at all, and her voice sounded like it might break under the weight of her fear. But she wouldn't back down, not until he listened to reason.

"Give it to me, Angel, before you hurt yourself."

"You're concerned that a paltry knife might hurt me when we're about to be ripped apart by iron shot?"

"Bloody hell! I don't have time for this," he growled, taking a careful step toward her.

"Stay back, Jackson. I swear, I'll use this on you." But the thought of doing so made her stomach heave. She swallowed, tightening her grip on the jeweled hilt.

"Grace—"

"We're in range, Captain!" the helmsman shouted.

Jackson jerked his attention starboard. Cursing, he sent her an irritated glare, then lunged for her, knocking the dagger from her grip. The knife skidded across the deck, clattering against a bucket of water. Pain exploded in her fingers, numbing her hand. She backed away, but he caught her around the waist, locking her against him.

"Macklin!" he growled.

"No! I'm not going below." She flailed her legs and tried to escape his hold, but his arm wouldn't budge.

"You want to stay?" He set her on the deck and spun her to face him, gripping her shoulders so hard she winced in pain. "Fine, then you'll stay with me. But I'm warning you, Angel, don't interfere, or you'll get us all killed."

"And spoil your fun?" she spat, feeling her eyes well with angry tears. "I wouldn't dream of it."

Just then, a boom filled the air, echoing across the sky like thunder. Everyone on deck went still. A white cloud of smoke ballooned from the gun port of the nearest ship. The steaming fog barely began to dissipate before the cannonball struck the ocean's surface no more than twenty yards from the *Sea Angel*'s bow. A funnel of water flew into the sky, spraying over the deck.

Holding her wrist in a bone-crushing grip, he shouted, "We have one pass. Mister Dillon, I want your cannons breathing fire!"

"Aye, sir!"

Grace tugged against Jackson, wanting free. She couldn't stand by and watch him destroy himself, his ship and crew. "Why can't we run, Jackson? Tell me why? We're lighter. The wind is perfect for sailing south. We can circle back later."

Not sparing her a glance, he shouted, "Helmsman, hold her steady."

"You know we can outrun them," she insisted. The warship fired again. Grace flinched, instinctively hugging up against Jackson until she saw the shot strike the water no closer than it had before.

Finally, Jackson turned to her, though when she saw the fury that turned his eyes to matching pinpoints of hardened copper, she wished he hadn't. "More is at stake than our lives, Angel. We have to reach the Colonies within three days. Any longer and all will be lost."

She stared at him, confused. "What are you talking about? What will be lost?"

"The rebels' cause."

"This is about the colonists and their uprising?" Her jaw dropped open in disbelief.

"I think they might resent you calling it a mere uprising," he commented dryly, turning away. "Now, if you please, Mister Dillon."

A cheer swept through the crew, but their cries were obliterated as a deafening roar tore through the air. The explosive sound echoed, rising, vibrating, growing so loud she thought the sky would break, or the sea would erupt and swallow them whole. The ship heaved, tossing her back, but her fall was cut short by Jackson's hold on her arm. Something popped in her shoulder. She cried out, she was sure of it, though she didn't hear her voice in the deafening rumble.

White acrid smoke clogged the air, burned her lungs. She couldn't see the other ships, could barely make out the deck before her. But she could hear. The ocean rasped as the *Sea Angel* sped on. Men were shouting around her, tightening lines, angling sails. Orders were called to haul the cannons back and reload them with enough chain shot to rip apart riggings and sails. Another order was given to restore the wheeled carts into their gun ports. Then the explosion happened all over again.

The deck jolted beneath her, tipping sideways with the force of the report. She latched onto Jackson's arm, ignoring the twisting pain in her shoulder. Saltwater sprayed the deck and coated her skin. The other ships were still firing. The *Sea Angel* shuddered, and took a jerky dive over a rising swell.

"Have we been hit?" she shouted.

"Hold on!" Gripping a ratline, Jackson wrapped his other arm around her, pinning her to his side. The bow rammed into an oncoming wave, jolted upright, then dove with the ocean's surf, taking them past the British ships.

Wind grabbed hold of the smoke, spinning it away in ropy threads. Crewmen were furiously reloading their cannons, their aim now directed well to stern. The warships were still facing east while the *Sea Angel* sped west. The huge galleys struggled to turn and pursue, but with over half their sails ripped and trailing in the water, and the tops of two masts a splintered ruin, they wouldn't be going anywhere fast.

Grace fisted her hands in Jackson's shirt, waiting for him to order the helmsman to turn about for another pass. With the *Sea Angel*'s speed and maneuverability and the warships sitting like lumbering logs, the vessels would make easy prey—one any true pirate who'd showed the loathing Jackson had, wouldn't turn his back on.

Dillon raised his beefy arm, then whipped it down, shouting for another volley. Cannons exploded, but their salvo fell short of their mark and fell harmlessly into the churning blue water.

She glanced up at Jackson, saw the harsh lines around his eyes, the determined set of his jaw. He gave a small nod, as if mentally affirming something in his own mind.

"Mr. Kent," he called. "North by northwest, if you please."

"Aye, Captain." Without a backward glance, the stout helmsman spun the wheel, turning the ship away from the wreckage and headed for open sea.

"You aren't going to sink them?" she asked, stunned.

Jackson looked down at her, his brow pulled in a frown. An unfathomable emotion passed through his eyes, then it vanished as if snatched by the brisk wind. "Do you have so little faith in me as to believe I'd send those men to their deaths?"

"Since I don't know you any longer," she said, feeling the pain of those words like a vise around her heart, "I hardly know where my faith in you should lie."

The corner of his mouth quirked with a half-smile. "You think I've made a bargain with the devil, Angel?"

"I don't know," she whispered. "Have you?"

"I wouldn't have attacked those ships had they not been in my way, but since they were, I had no choice. I couldn't allow them to stop me."

"Because of the rebels," she said, more as a statement of fact than a question. "What could possibly be so urgent?"

"I don't expect you to understand."

"I'm not a child any longer, Jackson."

"If only you were." Wind whipped his tawny hair about his face, shadowing the turbulent emotion that flared in his eyes. He bent his head, bringing his lips dangerously close to hers. His hand tightened on her waist, making her aware of not only her wild, desperate need to kiss him, but of their position, as well.

He still gripped the ratline with one hand while holding her with the other. In the turmoil, she'd wedged up against him, her legs straddling one of his. She could feel the tightness of his thigh cupped against hers, his hip cushioned against the flat of her stomach, the muscles in his arm that felt like a band of iron strapped to her back.

All around them, men were hurrying about, adjusting the yards, dumping the seawater they no longer needed, gathering shot and powder to store below. She felt their curious gazes as they passed. Heat burned in a flustered path from her scalp to her chest.

She shoved against him, surprised that he let her go. In a tone that would have made her headmistress at Wilmouth proud, she asked, "Are you going to tell me why you risked all our lives in order to reach the Colonies?"

He glanced around them as if to ensure that no one could overhear. "Not now."

She crossed her arms, and said in a low, warning voice, "Jackson."

"I think I liked you better when you were a malleable child," he said, walking away.

"I was never malleable," she retorted, following him, determined that he would answer her.

Bending, he retrieved something from the deck, then turned to face her. "Perhaps not, but you were easier to manage."

"The reason, Jackson," she insisted, "that you couldn't delay."

He glared down at her, his stance one of wearied impatience. "Where do you think the two warships we met were sailing to?"

"I've no idea. But obviously, you do."

"Aye," he said, looking out sea. Grace followed his gaze. The enemy vessels were specks on the horizon, appearing and disappearing as the *Sea Angel* alternately rose and plunged over the waves. "They were supposed to meet the British fleet sailing from England."

"What does this have to do with the rebels?"

He swore under his breath, then ignored her disapproving look. "I told you, you wouldn't understand."

She folded her arms across her chest. "Then pretend I'm the child you want me to be and explain it so I *do* understand."

For a long moment, she didn't think he was going to indulge her, but then he said, "King George has decided to make an example of the rebels, believing it will convince the rest of the colonists to stop disputing the king's laws."

"The colonists have refused to pay their taxes." She knew little of the politics in the New World. But she knew that much at least. It had been in all the papers. She even recalled her brothers-in-law, Daniel and Nathan, discussing the need to tax the Colonies to help repay England for running the French out of Canada, thereby removing the threat of invasion.

To further prove that she could indeed *understand,* she added, "King George has declared the rebels' behavior treasonous. If he wishes to keep control of the Colonies, he must take action."

"King George has taxed everything except the air the people breathe," Jackson ground out. "They consider themselves little more than slaves to the king's edicts."

"Slaves," she said, trying to brush off the word, but the animosity in his eyes wouldn't let her. "Surely they're overreacting."

"Eight of the king's fiercest warships are less than a week behind us. He intends to block the colonists' shipping routes, stop all trade, virtually sever their contact with the outside world. Those same ships carry enough soldiers to subdue the rebels. If the colonists aren't given enough warning, there will be a massacre."

The wind blew warm around Grace, but a chill seeped into her bones. *War and death and poverty. Starvation.* She rubbed her hands over her arms as memories from the past tried to return. Battles, politics, the king's agenda—they were things she couldn't control. Things that had nearly destroyed her life when she'd been a child. Her parents and her brother, Robby, had died. She'd been too young to know about healing, but what she'd learned since wouldn't do her, or anyone else, any good. Once men decided to begin a battle, people were killed en masse, homes were burned, lives were erased as if they'd never existed.

She wanted nothing to do with war, *nothing,* ever again.

The colonists' rebellion doesn't involve William, or me. Once they were married, they would be happy and content in their home at White Rose, concerning themselves with nothing more complex than how many children they wanted to have.

Despite her private reassurances, tremors rolled through her stomach. "How do you know all this?"

"After capturing the *Maiden Fair,* I discovered a coded letter among Captain Peters's things."

"If it's coded, it could state anything. You must be mistaken about the British fleet."

He gave her a smile so wicked it was unlike any she'd ever seen. "There is no mistake."

She looked away, suddenly afraid that the dreams hovering beyond the tips of her fingers were about to be ripped away. "I don't want any part of bloodshed, Jackson."

"I know you don't, Angel." He took her hand and pressed the *Sea Queen* blade into her palm. Catching her chin, he urged her to look at him. "That's why I'm not taking you to Boston."

Chapter Seven

"Would you care to repeat what you just said?" she asked, her voice so low it trembled.

"You heard me." No matter how angry she became, or how much she argued, Jackson vowed he wouldn't concede. "I'm not taking you to Boston."

She stared at him, drawing in one deep breath after another. He had never known silence to have a sound, or, more astounding—a texture—but now he knew differently. Silence from an angry woman was a tangible thing, as capable of delivering wounds as the steel edge of a sword. The air pulsed around them in heated waves, shifting, vibrating against his skin. His fingers tingled with the need to touch her, calm her, though he didn't dare try.

He mentally cursed himself. He'd intended to tell her of his plan to return her to England, but only after his business was done and they were well across the Atlantic, far away from the Colonies.

Now there was no going back.

She held her body as rigid as a chisel made of ice, her expression controlled, unreadable. If not for the tension he felt unfurling from her like bolts of summer lightning, he might believe she hadn't comprehended his words. The knife gripped in her hand was as steady as if it were an extension of her arm. He frowned at the blade, sensing he'd erred by returning it to her so soon.

"I see," she said quietly. "I suppose I can't argue with your decision. You're just trying to keep me safe, after all."

"I'm glad you understand." He wasn't only glad, he was shocked as hell.

"Oh, I do." She gave him a fleeting smile. "Especially since William isn't in Boston. He's in Medford, which is where you will be taking me."

"Grace—"

"You gave your word." She raised her hand, pointing the knife at him. She blinked, frowning at the blade as if surprised to see it in her grip.

"A promise I'll damn well break if it means keeping you alive."

Lowering the knife, she sighed. A resigned look darkened her eyes. "Where are you docking?"

"Excuse me?"

"You have prisoners in the hold below. You can't keep them forever. I assume you intend to turn them over to someone. And you have a coded message to deliver to the rebels. Where are you docking?"

"In Newburyport."

"Fine." She turned away, ducked through the hatch and descended the ladder.

He went after her. "What do you mean, *fine?*"

"I've decided to disembark in Newburyport." She hurried down the passageway, bracing her hands against the walls as the floor shifted beneath them. "I'm sure I'll be able to find my way to William."

At the threshold of his cabin, he caught her arm and spun her around, leaping back to avoid being stabbed with the dagger she still gripped. "You aren't stepping one foot off this ship, Angel."

"You aren't going to stop me."

"What . . . what happened?" a female voice squeaked.

They both turned to look inside the cabin. Miss Foxsworth sat on the bunk bed, her knees drawn up to her chest, her hair a tangled nest around her head and shoulders, her eyes red-rimmed and puffy from weeping.

"The danger's over, Sheila," Grace said, her tone filled with the compassion that sounded like the old Grace, not the stubborn, mulish woman she'd become with him. "However, we're sailing to Newburyport instead of Boston."

"Where in heaven's name is Newburyport?"

"I'm not sure. North I think. We'll hire a coach to take us where we need to go. It'll be an adventure," Grace said, her voice brightening. "No need to worry at all."

"But those British ships!" the woman cried. "I saw what happened to them."

"No one was hurt," Grace reassured her as she discreetly tugged against the hold Jackson had on her arm. He tightened his grip, not about to let her go. "Their sails were ripped, nothing more."

Miss Foxsworth dropped her forehead onto her knees, and whimpered, "I want to go home. I hate the Colonies and I hate this ship."

Grace started toward the sobbing woman, but Jackson pulled her into the passage and headed for his first mate's cabin—the room he'd commandeered after giving Grace his. Opening the door, he ignored her protests and drew her inside. Shutting the door, he leaned against it and crossed his arms over his chest, making it clear she wasn't leaving until he decided she could.

Meeting his gaze and matching it for stubbornness, she arched her chin and squared her shoulders. "So, you intend to keep me a prisoner, as well. Perhaps you should put me below and confine me in chains."

"Don't tempt me, Angel. The idea has merit."

"Don't call me that."

"What? Angel?" He quirked a brow and pushed away from the door. Straightening to his full height, the cramped room seemed to shrink, making it far more intimate than he cared to consider. "You used to like your nickname."

"The use of a nickname means there's something special between two people, defining their loyalty to one another." Her eyes glittered as they pooled with unshed tears. "There is no loyalty in you, Jackson. You live by your own rules and desires, and care nothing about those of others."

He flinched, feeling as though she'd slapped him again. Though this time the pain her words delivered stung sharper than anything she could deliver with the palm of her hand. "It's because I do care for you," *so much that it's beginning to terrify me,* "that I'm doing this."

"I want to go to Medford."

"No."

"I want to marry William Mason."

"Damn it, Grace. He's not the man for you."

"You don't even know him."

"He's a nobleman, that's all I need to know." Jackson felt a denial twist in his gut. An aristocrat was exactly what Grace needed, a genteel man of quality who would give her the security she'd always sought. Someone who could promise a life free of constant fear. A man so different from himself he couldn't help but grimace at his own crude existence.

"William is the man I want, Jackson!" She fisted her

hands at her sides and glared up at him with righteous fury, unaware how her words cut through him.

"You don't know what you want," he said, latching onto his belief and refusing to let go. *But I do know!* Not until that moment did he realize how much he wanted her, had wanted her since the last time he'd seen her—five years ago at her sister's masquerade ball. She'd been stunning then, ethereal, so tempting he'd been shaken to the core. He'd never acted on his need, knowing she didn't deserve a man like him or the nomadic life he could offer. But, damn his soul, he couldn't deny his desire now.

"Grace." He gripped the small of her waist with one hand and the nape of her neck with the other.

"Jackson, what are you doing?"

He answered her by pulling her to him, then sealing off her surprised gasp with his mouth. He heard the dagger clatter to the floor. Her taste flooded his senses: cool, wet satin, as rich as honey. Taking advantage of her surprise, he drank her in, plunging his tongue inside, taking more of her. God, he had to have more.

Her hands fisted in his shirt. She twisted, pushing, struggling to break free. Then she pounded her fists once against his chest, before going stiff as a lance in his arms.

"Kiss me, Grace," he whispered against her mouth. "Just once."

A helpless moan caught in the back of her throat, the agonized sound winding through his mind, fueling the fire that bled through his limbs. She trembled against him, hopefully not in fear. This was Grace, the only person he ever truly cared about, the only one he'd let inside his heart.

Yet, he could feel her panic, the fine tremors running down her back, jarring her shoulders, turning her breath to a jagged rasp. She should take her knife and bury it in his heart, he thought, feeling enough disgust to sour his stomach. He eased his kiss, already trying to find a way to apologize, but there was no way to atone for this. Lifting his head slightly, he paused. Her eyes were closed, her cheeks flushed a deep rosy pink—the same shade as her wet lips.

Her eyes fluttered open. Sunlight drifted through the small window port, warming her hair to liquid gold. Her throat, the slope of her full breasts, pushed above the bodice of her gown, glowed as pure as cream. He'd always thought her beautiful, even when she'd been a child in scraggly pigtails, but there was no trace of that child now. If only he could pull away, express his regret.

But her lips parted as if she were trying to seduce him into kissing her again. Her grip on his shoulders turned possessive and needy, the desire in her eyes hypnotic.

Calling himself a fool, he nuzzled her neck, moving his hand up her back, exploring the dip of her small waist, and following it around to the feminine curve that led to her breasts. He pressed her to him, and shuddered when she didn't resist. Heat pearled off her skin, soaking through their clothes, igniting the lust that his self-loathing had tried to cool.

Lowering his head, he kissed her collarbone and rolled his tongue over the soft skin. He kissed the upper swells of her breasts while cupping the lower fullness in his palm.

Grace arched her back, tensing, a hoarse gasp tearing from her throat. Jackson straightened but kept his hand where it was and grazed his thumb over the nipple he couldn't see.

A shiver jerked her body. She gave a wooden shake of her head, opened her mouth as if to object. Her breath was unsteady. Strands of blonde hair had come loose from its knot, trailing along her face and shoulders. *She looks like she's been ravaged,* he thought, *thoroughly loved, and bewildered by it.*

Good God, how could he do this to her?

He released her so abruptly she stumbled back, catching herself against the bed frame. He stared down at her, his chest heaving as he forced his body under control, but the blood pulsed hot through his veins, tightening his skin, making him ache with a need too strong to ignore.

He raked his hand through his hair. Kissing her, touching her, wanting her—all were reckless desires, reckless and foolish. Made worse because she'd responded, opening herself to his urgings, accepting him, *wanting* him in return.

Where would it have led? Had he thought he could toss her onto the bunk and lift her skirts? Spend his lust as if she were no better than a common dock whore? The abhorrent image had him growling out a curse.

And what would he have offered her afterward? Another apology? Or perhaps the grand opportunity to live with him at sea?

"I . . . I . . ." She swallowed, dropping her gaze, looking at the walls, the narrow desk, the floor, anywhere but at him. An awkward, agonizing silence swelled inside the room.

With every passing second, Jackson's anger at himself intensified. He ought to say something to break the tension, but every excuse that came to mind seemed trivial and inept. Besides, he didn't know how to apologize without explaining why he'd kissed her in the first place—and how much he wanted to do so again.

"Your kiss, Jackson . . ." Her voice was weak, trembling with uncertainty. "It changes nothing."

She was more right than she could possibly know, he thought dimly. Though they might be attracted to one another, she was engaged to another man she claimed to love. But whether she loved her viscount or not didn't matter. Jackson had nothing to offer her . . . except friendship. And he suspected he was in danger of losing even that.

"Don't worry, Angel," he said, feeling something inside him go cold. "It won't ever happen again."

She finally looked at him, her eyes bright with anguish. Nodding hesitantly, she brushed past him. He didn't try to stop her, letting the door swing shut on the sound of her footsteps hurrying away.

Standing alone in the cramped little room, he could still feel the imprint of her back and hips, the soft fullness of her breasts in his hands. Still taste the sweetness of her skin in his mouth.

He would have to remember those sensations well, he realized. Because they were all he would ever have.

Chapter Eight

Seagulls swooped against the hazy sky, their white wings spread to ride the wind, their sharp cries both demanding and forlorn. Grace hugged her wool shawl tight around her shoulders, but she couldn't suppress a shiver. A fine, vaporous mist that held a damp chill clung to her face and her hair, penetrating her wrap and sinking into her bones. It was barely past noon, though it felt closer to dusk. Gray clouds surged above her, blocking out everything except the faint outline of the fast approaching coast. Massachusetts.

This wasn't how she'd imagined arriving at her new home—sailing in on a pirate ship instead of the *Maiden Fair*, the day dreary and bleak instead of bright and exciting, her heart aching and cold instead of hopeful.

In spite of her resolve not to, she glanced behind her. From her place at the bow she could see only part of the *Sea Angel*'s deck. Wood gleamed like dark, wet satin, half lost in fog, a ghost ship heading into the unknown. Half the sails had been lowered, but those still raised were tight with wind, quietly pushing the vessel closer to port. Dillon kept a close eye on the men manning the thirty-odd cannons. Other crewmen were hurrying about, moving on silent feet, preparing to dock. The muted hush was unnatural. Not even the ocean made a sound as the ship sliced a steady path. Some might consider the ominous mood a bad omen. But she didn't believe in such things. Or, at least, she tried not to.

Where Grace had wanted a clear, beautiful day, the crew had welcomed the murky protection. Though they were flying the *Maiden Fair*'s flag, they had a hold full of loyalist prisoners. Avoiding a confrontation with British vessels seemed prudent. So far, the *Sea Angel* had slipped by undetected. For that she was grateful, for herself and the crew, but mostly for Sheila. After the battle with the two warships, the woman had refused to step one foot outside of the captain's cabin, remaining huddled in bed with the covers drawn up to her chin. It was just as well she rested, Grace decided. Once they reached Newburyport and hired a coach, she didn't think their trip would become any easier. And to be honest, Grace wasn't looking forward to traveling in a foreign land with a woman who despised everything within sight—Grace most of all. However much she was tempted to, she couldn't leave Sheila behind to fend for herself.

She took note of the ship and the hive of activity with only a cursory glance. What she was looking for she found at the helm.

Jackson had spread a chart on the binnacle box and was speaking to the helmsman, a short, bow-shaped man with a bristly mustache that covered his upper lip and half his chin. Jackson's brow was pinched in a frown, as it had been for the past three days—ever since he'd kissed her and realized his grievous mistake. For as long as she lived, she would never forget the horror reflected in his dark eyes or the blasphemous curse that had followed. Had he thought kissing her so awful? Or just a monstrous blunder?

She shut the memory away, willing the pain that had wrapped around her heart to go with it, but the piercing ache stubbornly refused to budge, burrowing in as if it meant to stay forever.

She forced her attention back to Jackson, tried to view him with a judicious eye instead of an emotional one. A scrap of rope tied his wet hair back from his face, making his cheeks look chisel sharp. She saw traces of the young man he'd once been in the way he stood with his legs braced against the deck, the stubborn tilt of his jaw. His movements were still absolute and controlled, his voice confident, self-assured. Yet, there was something different, something powerful and undefined that radiated strength and ability from every pore of his tanned skin, every turn of his head, every gesture of his arms.

He was older. More experienced. She thought that might be part of the change in him, but there was a darker side to Jackson, a harshness she'd never seen before.

"He seems more like a stranger now," she whispered.

Not a stranger, she silently amended. *He seems more like a man.*

The realization sent heat curling through her middle. He *was* a man—with a man's needs. The need to take control, to lead instead of being led. Finally comprehending what she was seeing, she felt numb.

The orphan boy she'd fallen in love with, the one who'd trained under Morgan, then had served with Jo, no longer existed. He'd grown up, changed, hardened into a forceful man. His kiss was proof of that. The old Jackson would never have attempted anything so . . . so . . . personal.

But he did kiss me. She might not have any experience with intimacy, but she'd sensed his desire. His hands had been possessive and greedy as they'd moved over her body. She'd felt every sensation, every pearling ripple he'd caused beneath her skin, and had been certain he'd felt the same as well. She'd thought he'd wanted more than a kiss—much, much more. From her, the woman she'd become, not the little girl he once knew.

And then he'd pulled away.

She tightened her grip on her shawl. *Don't think about his kiss,* she lectured herself for the hundredth time. *And for heaven's sake, don't think about how it made you feel!* Her private reprimands had done little good over the last few days, and they did nothing to settle her unease now.

It meant nothing. He only wanted to throw me off balance, convince me to return to England.

The frightening part was that it had almost worked. For an instant, before he'd pulled away and she'd seen the self-contempt in his eyes, she'd forgotten all about William. She would have willingly followed Jackson anywhere, agreed to anything, for the rest of her life, so long as he didn't let her go.

Fool, fool, foolish girl!

Turning back toward the coast, her heart lurched against her chest in surprise. They were less than two hundred yards from shore. A row of buildings, their shapes as vague as the muted colors they were painted in, lined the coast. Some were mere lean-tos of bleached and rotting wood. Small fishing boats fought the waves as they struggled back to shore.

Her fiancé was somewhere beyond those buildings, far to the south. William wouldn't be expecting her for another week. She wondered if it would take her that long to reach him. A breath shuddered out of her lungs. It wasn't fear, she reassured herself. But the knot in her stomach and the way her skin prickled felt horribly like dread. She'd meant it when she told Jackson that she wanted to sail to

Medford, wanted to marry William. That was her plan and she meant to see it through. She'd been honest, she stubbornly reaffirmed, regardless that the words still burned in her throat.

" 'Cuse me, Miss Grace."

Startled, she faced the man who'd come up on silent feet beside her. "Macklin," she said, forcing her heart to settle. "I didn't hear you approach."

"Bein' quiet tends tae be an asset in my line of work."

She couldn't help her disapproving frown. "Why do you continue pirating? Don't you value your life?"

He shrugged. "Ain't got noth'n' else better tae do." He gave her a shameless grin, then stroked the point of his beard with one finger. "Besides, what would Jackson do without me?"

"Maybe he would decide to settle down and do something useful with his life."

"Ouch," he said with a good-natured grimace. Then he sobered and spared a furtive glance over his shoulder. Seeing Jackson was still at the helm, he turned to her, saying, "The Capt'n 'as 'is reasons for smuggl'n.' "

"I assume it's for the money, not to mention the chance to get himself killed."

"Aye, there's that, but there's someth'n' else, too."

"Such as?" she asked, desperately wanting an answer to the question that had plagued her for years.

He shrugged again with enough nonchalance to make her immediately suspicious. " 'E won't talk about it, not even with me. But I have a feel'n'. 'Tis like 'e's tak'n' England's interference with the colonists personally. Can't say as I understand it."

Neither did she. Looking past Macklin, she watched Jackson pick up the brass bring-me-closer and study the seashore. With loose strands of his blond hair blowing in the wind, he looked fierce and strong, so self-assured. Capable of surviving against all odds. *But for how long?*

"I told Miss Foxsworth that we'll reach port soon. If ye're all packed, I'll bring your trunks up and 'ave them unloaded once we dock."

She stared at Macklin, certain she'd misunderstood. But when his meaning dawned, she asked, "Jackson isn't going to try to stop me?"

"Why would 'e? 'E's ordered a man to go ashore and hire a coach tae take ye tae your fiancé."

"I see."

"Or if ye prefer, we could send someone tae the man's 'ome and have 'im come fetch ye."

"No," she said absently, "that would take too long." Jackson was just going to let her leave? Without trying to argue with her again? She should be relieved, and it annoyed her that she wasn't.

"If that's what ye want, Miss Grace."

"How far is Newburyport from Medford?" she asked, refusing to interpret the stifling weight pressing against her chest.

"By land?" he mused. " 'Undred miles, maybe less."

"That far?" She'd traveled by herself before, this time wouldn't be any different.

"Why would ye want tae go tae Newburyport?"

"I don't. I want to go to Medford."

"Ye're in luck, then." Mac nodded toward the buildings taking shape, forming a town complete with a busy dock crowded with sailors and horse-drawn wagons. "This 'ere's Mystic River. We passed Noodle Island a ways back. Thought we'd 'ave tae dance with a warship for sure, sneaking around the way we did. Those by-blows are known tae guard the pass we took, ye know. But they must be off somewhere, snooz'n' the day away. Or maybe they're 'arassing the local villagers farther south."

"What are you saying?"

"We're 'ere."

"Where? Medford?"

"Aye." Grinning, he winked and turned away, calling over his shoulder, "Let me know when your trunk is ready and I'll see ye safe on American soil."

Grace stared after Macklin, certain she'd been manipulated, she just wasn't sure how. She quickly dismissed the sailor and turned her attention to his captain. For the last three days, Jackson had been sailing to Medford—*to Medford*—and hadn't felt compelled to tell her. Instead, he'd let her worry that he was taking her to Newburyport. She'd been certain that he intended to hold her prisoner until his business was done, then force her to return home with him to London. She'd been thinking of ways to escape, going so far as to consider dressing in sailor's garb and sneaking off the ship. Her only quandary had been Sheila. Considering the woman's weak constitution, she would have given their plan away before Grace could implement it.

But now her planning *and* her worrying had been for nothing.

Hurrying to the ladder, she hiked up her skirts, not caring if she revealed her petticoats and stockinged legs, and descended to midship. Marching across the deck, she stopped before him, folded her arms over her chest and demanded, "What made you change your mind?"

He considered her for a moment, his expression carefully blank, but she knew he understood what she was referring to. Cradling the telescope in both hands, he said, "You did."

"And how did I accomplish this?"

"Does it matter?"

She arched a brow, silently telling him that it most certainly did.

A muscle began to pulse in his jaw. "I've warned you about the rebellion threatening this area. The dangers here are real, Angel. People are fighting. More than I care to think about have already died. Yet, you don't seem to care about anything except coming to Medford and finding the man of your dreams. So here you are."

Prickling at his censorious tone, she tilted her chin. "Why didn't you tell me?"

He snapped the telescope closed and set it on the binnacle box with enough force to bend the brass tubing. "My reason doesn't matter."

"I beg to differ. For three days I've worried about what I would do when I reached the Colonies. I want an explanation, Jackson. You owe it to me. What caused you to change your mind?"

"Leave it alone, Grace," he ordered, his gaze heating in a silent warning.

"Not until you tell me," she insisted, propping her hands on her hips.

Clenching his teeth, he finally growled, "I shouldn't have kissed you."

Taken aback for an instant, she stared up at him. "Why did you? Kiss me, I mean."

Jackson sliced a look toward the helmsman who, in his attempt to *not* listen, was making it obvious that he was. Taking her by the arm, Jackson led her to the railing.

"I was angry." From the muscle pulsing in his jaw and the shards of brown ice shooting from his eyes, she thought he might be angry still.

"How flattering," she said, feeling miffed when she should be relieved that he hadn't been driven by some hidden desire. They were going to part company soon, possibly within the hour, and might never see each other again. They didn't need bruised feelings getting in the way. Lord knew she'd been heartsick over him enough when she'd been a girl. She didn't need to continue that pathetic habit.

"And because I wanted to," he added in a gruff tone, looking down at her. Though she knew the river was calm, the deck took a dizzying dip.

"You're a beautiful woman. But that didn't give me the right to take advantage of you. Besides," he said, his mouth quirking with a faint smile, "after our kiss, you made it clear that you still want to marry your viscount."

"I . . . yes, that's right," she managed.

"I realized it's not my place to stand in the way of what you want." He studied her, his gaze touching her brow, her cheeks, dropping to her lips. The creases around his eyes deepened, making him look so sad and vulnerable the pain around her heart twisted, urging her to reach up and smooth over the worry lines, brush the loose, sun-streaked hair from his face.

The temptation to feel the silky strands, glide her fingers over the rough bristle of his beard, grip his head and draw him down for one last kiss—one that would undoubtedly burn her soul to ash—was almost too strong to ignore.

Fisting her hands in her shawl, she held onto the last shred of her determination. "If you'll excuse me, I have some packing to do before we dock."

"By all means, Angel," he murmured with a slight nod. "You might want to change into your best traveling gown, seeing as you'll be reunited with your fiancé soon."

"Yes." She took a step back, not feeling the sudden bite of the wind as much as she felt the chasm opening up between her and Jackson. "I'll want to look my best."

Because within in the hour, I'll have everything I've ever wanted.

She spun away and hurried for the hatch. Hurried toward her future and away, far, far away from her past.

This is what I want, she reassured herself as she took the ladder to the lower deck, feeling Jackson's dark gaze follow her until she was out of sight. Moving down the shadowed passageway, she pressed a hand to her nervous stomach and whispered fiercely, "This *is* what I want."

The open-air buggy, with two plank seats of weathered wood and a small rear bed crowded with her trunks, waited at the end of the pier. The term "buggy" was a generous one, she supposed. But she wouldn't turn her nose up at her limited choice of transportation. If she had to travel by foot to William's home then she'd willingly do it. Anything to escape the *Sea Angel. And Jackson.*

Smoothing her skirt of lavender brocade trimmed with cream Brussels lace, she headed for the well-used wagon, feeling ridiculous for choosing such an elaborate gown. With its pointed stomacher, tight-fitting sleeves and daringly low squared neckline, it might be appropriate for an afternoon tea, but not for a ride in a rickety buckboard. She blamed her choice on wanting to make a good impression on William when she arrived on his doorstep.

And, she admitted with a pang of remorse, since this could very well be the last time she would ever see Jackson, she wanted him to remember her looking her best. A vain thought, she knew, but she couldn't help it. Regardless of what had transpired between them, she didn't want their memories of one another to be angry ones.

Approaching the wagon and the hired driver, she paused to ruffle the manes of the pair of shaggy-coated gray plow horses hitched to the yoke. Their large heads hovered mere inches off the ground, giving the impression they were tired, bored or asleep.

"I see you're ready to leave."

She tensed, not having heard, or even sensed, Jackson's approach. But, then, her nerves were in such a tangle, it was a wonder she could stand upright on her own two feet.

Forcing a smile, she turned—and froze. Jackson had changed from his worn sailor's pants and shirt to a chocolate-brown jacket, the brass buttons lining the front panels shimmering like dull gold—the same as his eyes. His matching breeches were tucked into knee-high black leather boots. Over his white linen shirt, his wine-dark cravat was crooked and haphazardly tied, but instead of looking disheveled, he appeared reckless, even arrogant. Breathtaking.

His clothes were far from perfectly pressed, and they were a little out of fashion, but somehow it didn't matter. He was freshly shaved, his hair neatly tied in a queue, and he was looking at her as if she were the only person in the world he wanted to see.

Finding her voice, she said, "I take it you're not sailing immediately."

He pursed his lips, looking thoughtful, though to her frustration she couldn't begin to guess what his thoughts might be. "I have something to take care of first."

"I see." A burning pressure squeezed her throat, preventing her from uttering the dozen things she wanted to say. Regardless that he would ignore her urgings, she had to convince him to take care. She should take his hand, kiss his cheek, tell him how much she would miss him. But her chest constricted, locking the words inside.

"What in God's name is that, may I ask?" Sheila shrieked.

Grace sighed and pressed her lips into a tight line. Jackson's mouth curled into a scowl.

Lifting a hand toward the wagon, Grace admitted, "I know it's not what you're accustomed to Sheila—"

"I should say not." Retrieving a handkerchief from her reticule, she pressed it to her nose to block the stink of dead fish, soot and pitch, still complaining, "The seats don't have even a strip of fabric to protect my gown and there isn't room for all of my trunks. And I'm sure it's safe to assume this contraption doesn't have one spring to its name."

"I . . . Sheila . . ." Grace began, unsure how to explain. "This wagon is taking me to Lord Kensale's home. Since we didn't sail to Newburyport as we'd thought, Macklin is looking for a better carriage to take you to your relatives in Abington."

Sheila fanned her face as if hoping to dispel the rank odors. Grace glanced at the stalls where vendors were offering baskets of fresh fish, surprised she hadn't noticed the smell before. But the small port was so similar to the one she'd grown up in, and the others she'd visited when sailing with Morgan and Jo, that she hadn't paid any attention to the narrow dirt roads and simple cabins.

"I've decided not to visit my family just yet," Sheila announced.

A warning chill raked over Grace's skin, so suddenly and so coldly, she could hardly breathe. "What do you mean?"

"I've decided to accompany you to William's . . . I mean, Lord Kensale's. It would be unforgivable of me if I let you stay under his roof without a proper chaperon. You wouldn't want your reputation ruined so soon after your arrival, now would you?"

This couldn't happen. Grace glanced to Jackson for help, but he was watching Sheila like a wolf waiting for a snake to strike. "I appreciate your concern, but really, there isn't any need for you to change your plans."

"Nevertheless, I intend to accompany you." She clapped her hands together and faced the driver. "My trunks are ready. See to them at once."

The driver, clearly in his mid fifties and bent at the shoulders, was too old and out of shape for the chore. He raised a brow at Jackson.

He gave an almost indiscernible nod of his head.

"Inform one of my crewmen to bring Miss Foxsworth's things down."

"Aye, sir." The older man moved off at a moderate gait.

"Well," Sheila mused once the three of them were alone. Her gaze slid from Jackson's neatly brushed hair, over his attire, then down to his polished boots. "You could almost pass for a gentleman, Captain Brodie." With a flash of something close to malice in her eyes, she added, "Almost."

Grace gaped at the woman. Evidently, now that Jackson couldn't threaten to toss her off the ship, Sheila's courage had returned, along with her sharp tongue.

"Why thank you, Miss Foxsworth." He bowed slightly at the waist. "You're looking lovely, as well. I trust your stomach has settled now that we're on solid ground."

She sniffed. "Where was this pleasant side of you when you captured us, Captain?"

"Tensions were high, for that I trust you'll forgive me."

"Forgive you for sinking our ship? I think not."

"Please, must we discuss this?" Grace whispered, glancing around, afraid someone would overhear. There were only dockworkers and a few merchants carrying baskets of goods nearby, and though they were eyeing the three of them, fortunately they were too far away to hear.

"And he didn't sink the *Maiden Fair*, Sheila," Grace added, determined to set the woman straight, especially now that she insisted on traveling with her to William's. "The storm caused the damage. Let's put it behind us, shall we? Jackson will be sailing from here soon and we can all forget about the storm and the *Maiden Fair*'s demise."

"I'm afraid not, Angel."

She glared at him, silently warning him not to use her nickname, a name that until now hadn't sounded quite so intimate. "What do you mean?"

"I mean," he said, reaching into his vest pocket and

pulling out a timepiece. After a quick glance, he continued, "I'm not sailing as soon as you might like."

Goose bumps scurried over her skin, leaving a chill behind that froze the breath in her lungs. She had the sense she was being caught up in a bad dream, a nightmare spinning like a funnel cloud. Around and around, sucking her up, tossing her around at the whim of others.

"But is it safe?" She glanced at the ship, knowing the *Maiden Fair*'s captain and crew were still locked in the hold.

"For now. Medford might be close to Boston, which the British control, but this is still rebel territory."

"But wouldn't it be best—safer—if you left?" She didn't want to think of him leaving so soon, or of never seeing him again, but more so, she didn't want to consider what might happen if the British authorities captured him.

"No."

"Jackson, why are you doing this?" Grace asked, not caring that Sheila was listening to every word.

He grinned, a cool, implacable pull of his lips. "Why, Angel," he said, his voice low and rough, "I'm doing what any friend of the family would do. I'm escorting you to your fiancé's side."

Chapter Nine

Sheila had been right; the buggy had no springs.

Grace gripped the edge of her seat and struggled to keep upright as Jackson negotiated the team of horses through town. He'd climbed into the front seat as if he owned the wagon, taking over the driver's duty while she and Sheila had crowded into the back. He jockeyed through narrow streets bustling with wagons of all shapes and states of disrepair, their beds filled with sacks of flour, salt and crates of potatoes. Horses and their riders skirted around them, sometimes using the wooden walkways fronting the buildings to gain some ground. People on foot darted ahead like schools of fish heading upstream.

Through it all, Sheila complained about everything from being subjected to such a horrid mode of transportation to the rancid smells to being forced to visit such a primitive region. After a few minutes and several attempts to reassure the woman that everything would work out for the best,

Grace tuned her out and turned her attention to the town of Medford.

Her new home. The muddy roads, the mercantile with its windows filled with barrels of fresh apples, stacks of glass jars and a display of crimson silk were now a part of her life. Farther ahead, she glimpsed a tavern, the sign carved and painted green like a horned frog, for which it was named.

There were sounds of hammering, a few dogs barking in the distance, the rattle of wagons. But regardless that there were people all around, few of them were talking. There were no shouts, no children laughing or playing. She glanced behind her, realizing the street vendors hadn't been promoting their goods, but were quietly standing beside their stalls, waiting, a look of helpless despair on their faces.

Grace faced the front, her senses becoming fine-tuned. She started to ask Jackson if he thought the people's behavior was strange, but the way he sat, straight-backed, his narrowed gaze seeming to absorb every detail at once, she realized it was more than strange; something was definitely wrong. Perhaps the effects of the war had begun to take its toll. She'd been young during the Seven Years' War, but she still recalled the worry that had darkened her neighbors' eyes, the solemn pull of their shoulders. Was the same thing happening here? She prayed not.

As they passed the wharf and entered the business district, the buildings were better maintained, most with fresh paint and solid porches. A few had bright yellow daisies and orange buttercups planted in tidy gardens. But even here a strange tension clung to the air, a quiet expectancy that pulsed with the beat of a drum. She tried telling herself it was her imagination, or worse, her own rattled nerves that had her sensing trouble where there wasn't any, but she couldn't shake the feeling. Something wasn't right.

Then she heard it—a mysterious rumble, like the buzz of angry bees. Jackson pulled the team to a stop. Standing, he searched the area ahead.

Without glancing at the driver, he asked, "Is there another way around?"

" 'Fraid not, sir. There's only one road through town and we're on it."

"What is it?" Grace asked, trying to see past him.

Jackson let out a curse and took his seat, clicking the reins against the horses' rumps. The wagon lurched forward, drawing an indignant gasp from Sheila.

"Have a care, Captain Brodie," she admonished. "Your passengers are women, not a ship full of prisoners."

"Grace," Jackson said, "whatever happens, you and Miss Foxsworth are to stay in the wagon."

"Jackson—" Grace began, but stopped when they passed the last of the buildings and entered the town square. People crowded the village green, pushing and shoving, all shouting at once so she couldn't understand what was being said.

Jackson kept the team as far to the left of the mob as he could, only slowing when rows of people blocked his path. He forced the wagon through, ignoring the angry shouts and the fists waving in the air.

"What is wrong with these people?" Sheila cried, scooting closer to Grace.

Grace could only shake her head, her own fear beginning to build. They were furious, their cries for justice a frightening roar. But furious at what? Had the brewing war taken a turn for the worse? No, God, please, no.

" 'E's guilty!" a man they were maneuvering past shouted.

Others nearby exclaimed, "Aye, 'e's guilty! Name 'is punishment."

Jackson kept the wagon moving, finally making a turn

and heading for a nearby alley. Grace spotted a platform in the center of the crowd, and what she saw on it made her gasp in horror. "Jackson, stop!"

He glanced back at her with a look that said he thought her insane. "You don't want to see this, Grace."

"Please, stop the wagon." She stood, unable to tear her gaze away from the center of the town square. She gripped his shoulder to keep her balance, felt his muscles clench beneath her fingers. "Oh, dear God. What are they doing? They aren't . . . they aren't hanging that man, are they?"

Following the direction of her gaze, he bit out a curse. "Sit down! I'm taking you out of here."

"No!"

Sheila grasped Grace's hand and tugged, trying to force her to sit. "Do as he says. We must leave here at once."

"No! We have to stop them."

"Are you out of your mind?" the woman demanded, jerking so hard, her nails dug into Grace's skin. "They'll kill us too if we don't leave here immediately."

Grace pulled free, her gaze locked on the spot across the commons where a man of middle years stood alone on the platform, completely stripped of his clothes, his arms tied behind his back. He stared into the distance, his face blanched of color, his expression one of humiliation and pained resignation.

Three men carried a large black kettle up the steps and set it beside the prisoner. A fourth man dragged a sack onto the deck and waved at the crowd when they erupted into cheers.

"What are they going to do to him?" Grace asked, her voice breaking with disgust and fear.

"Tar and feather, my lady."

"What?" Grace rounded on the driver.

The man shrugged with an indifference she couldn't believe. " 'E's a bloody loyalist, spying for the Brits. From what I hear, 'e used tae be a messenger for the rebels. Somehow the turncoat got hold of a battle plan and was mak'n' his way to the British line, down in Boston."

"That doesn't give people the right to torture him this way." She faced the swarm of townspeople and pressed her hands to her mouth. Her heart raced, but she felt cold down to her bones. She had to do something, had to stop them.

Two men lifted large paintbrushes from the kettle. Clumps of black gooey tar fell from the bristles. Even from this distance, she could see steam rising in vaporous curls from the hot resin. They began lathering their prisoner who jerked and shuddered each time the brush came into contact with bare skin.

"We have to do something to stop this."

"What do you suggest?" Jackson asked, his expression harsh and vigilant. "We're sorely outnumbered."

"Your man's got the right of it. There's noth'n' ye can do, though I don't know why ye'd want to," the driver said, straining to see the commotion. Then he eyed her warily. "Unless ye're a loyalist."

"Of course not, but I can't stand by and do nothing while they harm that man."

"If ye try to interfere, those folks will wrap ye in tar for sure. It won't matter to them one bit if you're a king's spy or a do-gooder."

"I don't care, I have to try." Grace gathered her skirts, ready to jump off the wagon, but Jackson leaped over his seat and grabbed her waist, stopping her.

"You accuse *me* of being reckless," he growled in her ear. "Are you trying to get yourself killed?"

"But Jackson . . ." She sucked in a breath, unable to utter another word. Having finished painting the man with thick black tar from his neck and over his stomach, along his arms, and down his bare legs, they upended the mesh sack, spilling thousands of white feathers over his head. Some of the wispy down swirled on the breeze, flying safely away, but more caught against the man, coating his body so he appeared the coward the punishment was meant to imply.

The crowd roared their approval, shouting, laughing, some dancing in place. Grace pressed tight to Jackson, thankful his arms were there to support her, certain she'd fall if he let her go. She wanted to turn away, close her eyes, but she couldn't. She stared in silent horror at the appalling scene. Despite all she'd seen as a child, the starvation, the suffering, living in daily fear, nothing had ever prepared her for this.

"I suggest we leave, Capt'n," the driver warned.

Grace glanced down at the elderly man. "Why? What else could they possibly do to him?"

"I don't think you'll be want'n' tae know, my lady."

Jackson tensed. She expected to hear one of his curses, but he took her by the shoulders and forced her to sit back down beside Sheila.

"How can people be so cruel?" She searched his face, knowing he couldn't give her an answer.

Kneeling before her, he cupped her cheek in his hand. His eyes darkened to flints of polished stone. "I'm getting you out of here."

She nodded, for once not having the heart to argue. As Jackson took his place and gathered the reins, she saw a finely tailored man from the corner of her eye leap onto the platform. He raised his arms like a preacher intent on calming his flock. She didn't turn her head to watch, having seen enough of the town and the people she would have to live among.

Dear God, how can I stay here? Jackson was right, I never should have left England.

"Good people of Medford," the man called out in a rumbling baritone that demanded attention.

Grace blinked and tensed in her seat, not wanting to hear what would come next.

"You see before you a traitor, a turncoat who tried to rob you of your freedom!" Angry cries surged through the mass of people, but Grace barely heard them. Instead, she concentrated on the man, not so much his words, but his voice.

"Elliott Prescott has aided King George's insidious plan to make slaves of us all. We shall make an example of him today, warning those who think to betray us."

"Oh, dear God," she breathed, pressing her hand over her mouth, too afraid to look up.

"Hold on, Grace, I'll have you out of here." He slapped the reins against the horses' rumps and shouted, "Out of my way!"

"Hurry!" Sheila urged, her voice trembling with panic. "These people are insane. I've heard about this barbaric country. They won't be happy with one killing. They'll want another one. And we're strangers! What's to stop them from coming after us?"

"Justice is a heavy duty we all must bear," the man continued. "Let it be time for the gauntlet!"

"No!" Grace cried out, leaping to her feet, but the mob broke out in a thunderous roar, drowning out her protest.

"Damn it, Grace, sit down."

"Wait!"

He gripped her arms. "Bloody hell, what's wrong? You look like you're going to faint."

She swayed, and wondered if she might succumb to the one ladylike trait she had never mastered. God, this can't be happening, her dream couldn't fall apart so quickly and so completely. She had to be imagining it, the horrible, unbelievable sight before her had to be an illusion, a nightmare!

Jackson shook her. "Talk to me, damn it!"

"That man, on the platform, the one announcing the punishment."

Jackson frowned as he followed her gaze. "What about him?"

"That's William." She had the hysterical urge to laugh while tears burned the back of her throat. "That's my fiancé."

For a staggering moment, Jackson thought his mind was playing tricks on him. *Her fiancé.* He'd known Grace was engaged—she'd reminded him often enough—but to finally see the viscount . . .

Something inside him tightened, turning into a dark, dangerous emotion as her mouth parted in dismay and tears pooled in her eyes.

"I'm taking you back to the ship," he told her.

"Did you say that was William?" Miss Foxsworth asked in a hopeful voice.

Jackson couldn't respond, and obviously neither could Grace.

Miss Foxsworth stood in the wagon and strained to see around them. "Oh, my! Look! It is William. We're saved. He'll protect us."

Grace stared at Jackson, her gaze distant. The color had drained from her cheeks, turning them ashen. He had to get her away. "Both of you sit down. We're leaving."

"No," Grace told him, slowly shaking her head.

"You can argue with me later. Now sit!"

"I have to talk to William. I can't believe . . ." She gathered her skirts, then suddenly leaped from the wagon.

"Damn it, Grace!"

She moved away, struggling to push through the crowd.

He jumped down, chasing after her. With only a few strides and well-placed shoves, he caught her arm and forced her to stop. "Are you out of your mind? Or are you just determined to get us both killed?"

"The William I know wouldn't . . ." She cast a pained look toward the platform. "He wouldn't do this."

"You obviously don't know him as well as you thought you did." He urged her away. "Come back to the *Sea Angel* with me and we'll discuss it."

"I have to see him now, Jackson." She tried pushing through the crowd only to be shoved back as people moved aside to form a clear path for the gauntlet.

"Do you know what they're going to do to that man?"

"That's why I have to talk to William!"

Indecision tore at Jackson. He had to protect her. She didn't need to see the beating the traitor would suffer. He wanted to toss her over his shoulder and carry her back to the ship, but hesitated. If Mason was so embedded in the rebellion it was best if Grace learned of it now—before their wedding took place.

Taking her hand, he ordered, "Stay behind me."

Jackson worked his way through the crowd, giving as many punches as he took, some in the ribs, his arms, once in his face. He felt Grace press tight against his back, felt the death grip she had on his hand. All of a sudden, the mass of people turned like the shifting tide and headed to his left. He couldn't tell what had happened, though he could hazard a guess. The gauntlet had begun.

He kept moving until he reached the platform, now empty save for one man. Lord William Mason stood center stage with his hands folded calmly before him, a closed look on his face. He was younger than Jackson had imagined, in his early thirties if he were any judge. If not for his commanding pose, Jackson wouldn't have thought Mason to be a member of the nobility. He had none of the pale, narrow features his aristocratic brothers possessed. His face was broad and rugged, brown from the sun. He watched the crowded with eyes that were both wary and hard, as if they'd witnessed the horrors of life and had been forever changed.

Except for the patches of gray at his temples, his hair was as black as pitch. He seemed both intelligent and strong, a man capable of protecting what belonged to him—especially his wife.

Jackson hated him on sight. Thoughts of kidnapping Grace came to mind, but it was too late. She was already stepping onto the platform. *Eager to see the man she wants to marry.*

"William?" she said, too softly to be heard above the clamor. She cleared her throat and tried again. "William!"

He glanced toward them. Spotting Grace, his eyes widened with recognition, then quickly darkened with alarm. "Grace, my God! You're here!"

"I . . ." She looked to where the feathered prisoner was fighting his way through the crowd, raising his arms to ward off the brutal, endless blows, delivered with weapons of all kinds—fists and boots, clubs, rakes and canes.

Hurrying to her, Mason took both of her hands in his, drawing her away so Jackson had no choice but to let her go. "You shouldn't be witnessing this, my dear."

"How could you be a part of this?"

He shifted his body so he blocked her view. "This is nothing for you to concern yourself over. When did you arrive? Forgive me, I should have been at the harbor to meet you, but—"

"Answer my question, William."

He stilled for an instant, his blue eyes going cold at her authoritative tone. "I don't expect you to understand."

"Then explain it to me. There's a war going on, I understand that much. Is this how you colonists fight? By humiliating a man? Stripping him naked, tar and feathering him, then throwing him to the mercy of an angry mob?"

"This isn't the place to discuss this," he said, his tone inviting no further argument. "I'm sure you need to rest after your tiresome voyage. Let me take you to White Rose; I think you'll find your new home ideal, truly beautiful."

"I want an explanation now."

"I'm not used to having to explain myself, my dear. To anyone. But I'll humor you this once." He smiled, a quick tilt of his mouth that didn't touch his eyes. "Once you've lived here for a time, you'll realize that things are done differently in the Colonies. That's what our war is all about."

"Since when do English lords turn against England?" Jackson asked, immediately suspicious. What would the man have to gain?

Mason eyed Jackson, from his face down to his boots. "And who are you, sir?"

Grace pulled her hands free of the viscount's hold. "William, this is Jackson Brodie, a friend of my family's."

He gave a slight bow as if they were in a drawing room and there wasn't a brawling crowd behind them. "Why didn't we meet when I was in London?"

"It's a long story." Grace nervously wrung her hands as raucous laughter erupted. "But this—"

William touched her shoulder to calm her. "Come with me to my carriage. I'll explain everything on the way home."

"I won't be delayed—"

"He's right," Jackson said. "Perhaps we should leave as the viscount suggested." He wanted to hear the man's explanations as much as she did, but the crowd might not stop at beating their loyalist prisoner. A hanging could be next, and he didn't want Grace anywhere near to witness such an event.

"Excellent. My carriage is waiting not far from here." Mason took her arm and started to lead her away.

Jackson caught her other arm, stopping her, not about to let her out of his sight. "That won't be necessary. We have transportation." As the crowd cried out for the man to stand up and keep running, he said, "You obviously have things here that need to be handled. I'll see Grace to your home."

Mason hesitated, clearly reluctant to release the woman he'd claimed. Finally, he nodded. "Very well." He pressed a kiss to the back of her hand. "I won't be long, my dear."

Jackson pulled Grace away, keeping her close to his side. Even faced with having to navigate a hostile, surging crowd, he was tempted to smile. He'd been worried about how to convince Grace to leave with him and return home. He'd worried for nothing. Mason had managed to ruin his relationship with his fiancée without any input on Jackson's part. Nothing Mason said would justify his actions. In Grace's mind, there wasn't a valid reason to hurt another person. Before the day was through, she would be desperate to end her engagement and leave for England.

And Jackson would be there to take her away.

Chapter Ten

Grace felt cold, chilled down to her soul. She shouldn't have allowed Jackson to drag her away from the town square. She should have stayed, demanded to hear William's excuse for condoning that man's punishment. But she'd been too shaken to fight, too shaken and too afraid.

Why had William been involved with such violence? She couldn't escape the question, or even imagine an answer. Did she know him so little? Good God, what had she gotten herself into? She briefly closed her eyes and reasoned that there had to be a valid reason William would approve—encourage—such brutality. *A valid reason to torture a man?* Had the world really become so cruel?

The wagon lurched over a series of ruts. Jackson reined the team of grays to a smoother portion of road, while the driver held onto his hat, and Sheila, for once, endured the trip in silence, though she'd made it clear she was miffed about missing the chance to ride in William's carriage.

With every inch of ground they covered, taking her closer to her new home, Grace felt a suffocating pressure compressing her lungs. She pressed a hand to her throat and focused on breathing, trying to think about anything but the last hour.

Her gaze settled on Jackson. It still surprised her that he had consented to bring her to White Rose. She'd expected to see that possessive heat in his eyes, the silent warning that he intended to follow his own mind, her wishes be damned, and return her to the *Sea Angel*.

She'd been so numb when leaving the riot, she wasn't sure she would have fought him.

Things aren't as bad as they seem; they can't be.

She might have had a tumultuous childhood, but the last few years had been safe ones—difficult at times, but safe. She'd simply been unprepared to face such violence. If she married William—not if, *when* she married him— she might have to deal with such brutality again until the war was settled. The thought sickened her.

"Heavens," Sheila whispered, "it looks like a dream."

For the first time since leaving the square, Grace took note of her surroundings. Tall, large-leaved maple trees, some choked with heavy moss, were evenly spaced along the road, thickening into a forest of oaks and elms that stretched out into the surrounding hills. Their enormous height seemed to scrape the sky, blocking out everything but soft, muted light. It was quiet here, with only the occasional chirp of a bird and the rustle of leaves stirred by the wind. The grass was clipped low, smooth as a carpet, and as the horses turned onto a level drive, the rumble of wagon wheels seemed to hush.

"It's beautiful," she murmured with surprise, amazed she could find beauty in anything considering what she'd just witnessed, yet she was painfully aware that arriving at her new home wasn't the joyous event she'd hoped for.

As beautiful as it is, how can I live here? Raise children with William? Be content if I'm surrounded by war and death? The answers eluded her. Perhaps they would always elude her, just as feelings of safety and contentment had all her life.

She sighed with disgust, growing angry with herself. She hadn't heard William's explanation yet, and already she'd judged him guilty. She'd even decided she couldn't be happy with him at White Rose. *I can be content here, but only if I try to make it work.*

It was her own fault things weren't proceeding as she'd hoped. She'd imagined herself sailing across the Atlantic on a perfect ship, arriving on a perfectly beautiful day, being greeted by her perfect fiancé, whence she would then begin her perfect life.

Well, there wasn't any such thing as "perfect." The sooner she accepted that, she thought, drawing her shoulders back, the sooner she'd make peace with her past and move on to her future.

But he encouraged those people to beat that man—

She shut off the thought, determined to hear William out when he arrived.

They reached a gate and a white brick fence extending deep into the woods, and, she assumed, around the estate. Jackson reined to a stop and told the gatekeepers their names. They immediately unlocked the black wrought-iron gate and swung it open on silent hinges. Within moments they stopped in the circular drive.

Grace sat in the wagon, too stunned to move, her gaze darting from one incredible scene to another. A wide, airy porch surrounded the first floor of the enormous home. The picturesque veranda silently tempted her to try one of the wicker rocking chairs that looked as comfortable and they did inviting. Four pillars, wider than the expanse of her arms, shot from the ground floor to the top of the second. Set against a backdrop of dense trees and greenery, the white house, with its forest-green shutters, slate roof and countless chimneys, was unlike anything she'd ever seen. It was breathtaking, beautiful. *Perfect?*

"I never dreamed William owned something so magnificent," Sheila announced, sounding disgruntled. She glared at Jackson. "Which makes arriving in this horrid wagon all the more humiliating."

Grace looked away from the woman, not wanting to see the envy that would cause her brown eyes to glitter. If not for her, William might have asked for Sheila's hand, and this might have been *her* home.

Leaping down, Jackson reached for Grace and helped her out of the wagon. As he turned to help Sheila, Grace started up the wide stone steps, the sweet scent of roses filling her lungs. Pausing on the landing, she turned and spotted a winding path of colorful flowers; red begonias intermixed with yellow daisies, purple morning glories, and a dozen others she didn't recognize. Interspersed through it all were the rosebushes for which the estate was named. Dozens of them, hundreds, and all full of white, velvety blooms.

"This is possibly the most wonderful home I've ever seen," Grace said with mixed emotions, awe and surreal detachment among them.

"It's all right," Jackson said, watching her closely. "If a big house is what you want." He directed a footman to see to their luggage, then joined her on the porch.

"Standing here, breathing in the flowers, I can almost believe the persecution that man suffered didn't happen."

"But it did," he reminded her, almost gleefully.

The pounding sound of horse's hooves drew their attention to the drive. William, mounted on a roan thoroughbred, raced toward them. He drew the lathered animal to a sudden, prancing stop at the foot of the stairs. Leaping from the saddle, he took the steps two at a time until he reached Grace's side.

Breathing hard, his black hair tousled from his ride, he took her hand in his, his grip so intense, she barely concealed her wince of pain. "I dispensed with my business as quickly as I could. I even borrowed a horse. I wanted to see your face the first time you saw White Rose."

She smiled, unsure how to respond to William's eager expression. His timing seemed off, her mood still pensive from the day's events. What had happened to Elliott Prescott? How had William "dispensed with his business?" She wanted to ask, but wasn't sure she was ready to hear the answers. "Your home is lovely, William."

"It's your home, now." He put his hand on her waist, his fingers firm on her side, possessive and too familiar. She stiffened in response, knowing it was foolish. He was her fiancé; she had to become used to his touch. He turned her toward the front door, effectively cutting Jackson off.

Grace glanced back and received the full force of Jackson's half-lidded stare. He stood still, his hands loose at his sides, yet she sensed he wanted to pull her way from William. But for what reason? Was it William he objected to, or her marrying at all? He didn't want her, that much she knew for certain. Yet, she felt the tension in him, the anger building beneath his casual pose.

Why now? she wanted to demand. Why do you act like you want me now that I'm committed to another?

She turned away, refusing to let his emotions affect her. She'd made her decision, and by God, she would live by it. As William led her through the tall double doors and into the foyer, Grace caught a last glimpse of the roses crowding the gardens.

Perhaps it was the sun, or the different angle, but it struck her that the delicate white blossoms weren't as beautiful as they'd been before.

* * *

Whiskey was solace to a tortured mind, Jackson decided, staring into the amber liquid before taking another deep drink. Or perhaps the Demon Rum was the shove he needed to send him over the edge.

Standing by a pair of French doors that led to a sprawling garden, complete with a four-foot-tall hedge maze, he watched the occupants of the room. Miss Foxsworth occupied the velvet couch, her back erect, her expression serene—an exhausting struggle for the woman, he was sure. He didn't know why she was here or why Grace tolerated her company. He felt certain that even his Angel's compassion had its limits.

He turned his attention to the woman who had all but monopolized his thoughts. Grace, wearing another of her snug-fitting gowns—this one in pale emerald—with a neckline scooped low enough to make him gnash his teeth, sat in a high-backed chair before the hearth. She stared into the low-burning fire, her gaze intent, as if nothing could fascinate her more than the golden flames. But he knew differently, knew her attention was fixed on every word uttered by William Mason, viscount of Kensale.

"Once you've settled," Mason was saying from his place by the mantel, his hands clasped behind his back, his expression annoyingly cheerful, "I'll take you on a tour of the shipyard. It's a shame your brother-in-law, Daniel, couldn't have escorted you here. I would have welcomed his opinion on the design changes I've made on my newest ship."

"I'm sure he and Morgan will come as soon as they're able." She turned her gaze up to Mason and gave him a beautiful smile. If not for the remote flare of anxiety that made her eyes sparkle like ice, Jackson would have thought her at ease.

"Yes, well, but you're here. That's the important thing." Mason sent a cursory glance to Sheila and Jackson before taking Grace's pale hand in his. "Accompanied by your friend, Mr. Brodie. Tell me, sir, how are you acquainted with my fiancée's family?"

Jackson stilled the urge to rip Grace's hand free from the man's possessive grip. No one else should be able to touch her. *No one except me.* In a controlled voice, he said, "My business is in trade."

"You work with Daniel, then? Excellent. Do you know anything about ships?"

"I have a fair knowledge," he said, ignoring Grace's glare warning him to behave. Miss Foxsworth choked on her sherry.

"I'd welcome your opinion on my newest sloop, the *Triumph.*" Smiling, looking pleased, he added, "She's a beauty if I do say so myself. Nothing like her, or as fast, on the seas."

"I look forward to it."

"I'd like to join you if I may, Lord Mason," Miss Foxsworth chimed in. "I do adore ships."

Mason nodded respectfully, his gaze sliding past the homely woman, missing her disappointed pout, to focus on Grace. His steel-blue eyes took on a proprietary cast, darkening, making his thoughts all too apparent. Jackson nearly crushed the crystal glass in his hand. If only he could rip the man's eyes out of his head without upsetting Grace.

"We'll have to tour the shipyard soon, in the morning perhaps," Mason said. "I intend to host a ball in your honor, my dear. Tomorrow night, as a matter of fact."

"So soon?" Her body straightened with renewed tension.

"There's no need to delay. I want everyone within fifty miles to know my fiancée has finally arrived. As a matter of fact, I've already spoken with my steward to have things moved ahead. Notices will be going out to our neighbors posthaste.''

"I must agree with Grace," Sheila broke in hastily, her attention flickering to the couple's joined hands. Though her features were carefully composed, Jackson wondered if she wanted to break them apart. If so, perhaps he'd erred in his judgment of Miss Foxsworth. If she objected to the proposed engagement, she couldn't be as bad as he'd first thought.

"We've only just arrived," she continued. "Surely you need time to plan. And truly, I don't have my land legs back yet. Why, the way the room keeps dipping and swaying, I'm sure neither Grace nor I will be able to dance one dance without falling on our faces."

"Nonsense!" Mason waved a brusque dismissal. "A celebration to announce our engagement is just the thing."

"But with the . . . the difficulties," Grace said, "wouldn't it be better to wait?"

"Perhaps Grace is right," Jackson couldn't help saying. "The ladies suffered a shock today. Perhaps the ball could wait a week or so." Giving him time to sail to Newburyport, complete his business and return.

Mason's mouth quirked with a tight smile. "As Grace's friend, Mr. Brodie, I'd think you'd want to see her settled."

"There's no need to rush her, if she's not ready."

"Once we're married, she'll have all the time she needs to adjust to her new life." Mason laughed then. "You can't blame me, now can you, for wanting everyone to meet my beautiful new bride-to-be?"

"No," Jackson said, amazed he could speak around the anger clamping down on his chest. "I don't blame you at all."

"You're invited, of course, Mr. Brodie," Mason said, petting Grace's hand as if she were a lapdog.

"Jackson won't be staying," Grace hurriedly put in. "He must sail tonight, on business."

"Indeed." Jackson felt his blood turn cold. So she wanted him to leave, did she?

"Yes, Mr. Brodie," Miss Foxsworth said, giving him a pretty smile that surprised him by softening her stern features. "Perhaps you'd better leave now. We wouldn't want you to miss the tide or the boat, or whatever it is you sailors call it."

Jackson studied Miss Foxsworth, wondering what she was up to. He'd expected her to delight in informing the world that he'd attacked the *Maiden Fair*, still held the crew locked in his bays, but she sat quietly, with a small, demure smile on her face. If he didn't know better, he'd swear she was taking notes and formulating a plan. If so, he liked the English shrew more and more.

Deciding to change the subject and stir the pot, he said to Mason, "I believe you were going to explain your involvement regarding the scene at the square today. I, for one, am interested to know what the man did to deserve such a punishment."

Grace shot a look at Jackson, grateful that he'd finally broached the subject she'd both anticipated and dreaded. If she had to listen to any more idle chatter about ships and balls she was sure she'd go insane.

"It's a grisly business, Mr. Brodie," William said, tightening his fingers around her hand. "One I'm not sure the ladies care to hear about."

Grace pulled free of his hold and pushed to her feet. "I want to know, William."

William frowned down at her. "Very well. Elliott Prescott was working as a messenger for the rebels. He was responsible for carrying letters, documents, missives of all kinds between various camps. Our generals rely on men like him to keep the lines of communications open. If we lose that, we'll lose this rebellion before it's truly begun."

Mason went to the desk and poured himself a tumbler of whiskey from a crystal decanter, then refilled Jackson's glass.

"Four days ago, General Porter, who's stationed near Waltham, sent Elliott Prescott to the rebels' main camp in Cambridge. Prescott carried vital plans that described General Porter's battle strategy to push back the British line that now surrounds Boston, making it impenetrable. Times and dates had been detailed, as well as the number of men he intended to attack with.

"Instead of riding for Cambridge, Prescott took it upon himself to head for Boston, straight for the enemy. Fortunately, men loyal to the rebel cause intercepted him. And quite by accident, actually. If Prescott had delivered those plans, hundreds, perhaps a thousand colonists, men who are farmers and merchants, businessmen fighting to save their livelihood, would have been ambushed and slaughtered."

Grace sank into her chair, feeling the blood drain from her face. "Perhaps he'd become lost."

With an amused smile, he ran his finger over her cheek. "You are so innocent. That's what I find so charming about you." Shaking his head, he added, "The man confessed, my dear. And Prescott knows his way around the Colonies the way I know my own land."

"But couldn't you have simply imprisoned him?" Grace asked. "Did you have to humiliate him? Subject him to public torture?"

"We had to make an example of him, or else others might try the same. If that were to happen, we might not be so lucky as to capture the man before grave damage was done."

Grace looked to Jackson for help, but quickly realized

she'd receive no aid from him. He arched a brow, nodding his head, silently telling her that he agreed with William.

Fine, she thought resolutely, if they thought tar and feathering a man was just, she'd let the subject go for now, but that didn't mean she intended to forget what she'd witnessed. No, she could never forget Elliott Prescott's pain or the townspeople's revelry in his disgrace.

"There's something I still don't understand, William."

"And what is that, my dear?" He smiled at her, his steel-blue eyes glimmering with affection, his black hair neatly combed into a queue. He was a handsome man, she reflected, strong, assertive, a true leader. He would make her a good husband, she reminded herself. She was certain of it.

"You're a viscount, with a seat in Parliament. Why aren't you supporting England in the rebellion?"

The smile vanished and a frown appeared, deepening the creases around his eyes. "That's a question many of my acquaintances have asked. I hadn't thought to hear it from my own fiancée."

"In lieu of the fact that spies are everywhere," Jackson interjected, studying William over the rim of his glass, "you have to admit that it's rather suspect to have a nobleman turn against his peers."

"Turn against?" William demanded. "I've done nothing of the kind. I've decided to support the cause that is best for everyone. Myself included. I may be a viscount, but my holdings in England are suffering, my income there is insufficient to support the upkeep of my estate. I had a choice, Mr. Brodie," William said, though his gaze swerved to Grace. "I could either sit by and lose everything I owned because of unpaid taxes, or I could act. I decided to act."

"By emigrating to the Colonies?" Jackson asked.

"And why here, of all places? It's so, so uncivilized," Sheila said, pursing her lips, decidedly perplexed.

William barked out a laugh. "But that is the beauty of the Americas. Anything is possible. I've proven that by starting my own shipbuilding company. It's booming, I tell you. There's money to be made in trade, as Grace's brother-in-law well knows.

"If England simply wanted to claim the Colonies, collect a fair amount in taxes, I'd agree with them wholeheartedly. But King George is determined to drain our newfound resources, savage the land and its people, and control all trade so the colonists become slaves to his dictates. And all so he can refill the coffers in England."

"You can't go against the king," Sheila gasped, her brown eyes widening with alarm. "You'll risk losing all of your holdings in England. Your title."

"Perhaps. But what good is a title if I cannot put food on the table?" William took Grace's hand again, his blue eyes focusing on her, warming as he held her gaze. "But my life is here now. And with Grace as my wife, anything is possible."

She shifted, uncomfortable with his public display of affection. Or perhaps it was the feel of Jackson's furious gaze boring into her that had her so uneasy.

Too much had happened in the last few hours. She needed time alone, to sort through everything. "I'm rather tired, William. If you don't mind, I'd like to rest before dinner."

"Of course, my dear. I'll ring for a maid to show you and Miss Foxsworth to your rooms."

As Mason left to summon a member of his staff, Grace met Jackson's gaze. His eyes glowed like burning amber. "Will I see you before you leave?"

"As you reminded me, Angel, I must sail tonight."

"Perhaps I should leave the two of you alone so you can say your good-byes." Miss Foxsworth gave them a secretive smile, then left the room in a rustle of starched satin.

Grace stepped forward, then stopped, rubbing her palms down her skirt. "Promise me you'll be careful."

"I'm always careful." Jackson closed the distance between them.

She wanted to tell him to stay where he was, knowing that if he moved any closer she might touch him, and if she touched him . . . A lump formed in her throat and the words stayed locked inside her. He took another step, not stopping until he stood so close she could smell the earthy scent of him. Soap and clean sweat and an elusive scent that was only Jackson. She clenched her hands to keep from smoothing the hair from his brow, feel once more the warmth of his skin.

"Will you come back to visit me?" she asked, her heart aching with the thought of never seeing him again.

"Do you want me to?"

"Of course." She managed a trembling smile. "We're friends, are we not?"

"I didn't mean do you want me to visit," he said, taking her chin between his rough finger and thumb. "I meant do you want me to leave?"

"You have to."

"Aye, I do. But I can take you with me."

"Jackson, please—"

"Tell me you want to stay." He bent close, so close the heat of his body wrapped around her. "Look me in the eyes and tell me."

"I . . . I've made my choice."

"You'd choose to marry a man you don't love?"

She shook her head. "Don't do this—"

"Tell me," he demanded, the words rough in his throat.

"Jackson, don't—"

He took her mouth with his, stopping her protest, shocking her senses. He wasn't gentle, or seductive. He took her, hard and deep, plunging his tongue inside her mouth, filling her with his taste. His hands raked over her back, tightening, crushing her breasts into his chest, igniting fierce sensations beneath her skin. Shivers rippled through her body, waves of them, hot and cold, urgent. Too potent and fast for her to fight.

Oh, God, Jackson!

She tried to stop the kiss, tried to pull free, but her body refused to obey. *I have to let him go! I can't do this.* Regardless of how wrong it was, she couldn't stop kissing him. But Jackson ended it for her. He stepped back, his breath ragged and deep, his eyes blazing with desire.

"Come with me, Angel." The low, grated tone of his voice seduced her like no kiss ever could. But she couldn't give in. She'd finally reached the Colonies. William, her new life. Pulling the dredges of her courage from the bottom of her soul, she fought giving in to Jackson's plea.

"I can't. Try to understand."

He scanned the room, the polished floor, the costly grandfather clock, the plush settee and chairs. "I understand. Perfectly."

She recoiled as if he'd slapped her. Did he think she'd chosen William because of money? Could he believe her to be so shallow? It was the stable home he offered, the security. Jackson knew her well enough to know that's all she'd ever wanted. She started to explain, but he raised his hand.

"I believe we've said enough." The desire faded from his eyes, dying like a candle's flame being snuffed out. "You've made your choice. I hope you can live with it."

He turned then and walked out of her life.

Chapter Eleven

Grace paused on the second-floor landing, her hand demurely placed on William's bent arm, certain she was about to become ill.

Chandeliers blazed, a thousand candles firing against crystal and glass. Diamond-shaped light reflected off mirrors and gilded walls, sending its golden drizzle over the curving staircase, along wide, oak-paneled halls, flowing into the grand ballroom that was alive with music and laughter. People dressed in colorful silks and satin swirled under those lights, enjoying the endless food, the flowing wine, the company of friends.

Grace descended the stairs with her fiancé, stopping when he did and smiling when he introduced her to one acquaintance or another. She scanned the room, the strange faces that regarded her with cursory looks and open inquisition, realizing she was searching for one special face, one she knew she wouldn't find. Jackson was well on his way to Newburyport to deliver his prisoners and the message regarding the arrival of a British fleet.

She was truly on her own now. She'd made her choice, and not even Jackson's kiss had been able to sway her. *But what if Jackson had promised to change, offered to stop pirating and risking his life? Would I have made the same choice? Would I have stayed with William?*

She glanced at her fiancé, the strong line of his jaw, the vibrant tone of his skin, the coal-black hair showing its first signs of gray. She didn't know what she would have done, and it didn't matter. Jackson hadn't made any promises, because he couldn't change. He didn't even want to try.

She knew she was being foolish, yet her stomach quivered with trepidation. She couldn't move without feeling half the room watching and taking note. *That is what the ball is for,* she reminded herself. This gave everyone the opportunity to see her, gain an introduction. There would be time later for her to make friends. This ball was no different from the countless others she'd attended in England. This was her debut; she had to focus on making a good impression.

With that thought in mind, Grace willed her spine to stiffen, her smile to ease, but still it felt strained. Everything was going so well, even if she was exhausted and the room swayed as if she still stood on the deck of a rocking ship. She would have preferred the ball to take place a week or two later, once she and William had become reacquainted again, but he'd been right; there'd been no need to delay. Tonight she was taking her first step to establish herself in her new community. There would be teas to attend, musicals, outdoor picnics. Everything she'd imagined as the wife of a prosperous, well-respected man.

Unless the war escalated. Unless more traitors were found.

The muscles in her back knotted once more. She studied

the guests. Had they been among the crowd that had screamed for Elliott Prescott's punishment? She agreed that Prescott deserved to be disciplined for his crime, but she wished there'd been another way to set an example. If only the rebellion would end, if only the two sides could resolve their disagreements in peace. But she wasn't so naive as to believe that men would willingly choose to talk out their difference if they could wield a weapon instead.

She'd been a child when she'd lost her home, her parents and young brother to war. All the security she'd known had been ripped away. She couldn't live through that again. Anything but that.

Spotting Sheila Foxsworth among a group of women, their heads bent close, all listening to whatever Sheila was saying, thoughts of war and Elliott Prescott were swept from Grace's mind and were replaced with a chill of foreboding.

She squeezed William's arm to draw his attention. "Will you excuse me, please?"

Smiling down at her with what she thought might be real affection, his eyes warmed to cobalt blue. "Don't be long. You've yet to meet General Rockwell. He's a great friend of mine, and the best commander among the rebel forces. I'm sure you'll get along splendidly with his wife."

"I'm sure I will."

He rubbed his thumb over the necklace lying flat and heavy against her collarbone. "I knew this would be stunning on you. You'll wear nothing but sapphires from now on, my dear. They bring out the fire in your eyes."

She touched her engagement gift, still shocked that he'd given her something so valuable, and so ... large. Six teardrop sapphires, each one the size of a man's thumb, were fastened to a collar of solid diamonds. She knew the necklace was grossly expensive, knew it caught the eye and envy of every woman in the room. And she knew it didn't suit her. She hadn't been able to tell her fiancé she'd prefer something smaller and less garish. So she'd worn the necklace to please him, hoping she wouldn't have to wear it again any time soon.

Withdrawing her hand from his arm, she made her excuses and crossed the ballroom, feeling as if she were an ungrateful ninny. No, worse than that—a fraud. The necklace she wore was meant for a lady, yet she still wore the *Sea Queen* blade, snug in its leather sheath, strapped to her thigh. Locked behind William's stone wall, she wasn't afraid for her safety. So why hadn't she removed the dagger? Hidden it in one of her trunks where it belonged? Perhaps Sheila had been right; at heart, Grace was a pirate, a fisherman's daughter, and she'd never be anything more.

She closed her thoughts against the doubts and set her mind to the problem at hand.

"Miss Foxsworth," Grace said, stopping beside Sheila and bestowing her best, and hopefully, warmest smile on the group. "I see you're enjoying yourself."

"Yes, Lord Mason has been a most gracious host." Sheila ran her fingers over the satin edge of her silver and lace bodice. The color didn't suit her wan complexion or her dull hair, but it made her almond-shaped brown eyes glow as if they were lit from within. "I believe this ball could compete with some of the best in London."

"Lord Mason has never been one to spare any expense when it comes to entertaining," one of the ladies said, Lady Sheldon, if Grace remembered right. The woman's gaze flickered to the necklace as she added, "Or on jewelry, it seems."

Before Grace could respond, another woman spoke, "Miss Foxsworth was telling us of your horrible journey. Rough seas, storms. My heavens, your ship was damaged."

"It was a difficult trip," Grace said, "but we made it through."

"Were you really captured by pirates?" the woman whispered with horror.

"I . . ." Grace faltered, feeling the blood drain from her face. "No . . . no, of course not."

"But I heard that you had been." The woman's furtive glance at Sheila implied where such a rumor had come from.

"I'm afraid you've been misled."

"Really?" the woman mused. "Hmmm."

Grace looked at Sheila, who arched a brow, her half-smile taunting.

"But you were forced off your ship, were you not?" Lady Sheldon angled her head as if daring Grace to deny the fact.

"We were grateful to leave the *Maiden Fair*. She was sinking."

"Then you didn't know the man who abducted you?"

"We weren't captured, ladies," Grace assured them, her jaw aching with the effort to keep smiling. She even managed a small laugh. "The storm damaged our ship beyond repair. We would have drowned if it hadn't been for another ship coming to rescue us."

"But didn't you know the captain of the other ship?"

The carefully blank stares burned Grace's skin as surely as if they'd been sticking her with red-hot pokers. "My brother-in-law owns a large trading company in England. I know many captains."

"Such as your sisters?" Lady Sheldon's cool voice sliced like the edge of steel. "They were captains too, were they not?"

One of the ladies began fluttering her lace fan, whispering behind it to her friend. "Pirate ships! Can you believe it? Surely Lord Mason doesn't know."

Grace locked her knees to keep herself standing upright. Sheila had told them—*everything*. A tremor erupted beneath Grace's skin, building, growing hot. When she'd accepted William's proposal, she'd blamed herself for the bitter pain Sheila had suffered and had tried to make it up to her by being her friend. Her efforts hadn't been enough. And now, the woman had purposefully ruined any chance Grace might have had at a new beginning.

Anger such as she'd never known poured over her, nearly suffocating her with a fury she had no experience dealing with, didn't begin to know how to control. She would never belong, never find the safe home she'd lost as a child. She saw her future in the women's narrowed, speculative gazes; they would never forget her past, and they wouldn't let *her* forget it either. She would always be an outcast.

I've been a fool, an absolute fool. Life in the Colonies isn't going to be any different from the one I've left behind.

Using every ounce of training she possessed, she made a small curtsy. "If you'll excuse me, ladies, I need Miss Foxsworth's assistance with my gown."

Gripping Sheila's arm in a hold that made the woman gasp, she turned away, pulling Sheila as she went. Behind her, she heard the outbreak of urgent whispers, but kept going, giving Sheila the choice to either accompany her or create a scene.

Shaking down to the soles of her slippers, not knowing what she intended, just that she had to do something, Grace headed for the French doors that opened onto a balcony overlooking the shadowed gardens. Once outside, she continued into the darkness, away from the light, the noise, the voices that would be spreading rumors like a disease.

"Release me!" Sheila demanded, futilely tugging her arm, but she was helpless against the strength of Grace's anger.

Reaching a tall hedgerow, she stopped and demanded, "How could you?"

"I don't know what you're talking about." Sheila's chin came up, her gaze glittering like jagged stones in the moonlight.

"You told them about my past, about my sisters. You had no right, Sheila."

"Do you intend to lie to these people? Pretend you're something you're not?" Reaching out, Sheila flicked Grace's necklace with her finger. "This should be mine, as well as this house, these grounds. This ball should have been held in *my* honor, not yours."

"I'm sorry William didn't choose you, Sheila, truly I am." If only he had offered for her, Grace thought. If only . . . "There were other men who wanted to ask for you, but you'd—"

"I didn't want other men, I wanted William. And you knew it. Let me warn you, Grace Fisk, I still mean to have him. Do you really think my mother *forced* me to sail to the Colonies? I have no relatives in Abington." She jerked free, her eyes turning glassy with malice. "I joined you because I have every intention of showing William the base creature you really are. Once he knows the truth, he'll end your engagement."

"He knows about my past and he doesn't care."

"William's pride will force him to care." Sheila tilted her head back to stare down her nose at Grace. "Do you think he asked for you because he fell in love with you? That he will stand by your side when his friends shun you?"

Grace wanted to argue that William would defend her, but the words wouldn't come. He'd been kind to her, but she didn't really know him—his involvement in the rebellion was proof of that. Would he support her? Or would he turn his back on her, too?

"William spoke to me often about how he planned to

expand his shipbuilding empire," Sheila said, her tone hurtful. "And now he can because of your connection with Daniel Tremayne. That's the *only* reason he settled for a commoner like you."

Grace crushed her skirt in her fist and felt the *Sea Queen* blade through the layers of her gown. She was tempted to draw it the way Jo would and . . . and do what? Frighten Sheila? Attack her? Stop her from speaking the truth? And by doing so, give Sheila another story to further rip her reputation to shreds?

No, there had to be a way to stop the scandal. She could deny everything, or admit to her past and laugh it off. If William laughed with her, perhaps all would be well. It was either face the censure or run. Since the day she and her sisters had boarded the *Sea Queen* and had turned their lives around, none of them had run from anything. No matter how tempting it was, she didn't intend to start now.

Grace gathered her skirts and hurried back to the house, trying to close her ears to the cutting sound of Sheila's cruel laughter. She had to find William, warn him. Together they could come up with a way to avoid a disaster. He was well respected; people would follow his lead. Surely she was worrying for nothing.

She crossed the bricked patio and burst through the French doors, only to come to a sudden and staggering halt.

A hush fell over the room. Every eye turned to watch her. William stood at the forefront of the crowd, a glass of champagne in his hand, a dark, questioning frown on his face. And beside him . . . beside him . . .

"Hello, Angel."

Jackson had never seen Grace look so beautiful, or so close to fainting.

"No," she whispered so low only those standing nearest to her could hear. She swayed slightly, and her hands clenched in the burnt-gold fabric of her gown. Her blue eyes grew round with disbelief, outshining the gaudy necklace sparkling around her throat.

When she'd been a child, playing on the deck of the *Sea Queen*, he'd seen traces of the lady she'd one day become lurking beneath the pigtails and dirt. But he'd never imagined her like this. Tonight she was a princess draped in spun gold, her blonde hair twisted into threads of sunshine around her head. Thick curls cascaded over one shoulder to rest on the upper curve of her ivory breast. She was stunning, ethereal, the most beautiful woman he'd ever seen.

And she isn't mine.

Jealously raised its ugly head, tightening every nerve along his spine. He stepped forward, pried her hand free of her skirt and bent to kiss it. Her skin was cold and frail against his lips, her fingers stiff. He straightened and hid his worry behind a taunting smile. "I take it you're surprised to see me."

"Mr. Brodie," she said at last, glancing at the crowd of onlookers behind him. Hearing the rustle of fabric and the shuffle of slippers and boots, he knew their audience was drawing closer. "I hadn't thought to see you tonight."

"And miss the opportunity to congratulate you on your upcoming nuptials? Nonsense."

Mason joined them, sliding a possessive arm around Grace's waist. "We're glad you could make it. Aren't we, my dear?"

"Yes, of course."

Grace had never had the ability to lie, and she was doing a poor job of it now. Jackson clenched his jaw. She wanted him a thousand miles from her. Perhaps he shouldn't have come, but he was here now, and he'd be damned if he would leave.

"Let me introduce you around, Mr. Brodie," Mason said, extending his glass of champagne to encompass the room.

"Why don't you allow me that honor, Lord Kensale?" Miss Foxsworth suggested, sweeping through the French doors behind Grace. She positioned herself beside Jackson, taking his arm.

With a satisfied smile that Jackson thought might be relief, Mason said, "That's very thoughtful of you, Miss—"

"No!" Grace drew a breath as if surprised by her outburst. "I mean, as my friend I should be the one to see to that duty."

"Yes." Miss Foxsworth drew out the word, layering it with suggestive meaning that had both Mason and Jackson frowning at her. "Your very *close* friend."

Jackson looked from one woman to the other. Something had happened between them, some event that had left Grace pale and shaking and Miss Foxsworth baring her claws. He had to get Grace alone and question her, but with a hundred guests gathered around listening to every word being said, and Mason holding onto her as if she were his property, he didn't see how that would be possible.

Disengaging his arm from the woman's grip, he bowed slightly to Mason. "Perhaps introductions could wait. What I'd prefer right now is a dance with the lady of honor."

"Of course." Mason's smile never faltered, but something that was definitely not humor flickered in his eyes. Turning toward the small orchestra, he motioned for them to resume playing. Kissing Grace's hand, he said, "But the next dance is mine. I've yet to have a moment alone with my fiancée, and I must say I can't bare to be apart from her for long."

Taking Grace's elbow, suppressing the urge to smash his fist into Mason's overbearing grin, Jackson led her onto the dance floor. He took his place across from her just as the music started. He moved through the steps by rote, unable to think about anything except the turmoil darkening her eyes, the small lines of strain etched around her mouth.

She wasn't happy to see him, that much was obvious, but had he caused her distress? He didn't think so. When she'd burst through the doors she'd been pale, her eyes full of tears. She said nothing now, just moved with the music, her body stiff, her gaze fixed on his chest instead of his face.

"Have I told you how lovely you look tonight?" he asked as he passed her.

Her mouth pressed into a tight line, and for an instant he thought she would give in to her tears. "Thank you."

"It's been a while since we last danced."

The comment seemed to make her even more miserable, for her mouth curved into a sorrowful frown. "Yes, it has. And you hate dancing."

"Not with you, I don't."

"Why are you here, Jackson?" she asked, finally lifting her gaze to meet his.

Such an easy question, yet he didn't know how to answer it. By not sailing to Newburyport as he should have, he was risking thousands of lives. Yet, he hadn't been able to leave. Not yet. "I thought you'd be glad to see me."

"I am. It's just that . . ." As she stepped around him to resume her place, she glanced at the people dancing beside them. "This isn't the best time for you to visit. Things have been a bit strained."

"What happened?"

"Nothing." She gave a small, frantic shake of her head. "I shouldn't have said anything."

Stepping into the center of a circle, he took her hand and led her in a single turn, saying under his breath, "I'm not leaving until I'm sure this is what you want."

"You have to go, Jackson." Her fingers flexed, tightening. "I'll make this work."

"Tell me—" He stopped when they were forced to return to their places. The music came to a dazzling end. People bowed and curtsied, others clapped as they moved off the dance floor.

Spotting Mason working his way through the crowd, his mouth set in a grim smile, his narrowed gaze fastened on Grace, Jackson bit off a curse. He took her by the arm and started for the gardens. When she spotted William as well, she pulled back.

"Thank you for the dance." She smiled up at Jackson, but her eyes glimmered like blue fire, haunting and sad. "Perhaps you could come by tomorrow. We could talk more then."

"I'd rather have our talk now, if you don't mind." He couldn't stay another day; he'd risked too much by delaying as it was. But how could he leave? Grace was nervous and edgy, and though he tried to disguise it, Mason looked ready to rip out someone's throat. Jackson wanted to know the reason why.

"Grace, my dear," Mason said, taking her hand. A muscle pulsed in his smooth-shaven jaw. "It's time to claim my dance. Though it's rather warm in here. Perhaps we could take a walk outside instead."

"I . . ." She glanced at Jackson, her expression filled with apprehension. "Yes, that would be lovely."

With a nod, she turned away and disappeared with her fiancé through the French doors. Jackson watched her go, barely resisting the impulse to rip her from Mason's side. But she'd never forgive him if he acted like the pirate she accused him of being. Besides, before he decided what to do next, he had to know what he was dealing with.

Something had happened, but what? And why wouldn't she tell him? *Because she doesn't want me to interfere.* How many times had she insisted that this was the life she wanted? Yet, he found it hard to believe William Mason could make her happy. *But what can I give her besides a life of misery?*

He glanced at the guests, who watched with interest as Grace strode from the room. People bent their heads together, whispering behind their hands, nodding, their eyes widening in surprise. Spreading gossip, Jackson presumed, not caring for being left in the dark. Spotting Miss Foxsworth standing alone by a white column, her hands gracefully folded at her waist, her face carefully blank of all expression and her eyes burning like black fire, he knew he wouldn't be in the dark for long.

If he couldn't have his talk with Grace, the English shrew would serve just as well.

"Miss Foxsworth," he said, coming up beside her.

Sparkling brown eyes fixed on him before chilling like frost. "Captain Brodie. What an unpleasant surprise."

Deciding to forgo any pleasantries, he stated, "I believe it's time you and I had a talk."

She angled her pointed chin, her smile turning as coy as a hungry predator's. "Why, Captain, I believe you're right."

Grace maneuvered down the pebbled footpath, her hand on William's arm, barely aware of the other couples passing by, the music floating from the house, the gay laughter. Her mind spun with thoughts of Sheila's betrayal, Jackson's unfortunate and untimely appearance, and dread, heavy, gut-wrenching dread of what was yet to come.

She risked a furtive glance at William. His jaw was set, his gaze fixed ahead of them. Was he angry? She didn't know, couldn't read anything in his expression. The inability served to remind her that she barely knew the man she'd decided to marry.

Once they were well away from the gardens, on a lone path that ended with a stone bench surrounded by colorful flowers, he stopped, pulling his arm free so she could sit. Grace folded her hands in her lap, willing them not to clench. The tense silence grew, becoming so thick she thought a granite wall might have sprung up between them. Flickering light from nearby torches drew a multitude of insects, all darting dangerously close to the fire, playing with their lives, yet not realizing how precarious a position they were in.

Grace had no such delusions.

Did William know what Sheila had done? He had to; why else would he have insisted they take a walk instead of dancing?

"I'm disappointed, Grace." William stood over her, his raven-black brows pulled into a frown, his hands clasped behind his back.

"Excuse me?"

"I thought you'd be able to handle the situation."

She opened her mouth to respond, but had no idea what to say, so she snapped her jaw shut and bent her head to study a crease in her gown.

"I suppose everyone in attendance knows of your past by now."

Grace felt her heart sink to her stomach. She closed her eyes and held her breath. Here it comes, she thought, he was going to tell her to pack her clothes and return to England. Everything she'd hoped for would be gone, ruined, over.

"I'm sorry, William," she said.

"As well you should be. I admit I was surprised when Miss Foxsworth arrived with you, but I thought since you invited her, you'd be able to handle her."

Invited Sheila? Where had he gotten that idea?

"You're going to have to be stronger, Grace, if you are to be my wife."

"What?" She looked up at him. Did this mean he didn't intend to call off their engagement?

"You can't let her bully you." William took her hand and pulled her to her feet. "I expect you to control Miss Foxsworth from here on out."

"*Control* Miss Foxsworth?" Recalling Sheila's vicious attack, and her vow to ruin Grace and marry William herself, she didn't think the king of England could control the woman.

"She's made a fine mess of your reputation, and mine."

"William, I can't tell you—"

He placed a finger over her lips. "No simpering, Grace. As long as you do as I say, the damage will be minimal."

She nodded and he removed his finger. "I thought you'd want to end our engagement."

"Over something so easily repaired?" He shook his head and smiled down at her, though his smile seemed forced. "Nonsense. This marriage means too much to me."

Is it our marriage that matters, she wanted to ask, *or your business ties to Daniel?* The truth stung her heart, burning deep, though she knew it shouldn't. She'd known from the beginning that William had chosen her so he could expand his trading empire through Daniel. It didn't matter that William didn't love her now, Grace admonished to herself. He was willing to overlook her past when no other man in England would. He had the ability to give her the home she craved, the security that would ease the restlessness in her heart.

Holding onto that thought, she asked, "Do you really think your friends will ignore my being a . . . a . . . pirate?"

"You'd be amazed what people will overlook if properly motivated."

"Thank you," she whispered, feeling guilty for all the doubts she'd had about marrying him, doubts that had manifested after Jackson had barged into her life once again.

As if reading her mind, William said, "I'll forbid you very little, my dear, but after tonight, I don't want Mr. Brodie visiting you again. Ever."

Taken by surprise, she blurted, "Why not?"

"I've asked around about him. Friend or no, he's not the type of man we can associate with. I've heard rumors that trading cargo aboard his ship isn't his main priority."

Wetting her suddenly dry lips, she asked, "What do you mean?"

"I mean he's deeply involved with the rebellion."

"But so are you."

"I support the rebellion, my dear. I believe in the fight for independence, but I'm not involved any more than that. Remember, this is our home. If the British win this little skirmish, we don't want them penalizing us for taking sides."

She stared at him, too stunned to say anything. Not see Jackson again? She knew it was for the best, but still . . .

"Now, shall we return to our guests?"

She rose to leave, but William stopped her with a hand on her waist. She looked up at him, shocked when his mouth suddenly closed over hers. Tensing, she suppressed the instinctive urge to pull away. This was her fiancé, she thought frantically, the man she was determined to marry. He had every right to kiss her.

She tried to relax, focus on what he was doing. His lips were warm, soft, undemanding against hers. But they were the lips of a stranger, foreign. *Unwanted*. Not unwanted, she tried to argue. Just different.

He lifted his head and watched her, the creases at the corners of his blue eyes cutting deep with his frown. "My, but you are an innocent, aren't you."

Her mouth trembled with a smile. "Shall we return?"

Taking her arm like a perfect gentleman, he led her up the path. The closer they came to the house, the quicker her heart thundered against her chest, though she couldn't say exactly why. Everything would work out fine. William still wanted to marry her and his friends would come to accept her, flaws and all. The night had been a strain, but nothing had been ruined.

Yet, that was a lie, and she knew it, feeling her throat close with the desperate urge to cry. After tonight everything would change, because after tonight she would never see Jackson again.

Chapter Twelve

"Everyth'n's ready, Capt'n," Dillon said, ducking through the doorway of Jackson's cabin.

"Has Mac returned yet?" Standing at the bay of paned windows, Jackson watched the town of Medford sleep. He should be asleep as well. There would be no time to rest once they set sail to Newburyport. But he couldn't lie down, didn't dare close his eyes, because he knew what he'd see. Grace, as she'd been the last time he'd seen her, turning her back on him and leaving the room with the man she wanted. *William Mason!*

Furious, determined to learn what had the room abuzz with gossip, he'd approached Miss Foxsworth, but he hadn't had to pry any information from her—she'd been all too willing to share the sordid details. It seemed everyone now knew about Grace's coarse upbringing. Yes, Miss Foxsworth had been a busy woman, indeed.

No wonder Grace had looked so panicked, and had been so adamant that he leave. She'd known his presence would worsen the scandal. And it had. He'd felt like a leper walking among saints. And Grace must feel more like an outcast than ever.

Jackson ground out a curse, wishing he'd followed through with the impulse to wring the Englishwoman's scrawny neck when he'd had the chance.

" 'Aven't seen Mac yet," Dillon admitted. "If I be know'n' the bloke, though, he's either nose-deep in a cup o' ale or 'e got his 'and up some wench's skirt."

Brought back to the moment, Jackson muttered, "Let's hope neither is the case. Whether he's on board or not, we sail at dawn."

"Aye, Capt'n. We'll be ready." Dillon turned and left the room.

Two hours, maybe three, before they'd leave this god-forsaken port. He should never have brought Grace here. If he'd listened to his gut, she'd be locked in his cabin right now.

Jackson closed his eyes and tilted his head back on his shoulders, though it did little to ease the tension knotting his muscles. Berating himself was useless. If he had it to do over again, he'd still bring Grace to Mason and hand her over like some damned prize. Because this is where she wanted to be, with Mason, the man who would give her the world.

"Bloody hell!" he swore under his breath. "Stop brooding. You've got a bloody ship to see to."

Turning to his desk, he unrolled a sea chart, but had to study it three times before the coordinates sank in. Water lapped the *Sea Angel's* sides, the quiet, familiar sound echoing throughout the room. The air was heavy with smells of the sea, fishy brine and salty mist. Comforting smells, but even they faded as his thoughts turned back to the last kiss he and Grace had shared. She'd been so soft and sweet, everything a woman should be. His hands shaking, he clenched the chart in his fists.

Straightening, he ran his fingers through his hair. He had to stop thinking about her, or else the temptation to return to White Rose and see her again would overwhelm him. *Shut her from your mind. Mason is who she wants!*

A commotion in the companionway drew his attention. A quick knock on the door preceded Mac, who hurried in, his lean face flushed, his sleek black hair mussed and wild about his face.

"I trust you had a fair time with the ladies," Jackson barked, more forcefully than needed, but he was angry and Mac was the unlucky person who was going to bear the brunt of his temper. "You're my first mate. Why weren't you on deck while I was gone?"

Mac smoothed his hands over his hair, then grinned his cocky, mischievous grin. " 'Twas only for an ale or two, Capt'n. 'Tis early yet. We weren't expecting ye back so soon." He glanced around the cabin. "Where's little Grace? I thought ye were bring'n' her back with ye."

Jackson felt his skin heat and his stomach twist. "She's going to stay here."

Macklin nodded. "I see. I 'ope the lass is 'appy, then."

"Yes." Jackson faced the darkened windows, a silent dismissal.

Macklin ignored it. "There's someth'n' I brought from town that I think ye might be interested in."

"Later, Mac."

"Umm, this isn't someth'n' that will keep. Ye better take a look at it now."

"Damn it, Macklin, I'm going to throw you in the hold with the other—" Jackson spun around, stopping his verbal lashing as soon as he saw the woman standing at Mac's side. "Who the hell is she?"

"I'm not sure." Mac studied the woman from the top

of her coiled auburn hair to the sturdy leather boots protruding from beneath her gown.

"What do you mean, you're not sure?"

"She wouldn't tell me 'er name."

"Macklin," Jackson growled, "I'll warn you now, I don't have the patience for your games. Return the woman to wherever you found her."

"But, Capt'n, I brought 'er for ye."

"Sweet Jesus, Macklin! The last thing I want right now is another blasted woman! Get rid of her."

"You don't want to do that, Captain," the woman said in a throaty purr.

Jackson scowled at her, but she didn't cower, didn't flinch or hide behind his first mate. Dressed in a simple but finely made wool gown and matching black cape, she tilted her rounded chin and held his gaze, her expression inscrutable.

"I've no interest in whores," he told her.

Her cheeks filled with color, then her smoky eyes widened with outrage. "I'm no whore."

"Then who the hell are you?"

Her stubborn pose returned. "My name isn't important."

Jackson turned away, having had enough. "Take her away, Mac. Throw her into the river if she doesn't have the good sense to leave on her own."

His first mate, fool that he was, didn't move. "I think ye'll find 'er a keen lass." At Jackson's furious glare, he sighed and took the woman's arm. "I'm sorry, lassie, 'e must be hav'n' a bad day. 'E isn't usually so ornery."

"I'm not going anywhere." She jerked free of Mac's grip. "I told you I had to talk to your captain, and I'm going to."

Jackson's temper reached its peak. Ever since leaving Grace's ball, he'd wanted to smash his fist into Mason's face, but since he couldn't, he'd gladly shed his anger by helping an annoying woman off his ship. He rounded the desk, intent on throwing her over his shoulder, then over the topside railing.

She tensed, holding one hand out as if he were a devilish child needing discipline. "Five minutes, Captain, that's all I ask."

"That's more than I'm willing to give."

She took a hasty step in retreat, declaring, "They told me you'd be difficult, but I'd had no idea."

He stopped short. *"Who* told you that?"

She shook her head as if deciding against explaining her statement. "Five minutes, Captain. Please, it's important."

"If it's so important, then you'll tell me who the hell you are."

Compressing her lips into a disapproving line, she said, "Mira. My name is Mira, but that is all I can tell you about myself."

Folding his arms across his chest, he growled, "Five minutes. Start talking."

"Not here. I need you to come with me."

He arched a brow, not about to take one step off his ship. He didn't know who the hell she was, and he doubted Mira was even her real name. At dawn, he was sailing from Medford and leaving every lousy memory it held behind.

"Your time is running out."

"I have something to show you that I think you'll find very . . . interesting." The quiet edge to her voice raised the fine hairs at the nape of Jackson's neck. He didn't trust the woman, had no idea what she was up to. She could be setting a trap for all he knew.

"Whatever you have, show it to me now."

"I can't. You'll have to come with me."

"Out of the question. I'm sailing at dawn."

"But this is a place a man like you will enjoy."

Hearing the lure in her voice, he asked, "What is it you really want to do for me, Mira?"

She tilted her chin again, that inscrutable look returning. "The question you should be asking, Captain, is, what can *you* do for the rebellion."

With Macklin and Mira following behind him, Jackson led the way down the gangplank to the three waiting horses. He chose the big, black beast, his polished leather saddle shimmering in the torchlight that Dillon held aloft. Macklin had somehow acquired the animal. Stolen it, most likely, which gave Jackson yet another reason to return to his ship and leave town before sunlight broke the horizon.

I shouldn't be going on a fool trip, anyway, but if this involves the rebellion . . .

Securing his pistol into the back of his waistband, Jackson gained the saddle. The skittish horse tossed his head, rearing and snorting into the dark. Once his first mate and the woman were mounted, he said, "Two hours, Dillon. Be ready to sail."

"Aye, Capt'n. With or without ye. I know my orders."

Nodding, Jackson gave the horse a slight nudge, and they were off, hooves pounding the muddied earth.

The night was damp and wet, but his skin felt heated, his blood coursing hot. Two hours to see whatever Mira had to show him, then he'd return to sail the *Sea Angel* up the Mystic River. He'd delayed leaving port too long already, but someone had sent Mira to him, and he couldn't leave until he knew why.

The Mystic River swirled past the tiny peninsula in a silent, demanding current. The warehouse, a vast building of wood and stone, spread over the rocky ground and shot two stories into the inky black sky. Tufts of struggling grass, shell and rutted dirt made up the well-used road. The road was deserted now, asleep, as was everyone else in the settlement of Medford.

Or almost everyone.

Windows blacker than soot circled the building Mira indicated as their destination. There was no sign hanging over the front door, or any lettering to identify what kind of warehouse it was. Having left their horses tied to a fence post two lanes back, they'd walked the rest of the way on foot. Jackson eased his pistol from the back of his waist, watching the shadows that seemed to rise from the ground. He half expected someone to leap out and shoot him, or smash his fool head in. *If this is a trap, a head smashing is no more than I deserve for falling for it!*

With minimal light from the slivered moon, he couldn't see much of Mira beyond the dark hair that framed her large, mysterious eyes. He'd already discerned that she wasn't a barmaid or an orange girl or even a strumpet. Besides her well-made clothes, her horse was a finely bred mare. Then there was her accent, cultured, educated, as refined as her clothes.

Could this genteel lady be a spy for the rebels? It wasn't uncommon for women to pass messages or hide weapons. But he'd never heard of one who would willingly venture onto the docks in the dead of night. Having had enough of secrets, he asked that very question.

"Shh!" She hesitated long enough to glance over her shoulder. "You'll understand everything soon enough."

"Ye can trust 'er, Capt'n." Mac stepped up beside him. They paused, waiting as the woman peered around the side of the blacksmith's shed.

"Can I now?" Jackson asked, not hiding his sarcasm. "And how long have you known her?"

"Long enough."

"How long?"

"Well ..." Mac shifted, glancing sideways at Mira. "Truth is, I met 'er tonight. But I've got this feel'n'—"

"You always get a 'feeling' when it involves a woman." Jackson glared first at Macklin, then at Mira's shadowed form. "She could be a spy for the loyalists, you know."

"I don't think so, Capt'n. I was 'aving my dinner at the Lion's Paw, mind'n' my own business. She joins me, says she knows I'm a member of your crew and that she wants tae meet ye."

"Why?"

"She wouldn't say, just that it was urgent and—"

"Would you two like to see what's inside that building before or *after* you've woken the entire settlement?"

"What's in there, Mira?" Jackson demanded. He wasn't wasting any more time until he knew what she was about and which side she was on.

"Guns, Captain. Guns are being built in there."

"What's so unusual about that? We're in the middle of a damned rebellion."

"What's unusual is that the rebels have no idea these guns exist."

Mac whistled low. "British spies in the heart of rebel territory?"

She nodded.

"How do you know they're being built for the British?" Jackson asked.

She smiled, her white teeth pearling in the dark. "I have my sources."

He narrowed his gaze on her. "If you knew about this, why didn't you alert the local authorities?"

"We might be in rebel territory," she said easily, "but that doesn't mean you can trust just anyone with knowledge as dangerous as this. If I were to tell the wrong person, I might . . . disappear."

"The rebel camp isn't far from here. You could have gone to them."

"I'm careful about whom I choose to trust."

"And you chose me?" He quirked a brow, more suspicious of her then ever. "Why?"

She sighed with impatience. "I'm well connected in Medford. I hear things, but I'm not always inclined to tell what I know. But why I'm doing this, and why I chose you, isn't important. The guns are. Besides, I don't like having British cannons so close to my home. Now, if you want to see more, follow me. And for God's sake, keep quiet."

She'd held out the bait and he'd bitten it off, Jackson thought with a scowl, trailing her from one shadowed corner to the next. It could still be a trap, but he couldn't leave until he knew for sure.

Crouching low, they snaked up to the warehouse and passed the rear doors. Jackson gripped Mira's arm, stopping her. "Aren't we going in?"

"No," was all she said before pulling free and continuing until she reached a bank of windows.

Cool air brushed off the water in a steady breeze. Besides the building itself, there were no trees, no brush, no structures of any kind to block the wind or give them cover.

Sweat coated Jackson's arms and back as he crowded in beside Mira beneath a window centered in the large warehouse. He peered over the splintered windowsill. Faint light coming from somewhere to his left reached the ceiling of thick wooden beams. Dozens of fist-thick ropes hung from hooks in the ceiling, draping from one end of the room to the other, crisscrossing in a spider-web pattern. Attached to the ropes were large metal pulleys and hooks that were thicker than a man's arm.

Inching higher, he saw long strips of wood, all finely cut and sanded—strakes that would create the hull of a ship. The table directly below the window he gazed through was filled with copper rivets, tools for measuring and splicing, mallets and spikes. If he could see further down the room, he was certain he'd find more wood waiting to be softened and shaped, saws for cutting. But there were no signs of weapons being manufactured.

He pushed up from his crouched position, but Mira caught his arm. He told her, "I'm going to find a way in."

She shook her head, tightened her grip and pulled him down beside her. "Trust me, Captain. You don't want to do that."

He glanced at Mac, who shrugged and leaned against the wall, evidently content to do as the woman said.

She might think she could pick and choose what information she revealed, but he'd had enough of her coy games. "Mira," he warned, "unless you tell me—"

A thud sounded from inside the building, a door closing or perhaps something being dropped. He froze, listening. Footsteps echoed in the cavernous room, firing off like shots from a gun. He heard the muffled tone of someone speaking, and another person answering.

He peered into the room. A brazier on a far table had been lit, as well as several lamps. Yellowish light pushed into every corner, revealing more workbenches and tools, a pile of white sails. To the right he spotted a stack of unmarked crates. As many as thirty by his guess.

A black man, as solid as an oak mast and nearly as tall, his bare arms glistening with sweat, made his way around the piles of lumber and coiled rope. Hefting an iron crowbar, he wedged the lid of one crate open.

"No dallying, Ramous," a man Jackson couldn't see ordered. "I want to be done within the hour. You, George, go help him."

Another Negro, this man leaner and no more than twenty, joined the other slave. Together they worked the lid free and set it aside.

A white man stepped into view, his saddle-brown, calf-length overcoat swirling around plain wool stockings and dirt-caked shoes. His worn tricorne hat was pulled low over his dark hair, concealing part of his face.

With a short braided whip, he pointed to the larger of the slaves. "There's no time to check them all. One will do. Unpack it, Ramous, and be careful about it."

The two men went to work, lifting several black metal shapes the size of a man's palm. Setting them aside, they began digging through the crate once more.

"I can't tell what those are, Capt'n," Mac grumbled. "We're too bloody far away."

"Be patient," Mira said, then nodded. "Look."

The slaves retrieved several sheet-iron tubes and aligned them with the other items. Slowly, the puzzle began to piece itself together in Jackson's mind.

"Bloody son of a bitch," he swore, then he swore again. "Those are parts of a cannon. I recognize a vent piece, and those are timed fuses."

Then, as if to confirm his statement, they heaved out a long, dull-black tube, grunting loudly as they placed it on the ground.

"Sweet Jesus," Mac whispered. "Those crates are full of cannons."

"Howitzers, to be exact," Jackson clarified.

"The British 'ave smuggled in cannons unassembled?" Mac asked. "For what reason?"

"My guess is they're less likely to be discovered."

"What do you think their intention is, Captain?" Mira watched him, her expression speculative, as if she were waiting for him to take charge.

"I think King George is planning to stamp out the rebellion," he ground out under his breath, the muscles in his back knotting. It was too much of a concidence to believe smuggled guns would be in Medford just as British warships were bearing down on the Massachusetts coast. "This must be a key part in the British invasion. And if so I have to stop them."

"Capt'n," Mac hissed, "we already 'ave our 'ands full, if ye know what I mean."

"And now they're overflowing," Jackson said, feeling as if a grim shadow had fallen over him. "You're the one who brought Mira to me, Macklin, do you expect me to ignore this?"

"But . . ." Mac swiped a hand through his pitch-black hair. "Ah, bloody 'ell. What is it ye intend tae do?"

"Relieve that loyalist of his cannons," Jackson whispered with a cold smile. He still wasn't convinced the cannons belonged to the British, but if they did, then the rebels would benefit from his pirating skills. If by chance they already belonged to the rebels, well, Jackson hoped the general he turned the guns over to would understand. Either way, he was stealing those weapons.

"Look," Mac said in a hushed voice. "They're packing everything up."

Jackson watched the men from the corner of his eye, more concerned with how to get inside the building—quickly and without being seen—and retrieving thirty-odd crates of cannons. There wasn't enough time to accomplish the feat tonight. But tomorrow he could return with wagons and half his crew.

Stealing from a ship in the middle of an ocean was far different from pilfering heavy crates in the middle of a busy town. If it was as Mira suggested and there were few people to be trusted, he would be risking his men's lives, and his own, but what choice did he have?

"You'll never change, will you, Jackson?" He could hear Grace's voice, angry, tear-filled and trembling. *"You're as reckless as you ever were. Determined to put yourself in danger's path, dragging all of us down with you."*

She'd been more right than she'd known. He did look for danger, welcomed it. Now more than ever if it would help him forget her.

"We'll return to the *Sea Angel* and make plans to return tomorrow."

"Tomorrow may be too late," Mira said.

"Unless there's someone we can trust to storm this warehouse and confront the owner . . ."

Mira adamantly shook her head.

"Then we'll have to wait. Dawn is less than an hour away. I need wagons and men, which means we return tomorrow night."

Macklin scratched his black goatee. "Wagons won't be a problem—"

"They're leaving," Mira interrupted.

Jackson raised up and peered through the window. The slave named George was nailing the lid shut, while the one named Ramous was listening to the white man.

Ramous simultaneously nodded and bowed as he took a sealed envelope and tucked it inside his shirt. A muffled "Yes, suh," made its way through the window.

"Stop for nothing until you've delivered this to General Gage." The leader murmured something else Jackson couldn't make out.

"If I needed more proof that this man is a loyalist, he just gave it to me." Jackson tucked the pistol back into his waistband. "He's working with the British general who's holding Boston. They must have something planned. Something I don't think the rebels will like."

He exchanged a wary glance with Mac. "We'll have to stop the slave and take that letter he's carrying."

Mac winced. " 'E's a big one, Capt'n. 'E's not go'n' down easy."

"It doesn't matter—" Jackson stopped as the leader turned into the light, revealing his face for the first time.

He stared in disbelief. A furious buzz rushed through his mind—denial, shock, anger.

A growl rumbled from his chest.

Mac gripped his shoulder, shaking him. "Bloody 'ell, Capt'n, what is it?"

"I'm going to kill him."

"Kill the slave? What in God's name for?"

Rage shot through Jackson's body in a trembling rush His hands curled into fists, and his vision blurred, turning red and hot and dangerously violent.

"I've changed my mind," Jackson whispered, his voice cold.

"Well, thank the stars for that. There's no reason tae kill no slave."

Jackson didn't bother correcting his first mate. It wasn't the slave he wanted to tear apart limb by limb, but William Mason. A British loyalist. A damned turncoat! *Bloody hell, Grace . . .*

Why hadn't he made the connection before? Seen through the act? *Because Mason had incited Elliott Prescott's punishment, fooling everyone, me included, into believing he supported the rebels' cause.*

But Jackson knew the truth now, and the British spy wasn't going to get away with it.

"Burn it," Jackson growled.

"What?" Mac and Mira said in surprised unison.

"Do it. As soon as they leave. Make sure nothing but ash remains in the morning." Jackson rose. He had to reach his horse.

Mac caught his arm. "Where are ye go'n'?"

He glanced through the window, saw Mason hurrying toward the rear door, his brown overcoat whirling out behind him.

Something cold and savage worked through Jackson's veins, a potent sensation he hadn't felt since his parents' needless deaths—hatred for the Crown, for the aristocrats who ruined lives at a whim. He'd been too young to do anything about the injustice then. Too young and too stricken with grief.

But times had changed, and so had he. Feeling a deadly smile steal over his face, he whispered, "It's time to teach them a lesson."

Chapter Thirteen

Dawn was never going to arrive.

Grace glared at the mantel clock, a beautiful porcelain china case with sprays of flowers and turquoise shells. It probably cost more than a good horse, but she swore it didn't work. The three candles she'd lit flickered in the cool breeze that drifted through the veranda doors. The *Sea Queen* dagger rested beside the clock, its jeweled hilt glowing like heated gold. The knife was a curse, she decided, a plague that would haunt her for the rest of her life.

She should have thrown it into the ocean when Jo had given it to her all those years ago, then set a torch to the *Sea Queen*, sinking the ship for good. If she had, she wouldn't be in this horrid mess right now. Jackson wouldn't have returned to pirating, wouldn't have raided the *Maiden Fair*.

Wouldn't have saved us from drowning after the storm. She sighed in disgust.

All she wanted was for the sun to rise, glimmer over the beautiful gardens, wake the birds and start the new day. Because the new one had to be better than the horrible one that had just passed.

Glancing at the clock once more, certain the hands hadn't moved in ages, she decided time must have stopped, come to a grinding halt. It had been hours since the last guest had left White Rose. Hours that she'd spent pacing the length of her elegant bedchamber, going over every conversation she'd overheard, feeling once again every wary look that had pierced her back after she'd returned from her talk with William.

She'd been tempted to leave the festivities right then and retire to her room, but the urge to flee had only heightened her anxiety even more. She might not be the fighter her sisters were, but she refused to behave like a coward. So she'd remained by William's side, held onto his tense arm and listened to him discuss the weather, the poor selection of slaves being offered at market, the outrageous price of tobacco, knowing that everyone's thoughts were really on her.

Reminding her that she was still an outcast. *And will always be.*

Clenching her hands, she spun around to stalk across the carpeted floor once more. William had assured her that everyone would *forgive* her unfortunate upbringing. But she knew better. She'd lived with her notorious past for too long to know it couldn't be tucked away and forgotten like a dirtied gown.

The way she saw it, she had two choices; she could pack her trunks and leave, or stay and endure the disdain that was sure to come. Honestly, she didn't know which choice would be the hardest—admitting defeat or being ostracized . . . *again.*

Wandering onto the veranda, she rubbed her lower back

and winced. Her body hurt, her muscles sore and stiff from tension. Her eyes burned, too, partly from lack of sleep, and partly from the need to cry. But she refused to give in to tears, even if she did feel isolated and alone.

Even Jackson had abandoned her, she thought, her distress twisting with a familiar ache. When she'd returned to the ballroom, he'd been nowhere in sight. Later, she'd overheard two gentlemen discussing the pirate who had stormed from the house.

"Without saying good-bye," she whispered. Evidently, Jackson was angry with her, too.

"Well, fine." She crossed her arms beneath her breast. She didn't care that he'd left. In fact, she was glad he was gone. With him out of the way, the gossip would fade. Everyone would forget about her. They had a war to worry over. What was her paltry history compared to blood and death!

Grumbling to herself, Grace resumed her pacing across the veranda, the wooden floor cold beneath her feet. Goose bumps prickled up her legs and over her arms. She pulled her thin cotton robe around her, welcoming the crisp wind. Maybe it would help clear her mind, let her grasp a solution.

Turning to make another trip, she paused when she heard a thump, then the shatter of glass from somewhere below. Her heartbeat quickening, she rushed to the railing and scanned the yard. Wind stirred the bushes and trees, lengthening the shadows. White roses gleamed like fallen stars in the dark. She saw nothing else, no intruder slithering along the wall trying to sneak in. Perhaps a tree limb had fallen against a window or . . . or . . . what? She couldn't think of another reason for glass to break—in the middle of the night. It had to be a thief! She had to warn someone.

She ran to William's room, pausing only briefly before entering his bedchamber. Now wasn't the time for proper decorum. Dying embers in the hearth guided her to the huge high-post tester bed, where she stopped short. The bedcovers were rumpled, pushed back to the foot of the thick mattress, but the bed was empty! William must have heard the noise and gone to investigate. She stood still for a moment, indecision tearing at her. She could return to her room and wait to learn what had happened, or she could try to help him. Her skin tingled hot with adrenaline. Her palms turned sweaty, and her heart fluttered a wild beat against her chest. Her sisters wouldn't hide; how could she even think to?

Rushing into the hallway, she headed for the stairs, detouring long enough to snatch the *Sea Queen* blade from the mantel in her room. The hilt was cold in her palm, heavy and awkward. She didn't plan to use it, knew she'd probably injure herself if she tried, but if she found William, he might need it.

The hallway was dark, her feet making only a whisper of sound as she sped through the corridor. She took the stairs down, listening for any noise. Everything was silent, still, interrupted only by her own ragged breathing.

Reaching the foyer, she hugged up against a wall. When she'd heard the crash, she thought it had come from a small sitting room near the gardens. Deciding to start her search there, she eased down the long hallway, her eyes wide in the dark, her pulse pounding in her throat.

Please, Lord, if there is a thief in the house, let me find William first.

She hesitated near the doorway to the salon, her mind dizzy with fear. She clenched the knife in her sweaty hand, wanting to curse her own foolishness. What had she been thinking, leaving her room to search for a thief? Was she insane? If she found the man, what did she plan to do? Apprehend him? Intimidate him? Threaten him with her blade? Whatever she tried, she'd most likely end up dead.

But turning back now would be cowardly. She'd reached the salon unscathed; she may as well inspect it. *Then* she could rush back to the safety of her room. Faint moonlight washed through the open window, glinting like dull silver off the tip of her knife. Scanning the dark corners and unoccupied furniture, she thought everything was as it should be. Neat and tidy, richly decorated. Two heavy silver candlesticks sat upon the mantel beside the gold-leaf looking glass. A mahogany whatnot stood in the corner, its shelves filled with porcelain bric-a-brac and a collection of china plates. Valuables any thief would love to filch.

Grace crept across the room, frighteningly aware that she stood in the open, wearing only her flimsy robe and gown, and gripping a useless dagger for protection. She should have paid more attention when Jo had practiced sparring on the deck of the *Sea Queen*. Was it parry then strike, or strike then parry?

Oh, God, what am I doing here?

At the window, she stared at the shattered glass glittering like fallen tears over the wooden floor. To her dread there wasn't a tree limb in sight.

Which meant someone was inside the house—with her!

An icy chill ran down her spine. She had to get out of there, now! But her feet refused to budge. Without turning her head, she looked to either side of her. Nothing stirred. She took a step backward. When nothing happened, she turned and headed for the doorway, one slow step at a time, afraid to move too fast, afraid she'd draw the thief's attention. She thought about calling out for William; he would surely hear her, come running, but her lips refused to obey her mind, and even if they did, no sound could possibly work past the thick knot of fear in her throat.

She'd made it to the hallway, now the stairs. If she ran, she could be in her room in less than a minute. A prickle of awareness skimmed her neck and slithered down her spine. She knew she was being watched. *Oh, God!* She could feel his eyes following her, waiting, planning.

She almost moaned out loud. *Go!* a voice screamed inside her mind. *Go! Run! Now!*

She bolted down the darkened hallway, her feet muffled thuds against the carpets, her heart a frightened roar in her ears. She glanced behind her, thought she saw a shadow move. William? But wouldn't he call out? Even if he thought her the intruder? No, it had to be the thief!

Willing her feet to go faster, she turned down a second hallway. The foyer loomed ahead, a dark expanse of rich paneling and marbled floors. The stairway, she had to reach it. He wouldn't dare follow her upstairs, where he might become trapped.

Gripping the balustrade in her free hand, she took the stairs two at a time. Her bare foot caught in her gown, tripping her. She banged down hard on her knees, crying out. She pushed up, started climbing again, only to be jerked backward. A large hand clamped around her waist, another pressed over her mouth as she was lifted into the air.

She registered the length of a hard body at her back, far larger and stronger than her own. Larger even than William's. Her fiancé hadn't mistaken her for the intruder. Which meant . . .

Flailing her legs, she twisted, tried to bite the hand crushing her lips against her teeth. Her attacker adjusted his fingers, covering her nose as well, cutting off her breath. It took only seconds for her to start fighting to breathe instead of fighting to escape.

The man whispered close to her ear, "Will you behave?"

Eyes wide, her heart pounding in her throat, she nodded. He eased his grip on her face. Grace drew in a deep breath that smelled of leather and sweat.

"Do as I say and everything will be fine." His voice, tight with anger, silently conveyed that he meant what he said.

She nodded again, willing to agree to almost anything if only he'd let her go.

The man eased her down until her feet touched the floor. Grace could have wept in relief. Maybe he was an honorable thief; maybe he'd keep his word and release her.

A bang echoed through the house, coming from the kitchens, she thought. William? She could only hope. Or perhaps one of the servants? Now was her time to act. Remembering the knife in her hand, she swung it up and back, loathing the thought of stabbing someone, but she had to escape.

"Bloody hell!" he swore, gripping her wrist in a crushing hold, then ripping the knife from her hand.

She gaped at the shadowed man. She knew that voice. "Jackson?"

He didn't answer. Instead, he jerked her off the floor and whipped her around so fast she lost her breath. He darted down the hallway, entering the first room he came to—the dining hall—releasing her long enough to shut the door softly behind him.

"What . . . what are you doing here?" She pressed her hand to her forehead and took a steadying breath. "You frightened me half to death! How could you?"

"If you'd been abed where you belong, instead of wandering about half dressed . . ." She could feel his hot gaze rake down the front of her, the effect as potent as a touch of his hand. ". . . our reunion wouldn't have been quite so . . . unpleasant."

"You may be a pirate, Jackson," she whispered, the words sharp and bitter, "but even this is beneath you. How could you steal from William?"

"It's quite easy, actually. He has what I want." She

couldn't see his face clearly, but the ruthless edge of his voice was unlike anything she'd ever heard. Still gripping her wrist, he pulled her against him, his head cocked as he listened through the door.

"This is insane. You have to leave before you're discovered."

"I plan on it, Angel."

Her thoughts a crazed jumble, she stared at him, trying to understand the man Jackson had become. Was this some sort of punishment? Revenge? Or was stealing so much a part of him, it didn't matter who he stole from? "Jackson, why are you here?"

"I'm taking back what's mine."

"What are you talking about?" she demanded.

"You."

"What? I don't belong to you!"

"Perhaps not, but you're not going to belong to Mason either."

"That's not for you to decide, Jack—"

He clamped his hand over her mouth, effectively shutting her up. In the faint light, his eyes glared a warning for her to behave. She pushed against his chest, twisted, even tried to kick him, but he crushed her to him, ending her struggles. His arm wrapped tight around her waist, molding her breast to his chest, her smaller thighs to the hard length of his. Heat rolled off him, singeing the air, her skin, filling her mind with his masculine scent. He had her well and trapped, with his strength, and with his presence. Fighting was useless.

As soon as she stilled she heard the sound of footsteps coming closer. William? She squeezed her eyes shut, praying whoever it was wouldn't find her. Her fiancé might have forgiven her for the events at the ball, but he'd likely not forgive her, or even bother listening to her explanations, should he discover her in a darkened room, with Jackson.

Weary to the bone, she dropped her forehead against Jackson's chest. She felt the strong beat of his heart, raging as fast as her own. His body felt taut, on the verge of breaking loose, like a wild animal determined to escape its cage. She sensed the anger in him, a bottomless well of fury.

"*I'm taking back what's mine,*" he'd said. *Her?* Did he really want her? Or did he just want to take her away from William?

As soon as the footsteps passed them by, Jackson eased the door open, then shut it again with barely a whisper of sound. "Seems your fiancé has decided to come home at last."

She glanced at the door. "What are you talking about? William has been here all night."

"Afraid not, Angel."

Grace tried to ask what he'd meant by *that,* but he didn't give her the chance.

"We're leaving now," he told her.

"We? *We* aren't going anywhere." She wrenched around, tried to pull free. His arm tightened, securing her as easily as a thick iron chain. "Let me go, Jackson!"

"Make one more sound, Angel, do anything to attract notice, and I'll tell William you invited me to your bed."

"You wouldn't!" She froze, gaping at him in disbelief.

"Would you care to test me?"

She snapped her jaw shut. If she willingly left with Jackson her future at White Rose was doomed, yet if she called for help, she had no doubt that he'd follow through with his threat and spin any lie necessary to ruin her. William would be forced to end their engagement.

Either way, she lost.

At that moment, she hated Jackson, hated him with all

her heart. Angry tears burned her eyes. Her breath grated hot against her lungs. Arguments filled her head, but they were useless. Nothing she said would change his mind. A frayed, weary part of her didn't even want to try. She was tired of fighting, tired of trying to be the perfect lady who yearned to be accepted, only to fail time and time again.

Within moments, Jackson had her out of the house and through the gardens, carrying her when she fell, the pebbled ground scraping her bare feet. As they reached the towering white-bricked wall, the first pink of dawn was brightening the sky. He helped her up onto the wall and ordered her to jump to the other side.

She glanced down and gasped at the distance. "Are you out of your mind! I'll break my leg."

"No, you won't," he growled, clearly irritated. "Just close your eyes and go."

She stared at the ground, far below, realizing he was right, she wouldn't break her leg, she'd break her neck.

"Go, Grace!"

Drawing a deep breath, she started to jump, but hesitated when she spotted a black horse tied to a tree a few yards away. An idea occurred to her. If she jumped and was quick to get up and run, she could reach the horse and escape. She smiled, feeling a powerful thrill rush through her. Perhaps she was more like her sisters than she'd thought.

Her decision made, she held her breath and pushed off the wall. She landed with a bone-jarring grunt, falling onto her side and planting her face in dirt and leaves. Hearing Jackson struggle up the wall on the other side, she half crawled, half ran to the horse. Jerking the reins free of the tree branch, she tried to put her foot in the stirrup, but the animal flinched away, snorting and tossing his head, flicking her in the face with his long black tail.

"Hold still," she pleaded. But the animal circled around

her again and again. Knowing she had only seconds, she leaped up, grabbed the saddle and held on. She reached out with her foot . . . and found the stirrup!

Heaving herself up, she threw her other leg over the horse's back and gathered the reins. She had to reach the front gate. The guard would let her in. Somehow she'd explain everything to William. She straightened, ready to kick the horse into a mad run. A hand clamped tight around her leg. She gasped, her heart stopping mid beat as she stared into dark brown eyes that burned with rage.

"Leaving without me, Angel?"

Fury raged like fire through Jackson's veins, but he thought his emotions might seem trivial compared to Grace's. As he pushed the black gelding through the break-ing dawn, she sat before him, her nails digging into his wrists like the claws of an angry cat. She hadn't spoken another word since they'd fled from White Rose. He'd expected her to demand an explanation, then flay him with another argument when he told her why he'd stolen her from Mason. But she just looked ahead, her back straight, her jaw clamped as tight as an oyster shell.

Her thin cotton night rail and robe, damp with morning dew, was molded to her arms, the full curve of her breasts, the nipples showing through dark and pebble-hard. The sight of her looking so feminine, so completely at his mercy, tightened his gut. He'd offered her his coat, but she'd glared at him in silent refusal.

He supposed she had every right to be upset and con-fused, even irate. After all, he'd just ripped her imaginary world to shreds. He'd do so again without a moment's doubt. She didn't know what kind of man she'd decided to marry. But before the day was out, she would.

Not until they passed through the town square that was

just now coming to life, did Grace turn to him—to plant her face in his chest.

"How could you do this to me?" she demanded.

He understood her anxiety. "No one will recognize you."

"Heaven help me, Jackson, I could shoot you for this. I'm in my nightclothes!"

He glanced at the fishermen heading for the wharf, merchants slowly making their way to their shops and open-air stalls, their gazes following Jackson's passing. He spurred the horse faster. Lather coated the animal's neck and flanks, but he couldn't slow, and not because he worried for Grace's reputation. He still might reach the *Sea Angel* before she sailed. He had to try, at the very least, because getting Grace to safety was all that mattered.

Reaching the docks, Jackson slowed his mount and cursed long and loud. Grace gave him a scathing look and pressed her lips together in disapproval, but she didn't reprimand him as he expected. He wouldn't have heard her if she had. Vexation buffeted him from all sides.

The *Sea Angel* was gone!

Bloody hell and damnation!

His crew had done as ordered, sailing with the new tide. He scanned the horizon, but found no trace of the three-mast ship. She was well on her way to Newburyport. In two days time, Macklin would deliver the missive Jackson had decoded, as well as the loyalist prisoners, to a trusted ally.

Touching his sore ribs, Jackson felt for the new letter he'd tucked inside his coat. Catching up with the slave, Ramous, had been easy; taking the message William Mason had given him to deliver to General Gage, had not. Wrestling the towering, muscled slave, taking more blows than he gave, Jackson had feared his days were at an end, but a well-placed punch to the giant man's nose had made Ramous see reason.

Jackson glanced around the now-bustling docks. A thick cloud of smoke hung in the air. Nearby he heard a faint conversation about a fire raging out of control near the shipyard. He smiled, certain Mac and Mira had done their work. Jackson wished he had time to see the glowing remains of the warehouse, the cannons' charred cases, but the warehouse was too far away to risk seeing it for himself.

He had to leave town, now, before Mason learned that both his fiancée and his letter had gone astray. There were several ships along the pier being loaded with crates and barrels of supplies. He could buy passage on any of them, but when would they leave, and who were they loyal to?

They were questions Jackson couldn't afford to find out the answers to.

"Unless you intend for us to swim to Newburyport, I suggest you return me to White Rose."

Jackson stared down at Grace, relieved that she'd finally spoken to him and angry that the first words out of her mouth were to be returned to her blasted fiancé.

"You're staying with me," he told her.

"Even if I don't want to?"

A pair of sailors sauntered past, eyeing Grace and smiling broadly. "That's the way I'd keep my woman," one man said to the other. "In her nightclothes so's she'll be ready any time 'o the night!"

Grace's body tensed as stiff as a board. Jackson scowled a warning at the men until they turned and hurried off. Shrugging out of his coat, he placed it around her shoulders. This time she accepted it without complaint, then tried futilely to cover her bare feet with the ends of her gown.

He spun the gelding around and started back through town. Grace gripped his arm, shaking it urgently.

"Where are you taking me?" she demanded.

"We'll have to ride north to Newburyport. It's not too far—"

"No!" She twisted in the saddle to look at him, her face pale with horror.

"Damn it, Grace. Against my better judgment, I've done everything you've asked of me. But no more."

"You've—you've—" Her cheeks flushed with outrage. "I had to fight you every step of the way to reach Medford, regardless that you have no right to have a say in how I choose to live my life."

"The hell I don't."

"Don't curse at me, Jackson. Now take me to White Rose."

"We're going to Newburyport."

"I can't!"

Aware of the curious eyes and ears around them, he spurred the gelding into a trot, forcing Grace to hold onto him, and effectively shutting her up. Or so he thought.

"I don't know what has gotten into you, Jackson. But I can't travel to Newburyport like this. I can't."

"Why not?" he asked, only half listening to her. Three men emerging from the Custom's House paused to stare at them. Perhaps they were only surprised to see a man and a half-dressed woman on horseback trotting through town, or perhaps they recognized Grace as Mason's fiancée. Either way, he had to get them out of sight.

"I'm in my nightclothes, for heaven's sake." She glanced over her shoulder, giving him an imploring look. "Please, don't do this to me. Take me to White Rose."

"No."

"Why?" Her eyes welled with tears. God help him if she let them fall. He'd never been able to withstand her tears. But she sniffed them back.

"I'll explain everything later, but right now we have to get out of here."

Before she could respond, he put his heels to the horse's sides and sent them racing down roads and through alleyways, then finally onto a road heading north. He kept up the grueling pace, determined to put as much distance between them and Medford as possible, knowing he'd have to veer off as soon as travelers were out. The fewer people who saw them, the better.

He had no doubt that once Mason learned who had stolen his bride-to-be, he would come looking for him.

Jackson was counting on it.

Chapter Fourteen

The settlement had no name. Too small to be considered a town and barely large enough to be termed a village, the shabby cottages of wattle, with thatched roofs and broken fences, lined a single road. Pigs rooted through the mud for scraps of food and chickens scratched alongside them, roaming free, seeming to expect the right of way to horses and people. The place had an unstable, temporary feel to it, as if the villagers might pick up and leave at a moment's notice.

Situated among the squalid homes was a tavern with the unlikely name of The Snowflake Inn, a tap house that had two rooms abovestairs for passing travelers. Grace occupied one of those rooms now. Though cold and musty, the floor was swept free of dust. A small rickety table and two hard benches filled one corner. The bed was a surprise, however. Large enough to accommodate two, its interlacing ropes supported a straw mattress and clean sheets. She ran her hand over the faded quilt, thinking it looked like pale wildflowers had sprung up right inside the room.

She lay back, burrowing her head into the soft feather pillow. Her muscles cried in protest and her stinging eyes begged for her to sleep. But how could she? She'd been abducted . . . by Jackson of all people!

She expected him to return at any moment with plates of food, ale and an explanation for his atrocious behavior. But nothing he said would convince her to forgive him. Nothing!

She'd insisted she be given her own room, but he'd ignored her, renting only one. They weren't staying long, he'd said, only long enough to rest the horse and eat a meal. Evidently he intended for her to sleep in the saddle.

Just as her anger started to rebuild, the door swung open, banging against the opposite wall. Jackson entered, swallowing up what little space there was and filling the room with vibrant energy. His sun-streaked hair was pulled back from his face and tied with a leather strap, making his eyes sharper, so dark a brown they seemed black, glassy in the gathering dusk. His gaze swept over her, skimming the length of her body, pausing a breath too long at her breasts. Tingles ignited beneath her skin.

Where she'd been tempted to drift off a moment ago, now she was wide awake, her heart pumping against her chest. She scooted off the bed and sat on one of the benches, diverting her gaze as she lit an oil lamp.

Without a word, he set the tray he carried before her. She stared at the pile of food, and her stomach gave an unladylike rumble. There was a wedge of creamy yellow cheese, a roasted hen, still steaming from the oven, sliced cabbage, a loaf of freshly baked bread, two tankards brimming with ale and a lime.

Frowning, she picked up the green fruit and asked, "What is this for?"

"That's mine." He took it from her hand and claimed the opposite seat. Pushing the tray of food toward her, he said, "Go ahead. Eat."

She thought about refusing, but discarded the idea. If she planned to escape she'd need her strength. And she did plan to escape. Though returning to White Rose and William wasn't something she wanted to face. William had to know she was missing by now. Was he worried? Was he searching for her? Or was he glad she was gone? She could imagine Sheila concocting some story that would only deepen his anger. And considering his reaction to Sheila's betrayal the night before, he would probably believe anything the woman said. She had to reach William, before Sheila poisoned him against her.

Why bother? a weary voice asked from the back of her mind. She told the doubting voice to be quiet, but her conscience refused. *If he has so little faith in me, how can I make a life with him? And if I tried, what kind of life would it be?*

She pushed a hand through her hair, annoyed with herself. She couldn't think this way or else she'd lose sight of her dream. Marrying William would be wonderful, for both of them; she just needed the chance to prove how well suited they were. She looked at Jackson, noticed the way his brow was furrowed as he concentrated, the carved lines of his jaw and cheeks like rough marble, strong and enduring. And so different from William. Where Jackson was light and bold and adventuresome, William was dark, stable, a man of business.

But is William the man I want?

"Oh, shut up," she snapped out loud, not meaning to.

"I didn't say anything," Jackson said, arching a blond brow.

Mad at herself, at Jackson, at the entire world, she snatched up the bread, ripped it in half and took a bite, her mind furiously at work. First, she had to find some clothes; she couldn't travel through the countryside alone, wearing only her night rail and robe. Then she'd find her way back to William; she had no choice. She had to face him, see if there was some way they could salvage her reputation and put her past behind her.

Or she could do as Jackson insisted and return home to England.

She closed her eyes, sighing deeply. No, she couldn't give up hope. Everything she'd ever dreamed of lay in William and White Rose: the home, the devoted husband, the children she could love and protect and watch grow. She couldn't just walk away from all of that without trying. Because if she did, she'd have nothing. No home, no future. *No Jackson.*

With only one course to follow, she straightened her shoulders, ready to demand Jackson justify his behavior, but the words stuck in her throat.

"What are you doing?" she asked instead.

Drawing her *Sea Queen* blade from the waist of his pants, he sliced the lime in half. Holding one portion in his large hand, he squeezed the fruit so juice dripped onto the blank sheet of paper he'd placed in front of him.

"Watch." His gaze flickered up to her, and his mouth lifted with a wolfish grin. "I think you'll find this interesting."

"You consider wasting a perfectly good piece of paper and costly food interesting? I believe you've spent too much time at sea, Jackson."

"Have I now?" With his grin turning cynical, he moved the tray of food aside and slid the paper in front of her. "Watch."

He continued squeezing the fruit, moving his hand so the drops wet the entire page. Foolishness, utter foolishness and she'd had enough. Her night rail and robe weren't elaborate, but perhaps the inn's proprietress would take them in trade. She pushed to her feet and opened her mouth to inform Jackson she was leaving. Once again, words died in her throat.

Before her eyes, black lettering appeared like magic on the blank page. "How did you do that?"

"It's a military trick, used to pass secret messages." He watched her, his brow furrowing with a somber frown.

Confused, she shook her head. "You have another of Captain Peters's letters?"

"This one isn't from the *Maiden Fair*'s captain."

For some reason, perhaps it was the grimness she heard in Jackson's voice, the fine hairs at the nape of her neck raised in warning. "Then to whom did it belong?"

"I think you know."

"Don't play games with me, Jackson. I'm tired and furious enough as it is. If you have something to tell me, then do so!" She pressed a hand to her forehead, hating her shrewish tone, but heaven help her, she felt out of control, helpless, as if her life had been caught up in a cyclone.

"I took it from a slave who is owned by your esteemed fiancé."

She crossed her arms beneath her breasts. "If you're implying that William has something to do with the rebellion, I already know that. We saw him in the midst of it when we arrived."

"Aye," Jackson mused. "Tar and feathering a British loyalist made a good cover for your viscount."

"You're talking in riddles." Exasperated, she glared at him. "Say what you mean, because I intend to leave here, regardless of whether you approve."

He stood up so abruptly the bench toppled over and skidded across the floor, banging against the wall. "You aren't going anywhere near Mason again, Angel, so don't even try."

"You can't stop me!"

"The hell I can't."

She drew in a breath, tempted to stomp her foot in a fit of temper. Had she been eight years old again, she might have. Instead, she forced her emotions under control. One of them had to act logically. But when Jackson was involved, it seemed that duty always fell to her.

"You know I want to marry William," she said calmly.

A muscle clenched in his jaw, and his eyes darkened, warning her that he didn't care to hear anymore.

Before he could interrupt, she said, "You also know that I've always wanted to live in a place where I could build a life, have children."

"Aye, someplace safe." The anger drained out of him. She wished it hadn't, because now he watched her as if she were something precious, something he valued, something he longed for but couldn't have.

"Yes, someplace safe, some wonderful place I could make my own." *Something that you refuse to give me.*

"I know, Angel."

"So now that I finally have the chance to have all of that, why are you so determined to take it away from me?"

"It's an illusion. What you're looking for isn't here." He picked up the wet paper, shaking it. "At least not with Mason."

"You may be right, but I have to go back and try." She sighed, dropping her gaze to the table, part of her wishing she weren't so stubborn. "Though after last night, it may be a waste. William may not forgive me."

Jackson drew in a furious breath. Slapping the letter on the table, he clenched his hands and paced in a tight circle before rounding on her. "You've done nothing that needs forgiving. Read this letter and you'll understand why."

"I don't want to read it."

"Damn it—"

"Don't curse at me."

"It's either curse or smash my fist through a wall," he ground out. "Mason is dirt beneath your feet, yet you want his acceptance. I don't understand why, Angel, I've tried, but I don't understand. You're perfect the way you are, with your common blood and pirating past."

"Thank you for the compliment, but coming from a fellow pirate—"

"It means nothing?" he asked softly, his gaze narrowing on her.

She swallowed. How had they come to this? Fighting like enemies? "That's not what I was going to say."

"Then pray continue." He swept out his hand, mocking her with a half-bow as if he were an English lord and they were standing in a grand salon.

"You know about my past, Jackson," she said, holding on to the emotions boiling up inside her. "How I lost my parents, why Morgan, Jo and I were forced into pirating."

Retrieving his bench and resuming his seat, he regarded her for a moment, then nodded for her to continue.

Turning away, she ran her hands through her tangled hair, and tried to put her thoughts in some sort of rational order. Somehow she had to make him understand why marrying William was so important to her—and in doing so, maybe convince herself that marrying a man she didn't love was the right thing to do.

"You know we resorted to pirating so we could save our home," she began. "The trouble is, we lost it anyway. None of us could have known that once we set foot aboard the *Sea Queen* our lives would be irrevocably changed. But they were."

She paced to the small window and looked out over a garden choked with weeds. Dusk was fast approaching, the lengthening shadows hiding the worst of the refuse and sorely built homes. "After Morgan married Daniel, we didn't return to our cottage in Dunmore, though Jo and I had wanted to. We went to London instead, and lived with Daniel.''

"You can't convince me that you suffered under Daniel's care," he scoffed.

"Of course not." She closed her eyes, remembering how awed she'd been by her first glimpse of Westminster, the Tower of London and Buckingham Palace. As incredible as the city was, it had also been frightening. She'd witnessed poverty unlike anything she'd ever known, thousands of people crowded into squalid homes that were dark and filthy, covered with layers of soot. The poor labored every day of their lives, their faces grim with the knowledge that nothing would ever change—that they'd been born into a hand-to-mouth existence, and that they'd die the same way.

"At first, living in the city had been exciting, incredibly wonderful. If I wanted something, all I had to do was ask, and my wish was granted. Perhaps it was too much too soon, or perhaps I felt as if we hadn't earned the right to live in such luxury. I don't know," she said, frowning into the dark. "I only know the abundance of wealth frightened me.''

"It was a lot for a child to take in. I was there, I understand."

She nodded, remembering that he had been with her and her sisters in the beginning, but he hadn't stayed. Jackson had hated the city, the noise and crowds. He'd left to live in their family cottage with her Uncle Simon in Dunmore.

"I'd never liked living aboard the *Sea Queen*—"

"Tell me something I don't already know," he muttered under his breath.

"But until I reached London, I'd never realized how truly fragile life could be. If we hadn't turned to pirating, we could have ended up living in a shanty along the harbor, begging in the streets for a copper.''

"But that didn't happen," Jackson said.

"No, it didn't. And with Daniel to take care of us, I knew we would always have a roof over our heads, food to eat. But then I learned the bitter lesson that only those born with blue blood were allowed to join the ranks of aristocrats. No matter what I did, I would never be one of them."

"I'd count that as a blessing." He leaned back against the wall, his gaze intense as he folded his arms across his wide chest.

"But I wanted to belong, Jackson," she told him. "I began to feel safe, and I wanted that feeling to last forever. I wanted a home like Morgan's, a husband like hers."

"There's no reason you couldn't continue to live with them."

"As a dependent sister-in-law? I wanted my own home."

"Then you could have returned to Dunmore."

"Could I?" She looked at him thoughtfully, then shook her head. "I don't think so. I no more belonged in my small village than I did among the nobility of England. Which is why I went to Wilmouth School for Girls, to learn to become a real lady. But everyone in London knew about my past, and they seemed determined to make sure I never forgot where I came from. Despite my connection to Daniel, no respectable lord wanted to marry a pirate, which is why I chose William."

"So you could start over in the Colonies?"

"Exactly." Speaking her fears out loud for the first time, she felt a strange weight lift from her chest. "So now you understand why I must go back to him."

Watching her with a hooded expression, he toyed with the edge of the secret message on the table. "I understand nothing of the kind."

Her mouth dropped open, but she was too incensed to

say a word. Snapping her jaw shut, she ground her teeth and propped her hands on her hips. Crossing to him, she glared down at his upturned, arrogant face, barely resisting the urge to slap it. So help her, she'd never been so angry in her life. She'd poured her soul out to him, explained why she had to marry William, yet he was too thick-skulled to grasp her dilemma.

"Then understand this, Jackson Brodie," she said, coming so close to him, she could feel the sudden tension leap from his skin, like tiny sparks singeing the air. "I'm not going anywhere with you. With or without your help, I'm returning to White Rose."

"And how do you intend to do that?" he asked, raising a blond brow.

She gripped the bodice of her night rail. "I'll sell this if I must. Trade it for a mule and a wool dress."

He looked to where her hand fisted in the soft fabric of her gown. His pupils darkened, thinning to pinpoints of black. The brown of his eyes flashed with gold, a sure sign his temper was aflame. She saw further evidence in the flare of his nostrils, the sudden flush of his tanned cheeks. She'd pushed him too far, but she didn't care. She might love him, wish *he* could give her the security she needed, but he couldn't. She'd known that all along, which was why she'd created a new dream, and, by God, she was going to see that her dream was fulfilled!

They glared at each other, their angry breaths grating the silence.

Finally, in a chest-rumbling growl, he warned her, "If I have to truss you up and bind your mouth, I'll do it, because you're coming with me."

"Oh, no I'm not."

"Grace—"

"You won't change my mind by scaring me, Jackson."

"Fine, then I'll try something else." He gripped her

waist and jerked her to him. Gasping, she stumbled and fell against him, half against his chest, half on his lap.

Twisting his hand in her hair, he brought her head down to his and kissed her mouth. Shock numbed her senses. Heat exploded from every spot they touched, their joined lips, their chests, their legs. His hand skimmed down the side of her face, to her neck, over the curve of her unbound breasts. His palm cupped her fullness, his fingers squeezing tight. Spikes of pleasure tightened her nipple, the sensation so intense, she arched her head back and sucked in a breath.

Her mind in a swirl, her mouth full of his taste, she pleaded, "Jackson, no . . . we can't."

He didn't answer or stop, but kissed her throat, the pulsing vein along her neck. His mouth was hot, his teeth smooth and hard as he nipped her skin. A warm, tingling shudder spread over her limbs.

"You—you can't convince me to stay with you this way."

He raised his head, meeting her gaze. His eyes were dark and sensual, the look in them possessive. "Oh, I think I can."

Then he took her mouth again, claiming her, branding her with the invasion of his tongue. He became the wild animal she'd likened him to, kissing and taking, plundering her to the depths of her soul.

His hands were everywhere, exploring her stomach, the length of her back, the curve of her bottom. Each touch was more intimate than the last, more forceful, masterful. He knew where to touch her and how, knew what would draw the gasps from deep in her throat. He skimmed his palm down her thigh, his fingers tickling the backs of her knees before seeking her calf.

She had to stop him; they were going too far. She'd wanted this from Jackson all her life, but she knew it was wrong, knew they weren't meant for each other. But, God, to feel the heat of his lips against her skin, to have his scent explode inside her mind—it was heaven and hell, all rolled into one. She had to fight him, fight her own feelings for him. She couldn't let him further inside her heart, knowing he'd break it for sure this time.

Then she felt his calloused hand on her bare leg. The new, forbidden sensation made her clamp her legs tight. She broke their kiss, pushed against his chest.

He tightened his arm around her waist, refusing to let her move an inch. "Don't stop me, Angel."

Her mind spun with confusing thoughts and needs. Looking away from the desire burning bright in his eyes, she tried to think straight, grasp any solution, any rational idea. Recalling their conversation, she stammered, "You . . . you can't intimidate me, Jackson, and I . . . I won't let you seduce me."

His hand moved up to her knee. Tensing, she grabbed his wrist, stopping him from moving higher, then realized her mistake. Using only his thumb, he circled the sensitive inside of her thigh, around and around, over and over again, heightening her awareness, making her skin tighten and her breasts ache.

Such a simple act, yet she felt the effects deep in her core, a twisting between her legs, a yearning that tingled with the need to open up and find release. She trembled, tried to say his name, but couldn't. Her cheeks were hot, her entire body burned, felt restless and taut, stretched like a rope on the point of breaking. She shifted, needing to stand, but only succeeded in pressing his erection deep into her leg. He clenched his jaw and sucked in a breath.

"Jackson . . ." she whispered.

"Let me make love to you, Angel." His voice, so deep, so strong and arousing, was a form of seduction in itself.

How could she refuse him? Yet, she had to. *She had to!*

His hand moved higher, inching up. She shook her

head, but when he reached her hip and his thumb dipped into the crease of her leg, the room spun around her. She curled her hands in his shirt and held on. How could she react like this? How could she want him so much, knowing she shouldn't? She didn't know the answers, and knew she was on the verge of not caring.

Kissing her neck, he worked up to her jaw, grazing it until he reached her lips. His kiss was hard and controlling, taking, his tongue plunging into her mouth just as his fingers plunged between her legs.

She gasped, but he swallowed the sound. His fingers were hot and firm against her sensitized flesh. He added pressure, moving slightly, then released her. Added pressure, then released. He did it again and again, building the already unbearable ache. She tried to cry out for him to stop, but the words only circled within her head, never making it past her throat.

But she didn't really want him to stop—not yet. She'd never felt so tight, so ready to explode, so fragile she thought she might shatter. She'd always known it would be this way with Jackson, had always sensed that he would be the one to make her soul fly apart.

In a way William never would.

She shut the thought away as soon as it formed. She wouldn't think about William now. She couldn't. Every thought, every sensation, every beat of her heart was fine tuned on Jackson, on what he was doing to her, what he was making her feel.

"Part your legs for me."

Her cheeks flushed with embarrassment, but she did as he asked. He slipped his large finger inside her, shocking her with the invasion. But he withdrew it almost immediately, rubbing the moist finger against her nub.

She arched against him, gasping, all thought gone, every nerve, every cell in her body reaching, reaching.

"Jackson," she whimpered.

"I'm here, Angel. Let it go."

She didn't know what he meant by that. Let go? God help her, it was all she could do to hold on, keep herself from flying apart. But Jackson's next move shattered what little control she had left. He closed his mouth over her breast, suckling her through her cotton gown. Heat burst inside her. His tongue laved her hardened nipple, while his fingers loved her core.

"Jack . . ." Her breath caught in the back of her throat. She tensed, stiffening against his hand, pushing her breast into his mouth. The shudders tore through her, waves of them, spikes of sheer pleasure that came and went, rolling through her like a storm.

Dragging in one ragged breath after another, she opened her eyes, and found Jackson staring at her with such possessiveness, such frightening intensity, she couldn't speak. But he had no such trouble.

"Make no mistake, Angel," he said, though he growled the words like a warning. "You belong to me."

Chapter Fifteen

"I belong to no man, Jackson," Grace said, stunned by the defiance in her voice considering her mind still swirled in a burning haze.

"You belong to me, Angel. You always have." His eyes glowed like twin spears of gold, focused and a little wild. "I think it's time we made it official."

He shoved up from the bench, cradling her in his arms as if she weighed no more than a baby lamb. Two determined strides had him at the edge of the bed, and without any doubt she knew what would come next.

"Jackson, no."

He laid her on the mattress none too gently, placing his hands on either side of her head. Towering over her, his eyes blazing with hunger. The loose strands of his hair curled around an iron jaw clamped tight with need. The passion he'd brought to life within her throbbed in response. Heat spread, twisting like coils of rope throughout her veins.

With a desperate moan, she ducked beneath his arm, hurrying to the far side of the room, knowing it wasn't far enough. He wanted her, and God help her, she wanted him as much. But it couldn't be like this. She was engaged to another man, she had dreams. Dreams that seemed faint, distant, trivial as Jackson straightened, turned, his body tense, his chest expanding, stretching his linen shirt with each breath he took. His erection strained against his wool pants. The sight stole her breath.

"Do you know how much I want you?" he asked softly, taking a step forward.

"Don't." She pressed her hands to her stomach. Her nerves quivered, yearned for what he could give her.

"Or how *long* I've wanted you?" He took another step, his broad shoulders blocking the window, the walls.

"A week? Two maybe?" she asked. "That's nothing."

He shook his head. "I wanted you the night of Morgan and Daniel's masked ball. Do you remember that night?"

"That was five years ago."

"I'd left London that night because I knew you wanted a man with a title and wealth. And I'd foolishly believed that's what you deserved. But I was wrong. What just happened between us proves that."

She retreated until she butted up against the wall. "Jackson, what we just did, it was . . . it was . . ."

She couldn't say *wrong*, because she didn't believe it. What he'd done to her had been incredible, beautiful, so wonderful she wanted it again. She wanted everything Jackson could give her, shook with the force of her need, and that's what frightened her the most. Because it would be a fleeting passion, nothing more.

He planted his palms against the wall on either side of her shoulders, then leaned so close she felt wrapped in his scent of heat and sweat, of something primal and male.

She expected him to kiss her, break down the last of

her defenses, but he surprised her by asking, "Do you love me?"

Frustrated tears welled in her eyes. She'd loved him forever, and he knew it. "Don't do this."

"We belong together, Angel. You know it."

"You're a pirate, Jackson. You belong on board the *Sea Angel*. I won't live like that again. I can't."

"But you can live with a traitor like Mason?" he demanded, biting off the words. "A man you don't love?"

"I . . . I . . ." She didn't know how to respond. She'd never expected to fall in love with William, not when Jackson had seized her heart twelve years before, but she couldn't tell him that. Then she registered the first question he'd asked.

"What do you mean, 'traitor'?"

Jackson straightened to his full height. Anger flashed through his burning eyes. His jaw tensed with something other than need. "I'm afraid your fiancé isn't the wounded viscount he's led us to believe."

"What are you talking about?"

He lifted the secret message, angling it to the light so he could read it again. The corner of his mouth twitched with a bitter smile. He held the letter out to her. "Here. I know you don't want to read this, but unless you intend to remain clueless about your fiancé's activities, I think you'd better."

Taking the paper with a trembling hand, she stood beside Jackson, trying to ignore his presence, and failing. How could she ignore him when every part of her body cried out for his touch? *Stop it!* She shook her head to clear her thoughts and focused on what she held.

The paper was ordinary, without any personalized lettering to identify the sender. When she glanced to the bottom, her heart thudded hard against her chest. *It's signed by William. But that doesn't mean anything.* Willing herself to believe that, she began to read.

> *My esteemed General Gage,*
>
> *I pray this letter finds you well and prepared to act within two days' time. The supplies I promised will be awaiting you at Roxbury Hill. I trust you will have a regiment in disguise and in place, ready to deliver the final assault.*
>
> *My only regret is that I will not be on hand to see His Majesty's troops destroy the rebels, ending this atrocious affair. The rebellion must be crushed, else it will be the ruin of us all.*
>
> > *Respectfully Yours,*
> > *William Mason*
> > *Viscount of Kensale*

She glanced up. "I don't understand. What does this mean?"

Jackson took the paper, folded it and tucked it inside his shirt. "It means your charming fiancé, the man who orchestrated Elliott Prescott's punishment for being a loyalist, is, in fact, a spy for England."

"Don't be ridiculous," she said automatically.

"You read the letter. It's the truth. He's a turncoat who's betraying the very people who trust him." Jackson hefted his tankard of ale and took a deep drink, watching her over the metal rim.

Grace rubbed her brow, trying to take it all in. This involved the rebellion, and she wanted no part of it. "Even if he is a spy, what does it matter?"

Jackson gripped her arm, forcing her to look up at him. "It matters because he's setting a trap for the rebels. While he befriends them, he's plotting to have them butchered."

"That can't be true," she insisted, struggling to ignore the warning voice inside her mind. William couldn't be so devious. He couldn't be! "You're overexaggerating, Jackson. It's only a note. About supplies."

"I've seen those supplies, Angel. Powerful howitzers that can shred a dozen men to pieces with a single shot."

Her stomach heaved with just the thought of men being ripped apart, dying in pools of their own blood. Why couldn't men learn to live together in peace? Or was that an even more ludicrous dream than her finding a safe place to live?

She heard herself ask, "Why does everything always come back to war?"

"It's too late to complain about a war now, Angel." Setting down his empty mug, he lifted hers, pausing with it halfway to his mouth. "I warned you what you would find here."

She bit down on her lip and whispered, "It doesn't matter. The fact that he supports the British instead of the rebels, it doesn't matter. I still have to talk to William."

"Bloody hell!" He slammed the tankard on the table, sloshing the foaming liquid onto the scarred surface. "Have you not heard a word I've said? He's a traitor! A spy! He's not to be trusted. Now that you know the truth, how can you possibly have anything to do with the man?"

She rounded on him, her eyes blazing, her chest aching with a smothering pressure. "Because this isn't *my* war!"

"It became your war the day you decided to move here," he ground out through clenched teeth. "Can you really ignore the fact that your fiancé is planning a massacre?"

She drove both her hands through her hair in frustration. "If William is a British loyalist, why does that make him so much worse than you being a rebel?"

"How can you even ask such a question? Especially after what you and your sisters suffered!"

"Because I need to know the answer. I see no difference between you and William. Each side claims to be in the right and the other in the wrong. Each side has proven they'll go to any length, kill as many people as they think necessary, in order to claim a victory." Shivering, she faced him. "Explain to me how the two of you are so different."

"The rebels are fighting for their independence, Angel. Something the British won't allow. They want to continue taxing the colonists, suppressing them, treating them with no more regard than they would a slave."

"The king merely wants to keep control of a territory that is rightfully his."

"He won't be controlling the Colonies."

She drew a shuddering breath, though it did nothing to calm the turmoil rolling inside her. Jackson was consumed, obsessed, driven like a man who would willingly die to defend what he believed in. "I see we'll never agree on this issue."

"If you're referring to the fact that you support your fiancé betraying the very people he claimed to want to help, you're right. We'll never agree. He's not the honorable man you want him to be, Angel. If he supports the Crown, fine. He should stand up and say so, not betray his friends by lying."

Put in those precise words, Grace felt a stab to her conscience. Jackson was right. Spying was wrong, deceiving people who trusted you was worse. *He'd lied to me, as well.* Why had William done it? What possible motive? And regardless of his reasons, could she ignore them? Could she still marry him knowing the peaceful home he'd presented was a deception? That he was just as embroiled in the rebellion as Jackson was?

Just as reckless, just as willful, just as certain to die if he were caught.

But Jackson wouldn't have planned a battle, supplied weapons, knowing hundreds would be killed. He'd proven that when he'd sailed away from the two British warships instead of sinking them. She wrapped her arms around her waist, feeling ill, feeling the last of her determination to hold onto her perfect future fall away. Her dream had been a fantasy, she thought dully. An illusion, as Jackson had called it.

"Eat. We'll be leaving as soon as it's fully dark." He took her arm, his touch far more gentle than the harsh look on his face. Leading her to the bench, he forced her to sit.

She lifted a piece of bread and stared at it, thinking how unreal it felt in her hand. War surrounded her. She couldn't escape it, no more than she'd been able to escape who she truly was. A commoner. Picking up the *Sea Queen* blade from where Jackson had left it on the table, angling it so the embedded ruby, sapphire and emerald sparkled in the yellow light, she amended her last thought. She wasn't just a commoner. She was a determined woman who'd survived being a pirate.

And she wasn't going to let her dream end this way.

"You're heading the wrong way, Jackson." Grace tilted her head back to study the sky. "The moon's in front of us, when it should be to the left. We're heading west, not north."

"Three days on land and already I'm lost," he teased her, guiding the black gelding down the dark, invisible road. "It's fortunate that you're with me."

She shot him a tolerant glare, her blue eyes glowing like clear ice beneath the moon. "Where are you taking me? Obviously, not to Newburyport."

"We're heading into the heart of rebel territory."

As soon as he'd read Mason's letter to General Gage, Jackson had known he had to reach the rebels' post in Cambridge. He prayed General Artemas Ward was still camped there. The two dozen cannons in Mason's warehouse were destroyed, sitting in their own ashes, but that didn't mean there wasn't an ambush planned at Roxbury Hill. Were the British warships planning to land near there? For a surprise invasion?

If the rebels' defenses at Roxbury Hill were breached, the British would be able to push out of Boston and march on Cambridge. If they defeated the rebels there, the British troops could press further north, into Canada, ending the war and the colonists' bid for independence.

Jackson swore viciously under his breath. He had to warn the general or the rebellion would be lost.

Grace glanced at him, her brow furrowed. Hesitantly, as if she didn't really want to know, she asked, "What is it?"

He pulled her back against him, grateful when she didn't resist. Putting his lips to the cool, silken hair she'd left unbound, he breathed in her scent, warm and feminine. "I have a dilemma, Angel."

"You mean our situation is worse than I thought?"

"I'm afraid so."

She sighed, pulling her worn and patched cloak around her sorely patched dress. He hadn't wanted her to trade her gown and robe, preferring her unbound, her soft body unimpeded to his touch. But that was a temptation neither of them could afford right now, never mind that she couldn't continue riding about clad in her night rail and robe.

"Tell me," she said, "what is your dilemma?"

Were it another time, another place, he would have smiled at the tenacity in her voice. Something had happened to her back at the inn, something had changed her. Not just "something" Jackson thought. All it had taken was her learning that her fiancé wasn't the peaceful nobleman she'd thought him to be, being caught in a rebellion that was quickly turning into a war, and his own unwillingness to leave the conflict and be the man she needed.

He clenched his jaw. "I have a choice to make."

"Why do I have the feeling that I won't like whichever one you decide on?"

"Come now, Angel. This could be a great adventure."

"An adventure? We're riding through the dark of night where at any moment brigands could attack us. My new dress has more fleas than wool." To prove the point, she viciously scratched an area above her ribs. "And I'm heading into the middle of a rebellion, when all I want is to be as far away from it as I can get. That is not my idea of an adventure."

The gelding stumbled, nearly tossing Grace from her seat. Jackson caught her around the waist and secured her before him. His hand brushed her leg, and he felt the distinctive shape of the *Sea Queen* blade. Using the leather thong he tied his hair back with, she'd insisted on strapping the knife to her thigh. A rueful grin formed on his lips. She might not want an adventure, but she was prepared for one. She had never thought she was as strong as her sisters were, but Jackson knew his Angel had more strength than the other two combined. She just didn't know it yet.

"The rebel forces at Roxbury Hill need to be warned, but they're fifty miles to the south," he told her. "With only one horse, it will take us too long to reach them."

"You could have left me at the inn."

He could have, but letting her out of his sight was out of the question. She may now doubt Mason's integrity, but she would still try to confront him, and Jackson didn't want her anywhere near the man.

"As much as they need to be warned, they need reinforcements even more," he reasoned out loud. "Which means we're going to Cambridge."

"And then what?"

"We give General Ward the letter."

"And then we leave?" she asked hopefully.

"And then we leave." As much as he wanted to be involved in defeating the British, he intended to take Grace to Newburyport, place her on board the *Sea Angel* and set sail across the Atlantic. Where for two months, he'd have her all to himself. He'd have to cherish every moment, he thought, resting his chin against her cool hair, because they were all he'd ever have.

Chapter Sixteen

The predawn air was silent and damp, the ground-eating fog the color and thickness of old steel. A chill passed through Grace as she hid behind a fat bush, its prickly limbs stabbing her each time she moved. She'd wrapped the horse's reins tight around her fist, though she doubted the huge black would try to flee. Exhausted, his shiny coat lathered, he stood with his head down, one rear leg cocked as if he were already asleep.

Poor animal, she could sympathize. Having gone two days without any rest, Grace felt the effects in her aching legs, her stiff back, the fuzziness weighting her mind. If it weren't for the fact that she was scared half out of her wits, she'd gladly stretch out on the wet grass and go to sleep. But she didn't dare.

Where was Jackson?

She peered over the bush. Trees loomed on all sides of her, monstrous shadows that shifted with the gray, billowing mist. She was in the middle of a forest, with no sign of the blasted man who'd abducted her so he could protect her!

For the fifth time since leaving the inn, Jackson had forced her to dismount and hide behind a thicket, ordering her not to move until he returned from investigating some noise or to trail a passing horse and rider. Only when he was satisfied that they were safe did he let her continue their trip.

But this time he'd been gone for nearly half an hour.

"Fool man," she whispered. Irritated at him, at herself for listening to him when her instincts told her to run, and at the entire situation, she sat back on her heels and fingered the *Sea Queen* blade through her rough skirt.

More than once she'd considered mounting the black gelding and leaving Jackson. The only thing that kept her from fleeing now was not knowing where she was. Medford was to the east, but did she dare try to make it back on her own? She sighed, disgusted with her own apprehension and unwillingness to take a chance.

She'd thought the precautions he was taking were ridiculous, and had told him so. They were in rebel territory. They should be safe. Perhaps William was a spy, but that didn't mean everyone in the entire colony was a spy, too.

But Jackson's argument had been valid. William might be searching for her. And Grace knew that if her fiancé found her *with* Jackson, before Jackson delivered his message, a new rebellion would take place right in front of her eyes.

The thought of William combing the countryside for her shouldn't make her chest tighten with anxiety, but it did. If he found her, what would she do? What *could* she do? Question him about his involvement with the rebellion for certain. After that, she didn't know. Return to White Rose? Continue to plan their wedding? Continue dreaming about the children they would one day have? She grimaced, trying to picture their life together, but this time the images were fuzzy, pale and indistinct, like a chalk drawing washed away by the rain.

Hearing a clopping noise, she perked up to listen. Horses, she realized, several of them. Feeling a tug on the reins she held, she turned just in time to see the gelding lift his head, his nose in the air. He whinnied low, but the sound exploded in Grace's ears. She leaped up and clamped her hand over his muzzle. Holding her breath, she searched the dark, expecting shouts of "Who goes there?" and "Come out or we'll shoot." There was only the occasional chirp of a cricket and the heavy fall of hoof after hoof. She waited for the riders to come into view, wondering if Jackson was anywhere near, and if so, had he heard them? Or would he be caught by surprise and captured?

Grace gritted her teeth, annoyed that she was becoming as paranoid as Jackson. *It's all this hiding and waiting that's driving me insane with worry.* Still, she lifted her skirt and withdrew her dagger just to be safe. The distinctive plodding of horses' hooves grew louder. Shadows shifted, taking shape into three horses lumbering along the road, their heads swaying low. Their riders seemed just as lulled by the horses' steady gait. The men sat slumped in their saddles, their dark, shapeless coats buttoned up tight, their hats pulled low over their heads.

Grace nearly sighed with relief. Farmers most likely, on their way to market. Or merchants traveling to a nearby town. Though they might be decent men, she wasn't foolish enough to risk asking them for help.

Holding tight to the reins, she whispered nonsense into the horse's ear and patted his broad forehead to keep him quiet. The men rode past, not fifteen feet from where she hid. Sweat broke out over her skin and dripped down her temples. Where was Jackson? He had insisted on dragging her along so he could protect her! Instead, she was shivering in the dark, with nothing but a weary horse and a knife she didn't know how to use as her only defense!

Surprising herself by uttering a curse she'd learned from Jo, she listened until the trudging sound of horses' hooves faded. She kept still for a while longer, until she was certain the men were long gone. Searching the dark once more, shivering with cold and fear and anger, she made a decision.

She was through waiting!

Returning the knife to its makeshift sheath, she put her foot into the stirrup and hefted herself up into the saddle. She couldn't let Jackson take her to his ship, where he'd force her to return to England. She had to see William first. As his fiancée, it was her duty to give him a chance to explain his actions before she made any judgments. Jackson had told her they were on the road leading to Cambridge. As long as she stayed on it, she should reach the camp. Then she could ask the general in charge to give her an escort to White Rose.

If Jackson caught up with her before then, well, she'd deal with him. And if not . . .

Nudging the gelding, she emerged onto the road and headed west. An icy breeze swept past, grazing her neck, sending a chill down her spine. She refused to be afraid; there was nothing to be afraid of. But despite her own admonition, she looked behind her and drew back on the reins and worried her lower lip. She'd never been one to act rashly, but being abducted against her will, learning her fiancé was a spy and nearly losing herself in Jackson's arms, had her emotions in a whirlwind. But she had to go. She couldn't let Jackson decide her life.

"Well, what 'ave we 'ere? I told ye I 'eard another 'orse."

"It seems you were right, Charley."

Gasping, Grace faced front, her heart lodging in her

throat. Two men on horseback blocked the road, their bodies huge, bulky shapes, their eyes glittering like sooty stones in the dark.

"What are ye doing out here, missy?" the thin man to her right asked.

Grace shivered, feeling their gazes slide over her body. She stiffened her spine. *Don't show them how frightened you are.* Summoning her fleeting courage, she demanded, "I'm on my way to Cambridge. Please let me pass."

"Why don't ye go around us?" the fatter of the two men said.

"Search the area." The taller man waved his arm, dismissing his partner. "I want to know if there's anyone else nearby."

She watched the first man disappear into the surrounding brush. Her heart skittered against her chest. *I have to run, now!* She heeled the gelding, but the man before her shifted his mount, cutting her off.

"Let me by!" she insisted, hearing the fear in her voice. "You have no right to stop me."

"Is that so?" The man grasped her reins.

Grace didn't think, she just acted, kicking the gelding hard in the sides. He lurched forward, only to toss his head up, crying out as the man jerked the bridle up hard.

"Let go!" she demanded.

The gelding danced sideways, trying to break free. She slapped the man's arm with the ends of her reins, striking him again and again, but he didn't release his grip.

"Damn ye, woman," he seethed. "I'll teach ye to hit me."

"Let go of me!" She pulled the reins, heeled the animal's sides. The gelding turned, but the other horse followed, matching step for step, butting up against the black, knocking him off balance.

Her horse stumbled. Grace grabbed the saddle, nearly

tumbling off. *Jackson!* She tried to scream his name, but fear became a knot in her throat. She should have listened to him and stayed hidden! Why hadn't she listened to him?

"Ye ain't going nowhere." The man seized her hand and tried to pull her out of her saddle.

Grace squeezed her legs tight around the horse's sides and held on.

"Ye want to fight, do ye?" Laughing, the man jerked her again, nearly wrenching her arm from its joint. Streaks of light flashed through her mind. She cried out; a numbing tingle spread through her shoulder and down her back. She felt herself sliding from the saddle, falling. The man kept his bone-breaking grip on her wrist, so only her feet banged to the ground.

"Are ye through?" he asked her, his cold voice menacing. "Because if ye ain't . . ." He let the rest of his threat speak for itself.

She gulped a breath. "Who are you? What do you want?"

"I ask the questions, wench, I don't answer them. Now are ye through fighting me? Or do I need to break your arm?" He gave her arm a slight twist to prove he meant his words.

Grace gritted her teeth, her fear blurring with a rush of anger and pain. How dare this man treat her this way! He had no right. It was foolish of her, but she refused to cower. Trembling, she said in as strong a voice as she could manage, "If you intend to rob me, then you're going to be disappointed. I have nothing of value."

"I don't know about that." Though she couldn't see his face, she heard his smile. "In the dark, even a homely wench can be of use."

"Why you—" Grace tried to lift her skirt with her free hand. She had to reach the dagger. She wouldn't let . . .

"Is there a problem?"

Grace turned as much as she could and looked behind

her. She almost sank to her knees in relief. A shadow parted from the trees. Jackson had never looked so tall and strong, or so furious. He took slow, casual steps, his hands loose at his sides, his gaze fixed on the man who held her.

Hearing a telling click, she glanced up to see her abductor holding a pistol trained on Jackson. Her heart froze in mid beat. She turned back to shout for Jackson to run, but the fury in his eyes stopped the words in her throat.

She knew then that they would kill each other. Even if the man shot Jackson, she knew he wouldn't stop. He'd keep coming, driven by anger and his need to protect. She couldn't let it come to that. Somehow she had to keep them from fighting. And there was the second man to consider. Surely he would be returning soon.

Lifting her skirt the rest of the way, she gripped the dagger's hilt. The curved gold fit her palm, smooth and cold, the weight heavy. She didn't think, couldn't think about what she intended to do or she'd reconsider. Clenching her jaw, she swung her arm and stabbed the man in the thigh. She felt the blade tear through cloth, rip open skin, the flinty steel sinking until it struck bone.

Bellowing a hoarse cry, the man released her. His horse pranced sideways, butting Grace and knocking her out of the way.

Jackson caught her around the waist, spun around. "Run—" He slid to a stop.

Four men on horseback lined the road behind them, each with a pistol raised and cocked to fire.

The man she'd stabbed bit out an order. "Bind them and bring them with us. I'll deal with them at camp."

"Who are you?" Jackson demanded.

"Someone ye should not have crossed." The man's black eyes glittered with warning. He reached into his saddlebag and withdrew a white cloth, tying it off around his bloodied thigh.

"We're on important business."

"Aren't we all?" another man said, jerking Grace out of Jackson's hands.

"Please, you have to let us go." Grace flinched when the bandit took her knife and gripped it in fingers the size of plump sausages. He wiped the blood on her skirt, then stuck the blade into his waistband.

"That's mine," she told him, trying to snatch it back.

"Is it now?" He laughed and caught hold of her wrist. "Well now it's mine."

"Let her go," Jackson warned, ignoring the bandit who was tying his hands behind his back. Another man stepped up to him and smashed his fist into Jackson's jaw.

"No!" she cried.

Jackson stumbled back, gained his footing and shook his head. Blood dripped down his chin and stained his shirt. He spit a dark stream into the dirt.

She trembled, so cold with fear she could barely think or move. Jackson watched her with eyes as dark and dangerous as the robbers who'd captured them. Panic screamed through her mind. She could read his intent in his eyes. He wasn't going to let these men take him without a fight. She had to stop this nightmare, but how? Her last attempt to free them had only made their situation worse.

Slowly, Jackson's gaze sliced up to the man she'd stabbed. In a carefully controlled voice, he asked, "What side are you on? Rebel or Brit?"

"Why, the rebels, of course." The laughter that followed from all five men sent a shiver of dread up Grace's spine.

Another man ran his hands over Jackson's body, retrieving the pistol from his waistband. Then he reached inside Jackson's coat and found the letter. He immediately handed it to the man who appeared to be their leader.

He tilted the letter, trying to find a slice of moonlight to read by. "Well what 'ave we 'ere? A letter to General Gage. How interesting."

Grace's heart stopped beating. They were in rebel territory, carrying a message addressed to a British general. They were going to be accused as spies. Oh, God. "This isn't what it looks like."

"Shut up, Angel," Jackson warned.

She ignored him. "We aren't delivering the letter to the British."

"Angel—"

"We're taking it to Cambridge, for General Ward, so he can send troops to Roxbury Hill."

"Is that so?" The man's hat shadowed his face, but she could have sworn that he was smiling down at her.

"Yes, so if you'll let us go, we'll forget any of this ever happened."

"That's an interesting story, *Angel*. But one I find 'ard to believe."

"It's the truth!"

"Perhaps, but until I'm certain ye aren't a spy, ye'll be staying with us."

"But—"

"Let's move," he called to his men. Reaching down, he grasped her arm. "Ye, Angel, will ride with me."

She tried backing up, looking to Jackson for help. He struggled against the two men who were forcing him toward the black gelding.

"Don't touch her!" Rage sharpened every angle of his face. One of the captors hit Jackson in the temple with the butt of his pistol. He slumped in the man's arms, his head drooping against his chest.

"No!" She lunged for him, but the man gripping her arm held her back.

"Unless ye want to see 'im dead," the man taunted in an amused voice, "ye'll behave."

With no other choice, she allowed herself to be lifted into the saddle. The man held her before him, his arms tight around her waist, his breath a hot rasp against her neck.

She kept her gaze pinned on Jackson as they threw him across the gelding's back and willed him to wake, assure her that he was all right. He didn't stir, didn't lift his head and open his eyes. *Jackson! Please* . . .

This was her fault. If she'd listened to him, if she hadn't felt compelled to see William, none of this would have happened. Why hadn't she stayed hidden? *Why!*

Because I thought that if I ignored the rebellion, it would go away. It wouldn't dare touch me. She'd been a fool, an impatient, naive fool!

Somehow, she had to make this right. Somehow . . . But what could she do? God help her, what could *she* possibly do?

The throbbing spread throughout his skull, a hard, pounding that centered behind his eyes, pushing down his neck, tightening nerve endings into painful knots. Lying on his side, his arm numb from his weight, Jackson was reluctant to move, knowing the pain would only worsen. He didn't know where he was, and Grace . . . The last he'd seen of her, she'd been at the mercy of the leader, a man who thought them to be spies.

He swore softly and winced when streaks of lightning flashed behind his eyes. Gradually he eased his lids open, trying to bring his hand up to shield the dim light, but his arms were bound behind him.

"Be still."

The soft whisper brought Jackson's eyes open and his

mind alert. Grace hovered above him, her tangled blonde hair framing her pale face. She tilted a flask to his mouth.

After a drink of warm water, he asked, "Are you hurt?"

"Other than feeling like a rabbit caught in a coyote den, I'm fine." She ran her fingers over his brow. "How's your head?"

"I'll live." He glanced beyond her, saw a wall of aged planks, so warped that strips of light leaked through the cracks. The air smelled musty and stale.

"Where are we?" Struggling to sit up, he gritted his teeth. Damn it to hell, everything hurt from his head to his cracked ribs. "And where are those men?"

"We're in a barn, or what's left of a barn. And our hosts," she quipped sarcastically as she helped him up, "are outside."

"Why haven't you untied me?" he asked, tugging on his ropes.

"Because until a few moments ago, one of them has been in here with us."

"They left you untied?" Seeing the obvious, he was already making plans for their escape.

She nodded. "Evidently, they don't consider me a risk."

"Any idea what they're doing out there?"

"I overheard them discussing the letter. They sent one of their men to bring their leader."

"I thought the man you stabbed was their leader."

"Evidently not." She grazed her fingers over his temple again, grimacing, her crystal-blue eyes glistening with tears. "I was afraid you would never wake up."

"I'm all right, Angel," he assured her.

"Jackson, I'm so sorry."

"Don't. We're going to get out of this."

She nodded. "What do you think they'll do to us?"

"Considering they've brought us to an abandoned barn instead of a town, I can't imagine they plan anything good." He scanned the floor, littered with rotting hay, the bare walls, the rafters, looking for a weapon of any kind. "Find something to cut these ropes."

She left, quickly returning with a rusted piece of metal. "It's small and dull, but it's all I could find."

"It'll have to do."

She knelt behind him and began sawing through the rope. A moment passed with her breath growing louder, frantic. A sob escaped her. "It's not cutting, Jackson. If only I had my knife."

"Keep trying, Angel, you can do it." He gritted his teeth and tried to think of another plan. He had to get her away from there, with or without him.

The thunder of hooves and sudden shouting drew their attention.

"Oh, God, Jackson." She gripped his arm, her eyes wide, her face draining of all color as she stared at the closed door.

"Let me do the talking, Angel. Do you understand?" He narrowed his gaze on her and waited until she gave him a reluctant nod. "I'm not without influential friends in the Colonies. Once these men listen to me they'll let us be on our way."

"I hope you're right." She brushed the hair from his brow with trembling fingers. "Believe it or not, right now I'd rather be on board the *Sea Angel* than anywhere else."

He returned her wavering smile. "We're going to get out of here, Angel."

But then the wide, double doors swung open and threw them into hell.

Chapter Seventeen

"William!" Grace pushed to her feet, choking back her shock. She hadn't known who to expect when the "leader" arrived, but it hadn't been her fiancé.

He stopped short, his dark brows shooting up with surprise. He wheeled on the slender man beside him. In a cold voice that should have sliced the man in half, he said, "Leonard, you failed to mention that you had found my bride-to-be."

Leonard, the man Grace had stabbed, turned as gray as the collar of his waistcoat. His gaze scanned her tattered gown, her disheveled hair, then settled on her face. "My lord, it was dark, and, begging your pardon, but she don't look anything like she did at the ball."

This wretched man had been at White Rose? Grace hadn't seen him, but then she'd been too distracted with Sheila and Jackson, and trying to avoid a potential scandal to notice everything that had been going on around her.

William narrowed his gaze on her. "I've been worried

about you, my dear. After I found the broken window in the parlor, then realized you were gone, I could only imagine the worst, that you'd been abducted. I've had men searching everywhere, but I hadn't thought to find you here." He arched a brow, turning his features sharp. "And in the company of Mr. Brodie."

"William, I'll explain everything, but first—"

"I kidnapped her."

Grace spun around to stare down at Jackson. What was he saying? She almost asked if he was insane, but the look he shot her, warning her to keep quiet, made her pause. He sat helplessly on the filthy floor, his hands tied behind him and his clothes rumpled and dirty, yet he seemed more in control than ever, as if he knew what he was doing.

"Is this true? Were you kidnapped by your 'friend'?" Removing his hat, William stepped further into the barn, giving Grace her first real look at him. He seemed disarrayed, as if he'd hurriedly dressed. Shadows of exhaustion rimmed his steel-blue eyes. His knee-high riding boots were covered with dust, as were his black breeches and forest-green coat. His hair had escaped the ribbon tying it back in a queue. Black strands hung limp alongside his face, making his cheekbones more prominent, his mouth a grim line of disapproval.

"I . . . I . . . Jackson—"

"Come now." William took her hand in his. "You can tell me the truth."

The silky smoothness of his voice sent a chill up her arm. Her skin prickled, jarring her with a shiver.

"She didn't want to leave, Mason," Jackson said. "I took her against her will."

"Is this true?"

"Well . . . yes." What was Jackson doing? Trying to save her reputation? Why would he bother when he'd been so determined to keep her away from William?

Her fiancé sighed and smiled down at her, though the effort didn't come close to reaching his eyes. "I knew you wouldn't dare leave me without good reason." Glancing over his shoulder, he called, "Did I not tell you Leonard?"

"Aye, my lord." The man limped closer, a bloodstained cloth tied around his thigh, his belligerent gaze on Grace. "Ye said she was a loyal dove, too innocent to betray ye."

"But not so innocent as to hesitate in stabbing a man, eh, Leonard?" Reaching into his waistcoat, he withdrew her dagger. He turned it over, studying the three glowing gems. "This is quite a valuable piece, my dear. How did you come by it?"

"It's mine, a family heirloom." She held out her hand. "I'd like it back, please."

"Do you mean to tell me that when Mr. Brodie abducted you, he let you take your knife along?"

She dropped her hand, clenching it in the folds of her skirt. "Not exactly. When I heard a window break at White Rose, I went to wake you, but you weren't in your room." She paused, recalling what Jackson had said, *"Seems your fiancé has decided to come home at last."*

"Where were you?"

"Looking for the intruder, of course."

Was that the truth? Or was he lying? She wished she knew. "I retrieved my knife and went to investigate."

"Let me guess," William said, his voice soft with sarcasm. "You found Mr. Brodie?"

"I didn't know it was him." She glanced at Jackson. For a man who'd warned her to let him do the talking, he was being suspiciously closemouthed.

"Then why didn't you use this on him?" He angled the knife in the air. "You seemed to have no qualms about stabbing Leonard."

"She did try," Jackson finally said.

She frowned at him, wondering if he was purposefully

trying to provoke William's temper. Then it dawned on her. When Jackson did speak, it was to make himself look like a *villain* and her, a *victim*.

She faced William. "I stabbed your man because I was terrified. He threatened me."

"Leonard said you tried to interfere when they were subduing Mr. Brodie."

"Of course I did. I didn't know who these men were. They could have been murderers or cutthroats. Jackson might have taken me against my will, but I knew he wouldn't harm me."

A smile tweaked William's mouth. "You are far more fearless that I'd given you credit for. Very well, here's your knife. I'll allow you to keep it, but only if you give me your word that you'll put it away once you're home. Handling a weapon isn't very ladylike. And from now on, you'll leave apprehending intruders to me."

Nodding, she took the dagger and closed her fingers around the warm metal hilt. It felt solid in her hand, the weight familiar. Perhaps it was her imagination, but a tingle moved up her arm.

William knelt so he was eye-level with Jackson. "I'm curious, Mr. Brodie, why you would hand deliver Grace to me, only to break into my house and steal her away?"

"Why, to keep her out of your double-crossing hands, of course."

Grace barely suppressed a moan.

William laughed, a deep, malevolent sound that raised the hair on her arms. "I do like honesty in a man." Reaching into his coat again, he withdrew a stained sheet of paper. "So let's continue along that vein, shall we? Would you care to explain how you came to possess this letter?"

An insolent grin pulled Jackson's mouth. "I think you know exactly how I came across that letter. That very *damaging* letter, I might add. You've been putting on quite a show. Leading the rebels around by the nose while you plot their defeat."

"Yes, it's worked very well so far. And it will continue to do so in the future."

Grace stiffened, not liking the finality of William's tone. Before she could interject, he asked, "Are you responsible for destroying my warehouse?"

"The warehouse and the howitzers you were hiding? Afraid so. I had intended to steal them—it goes against my nature to destroy something that could have helped the rebels. But then I saw who the bastard turncoat was. None other than the reputable Viscount Kensale. You can imagine my surprise."

"You should have stayed out of this, Brodie." William pushed to his feet, his unrelenting gaze fixed on Jackson. "Had you sailed when you were supposed to you might have lived longer."

"What do you mean?" Grace gripped William's arm. She couldn't have just heard her fiancé threaten Jackson.

"There now, my dear." William put his hand at her waist and steered her toward the door. "This will all be over soon. You'll be back at White Rose. Once you've bathed and changed your clothes, you'll forget any of this ever happened."

She stopped. "How can I possibly forget about this? You've lied, William. To me, to the colonists."

"For good reasons, my dear."

"And those are?"

"I'll make everything clear to you after I return home. Including how my future wife is to behave."

"I want to know now." She squared her shoulders.

His tolerant expression vanished. His eyes glittered with a cold so clear, she swore she could see inside him. See anger and contempt, a violence so foreign to her, she didn't know how to name it.

"I'm not used to explaining myself, Grace. But you're distraught, so I'll humor you. I meant it when I said the Colonies is now my home. But that doesn't mean I'm foolish enough to risk losing my seat in Parliament, my estates in Devonshire. I had to find a way to protect my holdings in England, while guarding my investments here."

"So you decided to play both sides?"

"Exactly."

"Why get involved at all?" she asked. "You're wealthy."

"And getting wealthier every day, I'm happy to say. England has paid me handsomely for providing valuable information, not to mention for using my ships to smuggle weapons. Don't frown so, my dear. You will reap the benefits of my connections. You'll lack for nothing. Clothes from France, the best carriages. You can travel the world."

"I've already traveled the world."

"But not in style. I can give you anything your heart desires. You have only to ask."

A tremor wound through Grace's body. She wanted to scream that he was a monster, but the words wouldn't come. She could barely breathe around the fury squeezing her chest like a fist. Everything, *everything* was a lie. William could no more provide a happy, stable life any more than he could feel guilty for betraying his friends and neighbors. The worst part, the realization that made Grace want to double over with the force of her anger, was that she'd suspected the truth about William all along. She'd suspected, but hadn't let herself really see it. Instead, she'd clung to her childish dream, proving just how foolish she really was, how very foolish and naive.

Rubbing her thumb along the *Sea Queen* hilt, she asked, "What do you intend to do?"

"That's not for you to worry over, my dear. Go with Leonard. He'll see you home."

She started to insist that she wasn't going anywhere, but catching Jackson's furtive shake of his head, she stammered, "I'd . . . I'd rather wait for you, if you don't mind."

He took her hand and brought it to her lips. "This is war business and doesn't concern you. It would be best if you do as I say and leave."

"What are you going to do with Jackson?"

"I know he's your friend, but he's a traitor to my cause. Besides which, he knows about my dealings with the British. I have to protect myself, and you. As my future wife, you must understand that."

"What are you going to do?" she insisted again.

Holding her arm, he forcefully pulled her outside into the hazy morning light. "I told you not to worry. Now, go to White Rose with Leonard."

"Not until—"

"I've had a rather trying night, Grace," he said, anger whipping through his tone. "I've answered your questions. I suggest you not try testing my patience any further."

Reaching Jackson's black gelding, William helped her up into the saddle. With every passing second, she frantically tried to think of some way to stop William, convince him to give her a few minutes alone with Jackson. Now that she had her knife, she could free him.

Leonard rode up beside her, his expression dark and brooding. She wasn't going anywhere with him. But how could she object without making William even angrier? She had to get away from both men, and the four others who were standing guard nearby. But what could one woman do against six men?

"William," she pleaded, "let Jackson go. He can't do anything to hurt you."

"I'm afraid I can't do that, my dear. It's my duty to take him to the British camp in Boston where he'll be tried as a traitor."

She gasped. "No!"

"Don't worry." He patted her thigh. "Who knows, it might go well for your friend. He's a pirate, after all. Perhaps the loyalists can convince him to change sides. We could use his talents as a ship's captain."

She looked at the crumbling barn, wishing she could see Jackson once more, speak to him. Plead with him to do whatever it took to stay alive. Would he renounce his beliefs just to stay out of an English prison? The answer was no, emphatically, out of the question, *no!*

Which meant she had to do something rash. First she had to escape Leonard, then she had to free Jackson. *But how?*

She tightened her fingers around the hilt of her dagger, her mind searching furiously for a plan.

"I'll return to White Rose as soon as I can, my dear," William was saying. "Perhaps we can have lunch in the garden while we have our talk?"

She nodded, barely listening. She would leave with Leonard, then do whatever it took to escape him. Once she was free, she could ride for Boston by herself, confront General Gage, tell him of her connections in England. He might be inclined to listen to her and free Jackson. She'd even promise to see Jackson out of the Colonies on the first ship they came across. It might work. It *had* to work!

"Once I'm home, everything will be settled and we can begin planning our wedding."

"Yes," she said absently. "That will be lovely."

"Take care of her Leonard." William swatted her horse's rump, sending her off.

"Aye, my lord."

Every step the horse took, Grace's body tightened, begging her to turn back, not to leave. Her limbs shook with the effort to continue on. She had a plan, a good plan, and she meant to see it through. She'd save Jackson from prison. She'd return to England and engage both of her brothers'-in-law help if need be. Anything to make sure Jackson was freed.

Not able to sit still for another moment, she turned in her saddle . . . just in time to see one of William's men throwing a rope over the sturdy branch of a tree . . . with a noose dangling from its end.

Chapter Eighteen

"Don't be getting any ideas, lady," Leonard warned, his dark, narrowed gaze taking in her shocked expression.

She faced front in her saddle, her heart racing against her chest. William was going to hang Jackson! Dear God, she had to stop him! She nudged her horse into a trot, realizing she had to be out of sight before she tried anything. *But try what?* How could she escape her guard and return to save Jackson? Her sisters were the ones who plotted attacks, fought duels with swords, took whatever risks necessary to gain what they wanted. But Grace couldn't engage in a sword fight—or even a knife fight— she didn't have that bold trait. *But I'd better find it, or Jackson will die.*

When they were barely a mile from the barn, surrounded by nothing except trees and scraggly brush, she said, "I apologize for stabbing you, Mr.—"

"Potts," he growled, rubbing his wounded leg. "Leonard Potts."

"Mr. Potts. But I was frightened. When you and your men came out of the dark the way you did, I thought my virtue was at stake."

His mouth quirked with an oily grin as his gaze slid over her body. "I suppose I could understand ye thinking that. Guess I should count myself lucky ye are as short as ye are, or ye might have stabbed me in the gut."

She shuddered, not having to fake the revulsion she felt, for both the man and the image. Yet, the knife she gripped gave her a desperate kind of strength. Did she dare try stabbing him again? And if she failed to incapacitate him, what would he do to her? Whatever she tried, it had to be fast, and it couldn't fail, because she sensed she'd only have one chance to escape.

"Oh, dear. I think my horse has a pebble in his hoof." Without waiting for a reply, she slid from the saddle. Careful to keep her dagger hidden, she ran her hand over the animal's front leg.

" 'E looks fine to me," Leonard complained, coming up beside her.

"Could you check, just to make sure?" She stepped back, giving him room. Her stomach rolled and her arms visibly shook. Good heavens, what was she doing?

As he bent to lift the gelding's hoof, she raised the dagger, aiming for his back. She hesitated. *I can't kill him!* Flipping the knife in her grip, she brought the hilt down and struck Leonard in the temple with a solid thwack. Without a word, he slumped forward, landing on his face in the dirt.

Gasping a shaky breath, Grace watched him and waited to see if he would move. He didn't, except to breathe, for which she was grateful. She thought to tie him up, but didn't have any rope, or any time to spare. Instead, she slapped his mount on the rump, sending it racing down the road.

Gaining her saddle, she stared down at the prone man. Blood dripped from his temple, and she expected he'd have a wicked headache when he awoke, but it was the least he deserved. She smiled to herself, feeling bold, even courageous. She'd done it, gotten what she wanted without causing any harm—or at least not very much harm—just as her sisters had when pirating the *Sea Queen*.

She turned the black gelding back toward the barn, ready to face whatever came next and praying she wasn't too late.

Jackson glared at the empty doorway, barely holding back a roar of fury. He'd vowed to protect Grace and punish Mason, yet he'd failed at both. Watching Mason lead her away with a proprietary touch, seeing Grace's expressive face pale with worry, Jackson had been filled with a rage unlike anything he'd ever known. He didn't delude himself by believing the viscount intended to release him. If he lived another half hour he'd consider himself lucky. But, Jackson swore, if he had to die, Mason would be dying along with him, because he refused, *refused* to leave Grace in the traitor's hands.

Gripping the rusted piece of metal Grace had dropped when she'd first spotted Mason, Jackson sawed the ropes, slicing his palms, his wrists. The slick warmth of his blood smeared his fingers, but he barely felt the stinging cuts. Now that Grace was out of immediate danger, he could focus on subduing Mason. But first he had to free his arms.

He heard the approach of footsteps and rising laughter, but he continued splicing the thick hemp rope, ignoring the burning strain on his muscles. Sweat beaded his brow and dripped into his eyes, blurring his vision. *Bloody hell!* Was he slicing the rope, or just his own damned skin!

From the corner of his eye, he saw two men enter the

barn. He froze, clenching the metal in his fist. He watched their approach, their taunting smiles speaking to what might come next. Lifting him by the arms, they forced him outside. Jackson blinked against the morning glare, then he spotted Mason sauntering across the yard. The man's blue eyes narrowed, the expression on his face so ripe with conceit, Jackson could almost taste it.

"You really have become a thorn in my side, Mr. Brodie." Replacing his tricorne hat on his head, Mason angled the brim so it shadowed his eyes. "And you've cost me a great deal. In both time and profits. Neither of which I appreciate losing."

"Your losses are just beginning," Jackson goaded. "I'm not finished with you yet."

Mason smiled. "But you are, Mr. Brodie. Finished, that is. Whenever a thorn aggravates my side, I do the sensible thing and pluck it out. Getting rid of it for good. Which is what I intend to do with you."

"And Grace? What do you plan to tell her?"

"Don't you worry about *my* fiancée. I'm very capable of handling her."

The anger Jackson barely kept under control threatened to erupt. He had to get free, because there was no way in hell he was going to let Mason "handle" Grace. If it was the last thing he ever did, he intended to make sure the man wouldn't have the physical ability to even utter her name.

Mason nodded to the two men holding him. They forced Jackson across the yard toward a thick line of trees crowded with prickly brush and clinging vines. One tree, an ancient oak with a base as round as a small room, stood out from the rest—and not because of its size.

The knotted rope draping a massive branch caught the morning breeze and swung back and forth like the pendulum of a clock. A cold chill snaked down Jackson's back.

"You won't get away with this," he said as another man arrived with a horse.

"Of course I will."

"My crewmen will come looking for me."

"And they'll leave when they're told you are being held in a British prison camp."

"You won't fool Grace." Jackson scanned the area, looking for any reason to delay the inevitable. He needed more time to cut through his bindings. Just a few more minutes! Once they put him on the horse, he had to have his hands free!

"Grace is sweet, innocent to how truly corrupt the world can be." Stepping up to Jackson so that barely a hand's width separated them, Mason added, "Considering you are merely her 'friend,' I believe you've overstepped your bounds, or does your *interest* in her run deeper that just friendship?"

Jackson returned the man's derisive grin. "I don't believe that's any of your business."

"But it is. I can understand you burning my warehouse, destroying my cannons. This is war, after all. One must expect victories as well as losses. But kidnapping my fiancée . . ." He leaned closer, his voice lowering so it sounded like the scrape of steel against stone. "You touching my fiancée is something I cannot forget, or forgive. Grace is *mine* and I won't have her sullied by the likes of you."

"After last night, Grace will *never* be yours," Jackson said in a tone that implied more had happened between them than his capturing her. He knew that if he didn't escape, he risked bringing Mason's anger down on her, but he had to break the man's control, distract him, buy more time.

Mason visibly trembled. Jackson expected him to pull a gun, shoot him dead now, but the viscount only stood there, scowling in anger. "Heed my warning, Brodie, she'd better be innocent still, or I swear I'll dig you up and hang you again. Then I'll make Grace wish she'd never been born. Think about that as you draw your last breath."

Turning away, he shouted, "String him up!"

While one man held the horse's reins, the other two men wrestled Jackson into the saddle. Once seated, he fumbled with the piece of metal and tried to slice the bindings the rest of the way, knowing it was useless. There wasn't enough time. He searched the yard for some way out, but there wasn't any.

Another of Mason's lackey's rode up and slipped the noose around his neck, the rough cording abrading his skin. Then the man tightened the rope, cutting off his air. Jackson gasped for breath, wondering if he'd pass out before the horse sped from under him and broke his neck.

"I'd ask if you have any final words, Brodie, but I've already heard all I care to from you." Mason turned away, laughing as he headed for his mount. Apparently he didn't intend to stay and watch. His next words confirmed it. "See you dispose of him properly, boys."

The whinny of a horse and the hurried fall of hooves drew Mason up short. Everyone faced the road, tensing. Several men drew their pistols. The distraction was all Jackson needed. He worked the metal over the rope, felt several threads give way. He jerked on the rest, but they held.

The men ran for cover just as a riderless horse rounded the line of trees. Jackson recognized the animal immediately; his black gelding, the same one Grace had been riding when she'd left. God, what had happened to her?

Mason ran to the animal and caught the loose reins. He glared at the empty saddle as if he were silently ordering Grace to reappear. "Everyone, mount up and find her.

And Leonard! If he's let anything happen to her I'll string his worthless hide up beside Brodie.''

"What 'bout this one?'' the man holding the reins to Jackson's horse called out.

Mason swung into his saddle. "Hang him for God's sake, and be quick about it!" Mason sped down the road the way the black gelding had come, the three other men following in his wake.

The horse Jackson sat on pranced to the side, trying to follow the others. The rope tightened around his neck, cutting into his skin. He gritted his teeth and nudged the horse with his heels, trying to signal the animal to back up, ease the rope's slack. Black stars flashed behind his closed eyelids. This was his chance to escape; he couldn't let it pass. With only one man left to guard him, he had to find a way to get the noose off.

"Say yer prayers, Brodie, cause it's time tae die.''

Jackson silently cursed Mason, and himself for failing Grace. God, what would happen to her? From the corner of his eye, he saw the man raise his hand to slap the horse on the rump. Only his hand stayed in the air and a stunned look entered his eyes.

His mouth dropped open, but another voice, a female voice, said, "Untie him. Now.''

Jackson couldn't believe it. *Grace?* Where had she come from? He twisted in the saddle to see her standing behind the guard, her jaw set, her eyes bright with anger. She would have looked stern, even threatening, if not for the wild halo of blonde hair surrounding her face and draping her shoulders. A feminine blush rode high on her cheeks.

To his surprise, the man hurriedly reached up and worked the knot loose. Once his hands were free, Jackson pulled off the noose and leaped to the ground. The guard raised his arms out to his sides, making it clear why he'd been so quick to follow Grace's order.

She held the *Sea Queen* blade at his back, the steel tip disappearing into the fabric of his shirt.

"I don't know how you managed this," Jackson said. He glimpsed the rip in her gown, baring her shoulder, the burrs and tufts of grass stuck in her hair, and guessed she'd crawled through the brush. "But I'll kiss you for it later."

She smiled hesitantly. "What do we do with him?"

Jackson pulled her away from the man, then reared back, landing his fist between the guard's eyes. He collapsed at their feet in a puff of dust and didn't move.

"Mount up." Jackson half tossed her into the saddle and leaped up behind her. "We'd better be long gone before Mason decides to circle back."

She faced him, touching his neck, reminding him of the stinging abrasions. Tears pooled in her eyes. "You're all right? Tell me you're all right. I was so afraid . . ."

He kissed her, fast and hard, crushing her to him. "I'm fine, Grace. Because of you."

She nodded. "Perhaps I don't make such a bad pirate after all."

Smiling down at her, wishing he had time to kiss the worry from her eyes and tell her how much he loved her, he put heel to horse and fled for Cambridge.

As far as military camps went, the rebels' main base was an immense disappointment.

Granted, this was her first camp to visit, and Grace supposed she wasn't one to judge, but in her opinion, the severe living conditions were yet another reason war should be avoided. Men crowded around dying fires, methodically eating what looked like beans from tin plates. Their clothes were filthy and patched from constant wear, their boots dirt-caked and worn thin. Yet, despite their disheveled appearance, their faces were set with a strange determination.

As she sat on a stool outside General Ward's tent, waiting for Jackson to finish his meeting, she nursed a cup of strong black coffee and returned several of the curious looks cast her way. She saw purpose in the men's eyes, a quiet resolve to continue their fight. Whether they sat by themselves or in groups, or were performing some duty, she sensed their apprehension, as if they were never really at ease. She'd expected the soldiers to be hardened, emotionless—seasoned to the hardships of their job.

Then she noticed something else that made her sit up and pay closer attention. Only a few men were dressed in the blue uniformed coats with puff lapels and breeches. Almost all the men wore homespun brown wool pants, heavy shirts and coats. Clothes meant for everyday wear, farming or hunting. She took a closer look at the men and realized they *weren't* soldiers, but farmers and tradesmen. *Men who should be home, caring for their families.* Instead, they'd left their homes and loved ones, so they could fight for a cause they believed would save them.

Just as Morgan, Jo and I did to save Dunmore.

She sat there, feeling numb, feeling astounded. Were the rebels justified in their decision to take up arms against King George? She didn't know for sure, but sensing their conviction to fight until the end, knowing every man around her was prepared to give his life to protect his home, she realized the enormous sacrifice they were making. Jackson included. He'd come so close to dying, and all because he'd gone to White Rose to rescue her instead of riding to Cambridge with William's letter.

She sighed, finally understanding why Jackson identified with the colonists. *She* should have identified with them, as well. But she'd been too self-absorbed, too frightened that the past would repeat itself.

A deep, burrowing shame worked its way into her heart. How could she have ignored the rebels' dilemma, pretended that their fears didn't exist, thought of nothing except finding a safe home for herself? She pressed her fingers to her lips and fought back tears as the truth sank in. All this time she'd been searching for a place to belong, when she'd really been looking for a place to hide from danger and risk. But no more, she swore.

She couldn't remain in the Colonies. She didn't know anyone, and she didn't care to face her *ex*-fiancé again. Which meant she had to return to England. *And do what?* She ran a hand through her tangled hair. Besides seeing her sisters again and being an aunt to her nieces and nephews, there was nothing for her there.

So where does that leave me? She pressed the warm tin cup to her forehead, but it did little to ease her brewing headache.

I can stay with Jackson. She pushed the provoking thought aside. She might have helped him escape from William, but that didn't mean she could become a smuggler. Being a pirate, risking her life and those of others, wasn't in her nature. She wished she could change who and what she was—God, things would be so much simpler if she could—but that would be like trying to turn black into white. It couldn't be done. Regardless that she failed to see William's true nature, and that she might never have the safe home she'd always wanted, she couldn't live on a ship, never knowing what dangers she'd have to face. Never knowing if she'd finally lose Jackson forever.

She heard a noise behind her, but was too focused on her own turmoil to turn around. A strong grip lifting her from her stool snapped her out of her pensive thoughts.

"I need you inside," Jackson said, his mouth in a grim line and his expression bleak.

She ducked through the tent flap, wondering what had

gone wrong. He ushered her to a desk strewn with maps and letters, quill pens and a brass inkwell. But it was the short man in a blue uniform standing behind the desk that captured her attention.

"General Ward," Jackson said, his voice tight with frustration. "This is Grace Fisk, William Mason's fiancée."

The general nodded in greeting, his aged, deeply creased face inscrutable. "Mr. Brodie has informed me that you can support his incredible story concerning Viscount Kensale. I must say, it turns my stomach to hear that a staunch supporter of the rebel cause *might* be a loyalist spy."

Stunned, she glanced at Jackson, understanding why he seemed so disturbed. "You don't believe Jackson?"

"How can I?" the general asked. "He has no proof."

"But there *is* a letter, addressed to General Gage. I read it. It mentioned supplies he was sending to Roxbury Hill, where there is supposed to be some sort of attack."

General Wade arched a graying brow, but otherwise didn't react.

She fisted her hands. "William . . . Viscount Kensale . . . took the letter from Jackson after his men caught us trying to reach you. My God, they almost hanged him." She reached up and pulled Jackson's shirt collar aside. "Look for yourself."

General Wade leaned closer, narrowing his gaze as he studied the red, swollen scrapes ringing Jackson's throat. He straightened, leveling Jackson with a critical look. "Why didn't you mention this before?"

"I've been smuggling goods and information for the rebels since the conflict began. I somehow thought my word would have been enough to convince you."

Grace demanded of Jackson, "Did you tell him about the letter you took from Captain Peters and the British ships sailing here?" Without waiting for his reply, she turned to the general. "Jackson's ship, the *Sea Angel*, is sailing to Newburyport right now with a secret message regarding warships carrying British soldiers to Boston. He also has a hull full of loyalist prisoners.''

When both men continued to stare at her in silence, she insisted, "You have to believe me. William Mason is a loyalist. He must be stopped before more people are hurt.''

"You are betrothed to the viscount?'' the general asked.

"I was, but no longer.'' That part of her life was over. William and the dreams she'd spun around him would become nothing more than a regretful memory.

"Did you know of his involvement when you became engaged to him?''

"Of course not. I thought he was supporting the rebels, which was bad enough.'' At the general's quizzical look, she hesitantly added, "I didn't want to be involved with the rebellion at all.''

"Yet, here you are.''

She sighed. "Yes, here I am.''

The general nodded, turning away to rifle through some papers on his desk. "I appreciate what it took for you to bring me this information. That will be all.''

"But what are you going to do?'' Grace asked.

"I have one of two choices; I could ignore your statement, since it pains me to believe William Mason might be a turncoat. I've known the man since he arrived in Massachusetts three years ago. He's done a great deal for the Colonies.'' When she started to object, he raised a hand and stopped her. "Or I can send reinforcements to Roxbury Hill, which is a gamble in itself. *You* could be spies, trying to divide my troops—''

"That's not—'' Grace tried to interject.

"But since Roxbury Hill is essential to keeping the British harnessed in Boston, I feel I have no choice but to heed your warning.''

Grace sighed with relief, feeling Jackson slightly relax beside her.

Jackson shook the general's hand. "Thank you."

"If what you say is true, then I'm the one who should be doing the thanking. Bringing me this information may save the rebellion from a quick defeat. But hear my warning, Mr. Brodie. If what you've told me is false, there won't be a hole in all the Colonies that you can hide in where I won't find you."

Taking offense to the general's tone, Grace started to argue, but Jackson ushered her out of the tent, half carrying her to their waiting horse. Once he stopped to let her mount, she turned to him.

"I can't believe you let him threaten you that way."

"It doesn't matter," Jackson said, smiling softly as he pulled a strand of clinging hair from her face. "As long as he sends troops to Roxbury Hill, I'll be satisfied."

No sooner were they both in the saddle, with Jackson reining the horse out of the camp, than they heard shouts behind them, ordering the men to prepare to march.

A shudder ran through her as she imagined what the farmers and tradesmen would find when they reached Boston. An ambush? Pain and death? She whispered a prayer for them all. The sun had already begun its descent, streaking the sky bloodred, turning the trees, brush, the rolling grass a deeper, richer green. The woodsy sent of smoke hung on the air.

"Are we going to Newburyport now?" she asked.

"Yes."

"It's over, isn't it?" she said, feeling strangely lost, restless, and on the verge of tears. Though she couldn't say exactly why she wanted to cry. For her lost dream? For the men who were marching into war? Or for the inability to stop the coming battle? *But we made a difference.*

"Yes, it's over." He pressed his lips to her hair and tightened his arm around her waist.

The dream was over. She had to face reality. Her future. And she had no idea what that might be.

Chapter Nineteen

When on sea, sail; when on land, settle.

The English verse rolled through Jackson's mind, over and over again, a simple chant that knotted his gut. He'd lived half his life traveling the ocean, content with a rocking deck, the temperamental winds, the lifestyle that was as nomadic as it was ambitious. He'd thrived under the glare of the sun, welcomed Fate's changeable nature, delighted in the days when he could challenge the odds.

He'd become a man on board the *Sea Queen*, had found his place in the world . . . dangerous though it may be. But despite the dangers, and the unpredictability—or maybe because of those very things—the sea was what he loved. It was where he belonged.

Watching Grace at the bow, her hair a tangled cape of gold, he wondered if he could give it all up. For her.

After leaving General Ward, they'd ridden hard for Newburyport, finding the *Sea Angel* ready to sail—less her loyalist prisoners and the coded message. Jackson had wasted no time in ordering the larboard braces forward and the sheets set for windward. He'd been determined to leave the Colonies without delay. In his mind, he knew Mason couldn't reach Grace now—the man was finally out of her life for good—but Jackson wanted as much distance between them as he could get.

Stepping up behind her, he bracketed her body with his arms, trapping her with the railing at her front and his body at her back. She stiffened, but only slightly before letting out a wistful breath.

"You surprised me," she said, nervously running her hands down her skirt.

Before boarding the *Sea Angel*, he'd made one short detour, for which he was now grateful. Grace deserved more than the two plain gowns he'd purchased for her, along with the necessary undergarments, but they were far better than the rags she'd traded her night rail and robe for. She now wore a simple dress of royal blue, the material shades darker than her eyes. The gown was a size too small; the fitted sleeves and bodice hugged her arms and waist, the scooped neckline revealed a dangerous amount of creamy flesh.

His body responded, hardening with a throbbing pulse. Grinding his teeth and forcing the sudden rush of desire under control, he said, "I've never been able to sneak up on you. What are you thinking that has you so preoccupied?"

She smiled, a troubled lift of her generous mouth. The hot sun overhead brought fire to her cheeks. "A host of things. Seeing England again, my family. I don't know how I'll tell them about William."

"They'll understand." Her hair fluttered against his chest, grazing his cheek, adding the scent of her sun-warmed skin to those of the briny sea air and oiled wood. A touch of heaven his soul longed for. He tightened his grip on the railing to keep from gathering her in his arms. It would be so easy to hold her—just a slight shifting on his part—and it would feel so right, but she'd been through enough in the last few days. And he knew more heartache awaited them both in England.

"Morgan and Jo didn't want me to marry William."

Her murmured statement snapped him back to awareness. "I thought you had their support."

"I did. Their reluctant support, in any case." She faced the ocean's gentle swells. The last glimpse of Americas' coast had vanished hours before so she watched a pair of sea turtles play on the surface, then plung into the glittering depth. "But they knew I didn't love him, and thought I was foolish to marry for anything less."

"They were right," he said. *She loves me, though, and I love her, but that's all I can give her, and that's not enough.*

She nodded. "Will you return to the Colonies?"

Drawing a breath, he wrapped the length of her hair around his fist. They had to have this conversation, but he wished it could have waited a while longer. "There's still more that needs to be done. I can't explain it, Angel. But I feel compelled to help them, to somehow rectify the wrong that has been done to my family and yours, to the thousands in the Colonies who are suffering the same way we did."

She faced him, her eyes bright, anxious, but free of tears. "I do understand. I think you should go back and help the colonists win their independence."

"You aren't going to try to convince me to stay in England?" he asked, feeling a pang in his chest when she shook her head.

"You wouldn't be happy there."

He saw the rest of her statement in her eyes. *She wouldn't be any happier in England than he would be.* But eventually she would be content there, he thought, once she was settled. Then, before the thought had completely formed, he said, "You could stay on board the *Sea Angel,* with me."

"And live every day in fear that you'll be captured, or that the ship will sink?" She ran her hands down the front of his shirt, her touch light, hesitant, as if she resisted grabbing onto him, afraid that she wouldn't let him go. "You know I can't do that."

He knew, so help him God, he knew. Pulling her to him, he pressed his lips to her temple and tasted the salty-sweetness of her skin. He wished he didn't understand, wished he could argue with her, try to convince her that they could make a life together, but he knew better. She deserved more. Deserved a man who would willingly settle down and marry her.

Jackson closed his eyes. If only he were that man.

"Sometimes things just don't go as planned." Macklin tugged on the tarred rope that secured a stack of wooden cages filled with white, clucking chickens. "Take me, for instance. My da thought I'd be a farmer like 'im. Work'n' the same patch of land year after year, barely surviv'n'."

Half listening, half lost in her own thoughts, Grace strolled after the first mate as he checked the ropes his crew had already secured. The ship danced over a swelling wave, sending the chickens into a frenzy, but Grace hardly noticed. There was something soothing about the blustery roll of the deck, the gusts of wind that tore at her braid and swirled her skirts around her legs.

"I probably would 'ave stayed on, but my da up and died on me," Macklin continued, then called two crewmen over to haul the barrels of gunpowder below, where they'd be kept safe and dry from the coming rain.

Grace stopped and stared at the young man. "What did you say?"

"I'm say'n' I always thought I'd be a farmer."

Seeing a somber emotion mingle with the ever-present sparkle of mischief in his brown eyes, she said, "I can't imagine you working the land."

"Me either. 'Tis a good thing, I suppose, that my da died when 'e did."

"Macklin!"

Giving her a knavish grin, he shrugged his shoulders. "I just mean things 'appen the way they're supposed to. Ye can't fight life, ye just 'ave tae take what it gives ye. Like ye marry'n' that viscount. Ye weren't meant for him any more than I was meant to grow wheat. And tell me if I'm mistaken, but I think ye knew it all along."

Grace couldn't argue, didn't even bother to try. She'd been determined to marry William, had turned a blind eye to the man he really was. Even when Jackson had shown her proof that he was a traitor, she'd refused to believe it, or let it touch her. It had taken Jackson's near hanging for her to realize the man she'd thought would fulfill her dreams had really been a nightmare in the making. She shivered, sick that she'd come so close to having him for her husband.

Crossing her arms, she leaned against the railing and watched the gushing waves. A storm was brewing, building beneath the ocean and surging above in the gunmetal skies.

They'd been at sea for six days now. Six days, during which she'd only spoken to Jackson when they happened to pass on deck, or during their meals with the crew. When she wasn't alone in the captain's cabin—he'd taken to sleeping with the crew—their conversations had consisted of the weather, the ship's heading. Nothing personal, such as what would happen when they reached England. If she didn't know better, she'd think he was avoiding her. So for six terminally long and lonely days, she'd tried to envision—and accept—what her life would soon be like. *Without Jackson.*

She closed her eyes and tried to imagine herself attending balls, struggling to make friends, agonizing over her manners and dress, and, heaven help her, her past. The images wouldn't come, and it dawned on her why. They weren't important. The parties, being accepted by the nobility, none of it mattered. That wasn't the life she wanted. *So what do I want? Besides the love of a man who can't give up the sea?*

She saw herself stepping off the *Sea Angel* at a crowded London dock, standing on the pier alone, with no direction, no idea what she intended to do. Her future was a blank.

There was nothing beyond that isolated, unnerving vision.

Absolutely nothing.

Mac stroked the point of his coal-black beard with the pad of his finger. "She's a sight, is she not?" he cooed as if the ocean could hear his phrase. "The most beautiful and stubborn woman God ever created."

"I don't know that I can agree with you, Macklin." Hearing the deep, graveled quality of Jackson's voice caused the nerves along Grace's spine to tighten.

"Capt'n." Mac nodded in greeting. "We're ready, should the storm turn hot-tempered on us."

Once the first mate moved away, Jackson said, "You and Macklin seemed to be having a serious conversation."

"I think he was trying to give me some advice."

"I should caution you. Macklin has been known to dispense rather . . . inopportune words of wisdom."

"Really?" she mused, feeling strangely sensitized by the warm breeze against her face, the vibration of the hull beneath her feet. She met Jackson's gaze, saw the gold flecks in his eyes flare with emotions she was almost too afraid to name. Longing, desire. Her skin rippled in response. Yet, she sensed uncertainty in him, as well, a hesitancy to act on his desire. But why? After what he'd done to her at the inn, what he'd made her feel, why would he hesitate now?

Because he doesn't want to hurt me? Because he knows there can't be anything between us unless one of us changes? If Jackson changed for her, would he still be the man she'd loved for most of her life? Or when he began to miss the sea, the nomadic lifestyle, would he grow to resent her?

Clearing her throat so she could speak, she said, "I think perhaps I should listen to Mac."

"Meaning?"

"He suggested that I shouldn't fight life, but make it what I want it to be."

"Macklin said that?" Jackson arched a brow in surprise.

"Something close to it." As the meaning sank in, she felt her slight smile fade. *Make life what I want it to be.* Like right now? she wondered. Live for now and worry about what would happen in England later?

The temptation to run her fingers over his cheek, feel the bristle of his day's growth of beard, lose her fingers in the length of his whiskey-blond hair had her taking a step forward. Those were things she could imagine herself doing . . . all too easily.

Jackson stepped back, out of her reach, thwarting her impulsive thoughts. "I'd best see to the ship."

She watched him leave, barely suppressing the urge to call him back. He wanted her. She saw it in his eyes, his fisted hands, the muscles in his arms that knotted and flexed. He wanted her, just as she'd always wanted him. Only he wasn't going to do anything about it. *Make life what I want it to be.*

Perhaps it was time she did just that.

Chapter Twenty

The squall hit like a bad-tempered woman.

Hot, stinging rain pounded the deck, slashed the crew's faces and bare hands, plastered their clothes to their bodies. Lightning split the sky with arms of jagged white light, ghosting the decks below and the men who fought to save the ship. The roar of the sea and the howl of the driving gale raged like monsters at war.

Gripping the wheel, using all his weight and strength to keep the bow into the teeth of the wind, Jackson sensed, for the first time in his life, that he might be fighting a losing battle. His hands stung from blisters, the muscles in his arms and shoulders burned as if they'd been set on fire. But worse, he didn't know how much longer the *Sea Angel* could withstand the abuse.

The storm tossed the ship over the ocean's back, lifting her onto the crest of a vicious wave, then plunging the groaning hull into the depths of hell. The ocean churned, spewing itself over the deck, ripping stored hammocks from their nets, loosening ropes from their knots. A small sail had already escaped its ties. It had flapped in the strangling wind before wrenching free and disappearing into the rain-soaked night.

Jackson prayed that was the extent of their damage, but he held out little hope. Seawater ran in a river over the floor, pouring down the hatchways, more than the pumps could handle. His thoughts went to Grace, locked below in her cabin, enduring the tempest alone. He didn't have to see her to know how frightened she was, terrified that they would all die before the next sunrise. Every impulse inside him screamed to go to her, make sure she was all right. Promise her that he would keep her safe.

Only his promise might turn out to be a lie. He'd always welcomed a bracing storm. And though she'd warned him to prepare for this one, no one had realized how violent it would be. This time Grace's fears might be realized. He might not win this battle. The helm wasn't responding, leaving the *Sea Angel* vulnerable to the wind. If he didn't do something soon, Grace would never reach England.

God, she didn't belong at sea; how could he have even considered asking her to stay with him? He'd been a fool, a selfish, egotistical fool! *Think, damn it, think!* She was too precious, and he loved her too much, to risk losing her.

"Capt'n, let me take the 'elm!" Macklin, tied by a safety rope, fought the ship's pitch to reach Jackson's side.

"I've got to find a way to keep the bow near the wind. If I don't, the rudder will crack." He searched the decks for some way to fight the surging waves, when an idea occurred to him. "Raise the main sheet."

Mac swiped a handful of wet black hair from his face and glanced up at the sail secured to the yardarm midship. "Capt'n, if I unfurl the sail, it'll rip apart, and possibly take the mast with it!"

"It's a chance I'll have to take. Now do it!"

Muttering that Jackson was insane, Macklin left to do as ordered, calling to three other crewmen to help. Despite the heaving deck and blinding rain, the ropes were quickly untied and the four men hauled the lines, raising the white sail up the mast. Wind tore at the sheet, snapping the canvas so taut, Jackson didn't know what miracle held it together. But it had to hold, he vowed. It had to, or they would all perish.

As the sail was tied off, Jackson spun the wheel to the left and felt the ship respond, slowly turning the bow full into the wind. He gritted his teeth against a smile. Maybe they had a chance. Just maybe.

Lightning flashed again, a rippling wave of light that shook the air, the sea, the very deck on which he stood. He saw his men struggling to retie lines that had come loose from the halyard down to the boom. They'd all been through storms before, all knew what had to be done. Jackson prayed it would be enough. He had to get Grace to safety. He had to. Nothing else mattered.

Just as the thought resonated through his head, lightning razed the sky. From the corner of his eye, he saw a movement midship. He stared at the familiar shape lurching against the heaving deck, certain it was an illusion, because it couldn't be real. *It couldn't be!*

But it was.

Grace stood beside the main mast, the raised sail whipping against the sky above her. Her clothes were soaked to her skin. With a rope tied around her waist, she held her arms out to her side, balancing herself against the plunging floor.

"Grace!" He screamed her name again and again, but the roar of the wind swallowed the sound. What in sweet bleeding Jesus was she doing? His pulse racing in his throat, he shouted, "Macklin, take the wheel!"

Without hearing Mac's reply, Jackson untied the safety

rope from around his waist. Gripping the nearby balustrade, he descended the ladder to midship. He lost his balance and banged hard onto his knees. The ship bucked, sending the bow into the air with the moan of a dying animal. Jackson was knocked onto his side. Gushing water swept over him, sending him sliding out of control. He reached out, but found nothing to grab onto. *Nothing!* Ahead of him, waves of water flailed against the ship's rail, swelling, rolling over the edge in a giant waterfall. It would take him with it if he didn't stop his descent. He had to find a way to stop! He had to reach Grace!

He flung out his arms, his legs, scrambled for footing against the slick deck, but nothing helped. The tide of water shifted, filling his mouth, obscuring his sight, flipping him around and crashing him into something solid. Pain exploded in his shoulder. He turned his head, realized he'd landed against the capstan.

He heard a panicked cry, knew it had to be Grace. *Hold on, Angel, please, God, hold on!* He gripped the capstan's arm and pulled himself up, wincing against the pain. He saw her then. Her eyes wide and stark in her pale face, were locked on him. She shouted something he couldn't hear.

Jackson knew that once he let go of the capstan, he'd have only one chance to reach her. Bracing his legs against the rocking deck, he lunged for her. She headed for him as well, reaching out, latching onto his shirt just as the hull crested a wave, throwing them both toward the stern.

"Jackson!"

He caught her around the waist as they were both flung backward. They landed against the deck like dolls flung to the ground, skidding across the surface, rolling over and over before they were wrenched to a halt. Grace cried out, her nails digging into his arms. Jackson looked down, saw the rope around her waist had saved them, but the force with which they'd stopped had nearly snapped her in half. She squeezed her eyes closed, dropped her forehead against his chest.

"Grace, are you all right?" he shouted above the roar of waves and wind. "Damn it, answer me!"

She didn't utter a word. Cursing, Jackson struggled to his feet and lifted her in his arms. He staggered toward the hatchway, blind to everything around him—the buffeting wind, the slashing rain, his crew consumed by their efforts to save the ship. Nothing mattered except getting Grace below.

Once in the companionway, he hugged her against his chest to protect her as he collided into the walls. When he felt a tug on the rope, he stopped to untie it from around her waist. Hearing her sigh of relief, he hurried on, his boots sloshing through the flooded hallway, slowing him down, increasing his desperation to reach someplace safe.

"We're almost there." She didn't move, didn't speak. If she were hurt . . . He couldn't bear to even think of it.

He kicked open the door to his cabin and hurried inside. The ship careened to the left, groaning as if it would rip apart. The lamp overhead swung and nearly struck him in the temple. Pale, erratic light wavered over the walls and blackened windows. The door slammed shut, locking out the water, the worst of the pounding noise. Lowering her onto the narrow bunk bed, he pushed the wet, matted hair from her face, and swore when he saw her closed eyes and the ashen pallor of her skin.

"Look at me, Grace!" he demanded. "Look at me and tell me why the hell you did such a foolish thing!"

She didn't make the barest noise. The only sounds were of the driving rain striking the windows, the grinding battle of wood against the sea, his own ragged breathing. He turned up the lamp's wick, then ran his hands over her shoulders, her chest and ribs, feeling for any broken bones, only slightly relieved when he didn't find any. When he pressed against her waist, she sucked in a breath.

"Don't . . ." Her eyelids flew open; her pained gaze locked with his.

Gathering the hem of her gown, he pulled it up only to have her grab his wrist. "What are you doing?"

"I have to see how badly you're hurt."

"I'm fine."

"Like hell you are," he growled, forcefully removing her hand from his. Without waiting to see if she'd dare object again, he shoved her skirt up until he exposed her waist, barely registering the sodden leggings outlining her legs, her slender hips, or the telling juncture in between.

Hissing a curse from between his clenched teeth, he ran his hand over the thick red welt circling her waist. Her skin would bear an ugly bruise by morning, but since she could have suffered a broken back, he'd consider a bruise lucky.

"Were you trying to kill yourself?" He shook with the force of his fear and sudden anger. "Or just scare me half to death?"

"I'm not the one who went running across the deck without a safety rope."

"I had to take mine off to help you."

"I didn't need your help," she said, shivering.

"Can you sit up?" With his help, she struggled upright, turning her head aside to hide her grimace. But he saw it. God help him, she was hurt! He attacked the buttons running down the back of her gown, but they were small in his hands, dainty, and the more he hurried the less his fingers obeyed.

Around a strained breath, she asked, "What are you doing?"

"I have to see how badly you're hurt."

"No you don't!" She tried to twist away, but winced. "The ship needs you." As if to confirm her statement, the cabin filled with an ominous sound as the hull plunged over a wave.

The ship righted itself, then took the next swell with ease, convincing Jackson that Macklin had the vessel under control. To Grace, he said, "You should have considered that before you decided to take a stroll on deck."

"The storm's worse than I thought it would be. I had to help."

"What could you have possibly done?" he demanded. He had to relieve Mac, but he couldn't go until he knew Grace wasn't in need of medical care. He tackled the buttons once more, finding they still wouldn't cooperate.

"Jackson, I can manage. Now please leave. The crewmen—"

"This isn't the time for modesty, Angel. The sooner I'm convinced you're all right, the sooner I can return topside."

She sighed, and he felt the tension drain out of her, yet when she spoke there was a stubborn edge to her voice. "It wasn't so long ago that I was a pirate, Jackson. I haven't forgotten how to secure a ship. I can still check ropes, make sure the sails are secured, or—"

"Or get yourself killed. Bloody hell!" At the end of his patience with her dress, he gripped the side panels and jerked them apart. Tiny blue buttons popped off and flew in all directions.

"What have you done?"

"Expedited matters," he growled, though he thought he might have made a mistake. Her wet shift was nearly transparent against her creamy skin. The fabric clung to her back, the curve of her waist. The sight was innocent and erotic. He touched his fingers to her waist. She sucked in a breath.

"Nothing's broken, Jackson," she said, her voice strangled. "I'll be fine.

He knew she was right. Yet leaving her went against every protective instinct he possessed. But he had to go. Standing, he ran his hand over his wet scalp. "Wrap yourself in a blanket, Angel. I'll return as soon as I can."

"I'm sorry, Jackson." Gripping her bodice against her chest, she looked up at him, her eyes clouded with worry. "I was afraid for you. I had to make sure you were all right."

He hesitated by the door and clenched his hands into fists, knowing that if he took one step toward her, he'd never leave the cabin. "There's no need to worry about me. Nothing is going to stop me from seeing you safely to England."

Not William Mason, not a storm, not even his own blasted heart.

Her decision was made.

Balancing the *Sea Queen* blade in her hand, it surprised Grace how calm she felt, how certain, as if she'd just now opened her eyes to see that everything had fallen into place, just as it was meant to be. Watching Jackson being swept across the deck, helpless against the pull of the sea, had been her nightmare come to life. Every part of her soul had screamed that he couldn't die!

Miraculously he'd survive, but she'd come so close to losing him that, just by remembering the moment now, her heart squeezed with a wrenching pain. *What if I had lost him? How would I have gone on? How . . . ?*

She ran her thumb over the round sapphire, then the ruby and finally the emerald. One stone for each sister, she realized. Each was smooth and hard, and possessed a unique quality all its own. Was it the knife that had given her sisters their strength? She didn't know. She only knew she felt different now, in control. Resolved to set her life on a new and different path.

Unless I do something to stop it, I could still lose Jackson.

After he'd left her to see to the ship and his men, her fear of the storm had faded, vanishing altogether. She'd *known* Jackson would keep them safe, and that the *Sea Angel* would persevere once again.

Now the rolling sea, restless from its battle, pulled the vessel on a fast, easterly course. Night still wrapped around the ship, sealing it tight. Having discarded her damp clothes, she wore nothing but a woolen blanket that smelled of Jackson and the sea. Grace stared at the darkness beyond the wall of paned windows. There were no stars or moon, just a deep, dark void that felt safe, suspended, as if all time had stopped, giving her this moment to do whatever she wished.

"Or make this time whatever I want it to be," she whispered, feeling her thoughts, her body, fill with a determination she hardly recognized. But it was a determination that felt good and right.

Securing the knife in its sheath and laying it on the desk, she turned the wick on the lamp down low. With soft amber light washing the cabin in warmth, she faced the door to wait.

Chapter Twenty-one

"I'll 'ave the crew mend'n' the sheets right away, Capt'n," Macklin said, his voice weary.

"Morning will be soon enough." Holding a lantern aloft to light their way, Jackson made another pass over the forward deck, taking note of what needed to be repaired. The list was long and growing longer with every step they took. "Sleep is what everyone needs right now."

"Aye, that they do."

"Assign a skeleton crew, then send the rest to their hammocks until sunup. We'll begin repairs then."

Macklin muttered a grim curse. " 'Tis a miracle any of us are still alive. With 'alf our sails gone and the rest ripped near to shreds, the fore mast split down the middle and the 'ull tak'n' on water, 'twill take another miracle to keep us from sink'n'."

"We've faced worse, Mac, and the cracks in the hull have been sealed." Jackson scanned the destruction, the ratlines that sagged from their hooks, swaying with the breeze, the shattered rails and scarred decks. It pained him to see the *Sea Angel* bearing such wounds, but she'd survived. He'd make sure she was put to right. "At least no one was hurt."

"Praise the saints," Mac said, taking the lantern and starting off toward the helm. "I'll take first watch, Capt'n."

"That's not necessary," Jackson said, though for the past hour, ever since the storm had lifted as quickly as it had struck, he'd wanted to go below and check on Grace.

"If ye don't mind, Capt'n," Mac said with a tired smile, "I believe I'd rather be asleep when the real work begins."

Forcing a scowl that only made his first mate chuckle, Jackson headed for the hatchway leading aft. He prayed Grace was asleep. He didn't intend to wake her; he just needed to make sure she was all right. He'd promised her that he'd take her to England, and he would, though with the ship's damage, it would take them weeks longer than normal.

It doesn't matter if takes weeks or months, he thought, navigating the darkened companionway. *Even if it took years to reach England, it would be too soon.* Because the moment he docked in London, Grace would step off the ship and out of his life for good.

At the door to his cabin, he slowly lifted the latch, taking care not to make any noise. Opening the door just as quietly, he froze, wondering if perhaps he'd fallen asleep on deck and the scene before him was part of a dream. Only the sharp hardening of his body told him he was awake and this was no illusion.

Grace stood near the windows, watching the black ocean beyond. She'd wrapped the blanket from his bed around her body as he'd told her to, but he'd never expected to find her wearing *just* the blanket, as she was now. His heart pounded against his chest, so loudly he was amazed she didn't hear it and turn around.

She'd braided her hair, pulling the length over her shoulder, the blonde shade paling in comparison to her skin, which glowed like velvety gold in the soft light. Holding the ends of the thick wool blanket in front of her, she let the rest dip low, exposing her bare slender back, revealing a hint of the indentation at her waist, the curve of her hips.

Blood rushed through his brain and filled his ears with a heated roar. He didn't trust himself to move, to speak. She was everything he could ever want in a woman. More than he'd ever thought to have. She was a vibrant, glittering star, shining bright, tempting him to reach out and pluck her from the heavens.

But I'm not the kind of man she needs! Except for love, what have I to offer her? A jaded life? An early and perhaps violent death? He'd known the truth all along, but this time, admitting it felt like having the best part of him ripped from his chest.

But how can I walk away from her? He didn't know. God help him, he didn't know.

He must have made a noise because she turned, her expression inscrutable, as if she knew some great secret that eluded everyone else.

"I . . . I thought you'd be asleep," he stammered like a smitten schoolboy. But seeing Grace this way, more beautiful then he'd dared imagine, he felt like an untried lad.

"The crew?" she asked, ignoring his statement. "Was anyone hurt?"

"Scratches and bruises, but nothing severe." He expected her to chastise him, order him to leave the room while she scrambled for clothes, but she merely nodded, her calm gaze staying on him, the strength in her crystal-blue eyes seeming to lure him inside the room.

"Is there something you needed?" she asked.

Why didn't she rail at him? Blush with embarrassment

instead of standing like a statue of Aphrodite tempting him to test his fate. He should leave, an inner voice warned, return to his hammock with the other crewmen. But sweet Jesus, how could he possibly turn away from her when he wanted her so much?

Silence hovered between them—she, quietly waiting, he, forcing the desire tightening his skin and heating his blood under control. As much as he wanted to touch her, taste her creamy skin, he knew it would be a mistake. "I wanted to make sure you were all right. Your waist—"

"I'm fine." Opening the gray blanket out to her sides, she dropped it to the floor. "But perhaps you should take a look to make sure." She watched him, as if unconcerned that she stood before him naked and glorious, offering to him what he'd only imagined.

He couldn't say a word, could hardly think. His breath lodged in his chest. His gaze left her face, moved over the white column of her throat to her breasts. They were full and round, perfectly shaped in the whispering light, the rosy tips pebbling as if feeling his gaze, or the imaginary touch of his fingers.

He clenched his hands at his sides and drew a breath, felt a tremor run through his limbs. Felt himself swell against the seams of his pants. His arms and legs, his chest, his entire mind filled with the taste of desire, the potency so strong and raw, so overwhelming, he thought he might jump out of his skin if he didn't hold her, fill his hands with her.

He looked past her flat stomach—the flesh at her waist that had begun to bruise—the curve of her hips to the golden triangle in between. Jackson trembled on the edge of control. He tried to think of a reason why Grace would tempt him this way. She held manners and proper behavior above all else. Didn't she know what this would do to him?

How it would end? Perhaps she didn't. Or perhaps she'd hit her head during the storm and was out of her mind?

A quick glance at her face and he knew, *knew* without a doubt that she understood where this would lead.

He stepped all the way into the cabin and closed the door behind him, but didn't go to her as his body demanded. Despite the confidence he saw in her sky-blue eyes, the emphatic set of her shoulders, she was an innocent, and because she was, he had to ask, "Are you sure you know what you're doing, Angel?"

"I'm sure." She angled her chin and her eyes glimmered with heat. "I know what I want."

"You wanted William Mason."

She shook her head. "Not the way I've always wanted you."

The control Jackson had barely been holding onto shattered into dust. A growl of need rumbled from his chest. He closed the distance between them and slid his arms around her waist. He filled his hands with the curve of her back, sweeping lower to her buttocks, molding her to him, clenching his jaw as pleasure pooled heavy in his loins. He ran his palms up to her shoulders, then down her sides, skimming the full swells of her breasts. She was so smooth and soft in his hands he wanted to touch all of her all at once.

Her arms circled his neck. "Kiss me, Jackson, the way you did at the inn."

The instant she issued the demand, their lips met in a claiming duel. Fire leaped through his veins. The taste of Grace, of honey and salty sea air, filled his senses. Where she'd been innocent the first time they'd kissed, now she matched his needs, molding her lips to his, seeking, taking, searching as if she couldn't get enough.

Lifting her in his arms, he carried her to the narrow bed, lowering her, intending to join her. To finally be able to lay with Grace, feel her beside him, exposed and at the mercy of his touch—he didn't know if he'd survive.

Only she planted her hands against his shoulders and pushed him back so he stood above her. Then she stated a single word that nearly robbed him of breath. "No."

"No?"

"That's right. No."

"Angel, if this is some kind of game—"

"It's no game, Jackson." Shifting onto her knees, she gripped the tail of his shirt and drew it up over his head, tossing the damp garment aside. She stared at his chest, touching every inch of him with her eyes. Reverently, she trailed the tips of her fingers over his collarbone, down the center of his chest, detouring to circle one hardened brown nipple, then the other.

Jackson held his breath and fisted his hands to keep from moving, or filling his palms with her breasts the way he wanted to. His stomach muscles convulsed and his hardened shaft pulsed with the need to be inside her, *deep* inside. But he waited. If his angel wanted to touch him, then he would stand here and let her . . . even if it killed him.

"Do you remember the day you were working on deck with your shirt off?"

He nodded, not trusting his voice enough to speak.

"Ever since that day I've tried to imagine what you would feel like." Curling her fingers, she ran her nails down his chest, pulling a shudder from him in response.

"And I've tried to imagine what you would taste like." She pressed her mouth to his skin, close to his nipple, then swirled her tongue over his flesh.

He hissed a breath through gritted teeth, trembling as desire burned hot through his limbs. *Sweet Jesus, help him!*

"Jackson," she said, her voice breaking, "even though I was engaged to someone else, I wanted you. But I was—"

"Could you do me a favor, Angel," he interrupted, "and find it within yourself to want the rest of me, as well?"

Grace smiled, her knees growing weak. Passion heated Jackson's whiskey-brown eyes, tiger eyes, turning them dark and wild, fervent with a hunger that exceeded her own. Any doubt about her decision to make love to him, any lingering embarrassment over her scandalous behavior of standing naked before him, offering herself—terrified he would reject her—dissolved like morning mist. She'd wanted him for most her life, yet she'd always been too afraid to risk her heart for him—too afraid of the pain she'd suffer if she ever lost him.

But she wasn't afraid now. She'd gladly risk her heart, her soul, her very life, just to have this one night with him.

Running her palms down the curve of his chest, his muscled stomach—smiling when he flexed against her touch—she untied the waistband of his pants. Keeping her gaze locked with his, feeling the beat of her heart in her throat, she pushed his pants down and let her senses absorb the feel of his lean hips, the coarse hair that dusted his long legs and tickled her palms. She couldn't believe her boldness; what must he think of her? She'd never been one to take control, but she didn't feel like her old self. She felt strong and willful, determined to take what she wanted.

And she wanted Jackson!

His skin was hot, singeing her fingers, urging her to explore more of him, touch what she'd only dreamed of. *Do it, Grace!*

Drawing on a well of courage, she slid her hand around his shaft. Jackson tensed, sucking air into his lungs. He gripped her upper arms as if he meant to push her away. Dropping his head back, his jaw clamped tight until she thought his teeth might crack. A visible tremor shook through him, but otherwise he didn't move, didn't tell her to stop. Not that she could.

She slid her fingers along his length, feeling him pulse against her grip, hardly believing she dared anything so bold. But now that she'd started, she couldn't quit. He was smooth and firm, and so hard with a mysterious kind of power that she trembled, igniting a desire inside her that heated her thighs, tightened her nerves, stretched her senses beyond their limits.

She found the tip of him, circled it with her thumb, gasping when Jackson hauled her up with a growled, "Enough!"

"But—"

"So help me, Angel, if you don't stop, this'll be over too bloody soon."

"Then tell me what I should do." She ran her hands up his sides, felt his muscles flex and constrict. His hair, streaked gold in the soft light, framed the fire in his eyes. There was an ungoverned fury within him, a whirlpool of passion that promised she would be a different woman—his woman—by the time the sun kissed the horizon.

Releasing her, Jackson removed his boots and pants and tossed them aside. Grace lay back on the bed, expecting him to join her, but he turned away and crossed to the desk.

Alarmed, she asked, "What are you doing?"

He opened one windowpane after another, allowing the cool predawn breeze to wash through the room. The flame in the lantern flickered, then steadied. The swirling air grazed her skin with a feathery touch, soft, erotic, teasing. The way she was sure Jackson's hands would feel if only he would join her!

Yet, he stayed by the windows as if some invisible bond held him back. His eyes became twin pools of gold set ablaze; his hands clenched and flexed, clenched and flexed. His gaze touched every part of her body, her breasts, her stomach, her legs, lingering at the junction between her thighs. He inhaled a deep breath, expanding his chest, sending muscles rippling and tightening along his body. He seemed on the verge of losing control, as if the wildness in him was on the brink of escape.

She didn't know what held him back, or why he bothered. This is what they both wanted. And as far as she was concerned, the time for waiting had come to an end.

"Jackson," she said, rising from the bed and crossing to him. "Would you prefer to make love by the windows?"

He stared down at her, breathing deep, seeming to fight some inner demon. "I don't want to hurt you."

"You won't."

"You deserve to be treated like a lady, taken slowly, so you don't become frightened."

"I'm not frightened, Jackson. Of you or anything you might do to me."

"You don't understand," he growled, gritting his teeth. He wrapped the end of her braid around his fist, drawing her closer and closer, until the tips of her breasts grazed his chest. In a voice that sounded rough and filled with pain, he said, "I've never wanted anything the way I want you."

"Oh, Jackson." Wrapping her arms around his neck, she pressed her body flush to his and gasped at the shock of feeling so much of him at once. She kissed him, opening her mouth to accept the force of his tongue.

He held her in a vise, deepening the kiss, turning it nearly savage. The fierce relentlessness of his passion should have frightened her, but it didn't. Instead, it had her straining against him, reaching for more of him to touch and hold. She wanted all of him—against her, around her, *inside* her. Inside, where the ache was building and twisting, gathering like a storm ready to strike.

Jackson broke the kiss to work his way down her neck, reaching her chest, kissing first one breast then the other, laving the nipples with his tongue until a hoarse moan rose from her throat and she thought she would go insane. He had to stop, or do something more, but she couldn't endure the teasing any longer.

"No, Jackson, please. No more."

"You want me to stop?" he asked, trailing his fingers down her thighs, then back up again.

"I want . . . I want . . ." She stared into his eyes and thought she could see inside him. "I want you to make love to me."

"You don't deserve to be rushed. I want to take my time with you, show you how it's meant to be."

She shook her head. Taking his hand, she led him back to the bed. "I'm not the fragile girl you once knew, or the young lady who's worried about her reputation."

"Are you sure?" he asked, though he didn't protest when he forced him to lie back on the mattress. When he circled her waist with his hands and lifted her so she straddled his hips, she gave a little yelp of surprise.

In a strained voice, he said, "You might regret this in the morning."

Grace held her breath, too shocked to speak. His swollen groin was pressed against her core, sending wave after wave of tingling desire spiraling through her stomach and up her chest. She couldn't suppress the shudder that gripped her, too overwhelmed that such a sensation existed.

Tightening her legs and rocking against him, she looked into his honey-brown eyes. "The only thing I regret is how much of a fool I've been. Now, make love to me Jackson Brodie."

She didn't give him a chance to respond, but leaned over and kissed him, using her tongue, her lips, setting a rhythm to match the rocking of their bodies. Her pulse doubled, tripled, her blood roared through her ears. Her skin felt tight, her limbs trembling and tense, her heart and soul screaming with demands she wasn't sure how to meet.

To her relief, Jackson knew just what to do. With a growl, he flipped her onto her back. Spreading her legs with his knee, he knelt between them. His hands were planted at the sides of her head, his arms shaking with strain.

Holding his gaze, she whispered, "Are you going to make love to me now, Jackson?"

"Aye, Angel. I'm going to make you mine."

She felt the tip of him at her core, pushing, stretching, turning the desire that had pulsed through her veins into something more. Something wild and fierce and breathtakingly surreal. He filled her until he reached her barrier. As he withdrew, she tensed, expecting the pain she'd heard about.

He thrust into her, breaking through. She felt a rip, a twinge of pain, but he thrust into her again, then again, shocking her with sensations that were too alive to ignore, too overwhelming to fight.

She felt she was set on a tide, being swept into its strength, helpless to do anything but join the storm, become a part of it, help it unleash its power. She locked her legs around his hips and gripped his arms, reached up and took his mouth in a kiss that turned into a mating of its own.

"Grace . . . I can't . . ." He thrust again, carrying her pleasure with him, turning it hot and frantic.

She arched her back, gasping as he continued to love her, pushing her higher and higher, making her feel things she hadn't thought possible. *There! Oh, God. . . .* Sensations ripped through her, tearing her thoughts apart, shredding her nerves into a thousand pieces. The wave that had

her hurtling though an unknown realm crested again and
again and again.

"Jackson . . . !" She called his name, wanted to laugh
and cry all at once. She felt full, flooded with light, with
life, with more love that she thought she could ever feel.

He tensed and threw his head back. A growl rumbled
up from his throat as he strained and strained. She felt
him pulse inside her, deep against her core. The corded
muscles along his arms and chest, his neck, were strained,
his jaw clenched as he spilled his seed.

She held him to her, held on . . . with no intention of
letting him go.

Chapter Twenty-two

Dawn had long since pierced the turbulent sky. Billowing gunmetal clouds, still heavy with the threat of rain, rolled above the sea, rumbling with an occasional warning. Yet, the clean, salty scent of the air, the steady rocking of the ship, told Jackson the worst had passed. Grayish light, streaked with hues of lavender and blue, filled the cabin, urging him to close his eyes and sleep.

But he couldn't. It was past time he relieved Macklin at the helm. The long list of repairs awaited him. Jackson didn't move. Instead, he ran his fingers through the tangle of blonde hair spread across his pillow, reveling in its softness, resisting the temptation to bury his face in its length and inhale its scent . . . *her* scent.

He didn't want to wake her, nor did he want to leave her. He wanted to touch her, make love to her, as they had for the past few hours, until exhaustion had finally overcome her and she'd fallen asleep. With Grace curled against him as she was now, he could easily ignore his duties, forget his ship was torn to pieces. None of that mattered.

Feeling the way her soft skin molded to his, hearing the small wisps of her breath, warm against his chest, being able to look at her, from her relaxed features to her small waist to the tips of her toes, those were the things that mattered to him now. Only one thing kept the moment from being perfect and letting him feel the contentment that hovered within reach.

The course of their lives hadn't changed. He had to take her to England. What would happen then? Would she say good-bye and leave him? Would he let her? Would she want to stay on board the *Sea Angel* with him? And if so, could he allow that, knowing she would be settling for a lifestyle she didn't want? Eventually growing to resent him, hate him?

Closing his eyes, he pressed his lips to her temple and felt something rip inside his chest. It would be better to lose her than have her grow to hate him. He loved her too much to have it otherwise. *He loved her.* The realization, the profound strength of those words struck a cord deep in his heart, making him admit that he'd always loved Grace, just as he'd always known they were destined for different paths.

He wondered if fate was testing him, laughing at him?

Not until she stirred did he realize he was squeezing her. Loosing his grip, he ran his palm over her back. Feeling the graceful curve of her spine caused a tingling twist in his groin. He drew in a breath, let his hand roam over her hip and buttock, then her leg, which was threaded between his own. God, she was beautiful. Slender and lithe, her skin pale as cream against his rough, tanned frame. The desire in him turned into a tremor of need. He didn't care what time it was, or that she might be tired. He wanted her, *had* to have her.

Cupping her breast, he squeezed the fullness. Soft and lush, so incredibly perfect. She arched against him. A moan escaped the back of her throat, warmed the side of his neck. Her eyes remained closed as she drew her foot up the inside of his leg. Tendrils of heat ran through his blood, coiling tighter as they reached his shaft, making it swell and harden.

"Jackson . . ." She sighed with a sleepy smile.

"Aye, Angel, I'm going to make love to you."

Gathering her beneath him, he found her core and entered her with one long, soul-shattering stroke. She closed around him, holding him tight, taking him deeper and deeper until he swore they had become one.

He didn't know what would happen once they reached England, but he had her now. God help him, for *now* she was his.

Chapter Twenty-three

"By using the canvas that was too shredded to repair, we sealed the cracks in the hull. I've half a dozen men sewing new sails for the fore and aft masts. The main mast split down the middle during the storm." Jackson raised his arm and pointed to where a wicked gash seared the length of the solid oak beam. "Without our main sails, the trip to England will take several weeks longer."

"Weeks?" Grace asked, biting down on her lower lip.

"I'm afraid so."

From their position high on the aft deck, she scanned the shattered railings, the spoked arms of the capstan that had snapped in two, the decking that had cracked under the pressure of the rioting sea. She sighed and pressed her lips together to hide her smile.

She couldn't be more pleased.

While it pained her to see the *Sea Angel* so badly beaten, she didn't regret the additional time she'd have to spend with Jackson, time she needed in order to form a plan so they could stay together. During the two days since they'd first made love, and the incredible nights that had followed, she'd thought of one idea after another, only to discard each and every one.

Though she loved Jackson with all her heart, she couldn't spend the rest of her life on a ship. Nor could she ask Jackson to give up the sea to live on land. There had to be a happy medium though; if only she could find one. She hadn't shared her thoughts with him, however. He was still determined to return her to England—the stubborn man. No, when she finally approached him with her idea of their staying together, she wanted a plan in place that he wouldn't be able to argue apart.

"Is there anything I can do to help with repairs?" she asked.

Jackson slid his arm around her waist and drew her into the curve of his hard body. "How are you with a needle and thread?"

"Pitiful, unless it's a handkerchief you want embroidered," she said, sounding breathless. Heavens, would she ever get used to the feel of his body against hers? She thought it unlikely. He was too overwhelming, too vital, and she loved him too much to ever become "used" to him.

Chuckling, he kissed her brow. "So that's what you learned at your fancy girls' school? Sewing initials and fleur-de-lis on linens?"

"Among other things."

"Anything useful?" he teased. "Cook hurt his leg during the storm. Perhaps I should send you to the galley to help him. Can you cook?"

"I'm afraid my talents lie elsewhere."

"And where might that be, Angel?"

She looked deep into his eyes, silently telling him what newly acquired skill she possessed that she wanted to use right now, while the morning sun glowed bright over the deck, while her body still held a pleasant ache from their lovemaking not an hour before.

"I have a ship to see to," he admonished, though the light in his eyes told her how tempted he was to whisk her to his cabin below. Emitting a growl of frustration, he muttered, "What am I going to do with you, Angel?"

You're going to keep me with you, that's what. Somehow . . . She felt a nervous twist in her stomach, fear that she was deluding herself, repeating a mistake, dreaming a future that couldn't be realized.

"Pardon me, Capt'n," Macklin said, coming up beside them. "The mizzen sails are ready to be raised. That'll give us a little dance and 'elp us on our way."

"Excellent. And the fore sails? When can we expect those to be ready?"

"By the end of the day, if the men's fingers don't give out before then."

"Bring the sheets home then, Mac." Frowning at the horizon, which rolled like a sea of glittering sapphires, he added, "We've been adrift for too long as it is."

"Are you worried?" she asked, feeling the return of the apprehension that was all too familiar, and hating it. She'd had enough of worrying and being afraid. She and Jackson deserved to be happy.

"No, just anxious to be on our way." When the smile he gave her didn't reach his eyes, she was certain that something was troubling him. "Besides, I don't like seeing my ship in such ruin."

"Your ship? Don't you mean *my* ship?" She arched a brow at him, determined to lighten his mood. "Jo gave her to me, remember? As I recall, you took her from Dunmore without *my* permission."

His gaze slid over her body, igniting tingles along her skin. Her breasts strained against her forest-green gown—

the only gown she had left. She'd yet to find all the buttons to the blue one. Her pulse warmed against the base of her throat. The languid feeling in her limbs became edgy and tense; the once-sated need inside her now rising with renewed intent. What she wouldn't do to have him alone. She wanted every minute she could steal. She didn't want to share him, but keep him for herself, spend the hours learning everything there was to know about him. How he felt and tasted, what made his eyes glaze with pleasure, what made him shout her name.

Grace shook her head, hardly believing how quickly her thoughts could turn lustful, scandalous. Good heavens, she was standing on a battered deck, surrounded by a wayward crew! A crew who undoubtedly had guessed what she and Jackson had been doing in his cabin for the last two days!

"Perhaps you'd like to captain her, then?" he asked, bringing her back to the moment.

"Hmm, no," she said, willing her flushed cheeks to cool. "I think I'll leave that to you for now."

"That's very wise of you. Come along, then. I need to check on the repairs Dillon is making."

She followed, having already seen the damage the cannons had caused below deck. She shuddered to even think about how lucky they were that no one had been killed, or that the hull hadn't been ripped to shreds, ensuring them all a quick death at the bottom of the sea.

Several safety ropes had come loose during the storm, sending the heavy carriages and iron barrels crashing into the walls and into other cannons, knocking them free. Two cannons had flown out through locked gun ports, splitting the strakes open wide. The result had been two gashed holes, the wood splintered and gagged as if a sea monster had taken a bite from the hull.

Just as they reached the hatchway leading to the lower decks, they heard, "Sail ho! Captain, sail ho!"

Grace froze, not having to turn to know that Jackson had tensed, his attention focused on the horizon along the stern. She could feel the sudden strain in the air, hear the unasked questions. Every crewman on board had stopped their work to wait for the orders that were sure to come.

"Can you make her out?" Jackson asked the sailor.

Holding the telescope to his eye for a moment, the man shook his head. "She has four masts, all full of sail, Captain, but I can't see her name. She's not like any ship I've ever seen."

"Her direction?"

"She's hauled her wind, and is gaining on us fast. We'll meet her by nightfall, if not sooner."

Grace looked at Jackson, saw his jaw harden. "Go below, Grace."

She ignored him and followed him instead to the helm.

"Mac!" Jackson shouted. "I need the aft sails now!"

"Aye, Capt'n," the first mate answered. "If I 'ave tae 'old the sheets up with my teeth, we'll 'ave sails!"

"Once they're up, I want all hands to clear the decks."

"Jackson—" she said.

"Check the braces, Mac. I don't want so much as a rope pulling free should we need to take a stand."

"Jackson—"

"Grace, I told you to go below."

"It's just a ship. It doesn't mean trouble," she said, though hearing the words, she knew how absurd they were. At sea, every ship you encountered posed a potential threat.

He stopped to stare down at her. She recognized the fixed purpose in his eyes, as if he'd withdrawn to prepare himself for battle, making plans to attack and seize, perhaps raid.

"You think I'm overreacting?"

She opened her mouth to answer, only to close it again.

She knew he would do whatever he had to to protect the ship and her crew. She shouldn't expect anything less.

He grazed his thumb along her jaw, then pressed a kiss to her brow. "Humor me, Angel, and go below where I'll know you'll be safe."

She nodded and watched him leave, calling out orders and retrieving ropes that littered the deck. His sandy blond hair was loose about his shoulders, framing his jaw, emphasizing the stark determination in his eyes. A mixture of emotions washed through her, tightening her chest, but she knew each feeling by name, and knew that each one had been inspired by Jackson. Pride, awe, respect, fear. But mostly, she felt love. So much love, it hurt to hold it all in.

Ducking through the hatchway, she descended the ladder, then hurried down the companionway toward the captain's cabin. Once inside with the door closed, shutting out the chaotic noise from above, she stood before the wall of windows. Inhaling one breath after another, she tried to slow her racing heart, ease the sound of her breath that grated against her lungs.

Everything would be fine. Jackson would see that they changed course and moved out of harm's way. *Except the* Sea Angel *was without half her sails,* a worried voice whispered from the back of her mind. The pumps were still struggling to empty the hull of water. And if they were forced to engage in a battle, how would they fare? Most of the cannons were crippled.

But it wouldn't come to that, she swore. She and Jackson hadn't come this far to lose everything now.

So she stood and waited, watching the glittering horizon, the faint white dots in the distance that were sails growing larger and larger and larger.

* * *

"The decks are clear, and the men are armed with pistols and swords. Everything that can be done, 'as been done, God 'elp us."

"The cannons?" Jackson asked his first mate.

"Those that could be rigged into use are manned and ready," Mac assured him. "We've fourteen in all. Two swivels forward and aft. The rest are fill'n' the gun ports, shot and cartridges at 'and."

Jackson nodded, confident Dillon had done everything within his power to prepare the men and weapons below. Between the brine of the sea and the sweat of anxious men, he could smell the telling whiffs of smoke from the lit linstocks, confirming the stout ship was prepared for battle . . . a battle Jackson prayed would never come.

Grace had said that it was only a ship that trailed them. But any ship, even one manned by honest sailors, could turn hostile when they crossed a wounded vessel. Easy prey wasn't to be passed upon, not when every sailor on the victorious ship shared in the spoils. And considering Jackson had ordered a course change three times, and each time the other ship had matched their heading, he doubted the captain's intentions were honorable.

No, they were being pursued. The question was, why? And by whom? Pirates? A British warship? A Spanish galleon?

Jackson climbed the ladder to the aft deck, nodded to the helmsman at the wheel and made his way astern. He passed two sailors who were taking bets as to how long it would be before the other vessel closed on them, and how long it would take the *Sea Angel* to sink her.

The knot that had formed in Jackson's gut when the ship had first been spotted gave a rending twist. With half his sails gone, he couldn't make a run for it. But turning to confront the vessel held little appeal. The *Sea Angel*'s rudder was sluggish; the better part of her armament reduced to scraps. Considering the agility of the other ship, and its speed, the *Sea Angel* would be rendered to kindling within minutes.

But he refused to continue running like a mouse being chased to ground. That wouldn't keep Grace, his men or the *Sea Angel* safe. While sailing with Morgan, when their ship had been named the *Sea Queen*, he'd learned how to beat the odds, use stealth and wit instead of the sword or cannon. Would any of those tricks work for him now? Perhaps, he thought, feeling a grim smile curve his mouth. Perhaps.

Turning to the helmsman, Jackson ordered, "Hard about Mr. Kent! All hands, brace the yards and haul aft the sheets!"

Macklin appeared at his side. "You've got a plan, I take it?"

"That I do."

"Care tae tell me about it?"

Speaking to both Mac and the helmsman, he told them, "Keep us directly windward. I want the sails full, and all the speed you can squeeze out of her."

"And then what, Capt'n?" Mac asked as he nervously stroked his beard.

"I'm going to set a trap."

"You want me to do what?" Grace asked, certain she hadn't heard right.

The crewman, Smith was his name, nodded, his dirt-smudged face growing red with exasperation. Forcing her to take the pile of dark clothing that looked identical to the black pants and loose-fitting shirt he wore, he said,

"That's what the Capt'n ordered, miss. And ye're not tae leave yer quarters."

"Why not?" she asked, though she needn't have bothered. In her heart, deep where she kept her fears hidden away, she knew the answer. Knew without any doubt what Jackson planned to do.

" 'E didn't feel obliged tae tell me, miss." Backing out of the room, he added, " 'E just said that ye're tae wear these clothes and stay 'idden away, just in case. . . ."

The door closed behind the little man before she had a chance to ask in case of what. She returned to the window, where all morning she'd watched the other vessel approach, breaking through the ocean's swells like an avenging shark, following their every move. Even if the *Sea Angel* had been whole and healthy she wouldn't have been a match for the ship bearing down on them now. Despite the heat sealing the cabin, Grace shivered with a sudden chill. What did they want? *Why won't they let us go our own way?*

Evidently Jackson had wondered the same thing, because ten minutes ago the *Sea Angel* had changed course once again, this time making a one-hundred-and-eighty degree turn to starboard—putting them directly in the path of the oncoming ship.

"We aren't running any more," she murmured. She looked away from the empty sea to the black clothing she clutched in her hands. Her disguise. As if a shadow had moved into the room, she felt a grim finality weigh her limbs down like lead. She was back where it had all begun.

A painful smile pulled at her lips as she whispered, "It seems I'm to become a pirate once more."

For the first time in his life, Jackson feared the sea might betray him. From one moment to the next, the wind shifted, stirring the ocean, sending swells billowing over the *Sea Angel*'s bow. The sails flattened, losing the pull of the breeze. With a groan, the ship was tossed over the waves, their speed slowing until they barely managed to hold their place.

"Balance the mizzen!" Jackson shouted to the crew. "Mr. Kent, keep us in the wind."

"She's not listen'n' tae me, Capt'n!" the helmsman complained, putting his weight behind the wheel.

"Bloody hell." All around him, his men were squaring the yards, securing the clew lines, anything they could to gain control of the ship. But nothing helped. He'd planned to approach the other ship and ask for assistance. By showing only a skeleton crew, the other captain would reveal his true intent, either by offering them aid or by threatening to blow them from the water. Not that Jackson would let the latter come about.

Once the other crew boarded the *Sea Angel,* Jackson's men, all dressed like sea demons, would be on hand to subdue them. In the past, he'd seen sailors tremble in fear and surrender when well-trained pirates swarmed their decks. If that failed, he would signal Dillon to fire the cannons before the other captain knew what happened.

Clenching his jaw, Jackson cursed the elements. "We'll have to wait for them to reach us instead. By now they must know we're badly damaged."

"Ye want tae reef the sails, Capt'n?" Macklin asked.

Jackson considered lowering the sails. It would help stabilize the ship, but then he decided against it. "There's no sense being completely at their mercy. I want to be able to move should the need arise."

"Capt'n," a crewman shouted from his perch atop the fore topcastle. "I can make out 'er name. She be the *Triumph.*"

Jackson frowned. He'd heard the name before, but

couldn't remember where or why. Retrieving his spyglass, he studied the vessel's sleek lines, the four towering masts, all full of gleaming white sails. She was narrow of hull, slicing through the surf like a sword cleaving air. She was unlike anything he'd ever seen.

Then a memory surfaced, and with it a voice he thought he'd never have to hear again. *"I'd welcome your opinion on my newest sloop, the* Triumph, *"William Mason had said with an arrogant smile. "She's a beauty if I do say so myself. Nothing like her, or as fast, on the seas."*

"Bloody hell," Jackson swore. "Sweet bloody hell!"

Chapter Twenty-four

"Is something wrong?"

Spinning around to find Grace behind him, thoughts of Mason were momentarily swept to the back of his mind. Jackson had told Smith to give her the pirate's garb with the express order to wear them, but he hadn't actually thought she would.

Now all he wanted to do was dress her in her one remaining gown and hide her in the darkest, safest corner he could find.

She looked so different from the woman he'd seen a few hours ago. He hardly recognized her. With her white-gold hair in a single braid down her back, her cheeks were more prominent, the set of her chin more stubborn and resolute. Even her eyes seemed clearer, shimmering with strength. The black shirt with the strings tied at her throat, the long sleeves rolled up to her elbows, and the pitch-colored, snug-fitting pants had transformed her from an incredible lady to a tenacious pirate. The ease in which she wore the *Sea Queen* dagger sheathed at her side made the transformation complete.

"You're staring, Jackson." A slight smile tweaked her lips before she frowned. Steadying herself against the ship's sway, she asked, "What's wrong?"

Recovering from his surprise, he realized that she might look every bit as fearless as her sisters had when captaining the ship, but the image was an illusion. Grace didn't have the heart for roving or setting traps.

"Didn't Smith tell you to stay below?" He took her arm to guide her to the hatchway.

Pulling free, she faced him. "He did."

"Then for God's sake, Angel, return there now."

She inclined her head, indicating the ship barreling down on them. "Do you know them?"

"Aye," he growled. "And so do you."

She arched a brow in a silent question, making it clear she wasn't about to leave.

With no time to soften the truth, he ground out, "It's Mason."

The healthy glow in her cheeks paled. "That's impossible."

"Do you recall Mason asking me to view his newest sloop?" Leading her to the railing, he said, "Well, there it is."

Her hand clutched the dagger at her hip. "Do you think William knows who it is he's chasing?"

Jackson didn't want to frighten her, but lying wouldn't help either of them. "I have no doubt he knows exactly who's on this ship."

"Sweet heavens. What are we going to do?"

"We're going to play a game of hide and seek."

She rounded on him. "He almost killed you, Jackson. Our pirate tricks won't work with him. He's too cunning, too . . ." She struggled to find the right word, then settled on, ". . . heartless."

"Considering the *Sea Angel*'s wretched condition, I'm afraid using one of our tricks is our only option." Stroking his thumb over her pale cheek, wishing he could kiss the fear from her eyes, he added, "I don't know why he's after us, Grace. Maybe he wants you back, or perhaps he wants revenge. By revealing that he's a traitor, we ruined the life he's built in the Colonies. Whatever the reason, and whatever his intent, I'm not going to stand by and let him win."

A wave slammed against the hull, suddenly pitching the *Sea Angel*'s bow into the air. Jackson caught Grace as she stumbled backward. As the ship settled to the sound of Mr. Kent cursing the rudder, Jackson held her to him. He ran his hand over her back, wanting to soothe the trembling he felt in her limbs. But he didn't have time. They had half an hour, maybe less, before the *Triumph* moved within firing range, and he had to have everything in place in case Mason tried to sink their ship before he bothered to ask questions.

"Go below, Angel." He expected her to argue, or plead for him to find another way. He wondered when her eyes would fill with tears. But none of that happened.

She straightened and pressed her palm to his chest, directly over his heart. "Tell me what I can do."

Relieved, he gave her a quick kiss. "Wait for me. When it's all over, I'll come for you."

She smiled, a sad, tolerant lift of her lush mouth. "I'm not going to hide."

Hearing the stubbornness in her voice, he told her, "You're not going to remain on deck where Mason might spot you."

"I'm not afraid of him."

"Damn it, Grace, it's too dangerous. And I don't have time to argue."

"Then don't. Just tell me what I can do . . . *besides* going below."

He swore under his breath, tempted to throw her over his shoulder, cart her to his cabin and lock her in. But from the determined set of her chin, the anger beginning to override the initial fear in her eyes, he thought she'd probably find a way to defy him. Rather than risk that, he decided to give her a duty that would hopefully keep her out of harm's way.

"All right." Seeing her relieved smile, he warned, "I wouldn't be so pleased if I were you. You can help Cook. He's never cared for the job of ship's surgeon. Nor has he much talent for the task."

She went paler still, but she didn't object as he thought—prayed—she might. Taking his hand in hers, she brought it to her lips and kissed it. "Promise me you'll take care."

"I promise."

"I'll see you again when it's over."

He nodded, then watched her descend the ladder and head for the hatchway, where Cook had already set up a makeshift hospital in the crew's quarters. A strange foreboding settled over Jackson, like the shadow of a storm. He tried to shake off the feeling, tell himself it was nothing more than anger at having to face Mason again, but it didn't work.

The intangible fear remained, warning that this time he wouldn't be able to save Grace, because he wouldn't live long enough to see her again. He clenched his fist against the impulse to go after her. He should have told her how much he loved her. Damn it, he should have told her.

Now it was too late.

Chapter Twenty-five

The first shot rattled the sky like thunder.

The deck vibrated; the hairs at Jackson's neck stood on end. Cursing, he ran to midship, the order to return fire nearly rolling off his tongue, but the volley fell wide of the stern and splashed harmlessly into the sea. He slowed, narrowing his gaze on the *Triumph*, knowing he'd been given a warning.

Beneath the fading echoes of cannon fire, the *Triumph*'s towering hull slid past the *Sea Angel* like a falcon circling a wounded dove. No more than three hundred yards separated them, an easy range for the other vessel's cannons. So why didn't they fire? Then he heard the shout from the other ship.

"Stand down your weapons and prepare to be boarded!"

"The bloody hell I will," Jackson swore.

Iron guns lined the *Triumph*'s belly three rows deep. Men hurried over the gleaming decks, scurrying up the ratlines to adjust the sails. More stood ready with cutlasses in hand or muskets cocked and shouldered. Raising his spyglass, Jackson had no trouble spotting Mason. Standing beside the helm, dressed in a royal-blue overcoat of costly velvet and cream pants that were pressed with a fine seam, his hair neatly done in a queue, he appeared as arrogant and contemptuous as ever. He said something to the man beside him, who repeated the demand for them to prepare to be boarded.

"What's the order, Capt'n?" Mac asked.

"Our plan hasn't changed. Except I want you to drop anchor and lower the aft sails. If they want to board us, they'll have to come over in a skiff. The seas are too rough to risk drawing the ships together with grappling lines."

"I'll pass the word that noth'n' 'as changed. The men will be glad tae hear it. Dillon most of all. 'E says it's been too long since 'e's put 'is pets tae use."

"The day's far from over. He may still have a chance yet." Jackson looked through the spyglass once more. "Tell their captain we'll be glad to have them come aboard."

"Aye, sir."

Yet after the response was given, the *Triumph* made no effort to back her sails and stop, but continued to stalk the *Sea Angel*, her cannons never leaving firing range. Which meant what? Jackson wondered. What were they up to?

Anticipation pricked his skin like hot ice, urging him to act. Did Mason want the ship and crew, or just Grace? Or did he want them all to sink into a silent death? Jackson wished he knew. The man toyed with them, just as he'd toyed with the rebels who'd trusted him to help.

As his frustration grew and control of his temper shrank, Jackson decided to end the wait and order Dillon to unleash his pets. "All hands, prepare—"

At that moment the *Triumph* dropped anchor and came to a relative stop. A skiff was brought around and four crewmen scaled down the ladder. Within minutes they reached the *Sea Angel*, but only one man came aboard.

Where Jackson had expected Mason, or at least the captain, this man was nothing more than a carpenter or a boatswain. No one Jackson would bother to hold captive.

"I've come tae take Mistress Fisk back tae the *Triumph*," the barrel-shaped sailor told him without the least bit of fear.

"Is that so?" Jackson shouldn't have been surprised, but sudden anger burned through his veins like fire. He barely resisted the impulse to send the man back to his vessel with a message that they could all go straight to hell.

"Aye. Lord Kensale says if ye give 'er up without a fight, 'e'll let ye go free."

"That's very generous of him." Forcing the muscles along his arms and back to ease, he asked, "How do I know Lord Kensale is aboard your ship?"

The sailor glanced over his shoulder. " 'E seems tae know who ye are. And from the look of ye, I think ye know why 'e wants 'is woman back."

His woman? With a calm he certainly didn't feel, he said, "I won't turn her over unless I'm certain she'll be treated well."

"She will be."

"Still," Jackson insisted, "I'd prefer to hear that from Lord Kensale himself."

"If ye want tae waste yer time, so be it. Ye can come with me."

Jackson shook his head. "I'd rather he come here."

"And risk ye killing 'im?" The man chuckled. " 'E ain't a fool."

Jackson glanced around the littered deck, the shattered rails, the ripped canvas that still hung from the main yard. "I lost most of my crew in the storm. And my ship . . .

As you can see, she's in sore condition. Hardly a threat to a vessel as grand as the *Triumph*."

"Very well." The man puffed up his chest. "I'll take 'im yer message, but don't expect 'im tae be pleased about it none."

As the sailor returned to his skiff, Jackson paced, hardly daring to breathe, watching the boat struggle across the swelling waves. Once the crew reboarded their ship, Jackson looked into the spyglass and saw the sailor relay his message to Mason. The viscount smiled when the man was done, nodded and turned to say something to his first mate. Mason crossed to the railing where the ladder led to the waiting boat.

Jackson's pulse quickened and his skin heated with anticipation. Within a few minutes he'd have Mason at his mercy, and with luck, the *Triumph* sitting at the bottom of the sea. He snapped the spyglass closed, and gave Mac a small nod to be ready.

The explosion erupted like a shouted roar, catching everyone by surprise. White smoke curled from the *Triumph*'s belly. The rumble drowned out the gasp from Jackson's men, his own curse. Before the cannonball struck the *Sea Angel*, another shot sounded.

Cartridge smashed through the railings twenty feet to Jackson's left. Daggers of splintered wood flew through the air. Men screamed in pain, shouted in confusion. The second ball struck the deck, crashing through the boards to the level below. Another volley fired, then another.

The *Sea Angel*'s hull shuddered, rocking as she was struck broadside. Black smoke billowed across her deck. Jackson shouted for Dillon to return fire, but it was already too late. Their anchor was down, half of their sails lowered. There was no way they could maneuver enough to put their guns to use.

Jackson heard the whistling sound and knew what it

meant. He felt his heart rise to his throat. In a flashing instant the hissing screech grew louder, then the ship exploded right before his eyes.

Her hands trembling, Grace forced herself to arrange the cloth she'd cut up for bandages into neat piles. The needles and coiled thread, the knife Cook had sharpened to a splintered edge, was lined up, ready for use.

What had the first cannon shot meant? The *Triumph* had fired one blast, then nothing? The *Sea Angel* hadn't been hit, nor had she returned fire. Was William playing a game of some kind? Testing Jackson, pushing him into a battle that could have only one outcome? She had to go topside, see for herself what was happening. She looked at the doorway but didn't move toward it, knowing her presence would only distract Jackson. It was best that she remained below where she could be of use.

Beside her supplies were three full bottles of whiskey to dull any pain and clean any wounds. The last time she'd had to treat an injury was when she'd been on board the *Sea Queen.* A lifetime ago, she thought, wiping sweat from her brow. She hadn't had to use her meager healing skills since then; she wasn't sure she even remembered how.

Please, Lord, don't force me to remember now.

"The 'ot water's a boil'n' like ye asked." Cook, a squat, broad man of unknown years, limped into the crew's quarters carrying a bundle of old canvas sails that would be used as bandages. In his other beefy hand he held a small handsaw.

A shudder ran up Grace's spine, and she whispered another prayer that the saw wouldn't have to be put to use. Jackson's plan to capture William had to succeed, because the alternative was unthinkable. She didn't know what William would do to them, had no idea how truly demented his mind could be. Considering that he'd tried to kill Jackson once, she didn't fool herself into believing William would let him go now. Which meant the odds of escaping weighed heavily against them.

"I think that'll about do it," Cook said, resting his heavy body on a low shelf nailed into the side of the hull.

"Do you know what's happening?" she asked.

"Likely we're wait'n' for the other ship tae show their 'and. But don't ye worry none. Capt'n knows what 'e's doin'."

"Perhaps I should go see."

"Now, miss, the Capt'n wants ye to stay put."

"But still—"

A muted roar vibrated the air. Grace froze, her heart lurching against her chest. She looked at the ceiling, knowing what the sound meant, knowing what would follow. The explosion rocked the ship, sending her sideways and knocking into the makeshift table of supplies. The bandages, knives and whiskey flew from the surface and smashed against the wall.

Another shot followed the first, ripping through the deck somewhere near the stern. She heard men shout orders, some screamed, the sounds high-pitched and piercing. Smoke leaked into the hallway, filling the crew's quarters and choking her lungs.

"We have to leave here!" she shouted to Cook. Taking his arm, she helped him to the companionway. Another cannon blast struck the hull; the ship lurched beneath her, throwing her against the wall. She pushed Cook, helping him up the ladder when a sudden chill grazed her skin.

"Jackson," she whispered. Urging the man to hurry, she scurried up after him. Once on deck, she came to a swaying halt. "Dear God."

Smoke poured over the ship like a stream of thick fog,

obliterating the stern and part of the mast. Sails were lowered; men scaled the ratlines, their bodies black with soot and red with blood. She quickly spotted the *Triumph*, circling like a victorious knight. Or demon, she thought, her jaw hardening, her hands clenching at her sides.

She started to cross to the helm where Jackson would surely be. The *Sea Angel* heaved to the side and the sky filled with the sounds of thunder. Only this time, her ship wasn't taking a beating, but delivering one of its own. Plumes of white smoke curled into the air as Grace watched, holding her breath to see if Dillon's aim was true. One ball struck the bowsprit, severing the thick beam that protruded from the bow of the ship. A harmless strike, just like the others that fell into the sea.

She spun away, determined to find Jackson. They had to get the sails up, move the *Sea Angel* if they had any hopes of surviving. "Jackson!"

An arm snaked out and snatched her to a sudden halt. "Watch out!" Macklin shouted.

The smoke cleared enough for Grace to see an enormous hole of splintered wood in the deck before her. If she'd fallen, she'd have been sliced to shreds.

"Where's Jackson?"

"Go below. This is no place for ye." Macklin gave her a shove, but she spun away, searching the deck.

"Where is he?" she demanded again, coughing as smoke singed her lungs.

"Ye can't 'elp him, Grace. Go below." Gripping her arm, he led her through the maze of debris and wounded men who moaned even as they struggled to rise and help.

She jerked free, trembling with fear. "Where is he?"

"The *Triumph*'s captain is giving us time to consider surrender'n'." Spitting on the deck, Mac said, "I'll show 'im what it means tae surrender. I'm in command, Grace. So go below."

"You're . . . Where is Jackson!"

"Ye can't 'elp him," he told her, the words torn from his throat.

At his telling glance, she looked to a spot near the binnacle box. There, alone on the shattered deck, his clothes torn from his body, his skin streaked red with blood, lay Jackson. Her heart quivered, her mouth went dry. She ran to him, falling to her knees at his side.

"Jackson, dear God . . ."

Countless cuts crisscrossed his chest, slashed his handsome face, his bare arms, turning his body into a river of his own blood. His eyes were closed, his head lolled to the side. He didn't move, didn't even seem to breathe.

He can't be dead. He can't be! She touched his chest, cringing with a shared pain. So much blood. It was warm and wet, sticking to her fingers and palms. Pressing her hand to the center of his chest, she felt his heartbeat, faint, but there. She dropped her head between her shoulders, wanting to sob with relief.

Instead, she drew herself up. She had to think, fast. What needed to be done?

She stopped two sailors who were running past. "Take your captain below. Tell Cook to see to him as best as he can until I can get there."

"Go with them," Macklin said.

"Grace . . ." Jackson whispered. His eyes were open, clouded with pain.

"Shh, don't talk." She smoothed her hand over his brow. "You're going to be all right."

"Listen to Mac . . . whatever happens." He gripped her arm, his hold so tight his fingers dug into her skin.

"We're going to get out of this, Jackson," she said, desperate to believe it. "Please, you have to hold on." But he didn't hear her. His eyes slid closed and he slipped into unconsciousness. The two men urged her aside and carefully lifted him to carry him below.

"There's naught ye can do 'ere," Mac said. "Maybe ye can 'elp 'im."

Pushing to her feet, she pressed a hand to her stomach, fighting the need to accompany them. Jackson needed her, and she needed to care for him; he might not live if she didn't tend him now. But they were all still in danger. Anger and fear pulsed through her veins. She watched the predator ship glide past, the gleaming sails seeming to wink at her in the sunlight.

"This is my ship," she vowed, "and I'm not about to let William destroy her."

Chapter Twenty-six

Ten minutes, that was all the time they had.

William Mason had shouted the conditions to their surrender himself, promising he would treat them fairly if they gave up without a fight. *Fairly, indeed!* He also wanted her brought to his ship.

Grace paced the deck, ordering the uninjured sailors to take the injured ones below, seeing that the fires were doused and the leaking hull sealed, finding any distraction to delay the inevitable. She had no idea why William still wanted her—she'd saved Jackson after all, and had helped expose William's traitorous acts. He couldn't think they were still betrothed, she thought as she studied the *Triumph*'s arrogant stance one hundred yards to their larboard side.

"My crew has as much chance of being treated fairly by William as I have of becoming the next queen of England."

My crew. The phrase sent a shuddering strength through her chest. She'd never thought to utter those words before, had never felt them the way she did now. She'd never been protective of the *Sea Queen*. But the *Sea Angel* was different. *She* was different. This was *her* ship, and *her* crew, just as it had once been Morgan's and Jo's. And just as her sisters had done before her, it was her turn to take control.

She narrowed her gaze on the *Triumph*. William thought he had them well and trapped, helpless, with no choice but to take his offer of salvation or risk finding a watery death.

"Is everything ready, Macklin?" she asked as the first mate emerged from the hatchway.

"Aye, though I think ye're as daft as they come."

"If you have another suggestion, I'd welcome it," she said.

He sighed. "If only I did. But what ye've planned, though it will take a miracle tae work, is better than no plan at all."

"Thank you for your confidence. But this *will* work. I promise," she added, surprised by the certainty of her voice, because she wasn't certain of anything right now.

Feeling a ripple of panic, she glanced toward the hatchway. "Jackson?"

" 'E's 'oldin' on."

Every impulse, every part of her soul, her mind, screamed for her to go to him, but she couldn't. Not yet. If she went to him now, she wouldn't have the strength to leave him. The decision to first see to the ship and crew instead of Jackson nearly tore her heart from her chest. But if she wanted to save him, she had to save the *Sea Angel* first.

"Dillon and his men? Are they ready?"

"Aye, every man on board who can still stand is ready tae send that devil tae 'ell." Studying her with narrowed black eyes, stroking his pointed beard that was in sore need of a trim, he added, "I can't let ye go alone, Grace. Jackson will skin me alive if I let ye confront Viscount Kensale with no one there tae back ye up.''

"I'm the only one who can face him now. I was engaged to the man. That should count for something.''

"Still," Mac argued, "we both know ye don't 'ave the 'eart for this kind of thing.''

Gripping the hilt of her knife, welcoming the warmth against her palm, she murmured, "Let's hope you're wrong.''

Grace climbed the wooden ladder affixed to the *Triumph*'s hull, her heart rising in her throat with each rung she scaled. Her four crewmen waited below in their skiff with orders to return to the *Sea Angel* if they didn't hear from her within fifteen minutes. She prayed that was enough time to convince William to let them go, otherwise Dillon would follow her orders and unleash his cannons on the *Triumph*, regardless if she was still on board or not.

She wished she had a better plan, wished she knew what William wanted from her. She could only assume the worst, which meant no matter what happened, she couldn't back down. She might be baseborn, but she had a powerful family who would retaliate if he dared harm her. William couldn't ignore that fact.

Her mouth dry with fear, she reached the railing and climbed aboard the *Triumph*. Standing on the deck, she wanted to shrink back from the countless eyes watching her. An eerie quiet hung over the ship. Her skin crawled with unease, though she didn't think the ship or the crew had caused the wary feeling. The deck, and the men crowding it, were clean and neat, unnaturally spotless. Yet, there was a weight hanging over the ship like a cloud, a darkness that felt corrupt, defying the bright shine of the sun. A score of men lined the main deck, more were perched like vultures along the ratlines to get a better view. Near the opposite rail, posing as if he were holding court, she spotted William.

Despite the heat of the day, he wore an elaborate blue velvet coat and matching vest, his cravat tied in a flawless knot at his throat. His cream pants were tucked into polished knee-high boots. He looked every bit the lord, a man of power and position, the glint in his eye confirming that he thought he'd won the game.

If not for the sharp angles of his cheekbones, the brutal edge of his jaw, he would have appeared stalwart, regal. Now he just looked cruel. How had she ever thought him handsome? How in heaven's name had she thought she could be his wife?

Taking slow steps toward her, he smiled, making her shiver in apprehension. "Well, well, well," he murmured, his steel-blue gaze raking over her body. "It seems my fiancée has transformed herself."

"Not at all. You're finally seeing me as I really am."

"A pirate?" he scoffed, walking a slow path around her. The feel of his disapproving gaze made her skin ripple with disgust. "I'm afraid you make as poor a pirate as you do a lady."

Not affected by his insult, she forced herself to smile. "I'm here to discuss our terms for surrender."

"You?" He laughed. "I had hoped to meet Mr. Brodie again. The man you seem to prefer. Though I can't imagine why." He glanced at the *Sea Angel*. "Where is he? Why is he hiding behind your skirts?" His brow arched at the irony of her wearing pants.

Not about to discuss Jackson with this wretched man, knowing she couldn't even think about him and his injuries or she'd lose her courage, she said, "What are your conditions?"

"I've been giving it some thought, my dear," William

said with a cunning smile. "You will all become my prisoners, of course, so don't even think to resist. I intend to take you to London and let the authorities deal with you. Pirating is still high treason, you know."

She sucked in a breath. If they were arrested for pirating, the sentence would be certain death. She couldn't let that happen. God help her, she couldn't!

Squeezing the hilt of her knife, she said, "This has nothing to do with pirating."

"Not only are you pirates, you're rebels, fighting against the king." He shook his head, smiling. "No, I'm afraid your fate is sealed. There's no hope for any of you. Everyone of you will be hanged." Reaching out he ran his finger over her throat. "Such a pity."

She flinched from his touch, barely resisting the impulse to draw her knife and force him back. "My family won't allow that to happen."

"Do you really want to involve your sisters in your troubles? The king might decide to punish them as well. I seem to recall something about none of you ever taking to the sea again. But, it's a long way to England. Who's to say any of you will make the trip in good health?"

He means to kill us all. Heaven have mercy. She saw it in his eyes, the half smile that crossed his face. "Give me one reason why we should surrender to you, William. The *Sea Angel* may not be able to defeat the *Triumph,* but we can surely try."

"Such bravery. Who would have thought you'd possess such a trait?" Clasping his hands behind his back, he squared his shoulders as if waiting for her to beg for mercy. She glared into his twisted face. Sighing, he added, "There is an alternative. Would you care to hear it?"

"I'll not play your games, William."

"But you have been playing, my dear. As my fiancée,

you were my pawn, a means to an end, and I would see that end fulfilled.''

"What are you talking about?"

He rolled his eyes as if any child should be able to grasp his meaning. "I may have lost my position in the Colonies for the time being, but I have every confidence that King George will prevail. And once he does, I'll return to White Rose and resume building my ships and expanding my trading business. Though to really succeed, I'll need my connection with Daniel Tremayne in place."

"When my brother-in-law learns what you've done, he'll do everything in his power to see you ruined."

"Will he?" William's smile turned deadly. "I think not."

"You are an arrogant bastard. I'll tell him—"

"Nothing," he interrupted. "Here is my proposal, Grace. I'll offer it only once, so don't reject it out of hand. If you agree to marry me, I promise to release Jackson and his vagrant followers. They'll go free. No trials, no hangings. You'll save them all. All you have to do is give me your word that you'll never tell your family what has transpired, and, of course, you must marry me. Today."

She gaped at him, too stunned to speak.

He turned to the man standing by the helm. "Captain Rogers will perform the ceremony right now."

Grace wanted to shout that he was insane if he thought she would even consider marrying him, but she swallowed the words. Trembling, she looked across the ocean's pulling swells, saw the *Sea Angel*'s battered jib, the damaged strakes in her hull, the men bruised and beaten watching from the deck. What was she to do? What would her sisters do?

In her mind's eye she saw Jackson in the crew's quarters, lying on a table, his body cut and bleeding. Was he still alive? *Please, God, please let him live!* He had to. Nothing else mattered. He had to survive his wounds, and she had to make sure his fate wasn't a hanging at Execution Dock. She spotted her crew rowing the skiff back to her ship. Dillon would fire the guns soon. Should she signal to stop him? Or buy their freedom by giving up her own?

"I have your word that they'll go free?" she asked dully, facing William.

He smiled, his white teeth glittering in the sun. "Of course.

There was only one way to save the *Sea Angel* and her crew, she realized. *And Jackson.* Feeling a calmness settle over her, her mind became clear, her thoughts sharp and focused. She knew what she had to do. "Very well. A wedding it is."

Pain jerked Jackson back from the black depth he'd sunk into. His skin felt on fire, burning, the agony going clear through his bones. Every breath he drew was a torment, rasping his smoke-singed lungs. He was hot, boiling on the inside, yet he shivered with cold.

He opened his eyes a slit, saw the dark boards of a ceiling above him. It all came back to him then—the storm, his damaged ship, the *Triumph* hovering like a buzzard over its kill. The cannon fire that had ripped through the main mast, ripping through him as well. Considering the pain in his arms, the tearing sensation in his chest, he knew he shouldn't be alive.

And Grace, she'd seen it all.

Hearing a noise to his right, he turned his head and winced at the agony that invoked. Cook worked frantically on another crewman, wrapping the man's bloodied leg with strips of clean canvas. Jackson struggled to rise.

Cook glanced up, his eyes widening with alarm. "There now, Capt'n," he said, leaving the sailor to fetch a cup of water and help him drink. "No talk'n' now. Ye took a bad blow tae the 'ead." Making a tsking sound, he added, "And everywhere else."

"How long was I out?"

"Not long enough. I've bandaged the worst of ye cuts, the nastiest bein' that gash on your chest, but sew'n' will 'ave tae wait until later."

Jackson forced himself off the table, the effort sending shards of pain through his upper body and setting fire to his limbs. His head spun. He touched his chest where blood seeped though the bandages.

"Capt'n, please, ye got tae lay back down."

"I have to help Mac . . ."

"Don't worry none about Mac." Making the sign of the cross, he added, "It'll all be over soon."

Jackson gripped the man's arm. "What do you mean!"

"The *Triumph* has demanded our surrender."

"Bloody hell!" Jackson started for the door, swaying as if the ship were battling a storm.

"Don't give up 'ope, Capt'n," Cook said. "Your lady 'as gone over tae negotiate the terms."

"Grace? Damn it, I told her not to interfere." He drew in a breath and fought off the darkness that threatened to consume him. He had to stop her. He focused on the door and headed toward it. She couldn't face Mason alone. Because this time she wouldn't escape.

"I suppose there's nothing to be done about your appearance," William complained from beside her.

"There's nothing *wrong* with my appearance," she said tightly, staring past Captain Rogers who had taken his place before them to perform the wedding ceremony. She relished the black sailor's pants and shirt she wore, felt stronger in them, as if they were armor that would protect her from what was to come.

In a tone that sent a chill down her spine, William said, "You used to be malleable, my dear. I suggest you become so again, or it will go badly for you. As I'm sure you're aware, a husband has *complete* control over his wife."

Grace clenched her jaw to refrain from spitting in his face. She wasn't afraid of him, and she had no intention of becoming anything other than what she was: a fisherman's daughter who'd been pushed to her limit. But she needed a plan, something that would stop the nightmare, because she didn't think she'd survive one day as William's wife.

"If you would join hands," the captain said.

"I'm not touching him," she snapped.

William gripped her right hand and squeezed until she winced in pain. To the captain, he said, "You may begin."

Grace barely listened to the man drone on about the sanctity of marriage, of loyalty and devotion, knowing she would start laughing hysterically if she did. Instead, she gripped the *Sea Queen* dagger in her left hand, tightening her fingers around the hilt, burrowing the three unique gems into her fingers.

What can I do? she silently whispered, desperate for some way to escape.

Stop him, she heard a voice whisper back. She wasn't sure if it was her own subconscious, or a memory of her sisters. Then she heard it again. *Stop him! You know what to do!*

Her fingers flexed over the carved gold hilt, the embedded ruby, emerald and sapphire. Could she do it? Threaten William, possibly kill him? She shuddered. What alternative did she have?

Captain Rogers looked directly at her and said, "Repeat after me; I, Grace Fisk . . ."

Her mouth had gone dry. She had to work her tongue in order to speak. "I, Grace Fisk."

"Solemnly swear to take William Mason as my lawfully wedded husband in the eyes of God . . ."

The captain paused; her cue to continue. Her hand trembled. *Do it!*

"Say the words, Grace," William ordered.

"I solemnly swear . . ." She paused, her skin heating, her mind refusing to finish the phrase.

"Say them, damn you!" he shouted at her.

Do it now!

"I solemnly swear—" She jerked their joined hands back and drew the dagger from its sheath. Before anyone could react, she pressed the tip against William's stomach. "—to put this knife through your belly if you move."

"What—" William gaped at her in surprise.

Several crewmen lunged for her. She pressed harder, warning, "Tell them to stay back."

"You won't hurt me, Grace." His stunned expression vanished and was replaced by an arrogant smile. "You aren't capable of hurting anyone."

She angled the knife's tip, felt it slice through his clothes. William narrowed his gaze as if daring her to continue. She smiled into his ruthless face and shifted the knife, felt the steel tip break his skin. Her stomach clenched and she felt cold with sweat, but she didn't ease the pressure. A dark stain spread around the blade, turning his velvet waistcoat black with his blood.

"Do you care to test me?"

Grimacing, William raised his arms and nodded for his men to back away. "You can't escape me. I've won. This little demonstration of yours will only cost you in the end."

She had to move fast. Threatening William would only hold the crew off for so long. She knew from experience when sailing on the *Sea Queen* that once the crew recovered from their surprise, they would act.

Grabbing hold of William's pristine cravat, she turned

him so they faced the *Sea Angel*. Her battered crewmen stood along the rails watching the *Triumph*. The skiff was nowhere in sight. She heard a vague shout then a thunderous cheer as sailors began racing over the deck. But where was the skiff? She needed her men on the *Triumph*, now!

"Tell them to stay where they are," William said, "or I'll order my gunner to open fire. You'll be responsible for sinking your ship. Is that what you want?"

"Say one more word, William, just one," she warned in a tone that would have made her sisters proud. "And I promise you, you won't be alive to know who sinks and who survives."

A muscle flexed in his jaw and he flushed red from his hairline down to his neck. Grace almost smiled. She'd done it! She'd bested William. She wanted to laugh and cry with relief.

"It's over, William," she whispered. "You've finally lost."

"This fight is far from over, my dear." His grin flashed an instant before he swept his arm down, hitting her wrist in a numbing blow. The blade flew from her grip and skidded across the deck.

Whipping her around, he locked his arm around her neck and squeezed. Against her ear, he gloated, "Before this day is over, my dear, you'll learn that I never, *ever*, lose."

Chapter Twenty-seven

Sweat dripped into Jackson's eyes, but he hardly felt the sting. Gripping the rope ladder, he pulled himself up another rung, felt the strain in his muscles but willed himself to continue. Below him, Mac held the ladder steady, ready to climb up once Jackson reached the *Triumph*'s taffrail. He considered it a miracle that no one on board had seen him and his men row the skiff across, but the *Triumph*'s crew had been distracted by other events—the likes of which Jackson didn't want to consider. His heart hammered against his chest, not from exertion or from pain, but because he knew he had little time.

He'd seen Grace standing at Mason's side, with the captain facing them. Which meant what? What had the captain been saying that had held an entire shipload of seamen spellbound? Jackson was afraid he knew the answer, knew Mason had found a way to manipulate Grace. But what was he forcing her to do? Agree to return to England with him? Threatening to punish her for betraying him?

Reaching the taffrail, he eased himself over and crouched low, breathing hard to fight the flare of pain in his chest. The bandage was warm and sodden with his blood, and his body shook with exhaustion. His vision blurred, but he sucked in a breath, willing the burning to ease. Just a little longer, he had to hold on a little longer.

Sailors were crowded around the main deck, some clinging to the ratlines for a better advantage. Below him, Mac had begun to climb the ladder, but Jackson couldn't wait; he had to make his move while the crewmen were distracted. He'd taken no more than three steps when cheerful shouts rose from his ship. The *Triumph*'s crew tensed, some started to move, but then held their places. Sweet Jesus, what had happened now?

Jackson rushed forward, pulling a pistol free from his waistband with one hand and a sword from its sheath with the other. He elbowed his way through the men, ignoring their angry grunts, until finally he broke through. He froze, every nerve coiling in his gut by what he saw.

"Let her go," Jackson demanded.

With his arm locked around Grace's throat, Mason spun to face him, his surprise quickly shifting to an arrogant smile. "Mr. Brodie, you decided to join us? We were just completing some unfinished business. I'm sure Grace won't mind if you watch." Mason tightened his hold on her, forcing her to stand on her toes to breathe. "Will you, my dear?"

Jackson leveled his pistol at Mason's head. "This is the last warning I'll give. Release her."

Mason laughed. "Or you'll do what? Shoot me? And risk hitting our dear Grace instead? I don't think so." He shook his head, not bothering to hide his amusement. "Put the gun down, Jackson, and I might let you live."

His muscles strained with the effort to hold the pistol steady. Sweat ran in rivulets down his face and along his spine. He was cold, and growing weaker by the moment. He had to act, but Mason was right, blast his soul. He couldn't risk shooting and harming Grace. But he had to get her away. Whether he lived or died, he had to make sure she was safe.

"You can hardly stand up, man," Mason continued almost gleefully. "Lower your weapons. You've lost. Accept it."

"Let her go first, and I'll drop the pistol and sword."

Grace shook her head, tried to argue, but Mason silenced her with a twist of his arm. "I'm no fool. You'll shoot me the instant she moves away."

"I honor my word," Jackson said, swaying. "Do you?"

"You do look as if you're half dead. You probably couldn't hit the deck if you aimed for it." Mason's disdainful gaze raked over Jackson. "And by the way, I don't appreciate you bleeding all over my ship."

"Release her."

"All right," Mason said with a smug grin. He nodded to a pair of sailors who looked like they'd gladly tear Jackson in half if given the chance. "I'll free her, but make one move and you'll regret it."

Mason eased his grip on Grace's throat enough for her to slip free and spin out of his grasp. She rushed to Jackson, touching his face and staring in horror at his blood-soaked chest.

"What are you doing?" she sobbed in a whisper. "You can't be here. He'll kill you."

Jackson held her to him for a mere second before forcing her behind him. Letting her go, when all he wanted to do was hold her to him, nearly stole the last of his strength. "The day is far from over, Angel."

"Your weapons," Mason said in a warning tone.

Jackson tossed both his pistol and sword aside. He prayed Mac and the rest of his men were on board. A handful of men against an entire crew. But they were bringing a surprise with them that should sway things in their favor—at least for a few moments.

Mason held out his hand and smiled as if Jackson's presence was a great diversion. "Grace, come here. I'd like to get on with the wedding now. And, please, no more interruptions."

She looked from Mason to Jackson, uncertainty darkening her eyes.

"A wedding?" Jackson said, finally understanding the scene he'd witnessed when crossing to the *Triumph*.

"He promised to let you go." Tears welled in her eyes but she didn't let them fall.

"And you believed him?" Fury boiled in Jackson's mind. "You aren't going to marry him to save me."

She tilted her chin. "If it means saving your life, Jackson, I'll marry the devil."

The viscount laughed as she crossed to him and grudgingly placed her hand in his. Jackson drew a steadying breath and willed himself to wait. There would be no wedding. So help him God, there wouldn't be.

The captain began to recite the marriage vows. Each word felt like a stab wound to Jackson's heart. He glanced up at the ratlines, the crowd of strange faces, searching for one of his crew. He didn't see them, but he did see a bottle with a flaming rag in its mouth sail through the air.

"Get down!" he shouted, leaping forward, grabbing Grace and knocking her to the ground. He landed on top of her, covering her body with his. He heard the beginning of Mason's angry shout, but the explosion that followed drowned the rest.

"Run! To the stern!" Jackson told her, rising and jerking her to her feet. "A skiff is waiting. Go!"

He spun around just as another bottle exploded near the fish davit, ripping the nearby shrouds free from their hooks. Smoke rolled over the deck, obliterating the men scurrying to put out the spreading fires. The viscount stood amidst of it all, his furious glare taking in the destruction.

"Mason!" Jackson no sooner shouted the man's name than the viscount rushed forward, moving so fast Jackson had no time to spin out of the way. Mason tackled him around the waist, knocking him hard onto his back. The wind was knocked from his lungs. A splintering fire tore through his chest, numbing him with pain. Mason pushed up and swung his fist, striking Jackson square in the face.

He willed himself to move, fight back. He delivered a blow and caught Mason in the jaw. The man reeled back, but returned with a vicious blow to Jackson's temple. Rolling onto his side, taking Mason with him, he gained enough leverage to rise to his knees. He pushed to his feet, felt the ship sway. He shook his head and clenched his hands. He let Mason gain his feet before he delivered the next blow. Anger filled every punch, reverberating through Jackson's arm, making the next strike harder, better aimed. He felt the wound in his chest split, the blood flow down his chest and legs in a warm stream.

He hit Mason again and again, taking the punches the man delivered but not feeling them. He vaguely heard shouts around him, knew people were running. He felt others waiting nearby, watching. It didn't matter. Jackson kept swinging even when he didn't know how he managed. His arms felt like lead, his feet like stone. But he couldn't stop. Grace should be on the skiff by now, but was she on the *Sea Angel*? Was she safe?

She wouldn't be, not until William Mason, lord of Kensale, was dead. Mason staggered back, his face bloodied, his left arm cupped against his ribs. Jackson reached back, preparing for the final swings.

The solid blow to his chest caught him by surprise. Fire erupted in his mind. He fell to his knees, gasping. Looking up, he saw Mason holding a piece of timber, the blood from Jackson's bandaged chest staining the sanded oak plank.

"You have just forfeited your right to live, Brodie," Mason sneered, bloodied spittle flying from his mouth. "Not that I ever intended to let you go. But where your execution might have been merciful, now I intend to watch you suffer."

Jackson knew he had to move, find a weapon, his sword, his pistol. Something! He wouldn't survive another blow like the last one. But his legs wouldn't respond.

Mason raised the board.

"Jackson!" Grace shouted.

He glanced at her as she picked something up and tossed it to him. Sunlight flashed on gold and steel. He caught the *Sea Queen* dagger, felt the three gems embedded in its hilt. Just as Mason swung the wooden strake at his head, Jackson brought his arm up. The blade sank into the man's chest, breaking cloth and skin, chipping bone. Blood poured in a warm flow over Jackson's hand, but it was Mason's shocked expression that held him.

The board dropped from the viscount's grip. He staggered back, and the blade pulled free. Everyone on board the *Triumph* went still.

"This isn't over, Brodie. I'll see you pay . . ." Mason's words slurred as he fell to his knees, then, with a last sucking breath, collapsed onto his back.

Grace rushed to Jackson's side and held onto him. He wanted to lie down. He'd be all right if he could just lie down. But he couldn't, not yet. The *Triumph*'s crew might retaliate. He had to get Grace off the ship. He had to . . .

"Hold on, Jackson," she ordered. "You've got to hold on."

"I told you to leave. You've got to get off this ship. Mac, find Mac. . . ."

"Damn you, Jackson, I'm not going anywhere without you," she cried softly, her tears washing his face.

Jackson felt the ship sway, or was it him? He ran his hand over her brow, tried to tell her to go, but his throat wouldn't work. Then the sound of her crying began to fade ... and the light dimmed ... and then there was nothing.

Chapter Twenty-eight

A breath of wind moved over Jackson's body, a soothing touch that made him want to sleep forever. But some internal voice warned that he'd slept too much as it was. He needed to rise and see to ... see to ... He tried to think, but the more he forced himself to wake, the more his body felt.

Pain. Everywhere, and all at once.

Fire seared a path from his chest, down to his waist. With gritted teeth he sucked in breath after breath and willed the burning to subside. He shuddered, gradually forcing the torment under control. He blinked his eyes open and recognized his cabin at once. Frowning, he turned his head, saw the open windows, the map fluttering on his desk, the piles of bandages and a tin of salve stacked on the seat of a chair. A blue dress lay in a discarded heap in the corner, the buttons ripped from their holes.

Grace.

Everything came back in a rush. Grace at Mason's mercy,

their brief fight, the viscount dying from a stab wound inflicted by the *Sea Queen* blade. But what had happened after that? Had his crew managed to subdue the *Triumph*'s men? Who had protected Grace? He had to find her. Jackson sat upright, then hissed out a curse. His vision turned red, spotting with shards of light as his skin stretched and burned. Catching his breath, he touched his fingers to his chest. Clean white bandages replaced the bloodied ones.

Throwing the thin blanket aside, he reached for his pants and slowly worked them over his bare legs, tying the strings loosely at his waist. Slowly, he reached the door and gripped the wall when his vision spun out of control. The companionway became a tunnel with no end, the ship's steady rocking making each step a struggle. By the time he reached the hatchway, sweat beaded his brow and dripped from his jaw.

Climbing the ladder, he gained the deck and shielded his eyes until his vision adjusted to the bright noon glare. Finally able to see, he stared at the destruction around him, grief pressing against his heart. The *Sea Angel* looked as if she'd barely survived a war. Everywhere he looked he saw splintered yardarms, ravaged shrouds and charred decking. Sounds of hammers and saws, the murmur of men's voices as they carried out repairs, carried on the breeze.

But there was no sign of Grace.

Out of habit, he checked the position of the few sails raised. He frowned. Something was wrong. His skin iced beneath the hot sun.

"Grace," he called, but his voice was little more than a hoarse croak. Limping across the deck, hearing the conversations fall away and the work quiet, he climbed the ladder to the quarterdeck where the helmsman had control of the wheel.

"Capt'n," Mr. Kent said in surprise. "I hadn't expected

ye up so soon. But it's glad I am tae see yer still among the liv'n'.''

The way his body burned with fever, Jackson wondered if he'd remain living for much longer. He scanned the deck below, searching for any sign of blonde hair, the billow of skirts.

''Where . . .''

''A day from port I'd say. Maybe less.''

He meant to say, where was Grace, but couldn't get the rest out. He clenched his hands, and fought to stay upright. Where was she? Bloody hell! Where was she?

Then he saw it, the towering four-mast ship sailing close to stern. *A guard dogging its prisoner?* Was Grace aboard the *Triumph?* Had the crew captured her? And if so, why had he been returned to the *Sea Angel?*

He breathed a curse.

''We're do'n' the best we can, Capt'n,'' Mr. Kent said, misunderstanding Jackson's fear. ''With barely a sail to catch the wind, we've 'aven't made good time, but at least we're still afloat.''

They were a day away from England? He checked the sun's position again. Their heading was wrong. They weren't sailing east, but west. Where the hell were they going? And at whose order? Mason's captain? Where didn't matter, he decided. Somehow he had to take control of the *Triumph*, find Grace—

''What are you doing?''

The frightened female voice made Jackson spin around. His head reeled and he barely caught hold of the rail before he toppled face first into the deck.

''Grace.'' His vision was a blur, but he could make out her blonde hair twisted in a braid, the forest-green gown that brought out the fire in her cheeks and the worry in her eyes.

"You should be in bed." She rushed toward him and pressed her palm to his brow.

"Grace, you're here."

"Of course I'm here," she said, her tone softening.

He glanced at the other ship. "The *Triumph*—"

"You're bleeding, Jackson. I swear, if you've ripped open your stitches after I spent hours sewing you up—"

"You swear? Angel, you never swear."

"Yes, well, a lot has changed."

"Tell me."

"You're going to have scars."

"Damn it, what in bloody hell happened?" Though his throat burned like fire, he told her, "If Mason's captain is taking us to England, our heading is wrong."

She sighed and took his arm, urging him toward a crate near the railing. "Sit down and I'll tell you everything."

He didn't budge. "You'll tell me now."

"You're bleeding—"

"Now, Angel."

"Fine." She folded her arms across her chest. "We aren't sailing toward England."

He stared at her, willing her to continue.

"Our heading is the Americas."

"Why would he—"

"The *Triumph*'s captain and crew are locked in the 'old, Capt'n," Macklin said, stepping up beside them. "Along with Viscount Kensale, who's feel'n' poorly but will recover from his wound, much to everyone's disappointment."

"He's alive?" He received affirming nods from Grace and Mac. Jackson knew he should feel relief that he hadn't killed Mason, but he couldn't find it within himself to feel compassion for the man.

Mac stroked his beard. "We've a skeleton crew manning their ship. Or should I say, Grace's ship."

She blushed as if embarrassed by Macklin's announcement. It was then that Jackson noticed the jeweled dagger dangling from her waist by a gold link chain. She'd always hated the dagger and what it represented. Now she wore it as if it were a part of her.

He cupped the side of her face in his hand. "Are you all right?"

She nodded and gave him a teary smile. "Seeing you up and awake . . ." The rest of her admission trailed off, but he saw the relief in her eyes, the love that softened her face.

She ran her fingers over his bandaged chest. "I'm sorry, Jackson. All of this happened because of me."

"You're speaking nonsense."

"Am I? If I hadn't tried to be something I'm not, an aristocrat of all things," she said with a disgusted sigh, "you wouldn't have been wounded, the *Sea Angel* wouldn't have suffered such damage."

Drawing her to him, he kissed her brow and inhaled her sweet scent. He squeezed her tight, ignoring the pain shooting beneath his skin. "But you're safe. That's all that matters to me, Angel. I couldn't have withstood it if you'd been hurt. I love you too much—"

"You love me?" She went still, hardly breathing as she searched his face.

"Of course I do."

"You've never said it before."

"Well, I do, which is why we're changing course and sailing for England."

She narrowed her gaze, her expression turning stubborn. "We're going to America, Jackson. If you want to travel to England, you'll have to do so at a later date."

"Damn it, Angel. Just because Mason is no longer a threat doesn't mean it's safe in the colonies."

"I hadn't thought it would be, but it's where I intend to make my home."

"Of all the bloody nonsense!" he growled, swaying when his head began to spin, but he'd be damned if he'd pass out now. "Did you learn nothing while you were in Medford?"

"Things have changed."

"Have they? How?" he demanded, sensing his entire crew gathering close to listen to their debate.

"I'm going to make an honest businessman out of you, Jackson Brodie."

"Excuse me?"

"I'm not an aristocrat," she said with a regal tilt of her chin. "But neither am I a pirate. I know ships and I've learned a thing or two from Daniel about trading. I'm going to become a merchant."

"Is that so?"

"Yes, and I need a partner. Are you willing?"

"You want me to help you start a business?"

"That's what husbands do."

"Husbands?" A buzzing began in his mind, the sounds of fear and hope and longing.

"I have to tell you, though, I don't intend to live on the *Sea Angel* permanently. I want a home in Newburyport. It seemed a good village to have a place of business and to raise a family."

Have children with Grace? Could a man be so lucky?

"You want to live at sea and on land?" He felt like a simpleton, repeating everything she said. She'd obviously thought her plan through, but he was having a hard time catching up. *Not a hard time catching up,* he amended, *but a hard time believing she really wanted a life with him.*

"We could build our lives there," she said in barely a whisper, yet he heard every word clearly.

"You want me for your husband? Do you know what you're saying, Angel?"

"I've wanted you since the day I met you, Jackson."

Tears rimmed her eyes, making them shine like the sea. "You make me what I am."

"Which is what?"

"Complete."

Jackson kissed her then, filling his soul with the feel of her skin, the honey taste of her mouth. He barely heard his crew's laughter and cheers. Grace had found a way for them to stay together, and he thanked God for that, because now that he had her, he never, ever, intended to give her up.

"Land ho!" came a shout from a crewman perched high above. "Capt'n, there be land!"

Both Jackson and Grace turned to scan the horizon, the faint, hazy slope of a shore merged with the cerulean sky.

"It's beautiful." She wrapped her arm tenderly around his waist. "Go ahead. Give the order."

Jackson thought no man had ever loved a woman as much as he loved her. She'd always wanted a family, safety, a husband to love. He intended to give her those things and more.

"Mr. Kent," he said, "take us home."

Chapter Twenty-nine

The bleached wood absorbed the glare of the sun, making the deck ripple in heated waves. Snow-white sails stretched tight in their hooks, catching the wind and straining the *Sea Angel* against the anchor that had her pinned a hundred miles off England's southern coast. Smells of wood and brine, of sweat and joy filled the air. And sadness.

Grace ran her palm over the railing, the wood so finely sanded the beam felt as smooth as silk. The heels of her boots echoed as she roamed the nearly empty deck. It was time to leave. There was no use in delaying. She'd made her decision; there was no changing her mind. Besides, it had to be done.

"We're ready when you are, Grace," her elder sister, Morgan, said from the hatchway. Morgan, whose dark beauty masked a strength that had saved the lives of so many.

"If you're determined to do it, then let's get it over with." Jo's cheeks were flushed pink and her green eyes flashed with a tumult of emotions. Grace hid her smile, thinking how temperate her sister had become. Jo hadn't agreed with her decision, but she'd accepted it. A few years ago she wouldn't have been so gracious.

"Let's go," Morgan urged. "Our husbands are waiting."

Grace glanced at the schooner anchored off their larboard side. Daniel and Nathan stood near the head, quietly watching. Behind them, Morgan's daughter, Sarah, and her brother, Joseph, were keeping watch over Jo's four-year-old, Matthew.

Jackson stood apart from them all, his tiger-eyes focused on her, his loose sun-streaked hair battling the wind. She could sense his thoughts, knew he wanted to be with her. She regretted asking him to give her and her sisters this time alone, and not only because he loved the *Sea Queen* as much as she did, but because she didn't think she had the courage to complete her task.

Feeling a subtle kick in her belly, she rubbed the spot where her first child stirred, and imagined she could hear his thoughts as well. It was time to let go of the past, because the future held so much promise.

Drawing a deep breath, she led her sisters to the hatchway, through the darkened companionway to the captain's cabin. Charts filled the cable-lined shelves along the wall. The narrow bed was neatly made, the desk clear and ready for use.

Grace removed the *Sea Queen* dagger from the sheath dangling at her waist by its gold link chain. She'd worn the dagger for the past four years, ever since the day she'd stood up to William Mason and had changed her life forever. William's had changed as well. After recovering from his wound, he'd spent two years in prison for treason. He'd been allowed to return to England, but he'd lost his shipping business and White Rose. The last she'd heard, his holdings in Devonshire were in near ruin.

She closed her thoughts to the past. She had a duty to perform. It was time to pass the knife on, just as Morgan had passed it to Jo, and Jo had given it to her.

"Are you sure you want to do this?" Jo paced the cabin, her hands propped on her hips, her fingers digging into her waist.

Grace turned the dagger over in her hand. Sunlight splintered off the three gemstones. One ruby, one sapphire, and one emerald. One stone for each sister.

"I'm sure," she said. "There's only one way for me to pass this dagger down."

"It's a waste, if you ask me," Jo said, thoroughly disgruntled.

Morgan wrapped her arm around Jo's shoulders, hugging her in a way Grace had never thought to see. "It's the way it should be. Go ahead, Grace."

Gripping the hilt in her hand, she raised the knife high overhead, then swung down, impaling the dagger into the desk's surface, exactly the way Morgan had found the blade all those years ago.

She stepped back, tears filling her eyes. *It's time to let go.*

Without a word, they retraced their steps to the main deck. Warm air whipped across her face, drying her tears.

"It's not too late to change your mind," Jo said from beside her.

She faced her sister, who gazed at the weathered deck with an expression of longing. "The *Sea Queen* came to us when we needed her."

"I know but—"

"We don't need her any longer, Jo. Because of her we survived the Seven Years' War. We—"

"You never liked living at sea. I don't expect you to understand how much this tears me apart. Setting her adrift . . ."

"Do you remember when you gave me the knife? I didn't want it."

"I remember. You wanted to be a lady," Jo scoffed. "You told me you wouldn't find a husband with a dagger strapped to your side."

She sighed, amazed that she had changed so much. Already she missed the blade's comforting weight. "I thought that by living on the *Sea Queen* and becoming pirates we would lose everything—our homes, our lives, any kind of safety. It took almost losing Jackson to realize what we had gained."

"And that is?" For the first time since boarding the ship, a small smile lifted Jo's mouth.

"Courage to face our fears. Purpose. Hope." She glanced at the three men waiting on the four-mast ship that had once been known as the *Triumph*, but was now named the *Promise*. "And love."

"They are handsome devils, aren't they?" Jo quipped.

Feeling the weight lift from her heart, she knew she'd made the right decision. She loved the ship, but it wasn't hers any longer. "It's time to go."

She followed her sisters down the ladder to the waiting skiff. Once Macklin raised the anchor and joined them, the crew made quick work of rowing them to the *Promise*, and before long Grace and her sisters were by their husbands' sides. Wind snapped the *Sea Queen*'s sails taut, pulling the ship toward the setting sun. Her bow rolled over the cobalt sea, taking each swell like a lover returning home.

"I'm going to miss the old girl," Jackson whispered into Grace's ear. He wrapped his arms around her thick waist and pulled her close.

"You have me now."

"Aye, that I do," he said, nuzzling her neck. "And I won't *ever* be setting you free."

"I already know what path my life will take." Tilting her head back, she stared into Jackson's eyes, the gold flecks flaring with the kind of love she would treasure forever. "It's time the *Sea Queen* found hers."

Epilogue

Colin MacClaine clamped his hand over Nsala's mouth and whispered, "Which way?"

The African guide nodded toward a faint animal trail that disappeared into a dense thicket of ebony trees. Colin released the guide, then motioned for the rest of his party to follow. They'd begun the expedition three months ago, yet only fourteen men out of one hundred and twenty still lived. They were being hunted, tracked down like the animals they'd become.

"They've found us." Edward Moore, the third earl of Cheshire, gripped Colin's arm. Straightening to his immense height, he scanned the surrounding forest. His dark eyes were inscrutable, but then, they always were. Edward's wealth had financed their trip, but money meant nothing in the Congo; his title meant even less, but the man had the uncanny ability to sense what others did not.

"Where?" Colin asked. *Not again,* he swore to himself. He'd slit the throat of every man remaining before he let the Kuma-Bira warriors pick them off with their slow-poison darts.

"On the banks of the last stream we passed. Eighty yards no more."

"If Edward says they're there, then I suggest we get the hell out of here." Brian Latham aimed his musket toward the grove of black-green trees. With his golden-blond hair dark with sweat, his jaw tight with anger, Brian no longer resembled the renowned archaeologist Colin had first met but a man furious that so much had gone wrong and none of his knowledge had been able to stop it.

"Nsala says we head west. Let's pray he's right."

The black-skinned man nodded urgently. "I smell *kiun guza, akida*. Poison water."

"The ocean." Edward watched the dangling vines and towering trees as if he expected them to come to life. Taking the musket from Brian, he ordered, "I'll bring up the rear."

Colin turned to run, but froze when an agonized scream rent the air. Mola, one of the African guides, collapsed to the mossy ground, a six-foot spear lodged in his chest.

"For Christ's sake, run!" Brian shouted, grabbing up the satchel that had sent them on their trip toward hell.

Colin took the lead, slashing a path with his machete as he ran. Thorny acacias ripped his pants, tore his shirt, left gashes he barely felt along his skin. Yet he swung the deadly blade again and again. He heard the others behind him, their frantic breathing, their footsteps crashing through brush. All round him startled animals shrieked in rage. Were the Kuma-Bira pursuing them? Of course they were, he thought, biting off a curse. They'd pursued them since the day Brian had discovered The Makoko, the burial tomb of Kuma-Bira's long-dead kings. No one, Brian least of all, had known the price the warriors had placed on the golden collar that marked the tomb. But Colin and his men understood now.

"Nsala," Colin shouted. "How much farther?"

"We here, *akida.*"

As if the African's words possessed magic, the clinging vines, the canopy of trees lifted away to reveal a rocky cliff. Colin looked down at the sandy beach one hundred feet below. Beneath the sun's glare, the Atlantic Ocean glittered like gold dust—the most beautiful sight he'd ever seen.

"We're almost home, lads!" Finding a narrow footpath, Colin led the way down, then took off down the beach, searching the cliffs for a place to hide, another trail that might lead to civilization. Something that could be used as a weapon, anything that would save them from being systematically hunted down and slaughtered.

He glanced behind him and saw Edward clear the cliffs and reach the water's edge, only to stop and stare out to sea. "Brian, Colin!" he called, then pointed. "There!"

Colin followed his gaze, his surprise quickly turning into a shout of joy. A ship! A bloody ship in a bloody lagoon!

"Hello!" Brian called, waving his arms. "We need help!"

Colin glanced back, his momentary relief chilling with fear. Kuma-Bira warriors lined the rocky cliff, their faces painted red, their spears raised. "Run!"

No sooner was the word out of his mouth than he heard the telling whistle of steel splitting air. Like a flock of startled birds taking flight. Everyone turned and ran. He heard a scream behind him, then another. A spear struck the ground an inch from his boot. Dropping the machete, he raced into the water, dove into the surf. He didn't know who the ship belonged to, but it wasn't leaving the lagoon without him and his men.

Straining his exhausted arms, kicking with his feet, he finally reached the ship's hull. "Throw down a rope!"

He listened for an answering call, the sound of running footsteps, but heard only the splashing of men swimming for their lives. Why wasn't anyone coming to help?

Treading water, Colin saw the Kuma-Bira descend the cliff. Would they swim into the ocean to finish off the few of them who'd survived? He swam toward the back of the ship, where he'd seen a rope ladder swaying in the breeze. Reaching up, he grabbed hold of the last rung and pulled himself up. He climbed over the railing and started to help the next man, only to freeze.

The deck was deserted, eerily quiet. Every instinct went on alert. He reached for his machete, then remembered he'd dropped it on the beach. Cautiously, he stepped among the ripped sails that dangled from their yardarms. Frayed ropes littered the decks like a horde of snakes. The wood was dull, weathered by salt and debris.

"Is it deserted?" Brian asked, breathing hard as he came up beside him.

"So it seems."

Brian crossed to the railing and lifted the worn satchel over the side. Colin held his breath, expecting the archaeologist to toss the Makoko Collar into the ocean's jade depths. *A fitting end to our first exploration.*

"So many men died." Brian's arm trembled. "And all for a piece of gold."

Edward gripped Brian's shoulder and pulled him back. "None of us knew this would happen. Had we known, we would have chosen another area to explore."

Brian nodded and drew a deep breath. "They aren't swimming out to us, but they aren't leaving either. We're safe for the moment, but knowing the bloody bastards, we won't be for long."

"Perhaps there are weapons below," Edward said, shouldering his musket like a seasoned hunter. Lowering his voice, he looked around them and added, "They can't go on much farther."

Colin glanced at their surviving party. He counted fourteen men in all. Fourteen out of one hundred and twenty. He felt sick in his soul.

He hurried down the ladder to the dark companionway, then headed toward the rear, unsure where weapons would be stored. He kept expecting—hoping—someone would appear. But the ship seemed to be abandoned. He knew exploring, tracking, surviving in the wilderness—skills he'd learned living in Scotland. In the wild, he was an expert. About ships, he knew nothing. Reaching a large cabin, he stepped inside.

"The captain's cabin," Edward said. Crossing to a cord-rimmed shelf, he rummaged through scrolls of paper. "There are maps, logbooks, ledgers."

"But no weapons." Brian turned to leave. "Perhaps there's something on the deck below. You two go check. I'll climb the mast and see if there's a village or town nearby."

"Wait." Colin stared at the desk, a wary tingle lifting the hairs at the nape of his neck. "What's this?"

He stared at the dagger impaled in the solid oak surface. As a symbol of what? Colin wondered. A warning? Or as a sign to fight? The gold hilt seemed to pulse, calling to him to pull it free. The ruby, sapphire and emerald embedded in its handle glittered as if they wanted to speak. The piece was worth a fortune, yet someone had left it behind.

Who and why?

"I think we've found our way home, lads." Colin heard himself say as he wrapped his hand around the hilt. Feeling a vibrating warmth, he jerked the knife from its bed.

"How?" Edward asked, setting the musket aside.

"This ship." Angling the knife in his hand, a smile lifted the corner of Colin's mouth.

"May I remind you that none of us know a bloody thing about sailing." Brian raked his fingers through his hair.

"Well, gentlemen." Sunlight reflected off the icy blade, drawing his attention to the words carved into the finely honed steel. *Sea Queen.* Colin decided that was as good a name for a ship as any. "We're about to learn."

Embrace the Romances of
Shannon Drake